P9-DCN-619

The Secret Stones

DEE HOLMES

BERKLEY BOOKS, NEW YORK

This is a work of fiction. Names, characters, places, and incidents are either the product of the author's imagination or are used fictitiously, and any resemblance to actual persons, living or dead, business establishments, events, or locales is entirely coincidental.

THE SECRET STONES

A Berkley Book / published by arrangement with
the author

PRINTING HISTORY
Berkley edition / April 2001

The Penguin Putnam Inc. World Wide Web site address is
http://www.penguinputnam.com

ISBN: 0-425-17924-9

BERKLEY®
Berkley Books are published by The Berkley Publishing Group,
a division of Penguin Putnam Inc.,
375 Hudson Street, New York, New York 10014.
BERKLEY and the "B" design
are trademarks belonging to Penguin Putnam Inc.

PRINTED IN THE UNITED STATES OF AMERICA

10 9 8 7 6 5 4 3 2 1

Chapter One

The last time she'd rushed to the hospital emergency room had been when Jessica was five. She'd been bitten by a dog, and while her daughter had charmed all the nurses, Mattie had been terrified of infection and rabies.

This time wasn't like last time.

"I'm Mattie Caulfield," she said to the receptionist. "My daughter, Jessica, was brought in after being in a car accident."

"Go right through those doors and take a left. I believe your husband is already here."

Mattie barely heard the last sentence. Her chest was tight from holding her breath and her ears were ringing. Somewhere between the phone call and the frantic five-mile drive to the hospital, her heartbeat had soared to rocket speed. *Please, God, don't let her die. Please.* She rushed through the doors and straight into her ex-husband's arms.

Stephen wrapped himself around her like a warm blanket. He held her secure, stilling her shaky body, whispering, "Shh, you're shivering like a wet puppy." His voice had the calming effect of a beloved friend ready to blunt any upsetting news, and Mattie leaned a bit harder into him. They hadn't been this physically close since before their divorce was finalized six months ago.

In a raspy voice she asked the questions that had cemented themselves into her mind since the phone call. "How did this happen? Is she okay? How bad is she hurt? What have you been told?"

Stephen pulled back, his eyes searching hers with the misty nostalgia Mattie had often seen when they discussed their teenage daughters. "You always did pop questions out faster than I could answer," he said, trying for a smile. "How did it happen? Well, from what I've heard, the driver lost control of the car, bounced off a guard rail, and flipped into a culvert. Jessica was badly hurt, and I haven't been told much about her condition beyond the good news that she's alive and they're trying to get her stabilized. They called Tom, and he's coming in."

Tom Egan was their family physician, and the fact that he was notified should have comforted Mattie, but it simply added another layer of worry. Was there something truly serious the emergency personnel hadn't told Stephen? Like a head injury? Paralysis? Or some dreadful prognosis that required gentle preparation by an old friend?

Stephen had guided her to a chair, and she perched on the edge; her body was tense and chilled despite the warm May night. Doors slammed, doctors were paged, somewhere the clang of a gurney was followed by a woman screaming. Mattie shivered. A doctor and two nurses came from the right, rushed through swinging doors, and disappeared. She wondered if they were working on Jessica. The big clock above the doors read 10:18. The five minutes she'd been here felt like five hours.

"Where were you, anyway?" Stephen asked.

He stood above her, hands deep in his pockets, jacket open, tie loosened, his hair more gray than she'd realized and mussed as if he'd dragged worried fingers through it over and over. His face looked strained; the dimples that added a boyish approachability she'd once found fascinating and endearing were now hidden in tired lines. She wanted to comfort him, but all she could manage was to press his arm. He was a handsome man, affable, a devoted father. Looking at him now, she could understand why her parents were confused and upset when she and Stephen divorced. Now he didn't seem smothering or insensitive, just . . . as her mother would conclude, strong and supportive.

"Is where you were a secret?" he asked when she didn't answer right away.

"Of course not." She reminded herself not to be defensive, that the question wasn't out of line, that she would have asked him the same thing—well, actually she wouldn't have. "I was at the shop getting the month's books ready for the account-ant."

"At ten o'clock at night?"

"It's been a busy week." Mattie owned and managed The Garret, an antiques and collectibles business begun by her family and handed down to Mattie when her parents retired the previous year.

"And Hannah? Where is she?"

"She's spending the night at my parents'." And then she gritted her teeth and refrained from telling him she didn't appreciate being questioned as if she were a neglectful mother. She'd like to believe she was being overly sensitive, but this wasn't a new discussion or a new insinuation. It cut especially deep now because of Jessica.

Mattie knew she had no obligation to explain perfectly normal activities—or even blissfully sinful ones, for that matter. She certainly didn't have to feel guilty for not being home. And that's why his questions irked her. To Stephen, her not being home was tantamount to carelessness and dis-regard for her family.

With her warm fuzzy feelings now evaporated, she folded her hands. "Do you know anything about the other girl?"

He glanced away, drawing a sharp breath, sadness thick-ening his words. "She died."

Mattie inhaled sharply, her heart tightening. "Oh, God."

"No seat belt, according to what the police said. Jess wasn't wearing hers either. How could they have been so goddamn stupid?"

"Not stupid, Stephen. Just kids believing they're invinci-ble." Again came that painful clench in her chest.

Stephen nodded toward some people who had just come

in. "That's the girl's parents," he said in a low voice. "I heard one of the nurses refer to them."

Mattie stared at the distraught couple. Heartbreaking empathy brought tears to her own eyes. That could have been her and Stephen. It could have been Jessica who had died. Mattie felt both a sweep of relief that it wasn't, and a tinge of guilt that she could feel anything approaching cheery when another family was in such distress.

The woman was literally being held upright, knees sagging, feet nearly rubbery, by the man beside her. He helped her to a row of green plastic chairs, eased her down, then hunkered beside her in disheveled grief.

Mattie didn't recognize the woman, but knowing she'd lost her daughter pressed in on her. She knew, at least by sight, the mothers of both her daughters' friends. Between school activities, choir practice, and PTA, it would have been difficult *not* to recognize the parents. "Who was the girl with Jessica?" she asked Stephen.

"Arlis Petcher."

The name meant nothing to her, but because Stephen seemed to know it, she assumed he knew her. "Was she Jessica's age?" Which was nearly eighteen, as her daughter reminded her almost daily.

Stephen shrugged. "Probably a new friend. You know how friendly Jessica is. Just like her mother." He beamed fondly at Mattie.

"She never mentioned her to me." Or had Jessica spoken of her and had Mattie been too preoccupied, as Stephen often accused her of being?

"Probably because you were busy at the store."

Well, you sure walked into that, she mused in disgust. Mattie scowled. "Why do you always have to make working a synonym for neglect?"

He raised both hands in a peace gesture. "Honey, don't be so defensive. You're here now. That's what counts."

Truthfully, she had been busy for the past few weeks, mostly with setting up the estate auction at Alice Landry's house. Then there was Wyatt Landry—"Mom's sexy boyfriend," as Hannah called him, giggling, whenever he came to the house. Jessica thought he was cool, telling her mother that if he made her happy, then that was good. All in all, Mattie's growing relationship with Wyatt had brought no adverse reactions from the girls, which pleased her. At first she'd been leery of the swiftness of their attraction, what with her divorce so new, but Wyatt hadn't been pushy or demanding. She'd liked him immediately when he'd hired her to handle the auction of his mother's possessions.

Tonight, she'd turned down a date with him because her books for the month *had* to be at the accountant's in the morning. She could only imagine Stephen's reaction if she'd been on a date with Wyatt when she'd been notified.

As for her not being home every minute, Jessica and her sister, Hannah, were seventeen and fifteen, respectively—responsible young adults, for heaven's sake. They were never in trouble, and Mattie hated that Stephen could make hackles of guilt rise along her spine with the most benign comments.

A police officer came through the doors and went over to speak with the Petchers. Mattie rose, settling her bag strap on her shoulder. "Wouldn't you think the police could wait a while?" she said in annoyance. "My God, those poor people have just lost their daughter."

"What are you doing?"

"I'm going to offer sympathy and find out what happened tonight."

"I think we should offer to do something," Stephen commented, falling in beside her.

"Do something? Like what?"

He shrugged. "They don't look as if they've got a pot to pee in, and if Jess turns out to have some culpability, well, we shouldn't just ignore that."

"I don't think this would be a good time."

"Not tonight," he said, as if she'd missed his entire point or even as if generosity had a timetable. "But sometime."

She nodded vaguely, not adverse but not entirely sure either.

The officer glanced up when Mattie and Stephen approached. While Stephen stood beside him, Mattie spoke to the Petchers.

"I'm so sorry about Arlis."

The woman appeared confused. "Who are you?" She rasped out the question as if she'd been smoking all her life.

"We're Jessica's parents."

As if those words had been a match to gasoline, the woman glared, then screeched, "You! You're sorry? You're sorry? Your kid did this and you're sorry? Get her away from me!"

"Mrs. Petcher," the cop said, "take it easy."

"I don't have to," she sobbed. "Her kid killed my baby as sure as if she'd gotten one of them guns and shot her!"

Mattie didn't move, although Stephen tried to pull her back. "I'd be angry, too," Mattie said. "I'd be screaming the place down."

As if Mattie's words gave permission, Mrs. Petcher took a step closer. Her voice breaking between fury and tears, she cried, "Jessica made my baby steal our car. My Arlis never did nothin' wrong, then she meets up with Miss Prom Queen and what happens? She's lyin' dead while your kid was drinkin' and speedin' and stayin' alive. She killed my baby—that's what she did. She k-killed my b-ba-baby!"

Mattie's face drained of color, and she felt woozy. What could she say? Being sorry bordered on insult. "I don't know what to say, Mrs. Petcher. . . . I . . ."

"Get her 'way from me, Chuckie, get her away. . . ." Mrs. Petcher began to sway, and her husband, who appeared unsurprised by his wife's outburst, settled her into a nearby chair.

Mattie, however, was startled. Not by the outburst—that she could understand; that was normal if the woman believed Jessica had been responsible. No, Mattie retreated in speechlessness because she was swamped by the implications for Jessica. Stealing? Drinking and speeding? Not her Jessica. No! There had to be another explanation.

When the officer finished with the Petchers, he told Mattie and Stephen that he would want to speak with their daughter as soon as she was conscious. Mattie asked about the accusations.

"We did find beer cans in the car, and damage to the car plus skid marks indicate speed."

"Was the car stolen?" Stephen asked.

"The Petchers claim no one asked permission to take it."

"But our daughter would not steal a car," Mattie insisted.

"We'll be doing an investigation, ma'am. Asking for witnesses to come forward, including any in the Petchers' neighborhood who might have seen the girls earlier in the evening."

Which of course didn't ease Mattie's mind. One girl dead and another in bad shape, witnesses who might or might not exist. And if they did, what would they say? Mattie felt fear coil deep within her as the enormity of the accident details began to settle in.

"Was Jessica driving?" Stephen asked.

"We haven't ascertained who had control of the vehicle. Neither was wearing a seat belt, and since they'd both been thrown, no one was behind the wheel when the investigating officers arrived."

"Christ," Stephen muttered. "Jessica could be in a lot of trouble."

"If you could let us know when we can talk to her, we'd appreciate it." The officer left, and Mattie and Stephen went to inquire if there was any news about their daughter. When the answer was no, they found a coffee station and helped themselves.

Mattie sat staring at the paper cup, trying to process the accusations and what she knew about Jessica.

"Honey, the woman was hysterical. She wanted to blame someone."

"I understand that, but what if she's right?"

Stephen scowled. "Don't you think that waiting for Jess's side of the story before we find her guilty would be prudent?"

"Of course I want to hear her side. But none of what I've heard tonight sounds anything like what our daughter would do. It's so bizarre that I can't help thinking that either there are some missing pieces here or we don't *really* know her.

Even her being with Arlis Petcher is odd. I'd never even heard of her before now."

"Well, apparently they had some kind of friendship, because they were together tonight."

"Yes, and for what reason? Jessica told me she and some friends were going to the mall, and then they were having a sleepover."

"Where was the sleepover?"

Mattie tried to reconstruct the exchange with her daughter. It had been like many they'd had—quick bits of chatter between errands and unspoken assumptions. Under any other circumstances, Mattie wouldn't have given Jess's vagueness a flip of concern. She'd always been proud of the closeness she had with both girls—a bond and affinity that didn't always require whole sentences and tedious details. Now, she wished she'd paid closer attention.

"I assumed it was at Callie's because she has the big house. No, I *know* it was at Callie's, because I asked Jessica if she wanted me to drop off some sandwiches and she said no, because I made them last time and Callie's mother was going to order in pizza."

"Then check with Barbara tomorrow. Simple."

"But what if she never intended to go to Callie's? What if she let me assume she was, when all along she'd planned on going somewhere with Arlis? Somewhere she didn't want me to know about?"

"Mattie, you're getting way ahead of yourself to the point of sounding like this was some cooked-up conspiracy."

"How can you be so calm? This is our daughter in trouble, and it sure doesn't seem that she was some innocent victim."

"Okay, I admit it doesn't look good, but . . ."

Mattie barely heard him. Her mind raced down roads that a few hours ago would have been unimaginable. "Oh God, Stephen, you don't think she was going to buy drugs?" At the drain of color in his face, she shook her head. "No, we know our daughter. She wouldn't. She wouldn't." But a small nudge in her gut whispered, *Maybe she would*.

Then a doctor approached and introduced himself as Dr.

Wallis. "We have Jessica stabilized, but she still hasn't regained consciousness and her condition remains critical. If you want to see her, you can, but only for a few minutes. She's in intensive care. Fourth floor. Tell the nurse on duty who you are."

The elevator ride only increased Mattie's anxiety.

Moments later, they stepped into the hushed air of the ICU. Walking softly to where their daughter lay among monitors and tubes and bandages immediately became a memory forever seared in Mattie's mind.

How could this have happened? Where will it all end?

Stephen drew her close as they stood listening to the heave and blip and tick of the machines. Mattie touched her daughter's cool cheek and felt the pulse in her jaw. Tears misted her eyes as she bent down and kissed her. "You're going to be fine, sweetheart. You're going to get well. We love you very much."

They stood for a few moments, holding her limp hands and brushing back her blond hair. Stephen nudged Mattie when the nurse approached; she told them that Dr. Egan was waiting for them in the floor's visiting area.

Their physician, obviously called from some social gathering—he wore a boutonniere and the faint scent of cologne—brought Mattie's fears rushing back.

If he'd been called in from a party, it must be very serious. After patting her hand and shaking Stephen's, he suggested they sit down.

Neither did, and Mattie felt the sweat break out across her back, immediately followed by a prickly chill.

"I saw Jessica before they took her up to IC, and I've spoken with Dr. Wallis, who's covering the emergency room tonight. While she's not out of danger, she's in better shape than she was when Rescue brought her in. She sustained some serious injuries in the abdominal area as well as internal bleeding." He paused. "She's slipped into a coma."

"Oh, no. . . . no. . . ."

"Jesus." Then, holding Mattie's hand, Stephen asked, "Is she going to die?" And although Mattie shrank from the question, she waited, breath held, for the answer.

"Come on, Stephen, you know I can't answer that."

Stephen scowled. "Don't yank us around, okay? You're not just some drive-by doc. We both know you have an opinion, and we want to know what it is."

Tom Egan remained quiet a few moments. "All right. From what I've read and what I've seen of trauma patients, and comparing their injuries to Jessica's, I would say the odds are good that she'll recover."

Both Mattie and Stephen let out the breaths they were holding. Mattie asked, "How long before she wakes up?"

"It's anybody's guess. Could be a few days, a few weeks, or a few months."

"Can't you be more definite than that?" Stephen asked. "When we were told you were coming in, we assumed you knew something more than the guys rolling the gurneys."

Tom Egan looked from one to the other, clearly not pleased at being pressed to answer questions. Mattie agreed with Stephen. She expected more, too.

"Actually, I do know something more than the guys rolling the gurneys. I wanted to tell you in case you didn't know."

"Didn't know what?"

"That Jessica was pregnant."

Mattie gaped at him and Stephen stared. "That's impossible. There must be a mistake."

Tom shook his head. "No mistake. We couldn't save the fetus." Then he frowned. "Mattie?" When she remained unmoved, unblinking, he took her hand, patting it. "I'm sorry to have to tell you this tonight. And from your reactions, neither of you knew. But I didn't want to put it off for fear word would get around and you'd hear it from someone else. It's just so sad when kids fear confiding in their parents."

Mattie's mind reeled, desperately sifting through her chaotic thoughts for some smidgen of missed information that would make all of this at least understandable. Right now it felt as if her daughter had been living someone else's life. "How far . . . ?" She swallowed, cleared her throat, but the words wouldn't come.

"How far along? Just a few weeks. I'm sure she intended

to tell you." He glanced toward the elevators. "We can ride down together. I have another patient I should see while I'm here." Again he patted her, and she wanted to fling his hand away. *How could he be so blasé, so routinely solicitous? Oh, your daughter's in a coma. And oh, you didn't know she was pregnant? And oh, she would have told you. And by the way I have another patient, so good-bye.*

Stephen put his arm around her. "Come on, honey, I'll take you home."

Mattie stiffened and pulled away. "No. I'm staying here tonight."

"Stephen's right, Mattie. Go home and get some rest. Jessica is in good hands."

"Rest? You think I can just go home and sleep, as if this was just another night?" She backed away from both of them, her voice breaking. "My daughter's been accused of awful things. She's in a coma for God knows how long, then you tell us she was pregnant. I would say, Dr. Egan, that rest is the last thing I'm going to do tonight or for a lot of nights to come."

Chapter Two

*Wyatt Landry couldn't be sure if he'd dreamed the foot-*steps or if someone was actually in the bedroom. His mother's house had more than its share of squeaky floorboards—he'd spent his teenage years learning to avoid them when he'd been trying to sneak into his room without the old man hearing him.

He opened his eyes, keeping his breathing even as a very defined shadow drew closer. Nope, he hadn't been dreaming. The figure crept from the open doorway, across the carpet, and to the bedside table.

The digital clock flashed 1:50, the light outlining his wallet, mail from his last trip down to his Newport house, a crushed pack of gum, assorted change, and the keys to his brand-new truck; so new that those keys were still attached to the dealer's metal tag.

In an instant Wyatt grabbed the wrist of the hand that reached for the tag.

"Aw, shit!"

"I'm sure this is an idiotic question, but what the hell do you think you're doing?" Wyatt asked his seventeen-year-old nephew.

"I just needed to borrow your truck."

"Borrow? What happened to asking permission?"

"You'd have said no."

"Smart kid." He released his nephew's wrist and turned on the bedside lamp. "I'm not real fond of saying yes to a thief. How'd you get in here?"

Kevin shuffled his feet, clearly wishing his uncle hadn't asked. Wyatt waited. He'd been a cop about a million years ago, so kids trying to weasel out of answering with silence didn't fly.

"I didn't break nothin'," he muttered.

Evasion didn't sail either.

Wyatt folded his arms and waited.

"Okay, okay. Jesus, you're like a bad conscience." Kevin straightened, lifted his chin, and met his uncle's gaze. "I got in through a window in the basement." Pause and silence. "I forgot to close and lock it when I was helping you clean stuff out yesterday." His eyes widened as Wyatt's narrowed. "Not on purpose! Swear to God! I was even gonna come back, but Mom wanted me to do some stuff. Then when I got over here and it was all dark and your truck was here, I figured you were asleep. I was gonna lean on the doorbell, but then I remembered the window." He let out a breath. "Since I figured you'd say no, I thought I'd just take it and then come back. You wouldn't of ever known."

"And if I'd happened to have gotten up and found it was gone?"

"I didn't think about that."

"Figures." Wyatt rubbed his eyes and took a closer look at Kevin. "Your mother know you're out at this hour?" The teenager lived with his mother, Wyatt's sister, in a split-level a few blocks away.

"She's out somewhere, or I would've taken her car. Come on, Uncle Wyatt. Like, this is life or death."

Wyatt tossed the covers back. "Uh-huh."

"It is! What do you think? That I'd take your truck for something stupid?" Kevin Bonner, dark-haired with swarthy skin and intense blue eyes, wore paint-splattered jeans and a Coors T-shirt. He planted his hands low on his hips, as if daring Wyatt to argue. Actually he wasn't a bad kid, but Wyatt wasn't ready to give him the benefit of doubt on the stupidity meter.

"Okay, what's the big crisis?"

"Jessica might die. She got banged up in a car wreck tonight, and she's in the hospital."

Wyatt felt a hot knot tighten in his gut. "Was she with Mattie?"

"I don't know. I mean, I didn't hear who was with her. I just know I need to get over there."

Wyatt liked Jessica Caulfield; she was a bright, engaging seventeen-year-old with enough good taste and class that his nephew would only benefit. Wyatt could easily imagine that Mattie was very much like her daughter when she was a teenager. Knowing Jessica was a little like knowing the young Mattie. Mattie, the woman who had dazzled his heart and had him considering a second plunge into the very tricky waters of a serious relationship—a state, like marriage, that he'd religiously avoided since his nasty divorce five years ago. Of course, he hadn't broached anything about his thoughts to Mattie. Not yet. First, he didn't want to scare her off, and second, he wanted her to make the break she needed from the emotional baggage her ex-husband showed such zeal in plaguing her with.

Tonight, with Jessica hurt, Wyatt imagined good old Stephen would be beating his devoted-dad drum for Mattie's attention.

"How do you know all this?" Wyatt asked as he pulled on a pair of khaki pants and a faded oxford shirt, and stuffed his bare feet into Docksiders.

"I got a 911 beep from a kid who saw the wreck. He said he watched Rescue come. Someone told him she was, like, out of it and hurt really bad." Kevin blinked quickly, rubbing his wrist across his eyes. Wyatt didn't miss the terror glistening in the teenager's expression. "I *gotta* go and see what's going on."

Wyatt swept up his wallet and keys. "Then let's do it."

Outside the house, the yard rolled toward the street, its frontage needing more color and fewer green bushes. The old brick driveway curved not for aesthetic reasons but because Alice Landry had saved old bricks and Wyatt's dad, tired of the piles in the backyard, had used used his non-existent bricklaying skills to turn them into a driveway.

Wyatt locked the door and followed his nephew across the lawn to his black Ford F-250. Kevin climbed into the passenger seat, folding his arms as tight as coiled barbed wire. His face was hard with worry and something else. Disappointment? Despondency? Fear?

"Hey, Jessica will be okay. It always seems worse when you don't have any details."

"We broke up."

This had escaped Wyatt's notice, but now that Kevin mentioned it, he realized that not having a girlfriend had been the reason why the teenager had so much free time the past few weekends. Free time that Wyatt had benefited from when he'd needed help lugging boxes down from the attic.

"So you're going to see an old friend instead of a girlfriend. Sounds like an okay plan to me."

"Aren't you gonna ask me what happened?"

The question presupposed that he was curious, which he wasn't. Teenage romance gone awry was hardly a barn burner of a story. Nevertheless, Kevin stared at him as if this breakup was indeed news.

Wyatt backed the truck onto the street. "So what happened?"

He shrugged. "She's been weird and touchy about stuff lately. Then she started hangin' with Arlis Petcher, and I told her she was gonna get her ass fried. She told me to mind my own business. She never showed for a couple of dates, and when I asked her what she was doing, she acted like I was draggin' on her life. I was pissed, so I let her know I didn't want to see her anymore if she was gonna be a jerk."

"And?"

"And I haven't seen her except at school."

"Sounds like you gave her a choice and she took the one you didn't like."

"When you act like a jerk, you make jerky choices," Kevin said, clearly convinced Jessica had messed up.

Wyatt smiled. Ah, yes, those bushels of jerky choices.

He'd played in that barrel more than a few times. "Can't argue with that. Still, you were going to steal my truck to go to the hospital. That sounds like more than curiosity about an ex-girlfriend."

"It's dumb, and I don't know why I give a shit."

Because you're a nice kid. To Kevin, he said, "Well, I sure as hell don't know either."

And that was the end of the conversation. Wyatt drove through the deserted streets, allowing his nephew his conflicted thoughts.

Briarwood, smack in the middle of Rhode Island, was Wyatt's hometown, although he hadn't lived here since moving away five years ago, after his divorce from Paige.

His parents had both died here—his old man, a potato farmer like his father before him, had died of a heart attack in the late eighties. His mother had sold some of the land and some of the equipment, but she'd kept the house and every treasure she'd collected. And at her death just six months ago, she'd still owned it all—the house and a shed and its contents, from age-yellowed tablecloths and sheets to antique dishes to dilapidated and dreary furniture. It was this staggering amount of junk that had kept Wyatt temporarily living in Briarwood.

He'd returned about a month before she died and had stayed, spending time with her, helping her to get her affairs in order. This last endeavor became complicated and emotional because his sister, Corinne, called his preparations ghoulish; Wyatt had dismissed most of the shouting and arguing because he knew she refused to believe that their mother had only weeks to live. He sympathized up to a point, knowing Corinne was in big-time denial—a state she clutched whenever she didn't like the truth. Wyatt had tried reason, and for his efforts had gotten hysteria, so he'd taken the position of mostly ignoring her.

After their mother died, leaving him executor in her will, Corinne accused him of weaseling his way back into their mother's life to get control of her estate—which, in Wyatt's opinion, was heavy on junk and light on value.

Corinne simply didn't want to believe that their mother's final wishes were that the house and all her belongings should be sold and the money used for Kevin's education. Never mind that the will was legal and Corinne's son would be the beneficiary. His sister wanted to keep *everything*, and every day she invented some trumped-up reason why she should, and why he was a bastard.

The last go-around had been just that afternoon, when Corinne insisted that a pair of small oils she'd found in the attic were painted by Alice Landry. Her impassioned declaration was indeed bizarre, because neither Wyatt, nor anyone he'd spoken to, had ever seen his mother hang a picture, never mind wield a paintbrush.

In Corinne's view, five years of not living in Briarwood equaled five years of not seeing his mother. It was ridiculous reasoning; he'd been home often, but in Corinne's world of instantly processed feelings and melodrama, coming home didn't count as much as living at home.

"You said your mother is out somewhere," he said to Kevin. "Dare I hope she's found herself a boyfriend?" *An unmarried one*, he thought to himself. Actually, the last one had been legally separated, but whether it was brotherly concern or brotherly self-interest, he figured that if his sister got interested in a guy, she'd have less time to dissect every porcelain bowl and picture frame in the house.

Kevin shrugged. "Yeah, maybe. I don't know." He sat up straight. "Look, there's a cop talking to the Rescue guys."

Wyatt pulled into the hospital parking lot, and a few minutes later he and Kevin were headed toward the emergency waiting room. The fluorescent lights made it all too white, too clinical, too disinfected; Wyatt was reminded of how often he'd walked past this particular area on his way to the elevators and up to his mother's room.

"Something's going on," Wyatt murmured, taking note of Mattie and her ex-husband coming out of the elevator with some guy in a tuxedo.

"I know him," Kevin said. "That's Doc Egan. He's got a kid on the football team."

Wyatt watched, keeping at a distance, but Kevin hopped around like he had sand in his shorts. "Doc has to be telling them something about Jess. I'm gonna go find out."

Kevin had moved three steps when Wyatt pressed the boy's shoulder and urged him back. "Let's wait until they're finished."

Kevin stopped, but never took his gaze off the three people talking about twenty feet away. Wyatt focused on Mattie. Slender and pretty in slacks and a sweater, her blond hair cut in a short and sassy style that highlighted her cheekbones— tonight she appeared young and vulnerable. When she turned slightly, it was apparent from the sag in her shoulders that she was wrung out and deflated. Wyatt noted with alarm how close she stood to her ex-husband, how Caulfield eased his arm around her, and that she not only didn't push him away but leaned into him. *So what'd you expect? Divorced or not, Jessica is their daughter. Two parents supporting one another at a tragic time. Just because you don't want Caulfield around doesn't mean squat.* But Caulfield wasn't her husband, and therefore Wyatt found his display of family unity irritating.

Caulfield was saying something, and Mattie was now pushing away from him and the doctor. Then she glanced in Wyatt's direction, her eyes capturing his, her mouth squeezed tight to keep from crying. He wanted to cross quickly, take her into his arms, and assure her that tears were mandatory, given the circumstances. With the conversation obviously at an end, Kevin nearly vaulted the distance. Wyatt followed.

Kevin asked the first question and Stephen supplied the answer. "A coma?" Kevin looked stunned, as if he were suddenly an extra in some horror flick. "Like, she's not gonna wake up for weeks or months?"

Stephen answered. "We don't know yet. The doctor hopes it won't be long, but she's badly hurt. We're just thankful she's alive."

Wyatt's gaze met Mattie's while Stephen explained the accident details. They stood only a few feet apart, Wyatt with his arms crossed and his head tipped a bit to the side; Mattie leaned against the wall, her hands fidgeting. To the casual observer they appeared to be two people waiting while the other man and the teenager exchanged questions and answers.

Are you okay?

I'm scared.

She's going to be okay. You have to believe that.

I feel so useless.

I want to hold you.

Me, too.

Wyatt continued to watch Mattie, paying little attention to Stephen or to Kevin, whose fear hadn't been lessened by the details, as Wyatt had predicted. Especially when Caulfield said, "Arlis Petcher wasn't so lucky."

"Arlis was with her? That jerk made all this happen? I warned Jess to stay away from her. She shoulda listened. Goddammit, she shoulda known I wasn't just blowin' smoke." Kevin's voice broke, and he shuddered, hands fisted as if to hold himself together.

Wyatt recalled the mention of the Petcher girl when Kevin told him about his breakup up with Jessica. Mattie's gaze bored in on Kevin, as if she were seeing him for the first time.

"You warned her?" Mattie asked. "When?"

"A few weeks ago."

"Weeks ago?" "Weeks" wasn't a long time, but for Mattie, who thought she knew everything about both her daughters' friends, and given tonight's tragedy, weeks seemed like months.

Stephen tried to soothe her. "We have plenty of time to hash this out, Mattie. And I'm sure Kevin will be more than willing to help us." Then, as if he'd appointed himself the conversation monitor, he turned to Wyatt.

"I don't think we've met," Stephen said, offering his hand; Wyatt shook it after a few seconds of confusion at the abrupt switch. Mattie grew silent and thoughtful, seemingly undone that she knew nothing of her daughter's friendship with Arlis. Wyatt and Stephen exchanged pleasantries and embraced civility as Wyatt wondered what all the shit was about not having met.

"Actually we have," Wyatt said. He hated games, and wasn't about to play this one. "I'm Kevin's uncle, Wyatt Landry. We met about six weeks ago at Mattie's front door, remember?"

"Oh, of course. I apologize. I simply drew a blank."

Sure you did. About as blank as flypaper in a cow barn. The man was amazing. His expression really was confused and puzzled. Enough so that Wyatt wondered if he was indeed telling the truth—that he hadn't remembered. Not because Wyatt believed their meeting had been a landmark of importance in Caulfield's life, but because possibly Wyatt had misjudged its significance to Stephen.

Mattie said, "I'm going up to see Jessica once more before I go home. Kevin, why don't you come with me?"

"Man, you mean it?"

"Come on. It's only supposed to be close family, but they won't hassle us at this hour."

"Wyatt and I'll grab coffee while we wait for you," Stephen said.

Five minutes later the two men were seated in a waiting room, holding cups of black liquid that tasted like old socks had been used for the filter. Wyatt glanced at his watch. It was 2:35 in the morning, and he was in a hospital waiting area socializing with Mattie's ex-husband—a scenario he wouldn't have conjured up even if he wrote fantasy fiction for a living.

"I understand Mattie is appraising some stuff for you."

"Yeah. My sister and I are cleaning out our mother's house."

Then, instead of asking questions or raving about Mattie, Caulfield redirected the subject. "I met your mother a few years ago. I believe it was about the time you moved away. She was part of a group of new computer users, and my company was giving instructional classes."

Wyatt, by the sheerest of efforts, showed no surprise. He recalled his mother taking those classes. There had been about twenty participants, and her enthusiasm had been all about her new friends and the wonders of the Internet. Not once had she mentioned the instructor by name. For Caulfield to remember his mother from a class five years ago but not remember meeting Wyatt six weeks ago strained credibility. "And do you still teach classes?"

"Actually, I do. Not for my company, but I do adult classes three nights a week at the high school."

"And during the day?" Wyatt knew Stephen had been let go from the computer company where he'd worked quite successfully for fifteen years. Mattie had told him that Caulfield's unemployment, coupled with her working full-time, had been a major catalyst of their divorce. Given that his current unemployed status, according to Mattie, was neither desirable nor charming, Wyatt figured Caulfield would bob and weave around an answer.

"Truthfully, I'm unemployed. When Halbertech got bought up by another company, there was a major employee shake-up. They fired some, laid others off—and none of those have been rehired, by the way. Others, like myself, were told we were the lucky ones. We were given the option of staying if we accepted a pay cut."

"Sounds like a lose-lose deal."

"My sentiments exactly. I looked around, even interviewed with other software companies for something else in my pay range, but none of the places where I wanted to work were hiring. The places that would hire me didn't pay enough to keep the girls in makeup and shampoo. In the end, the pay loss was so demeaning, I quit. Mattie couldn't understand why no money was better than some money." He was silent for a few seconds, staring into his coffee. "The way it all came down made it a lousy deal no matter which decision I made."

Caulfield's straightforwardness impressed Wyatt, and he was sympathetic that Caulfield had gotten royally shafted. On the other hand, for him to choose unemployment when he had kids to support struck Wyatt as dumb and short-sighted. He could have bitten the ego bullet, gone into a new company at a lower pay level, and worked his way up.

Then, as if Caulfield were expecting just such criticism,

he used the unemployment issue to ask, "You quit the police force here, didn't you?"

"Yeah, but if you don't mind, I'd rather not roll out the details."

"Hey, I understand. Walking away from a job you love is tough."

Wyatt nodded. On that, he and Caulfield agreed.

Later, after Caulfield had left, Wyatt walked Mattie to her vehicle. Kevin had gone to get a Coke and told Wyatt he'd meet him at the truck. The kid was pale and shaky after seeing Jessica, muttering to his uncle that she looked dead and it was all Arlis's fault and Jessica was stupid to have gone with her.

At the driver's door of Mattie's car, they stood silent in the cool darkness. Lights from the hospital created illumination and shadows behind them. A lone car with a pizza sign magnetized to the roof sped by, leaving a plume of exhaust in its wake. As Mattie turned to unlock the door, Wyatt touched her shoulder. "Not yet," he murmured.

He heard her quick intake of breath and slipped his arms around her, tugging her to him, her back to his front. When he turned her to face him, she nearly collapsed against him, as though waiting one more moment would have been her undoing. Her face burrowed into his shoulder.

"What can I do for you, babe?"

"Make all this go away."

"No secret stones to make magic, unfortunately."

"Secret stones?"

"When my sister was a kid, she believed I had the world's only secret stones, and if I gave them to her to hold, they would get her out of trouble."

"How did they do that?"

Her question amazed him. He'd expected laughter, he'd expected a passing comment about childhood fantasies and idealistic beliefs. His whole point in even mentioning the secret stones had been to lighten the heaviness that engulfed her. But she was looking at him curiously—as if, indeed, he'd once possessed magical stones.

And so, instead of blowing off her question, he answered

it as seriously as she'd asked it. "Let's say I was behind the scene doing the problem solving while she clutched the bag. Most of it was kid stuff—like when Corinne was ten and skipped school and then got into a fight with another girl. When Corinne bested her, the girl threatened to have her big sister take care of Corinne the next day. I had a talk with the older sister, who was thirteen, and we made an arrangement."

For the first time, Wyatt saw a genuine smile. "Let me guess." Mattie pondered a moment. "I think the grown-up word would be extortion?"

"Me? I was only fourteen."

"Fourteen going on twenty-five."

"I simply suggested that her old man would be pissed if he found out she was fucking a couple of guys I knew. This was the early seventies, when thirteen-year-olds having sex caused alarm rather than a yawn and a new government program to supply condoms to six-year-olds. Anyway, she backed off like I'd presented her with a nest of scorpions to play with. When she didn't show the next day, Corinne was convinced it was the secret stones."

"Did you ever tell her the truth?"

"Nope. She believed in those stones until the old man took them from her and told her to grow up and figure out how to solve her own problems. Magic, he said, was nothing but a cheap sideshow at a carnival."

"How old was she when he took them?"

"Around twelve."

"The truth ended her childhood idealism, no doubt. How regrettable. Did she solve her problems?"

"Some she did, a lot she didn't." He tunneled his hands into her short hair, rubbing his hands against her head in a gentle motion. He kissed her forehead, and then they stood, arms around one another, silent as though easing back to the present and the reality of Jessica's accident.

Finally Mattie sighed, and Wyatt felt her tension return. "I'm glad you came tonight. I didn't know how much I needed to see you until I looked up and there you were."

"I'm glad I came, too." He tried to tighten his hold, but

she allowed it for only a moment before pulling away, as though to prove she could stand on her own.

But she kept their hands entwined. "All of tonight has been a huge and frightening mystery because none of the details I learned make any sense. God only knows what I'll do with the details I still don't know. Right now, I feel as if my own daughter is a stranger." She told Wyatt about the trip out of town she'd been clueless about; Arlis Petcher, whom she'd never met and had never even heard of until tonight; and then the most unsettling detail of all—Jessica's pregnancy, lost before Mattie even knew it existed.

Wyatt, because he'd been a cop, was rarely shocked by even the most bizarre behaviors. But this, coming out of nowhere, stunned him. "Pregnant? Christ, are you sure?"

"That's what Tom said. Because of the accident, she miscarried. I don't know if I'm supposed to be thankful or sad or angry." Her eyes were pools of fear and honest confusion. "I can't quite grasp it. Jessica just wasn't the kind of kid who would get pregnant and not tell me."

Privately, Wyatt thought Mattie was being naive, but he kept that to himself. "Babe, I have no clue how teenage girls think, so I won't even venture an opinion. Until she comes out of this coma, the answers are, at best, guesses."

God, had he really made such an asinine comment? Sugary words that offered nothing but sounded earnest. Secret stone-type words.

She looked deeply frustrated. "I have to get home. Hannah's at my parents', and they all need to be told before they hear about it in the morning from someone else."

Wyatt cupped her face and turned it upward. He saw in her wide eyes a desperate need to sweep out the conflicts and tuck herself into the pretty, safe life she'd had just a few hours ago when Jessica had been her perfect daughter.

"You shouldn't be alone," he whispered, only fleetingly realizing that if he went with Mattie, his nephew would have to drive his truck. Funny, he mused, how that didn't matter now as it had at 1:50 in his bedroom. "Let me drive you home."

"Oh, Wyatt, how sweet of you, but I can't."

"Why not?"

"It would just be complicated."

"Driving you home is driving you home. How can that—?"

She touched his mouth to silence him. "Please don't argue with me," she said. Then, as if in a rush to leave, she pressed the button on her keys to unlock the car. "I need you to just be a sweetheart."

He sighed, but he didn't argue. "All right. Then let me offer this. If there's anything you want me to do . . . mind the shop for you, run errands, take you to Newport to make mad, passionate love. . . ." He grinned, hoping to raise another smile, and he did, but it was fleeting. Then the tension returned, and she seemed to have escaped into some other world. "Mattie?"

"I'm sorry. I just keep thinking about all the unanswered questions."

"I'm sure."

"Who was the father?" She looked at him with such abruptness that he almost took a step back.

"What?"

"Jessica's baby. Who was the father? The only boy she'd dated lately was Kevin." She glanced at Wyatt's truck, where the kid had slunk down in the passenger side. "He never said anything tonight. Not a word, not a question, not even a curious look, which I think is pretty pissy."

"Mattie, maybe he didn't say anything because he doesn't know anything."

"Or he does know and he hopes no one will ask."

"Did you tell him?"

"No. I need to talk to Stephen first."

Wyatt felt the sudden drench of cold water. "Ah, yes, the ever-present Stephen."

"He's her father," she said, as if this was news, but he also heard the edge of defensiveness. "And he's as worried and confused as I am."

Before he could think too hard about the hole he was digging for himself, Wyatt said, "Yeah, that seemed real clear tonight when you had your arm around him."

"You're jealous?" This seemed to astonish her.

"Call it what you want."

"That's very territorial, Mr. Landry."

"Very intuitive, Mrs. Caulfield."

"I don't know if I like it."

"Tough."

When she started to object, he kissed her. He kissed her hard, wanting to imprint his touch on her, to show her that despite the mess tonight, nothing had changed between them. Then, to his delight and relief, she relaxed, returning his kiss. She slid her arms up around his neck and pressed tightly to him. Almost a kiss of desperation, a kiss of deliberate persuasion that made him want to believe that as of this moment, she'd declared Stephen a nonentity in her life.

Which was exactly what Wyatt wanted him to be.

Chapter Three

By a few hours after dawn, the tossing and worrying
and new questions had tangled and twisted Mattie into such
mental contortions that she gave up the idea of getting any
sleep. So much for the wonders of Valium.

She pushed back the covers on her white four-poster, sat
on the edge, and rubbed her temples. The May sun flooded
the blue and yellow bedroom, its brightness drawing her,
wooing her to turn and watch the light splash on a dainty
daffodil fabric-upholstered Queen Anne wing chair she'd
bought last week at an antique store in Connecticut. She recalled her happiness at getting the chair for such a reasonable price and her giddiness on her drive home as she
pondered the trio of east-facing windows that showcased the
angled space in her bedroom. The area was most favorable
to adding depth to the room's focal point—her bed.

None of these musings were the least bit relevant now,
but thinking about pretty chairs and a froth of accessories
was less stressful, less horrifying, and required no struggle
for answers. Mind drift, she supposed.

Beside the chair stood a mahogany gateleg table on
which she'd placed yellow irises in a blue Minton pitcher, a
hammered brass and china lamp with long silk fringe on the
shade, and a silver box with an intricately carved M that Wyatt had bought for her when she'd dragged him to an antique

mall in nearby Fall River, Massachusetts. In the box she'd placed dried rose petals from a Valentine bouquet, then scattered some on the table. A book of poetry and an old pair of spectacles completed the tableau. She'd spent hours two days ago arranging and placing so that the eye found interest and beauty. For Mattie, the presentation process and its kick of satisfaction gave her as much pleasure as the hunt and the discovery.

After she'd assumed full responsibility for The Garret from her parents, she'd quickly learned to first experiment with her knack for compelling arrangements at home. With the exception of the silver box, all the items on the table would be taken to the shop and offered for sale in just such an enticing display. Innovative arrangements assured customers that she sold more than junk and elderly dust collectors—she sold elegance. This invaluable sales tool she'd learned from her mother.

When Louise and Carl Rooney had run The Garret, her mother's knack for the "exquisite presentation" had helped to establish the business as one of the most popular antique shops in southern New England. Tap into customers' instinctive appreciation of beauty, then make it blossom by showing them what they could do when they took the item home. Each display was precisely thought out, yet its charm was that it appeared to be just the opposite—some lovely things hastily placed and then casually abandoned.

Lovely things placed and abandoned. Always inanimate objects? Or had she been careless and allowed such fanciful arrogance to envelop her personal life?

Certainly in Mattie's ideal setting, she was ultimately in control of every detail; she was adept at magically making expectations become reality; life was so pretty and secure that a daughter would be incapable of even a tiny dabble at the fringe of troubling behavior. And though in context it sounded like a pink icing world that only unrealistic romantics would inhabit, Mattie had indeed encouraged her daughters to search for remarkable possibilities instead of settling for the current teenage mantra of cynicism. And for that she offered no apology or regret. Beauty and serenity were so much easier on the senses than nasty conflicts—like the painful reality of her damaged daughter.

Somewhere in this looming mystery, Mattie had disregarded a defining moment or missed a more subtle turning point, either through ignorance or through the carelessness of only half-listening to one of Jessica's convoluted chats, in which she could leap from college choices to which of the thirty-seven shades of brown lipstick she should buy—all in the space of a few moments.

On more than a few occasions, Mattie heard without hearing, processed without pausing to question; and no doubt Jessica was aware of it when she switched to autopilot listening. Mattie knew her daughters weren't totally blameless. Getting their way by not volunteering information they deemed a red flag was a game in itself.

Just the same, Mattie knew she'd been deeply distracted of late—by The Garret, by her developing relationship with Wyatt, by the pressure of the upcoming Alice Landry auction, and, the last day or two, by the books she'd been rushing to ready for her accountant. Somewhere along the way, not deliberately, she'd mentally abandoned her daughter's life.

Mattie pressed her temples, trying to ease the stubborn headache that had developed on that frantic drive to the hospital. If only she could find even a few reasoned possibilities to explain Jessica's behavior.

Stealing a car. Forming a friendship with a girl whose name she'd never once mentioned. And then, yesterday afternoon, Jessica had deliberately lied about where she'd been going. Mattie would have liked to believe it was just evading the truth, which sounded far less damning. But in the end, both were the same.

And the most shocking—the pregnancy. For all these weeks, Jessica had been *pregnant*. Even after hours of trying to digest that fact, Mattie couldn't. She'd scrutinized the past days for some hint, some out-of-kilter action. Yet she could bring nothing major into focus. In hindsight, even the normal became suspicious.

Such as two days ago.

Jessica had come into the shop, complaining she had no summer clothes. And Macys was having a sale, so could she have the credit card? Mattie, in the midst of closing the sale of a two thousand dollar buffet, had waved her away with a yes, joking to the buyer that her daughters had enough clothes to open their own dress shop, yet every summer they wanted more.

Now, of course, she wondered if the new clothes were to disguise a pregnancy. Then there was the more cynical possibility—a reward for having figured out how to rid herself of an embarrassing problem. Mattie flinched from this second thought. She simply couldn't believe her daughter was capable of such cold, calculating deviousness—but then the Jessica she knew seemed to have evaporated, the Jessica she knew wouldn't have been pregnant.

Although teenage pregnancy wasn't the shock and shame of a generation ago, in their family the subject had never been treated as ho-hum. Mattie had taught and talked, and Stephen, too, had made it clear neither he nor their mother would view such a situation as a minor mistake or as no big deal. Had Jessica feared telling them, and decided to get an out-of-town abortion? That possibility would explain the lies—both outright and by omission—and a new confidante in Arlis. And perhaps the fear of missing an abortion clinic appointment energized the car theft idea. Desperation turned good sense into bad behavior.

It seemed like such an easy explanation, and yet one she would not blindly accept. She wanted answers, and by God, she intended to get some.

Mattie dragged her fingers through her hair and closed the window. In the bathroom, the mirror reflected a woman with tangled blond hair and dark circles under her eyes. A woman looking more like fifty-eight than thirty-eight. She washed her face, brushed her hair, and pulled on the chenille robe Stephen had given her for Christmas two years ago.

From the top of the stairs, she heard voices in the kitchen. She peeked into Hannah's room and saw a lump of quilts and lacy pillows indicating her younger daughter was still burrowed in and asleep. She eased the door closed, thankful Hannah wasn't beset by wakefulness.

Just hours ago, Stephen had brought their daughter home, upset that he couldn't calm her hysteria. Mattie had held her and rocked her, and Stephen gave her a Valium to calm her. Mattie had taken one, too, before lying down with Hannah. Once her daughter was asleep, she'd returned to her own room.

Now, as she headed downstairs, the questions she'd promised Hannah she'd answer today would no doubt be asked by her own parents.

In the kitchen, besides Stephen, she found Louise and Carl Rooney. Her mother fussed with putting away dishes from the dishwasher and her father sat hunched at the oak kitchen table, reading the editorial page of *The Providence Journal*.

Well into their sixties, her parents could have been a cover couple for vitality and attractiveness in their seasoned years. Physically fit, they both walked every day, played golf, and were meticulous about their diets. Her mother was slender and fashionably dressed. This morning she wore a suit the color of lemon sherbet, a watered silk blouse, and low-heeled pumps. She was impeccably made-up, her hair fashionably styled with a gray streak that enhanced her looks rather than pointing out her age. Her scent—something French that Mattie could never remember—was as familiar as her mother's worried but sympathetic smile.

Stephen leaned against the counter, talking on the phone. Earlier, while she'd been soothing Hannah, he'd turned off the ringer on her bedroom phone. He'd volunteered to take all the calls and promised to wake her if there was one about Jessica.

Now she watched him, eager for news. But he shook his head, his face haggard and tired.

"No, Donna, we haven't heard anything since we left the hospital," he said to Donna Morris, a young mother who worked part-time for Mattie at The Garret. "She's resting, and I'm sure she'd appreciate you manning the store today."

He glanced over at Mattie, eyebrows raised. She nodded, glad that Stephen, at least, was thinking straight. She hadn't even thought about whether to open or close today. "Yes," Stephen was saying, "I'll tell her you're praying for Jessica. We all are. Thanks for calling."

His face softened when he looked at Mattie. "Hi, sweetheart. I didn't expect you to be up this early. It's just a little past eight. What can I get for you?"

"You don't happen to have any secret stones, do you?"

"What?"

"Secret stones?" her parents chorused.

Mattie closed her eyes, feeling light-headed, as if she were two bodies—one floating in the blissful innocence of yesterday and the other tethered in an odious darkness, searching for daylight.

Secret stones indeed. How could she explain them? Wyatt, she realized, would have been amused by their puzzlement. God, they probably thought she was crazy. Next she'd be ranting about bugs in her hair and tiny magicians huddled on the beach, sorting through stones to find the secret ones.

She reassured them with a smile. "Just fringes of a leftover dream. I didn't sleep very well." They all looked immensely relieved. Couldn't have the orderly, practical, and always rational Mattie babbling anything weird. Secret stones, she was pretty sure, would definitely fall into the weird category.

The phone rang again, diverting all the concerned gazes. This time it was one of Jessica's friends. Again, Stephen was patient and informative. Mattie's mother whispered, "That phone has rung at least a dozen times just since your father and I arrived. Stephen has never once rushed the callers, and I'm sure he must be exhausted from answering the same questions again and again." Wonder filled her eyes and she whispered, "Why, it's as if he's the one comforting them."

"It would seem that way," Mattie said, finding her mother's fawning a bit heavy-handed but not surprising. Stephen was good on the phone, a trait Mattie (and Stephen, too) would have attributed more to his years of being a salesman than to instinctive empathy.

Yet her mother's admiration went far beyond his telephone skills. Her parents adored and respected Stephen, and had been quite vocal about the divorce—her father distressed, her mother mortified. They'd let Mattie know at least once a week, in the six months since the divorce was final, that she'd made a huge mistake she would profoundly regret.

Admittedly she'd had many moments of guilt and a kind of mourning for a love that began nineteen years ago as Briarwood's most promising union, and ended as a lost, sad casualty. But profound regret? No.

"Is Hannah still asleep?" her mother asked.

"Yes, I looked in on her."

"And how are you?"

"Numb." She poured herself coffee, pausing at the box of Dunkin' Donuts on the counter. She knew her dad brought those. Whenever there was a family crisis, her dad bought Dunkin' Donuts by the boxful. She knew that if she didn't take one, he'd fuss and frown and insist, so she took a cream-filled, ignoring her stomach's lurch of rebellion, and was rewarded with her father's nod of satisfaction.

Carl Rooney was a small man, always boasting he'd had to work doubly hard to get tall sons. She'd never been clear on what "working hard" entailed, but whatever it was, his labor had been rewarded. Her brothers, Geoff and Mark, were both just about six feet, whereas she'd inherited her father's shorter stature, standing barely five feet four.

Now, he dusted doughnut sugar from his hands before refilling his coffee mug. Her mother went into the dining room and returned with a Limoges cup and saucer; she poured a dabble of cream, and then coffee, into the cup. Louise Rooney despised clunky mugs, anything plastic, and improper behavior.

"Have you called Mark and Geoff?" Mattie asked, sipping her coffee, relishing its caffeine hit on her senses.

Her mother answered. "I reached Mark. It was only three in California, and he sounded as if he hadn't even been to bed." She glanced at Carl, as if their son's late hours were incomprehensible. Mattie wanted to say that Mark's penchant for parties and women, when he wasn't earning a gazillion dollars in Silicon Valley, was a surprise only to his mother.

"I hope you told him not to come," Mattie said.

"Not to come?" Her mother looked horrified. "Why, I did no such thing. His niece is badly hurt, and a trip home to see her would be entirely appropriate."

Mattie lowered her head, but the sight of the doughnut brought a wave of nausea. "Mom, there's nothing he can do here."

"He can go and visit Jessica, that's what he can do. He can see how a family pulls together in a crisis." She took a small sip of coffee, the emerald ring gleaming on her right hand. It had belonged to Mattie's grandmother. Louise pursed her mouth, then added, "Perhaps he might find something valuable in all of this to aspire to."

Mattie didn't miss the obvious sarcasm. Both of her brothers' disinterest in marriage had been an issue that her mother had chewed on and criticized for years. She wanted lots of grandchildren, and she thought it uncivilized that she'd had three children and only Mattie had done the "proper thing."

Louise set her cup down gently on the saucer, as befitted a fine piece of Limoge. She moved closer, drawing Mattie into her arms and hugging her delicately, as if she might fly into a dozen pieces. She pressed their cheeks together, then pulled back to look at her closely. "Oh, Mattie, you look so drawn and pale."

"It's not a perky, bright-eyed day, Mom," she muttered, growing irritated by the pointless conversation. She should have stayed in bed and waited so that Stephen could spare her their chatter and diplomatically have sent them home.

"It's a terrible day, but wrecking yourself isn't going to help Jessica."

Like she'd arranged herself to look as dreary as a wet mop.

"Some makeup and that lovely rose suit with the white piping would do wonders," Louise continued. When Mattie frowned, she added, "Of course, it's your decision."

"Thank God for that."

"Louise, that's enough," warned her father.

"I was only making a suggestion. I just think it's important for Jessica's sake that we don't look as if we're in mourning."

Her father rolled his eyes, then patted Mattie's hand. "Your mother is just worried about you, and I am, too."

"Why is everyone concerned about me?" she snapped, unable to endure the fussing any longer. She pushed back from the table and rose to escape the claustrophobic air that suddenly swirled around the table. She wanted to fling open the back door and escape. Instead, she gave them both a direct look. "The one thing all of us should be focused on is that Jessica wakes up okay. Forget about me. I'm not the one wrapped in bandages and tubes. I'm not the one that might die. I'm not the one who did unexplainable things."

Her father straightened and exchanged a puzzled look with her mother. "What unexplained things?"

Astonished, Mattie realized that her parents knew none of the contributing details. She'd just assumed Stephen told them when he picked up Hannah. Hadn't they asked? Or had Stephen simply cruised around the questions so as to avoid showing Jessica in a bad light? Though that might be commendable, surely he didn't think the unsavory fine points would remain a secret.

Apparently noticing her confusion, Stephen walked to her and slipped his arm around her shoulders. "I thought they should be told by both of us."

"Why?"

He looked honestly perplexed. "Why? Because they're your parents, and I assumed you'd want to be the one to explain and answer questions."

It made sense, and yet it didn't.

"Will someone please tell us what's going on?" her mother asked.

And so Mattie did.

By the time she'd concluded with the pregnancy and the miscarriage, Mattie was genuinely concerned about them. Her mother had sat down, as if no longer able to stand, and her father looked waxen. They huddled close together, like a pair of frightened children. Oh, God, they shouldn't have to be dealing with this.

Mattie knelt before them, taking their hands and rubbing their chilled fingers. Gently, she added, "We don't yet know what Jessica has to say. There may be other circumstances that will explain all this."

"How many circumstances can there be to explain her getting pregnant?" he mother asked. Then, rallying her composure, she added, "It's disgraceful!" She looked beyond Mattie to Stephen. "I hope you intend to speak to that Kevin person she was dating. He has a lot to answer for."

"You're damned right," echoed her father.

"Mattie and I'll take care of it," Stephen assured them.

With all three staring at her for confirmation, Mattie took the easy way and simply nodded.

But allowing Stephen to handle this wasn't exactly what she intended to do.

Chapter Four

"The Garret. May I help you?"

"Run away with me."

Mattie laughed. "I've been wondering when you would ask." It was Monday afternoon, two days after the accident, and Mattie, unable to sit at home by the phone any longer, had decided to go to the shop. She'd already called and asked Kevin to come so they could talk, and she was waiting for him when Wyatt called. "Where are you?" she asked him.

"At the house. I'm headed for Newport in about an hour. I miss you."

"I miss you, too. Are you going to the brokerage office?"

"Next week, I'll go in for a day or two, just so my desk isn't completely buried." As a result of his own shrewd investments, and new wealth from the tech markets when they were in their infancy and skeptics were ignoring them, Wyatt suddenly became the guy to call for advice on the volatile Nasdaq. Wooed by the big-name investment houses, he passed them up for a local investment firm in Newport where he did consulting and pretty much set his own hours. He had, by choice, a limited client base and a waiting list of investors looking to improve their portfolios through his knowledge. With the upcoming auction, he'd limited his days in the office but kept in touch with clients by phone or E-mail.

Now, he said to Mattie, "The day is gorgeous. Boats will be cruising in the harbor, and I hear the city's already crawling with tourists. I was thinking you could drive down and we could have dinner." And in his mind he added *and make love*.

"I'd like to, but . . ." He heard her hesitation.

"Let me guess. Your ex beat me to it."

She drew in a sharp breath, as if surprised by his comment. "Don't be ridiculous. Why would I go out to dinner with Stephen?"

"Excellent question."

"I know you don't like him hanging around."

"How about if I don't like him, period?"

She sighed heavily, and he knew his irritation with Caulfield was giving her one more thing to worry about. Before she could say anything, he apologized.

"I don't know what you want me to do," she said. "I don't want to fight with you, but I can't just pretend Stephen doesn't exist."

"I know, babe, I know," he said softly, then added his own turmoil of apprehension. "You can call it old-fashioned fear, but I can't get past the fact that when all of this is over and Jessica is okay, Caulfield will have coiled his way back into your life."

"Oh, Wyatt, no. You're in my life, and I'm not interested in changing that."

"Thank God."

"But Stephen isn't disposable. He's part of my life because of the girls. I can't change that, no matter how much you don't like it."

This time it was his turn to remain quiet.

"None of this is about Stephen and me, Wyatt. Please tell me you believe that."

"I suppose so."

"I want you to know so."

Saying it didn't make it so, but because there was no point in circling a subject that didn't have the answers, he gave some ground. "I'm working on it." Then he asked, "How is Jessica?"

He heard the long sigh. "No change. In the meantime, I'm checking into those unanswered questions."

"Good."

"Kevin is coming here so we can talk."

"He'll want to help. He was pretty upset and worried for Jessica."

"Not surprising, since he's probably the father of the baby she lost," she said firmly.

Wyatt was glad they were on the phone, so she couldn't see his astonishment. When she'd told him of the pregnancy, he had heard only speculation about Kevin. What had changed since then? Nothing that he knew about.

Given all the other unanswered questions about what led to the accident, Wyatt wasn't ready to assume Jessica hadn't had a secret sex life with more boys than just Kevin. And even sex with Kevin was more assumption than fact. He hadn't asked his nephew any questions because . . . well, hell, because he just hadn't. A nosy uncle he was not—if Kevin had wanted him to know, he would have told him.

Finally, he asked Mattie, "How did you come to that conclusion?"

"What other one could there be?"

"That he's not the father? That they didn't have sex? I know that's a foreign concept in this day of 'all sex all the time,' but restraint is a possibility. That Kevin might be the good guy in all of this?"

"Meaning Jessica is a bad girl?"

Maybe. But he didn't say that. Why had he ever thought that switching the topic to Jessica would be less tense? *Okay, smart guy, you walked into this one. You gonna piss or punt?* He kept his voice low and easy. "Maybe she's just a mixed-up kid. Come on, Mattie. I know she's your daughter and you want to protect and believe in her, but aren't you being a bit too naive?"

"My God, you think she was promiscuous!"

"I didn't say that."

"Then what are you saying?"

Shit! The beats of silence that enveloped his tongue were ominous. And Mattie seized on his befuddlement.

"You believe she slept around, don't you?"

He sighed. "No, of course not. All I'm saying is that there just might be another boyfriend. Maybe a guy that she knew you and Stephen wouldn't approve of."

"Jessica wasn't like that." He heard the chilly indignation and withdrawal. He guessed it was more comfortable to tag Kevin than to open the door on another potential deceit by Jessica.

"Give Kevin a chance before you hammer him."

Another three beats of silence. "Of course I want to hear his side of the story, but I'm not going to accept a lot of dodging and denial. He needs to accept responsibility."

"Sounds like you've already judged him guilty."

"I'll know for sure after I've talked to him." Then, even and cool, she said, "A customer just came in. I have to go."

And before he could get out more than "All right," she hung up.

It occurred to him that his nephew, guilty of the deed or not, was about to be blindsided. Despite not liking that, he knew from his cop days that the best way to get an unprepared response was to ask an unanticipated question.

He reached for the cell phone to warn Kevin, started to punch in the number, then changed his mind. Nope. He was already in deep shit with Mattie just for offering an alternative. The kid was a big boy, and whatever involvement he had with Jessica, he needed to face it and deal with the consequences—no matter how complicated and uncomfortable.

While Mattie waited for Kevin, she paid some bills, added three new items to the on-line auction site that had become a new and profitable outlet for The Garret, and blocked out a schedule for Donna. The young mother was grateful when Mattie contacted her about working full-time.

By four o'clock, when Kevin still hadn't shown up and the usual browsers had slowed to a trickle, Mattie decided she'd close and see if she could track down the teenager.

Just as she was locking the back door, the front door slammed.

"Mrs. Caulfield?"

Mattie rounded the corner, and there he was. "Kevin, come in. I'd almost given up on you."

"Yeah, well, I almost didn't make it. My mom and Uncle Wyatt got into a brew about the boxes I dragged down from the attic."

"Oh, no."

"Mom doesn't want any of it auctioned off."

"It can be difficult to part with family things."

He shrugged, peeling a lingering cobweb from his messy hair. His clothes were dusty and his face smudged with a streak of dirt. "She never looked at the stuff before Gramma died. Now every box is like some treasure chest."

Mattie knew from Wyatt that Corinne had not been easy to persuade. Their mother's will had been very specific that the items be sold and the money used for Kevin's college education, yet Corinne kept taking items back. Mattie guessed Kevin's mother was having her own internal battle between what she wanted and what legally had to be done.

Now, Kevin glanced around as if terrified to move for fear of touching or breaking something. "I shoulda cleaned up, but after my uncle left, Mom wanted me to help her lug some more junk. Anyway, I knew I was already late, so I just came."

"I'm sure your mother and uncle will come to an agreement."

"Yeah?" He looked at her as if she might have some news he didn't.

"What I mean is . . ." What did she mean? That families resolve problems created by the deceased's will? On the contrary, she knew the opposite—that even in the best of families, a will can cause strain, hard feelings, and nasty insinuations. She cleared her throat. Why had she allowed herself to be drawn into this?

He gave her a crooked grin, as if he understood her dilemma. "It's okay—even my uncle can't figure Mom out. Besides, she's always been bitchy about Uncle Wyatt. If she were my sister, I'd tell her to get a friggin' life, but he doesn't like to piss her off. You like my uncle, right?"

"Uh, yes, I do," she said, amazed that Kevin was so talkative; his chatter was definitely better than those one-word mumbles or grunts so rampant among teenage boys.

"He's a cool guy. He's been like a dad to me, but he doesn't put up with any horseshit—oh, sorry—but you know what I mean."

"Uh. . . ."

"One of the things that got him and my mom smokin' was Mom telling him that Paige might come back. You ever met her?"

The bounce from boxes to Wyatt and Corinne arguing to Wyatt's ex-wife had Mattie wondering if Kevin hoped to steer her away from getting to the reason why she wanted to see him. "No, I never have."

"She's a knockout, but you don't have to worry." At this she raised her eyebrows. "No way, nohow would Uncle Wyatt take her back. He told me once he'd burn in hell first. Mom and she are kinda, like, friends, I guess, and he doesn't like it."

Mattie found herself intrigued by this glimpse into the inner sanctum of the Landry family. "Sometimes our choice of friends raises questions for others, but that doesn't mean the friendship is wrong." So true, Mattie decided, realizing that her words to Kevin could also apply to Jessica and Arlis. Although Mattie had never heard of Arlis until the accident, there was no question that some kind of friendship had developed between the two girls.

He shrugged. "My uncle asked Mom why, of all the women in the world, she had to latch herself to his ex-wife."

That sounds like Wyatt. "And what did your mom say?"

"Fuck you."

"Oh."

"He was cool. He never lets her really rattle him. Mostly he just lets her do what she wants, and then if it's a mess, he just takes care of it."

Ah, he just takes care of it. Those wonderful secret stones that solved all the problems. Mattie smiled.

"You wanted to talk to me about Jessica?" he asked, startling Mattie by his directness. He was, she realized, either a brilliant strategist when it came to conversation or as clueless as Wyatt had suggested he might be.

"Yes, I do. Why don't we sit outside?" She took a can of Pepsi from the refrigerator, handed it to him, and grabbed a bottle of water for herself. Because the patio was uncovered and hot from the afternoon sun, Mattie led the way to the side porch. The space was set up with a table, white wicker pieces cushioned in yellow, and a few wrought iron chairs recently sandblasted, primed, and painted a glossy black. As soon as she found a suitable table, she'd put the iron set up for sale.

Kevin sat in one of the wrought iron chairs. Mattie appreciated that he didn't want to soil the yellow cushions. Thoughtful without being told. More insight into this young man. He tucked his work-booted feet beneath the chair. He popped the tab, took a long swig from the can. Mattie figured he probably wished it was beer.

He leaned forward a bit, rolling the soda can between his palms. "How's Jess? I haven't been in today 'cause of all the stuff I did for my uncle and meetin' you, but I'm goin' tonight."

Mattie told him there'd been no change, then added that she wanted to talk to him about before the accident.

"I didn't see Jess or talk to her before."

"I meant the weeks before."

He squeezed the can in his palms. "What about them?"

"You and Jessica were going steady, right?"

"We were going out."

"Okay, out. You two were pretty serious?"

"I guess so."

Mattie sighed. "You were her boyfriend, she was your girlfriend, you went steady—that kind of serious."

"We went out."

Was this the same Kevin that a few minutes ago had strung dozens of words together? She was growing more than a little annoyed. *All right, forget about subtle, get to the point.* Invasive she was not, but clearly this called for a specific question. "Kevin, were you and Jessica having sex?"

The air around them flattened, as if all the sweet scents of spring had swooshed out and scampered away, leaving behind an airless stench. His throat flamed crimson, the color quickly flooding his cheeks; he looked trapped, and Mattie fully expected him to leap out of the chair and run as fast as he could. She almost wanted to tell him never mind, sex with Jessica was none of her business, but of course it was.

"Kevin?"

"Jesus, how can you ask that? Not even my uncle has asked me that."

So Wyatt preferred ignorance to asking embarrassing questions, too. She wasn't sure if that endeared him to her or irritated her that he hadn't saved her from this awkward situation. "Kevin, I need you to answer me. Truthfully."

He sagged back, his body language so tormented and embarrassingly clear that Mattie really didn't need a verbal yes, but she waited nonetheless.

"I wanted to, but she wouldn't."

Mattie blinked. "Excuse me?"

"Huh?"

Mattie shook her head as if to clear it. "You're telling me you wanted sex and she wouldn't let you?"

"Yeah," he mumbled, as if his private humiliation were on public display.

And then, to her horror, Mattie heard herself asking, "Why not?"

"She said she'd promised herself she wouldn't give it away just 'cause a guy wanted it. Didn't matter that I wasn't just *any* guy; she said she was gonna wait till she got married. That you told her that once she did it, she could never take it back."

Mattie stared at him. Yes, that sounded like her daughter. At last someone had said something that Mattie, without hesitation, believed.

". . . months ago. Then she got kinda weird and started breaking dates."

"Wait, Kevin. What did you mean 'months ago'?"

"The last time we, well, went out."

"You two broke up months ago?" Mattie asked, more confused than before.

"Well, we sorta just stopped dating. She started acting weird, and I saw her with a couple of guys—you know, sorta hangin' with them like she liked them. At first I thought she was, you know, tryin' to make me jealous—Jess always got noticed by guys. Then I saw her hangin' with Arlis and some of her loser pals. . . ."

"Wait. When did she start being friends with Arlis?"

He shrugged. "A while ago." At her frown, he said quickly, "Hey, I didn't write it down. A few weeks, a month ago. I don't know exactly. Anyway, I told her she was lookin' for trouble, and she blew me off. Told me to get a life and leave her alone. Hey, I'm no guy who goes beggin'—tons of girls wanna go out with me, so I left her alone. But then when she got hurt—well, I mean, I did like Jess and I was worried about her. That's why I came to the hospital when I heard."

A spoiled relationship, but clearly Kevin still cared. She was confused as to why Jessica simply quit seeing Kevin. Was she afraid to tell him about the baby? Yet he'd said they never had sex, but since a pregnancy proved that wrong, she wondered if Kevin was scared or looking to avoid responsibility. That seemed odd, considering what she knew about him, but if he were desperate . . .

Mattie had other questions, but she wanted an answer on the most crucial one. "Did you know that Jessica was pregnant?"

This time there was no redness or embarrassment, as there had been with the sex question. This time his face was as blank as if she'd asked the question in Dutch.

"No way!"

"The baby was yours, wasn't it?"

But instead of a sheepish yes or a hot denial, his expression went from blank to befuddled. "Jess pregnant? Nah. Impossible. Probably some dumb rumor. Girls are always yakking about getting pregnant. Who told you that?"

"Dr. Egan," she said flatly.

His expression collapsed as the seriousness of what she'd said sunk in.

"Jesus. Then I guess she was."

"It would appear so." Mattie waited, and when he said nothing else, she put down her bottle of water and rose to her feet. Standing over him as if he were a recalcitrant child, she said, "Kevin, I'm asking you a direct question, and I want a direct answer. Jessica's baby was yours, wasn't it?"

"No! I told you we didn't have sex."

"I know what you told me, but women don't get pregnant by themselves."

"And I'm not a liar!" He squashed the Pepsi can, spewing the remaining soda on his hand and up his arm. He flung the can into a nearby bucket, then got to his feet and started toward his bike.

Mattie grabbed his arm. "Wait a minute."

He jerked away. "For what? To find out I was a moron for believing her virgin bullshit? She's telling me no, then I find out she gave it away to some guy who never used a rubber? If she told you the kid was mine, she's a goddamned liar."

With that, he pulled away from her. Moments later he was riding his bike down the street and disappearing around the corner.

Mattie stared after him. As much as she wanted to believe he was lying to her, she knew he wasn't.

This put her even farther back than square one; now she had not even an idea who Jessica had sex with. Even more disturbing was the reminder of Wyatt's words. Perhaps her daughter had slept around. And then there was Stephen. . . .

With this insistent denial from Kevin, she dreaded telling Stephen. No doubt she'd get the blame for this mess and he'd argue that Jessica got into trouble because she, Mattie, hadn't been home enough.

Wyatt Landry drove down to Newport, still troubled by his call to Mattie. Their disagreement about Kevin would shake out soon enough; what Wyatt really feared was the seeming omnipresence of her ex.

Wyatt didn't like him, didn't want to like him. Every time Mattie mentioned Caulfield's name, Wyatt clenched his teeth to keep back the imaginative expletives that tumbled on his tongue.

But keeping quiet, or now standing aside and silently watching Mattie slowly move from finding Caulfield's attention pesky but forgettable, as had been true prior to the accident, to citing his solid fatherhood credentials and his ex-husband support, unnerved Wyatt. Whether his own motive was selfishness, possessiveness, or plain old jealousy, he hadn't decided. Maybe all three, but what he did know for sure was that his pissed level was tipping toward the red zone. That exchange about Kevin had been more pissy than productive, and the Mattie of before the accident would have not been so defensive and ready to hang Kevin. The woman he'd come to know and love—the sparkling smile, the mischievous whimsy, the sweet disposition—had been swamped by her overwhelming concern for Jessica.

Now he slowed at the toll booth, tossed in the token, and crossed the bridge from Jamestown to Aquidneck Island. Years ago, the span had been renamed for Claiborne Pell, a former Rhode Island senator, but to most of the islanders it was still the Newport Bridge. He maneuvered the tourist-clogged Newport exit, veering to the side roads, and headed for his house on Old Beach Road after stopping at the post office to pick up his mail.

At home, he checked the progress on the new roof and, looking at his shaggy lawn, decided to hire a kid from the next block to take over the mowing. Wyatt liked manicuring his own yard, but he was spending so much time in Briarwood, he couldn't keep up with the fast-growing grass.

Trio Yorke, a fourteen-year-old who could have given some of the local landscapers lessons, was the third son of a woman Wyatt dated briefly after his divorce. Kathy Yorke knew Wyatt's ex from a Save the Bay benefit dinner, but they'd never been friends. Kathy thought Paige was a self-important snob because her father had worked on the governor's staff. Kathy's dislike of his ex plus his own blistering fury over Paige's year-long affair with his friend and partner Bobby Dodd constituted poor ground to cultivate a relationship.

Royally blindsided by the double betrayal, Wyatt had come perilously close to murder. His personal life and his career as a cop were so scorched that most days he didn't even recognize himself. Getting serious about *any* woman was about as likely as a bull humping a flamingo. And though heavy interest in Kathy was not an issue, he found himself in an emotional quagmire when Kathy began making less than subtle suggestions about living together, about love, and about "having a future together."

Wyatt was amazed and annoyed by her assumptions— how could three mediocre dates and some equally mediocre sex add up to forever after?

"It's what women do," Andy, a bartender friend, had explained while pouring Wyatt his third Coors. "They want more than sack time; they want bonds and promises."

"Based on what? That Paige is a bitch and Kathy is nothing like her? No argument on either, but hardly the prelude to 'Here Comes the Bride.' "

"A total prick would string her along and then, when it got messy, dump her."

"You think that's what I'm going to do?"

"Yep."

"Andy the psychic," Wyatt muttered.

Andy leaned forward, lowering his voice. "And who gave you a heads up on your wife and Dodd?"

Wyatt's silence answered that question.

"Way I see it, you got two ways to go." Andy wiped the mahogany bar and dumped more pretzels into a basket. "Either lose her now or love her the way she wants."

Gripped by beer-blurry self-pity, Wyatt almost asked, "What about what I want?" but caught himself in time. Sure as dogs pee on hydrants, Andy would nail him with "We both know what you want," and then guffaw for about ten minutes. Wyatt knew what he had to do.

Love for Kathy wasn't even a possibility, but he was genuinely fond of her. He didn't want to hurt her, but he didn't want to lead her on either. While he mulled over continuing to feign ignorance of her intentions versus making a clean break, Kathy arranged a "romantic" weekend at a Cape Cod bed and breakfast.

After they arrived, he overheard an exchange about some stoic cattle rancher who'd come all the way from Montana with a ditsy redhead twenty years his junior, and gone home with a headful of sexual euphoria and a firm wedding date. Then there were other stories with the same "happy" ending. Plus the owner, an orange blossom addict, had put together a guestbook called "Happy Marriages Begin at Cape Sea."

In hindsight, he should have nixed the getaway, but playing it all out had been instructive, in that he reinforced his absolute disinterest; although he'd had no doubt that Andy would have called him a bona fide prick.

Kathy had wrongly assumed that during those two days he would be so caught up in the kiss and bliss atmosphere that he'd parade out his—she was sure he had them—previously hidden serious intentions. He'd pitied her because she'd been so naive, but he also resented being set up in such a ludicrous environment. Christ, he'd been thirty-five, and the last time his head and heart had been influenced by such syrupy machinations, he'd been on his way to the altar with Paige. And that had been as far from a happy ending as slow dancing in a hive of bees. So because he'd been both amused and pissed, he'd spent the weekend dodging her commitment hints.

Finally, late Sunday, when they were packing to leave, the confrontation exploded. Kathy tossed away the hints and zeroed in. She wanted a wedding date or at the very least an engagement, and they weren't leaving until she got it. His mistake, he realized, was in not nixing the weekend in the first place. Pushed into an "either-or" decision, he quit playing soft and easy. He made it clear that the only relationship he wanted with any woman was one that could be summed up on a cocktail napkin. That, of course, sent her from stunned speechlessness to an inferno of outrage in all of four seconds. He readily admitted to being cavalier and shallow, but he figured that was a helluva lot more forthright than wasting time with suck-up excuses and dishonest apologies. Needless to say, their trip home had been stiff and tense.

Then, to his amazement, Kathy called a month later, as if there'd never been a harsh word between them, and announced she was no longer angry at him—better a broken relationship than a broken marriage. Could they still be friends?

Since a leap from bastard to pal generally required a bridge, Wyatt was suspicious and kept his distance. But no apparent fallout occurred, and a few years later, when he bought a house a few blocks from her, she was there to welcome him to the neighborhood.

Recalling his bluntness with Kathy, Wyatt wondered if keeping his thoughts about Caulfield tethered had been the wrong approach. What he wanted to do was convince Mattie to tell the fuckhead to move to another continent, but he couldn't imagine her doing that with Jessica's outcome in doubt. What he probably needed to do was soften his own approach . . . something along the lines of . . . well, sharing his concerns. He shuddered at applying such a candy ass phrase to any conversation with Mattie. They'd been up-front with one another from the beginning, but now, with Caulfield buzzing around, Wyatt had suddenly been thrust into standby status. He didn't like it, but had no clue how to change it.

"You're the candy ass, Landry," he muttered aloud as got out of the truck with his load of mail. And he knew why—because his feelings for Mattie were vastly more involved—and, yes, *serious*—than dates and sex. And because he didn't want to lose her over a disagreement he probably couldn't win, silence became his response.

Good old silence, he mused, unable to avoid the parallel of those months with Kathy. Except for one mammoth difference. He didn't want to lose Mattie.

He glanced once again at the roof. Two-thirds done, he gauged, and after a few grunts and scowls from Jake, the head roofer, Wyatt secured a "maybe" that the work would be completed by the end of the week.

In the house, he tossed the stack of mail onto the kitchen counter and called Trio Yorke. He'd caught him just coming in from school, and the teenager happily agreed to a twice-a-week mowing—Wyatt offered him seventy bucks a week. He hung up and did a general check of the house, scratching the idea of moving back and doing the commute. It wasn't the miles or the driving that settled his decision to temporarily relocate in Briarwood, but the daily details of getting his mother's things inventoried for the upcoming auction. Plus, he liked seeing Mattie at odd hours.

Back in the kitchen, he sorted out the bills from the junk that he tossed in the trash unopened. Then he came to a letter from his ex-wife.

He'd had a bellyful of talk about Paige with his sister. Now this.

His chest tightened as he stared at the envelope—Paige's precise penmanship, the heft of the expensive vellum, and the return address in Providence. Of all the cities in America, she had to choose one that was twenty minutes from Briarwood. Coincidence? No way.

Since their divorce, Paige had lived in Boston, Manhattan, and Philadelphia. Between two of those moves, an inheritance came her way via her father's death. Money and beauty were a lethal combination, and no doubt his ex-wife was using both to her advantage.

This Providence address was near Brown—an East Side artsy, intellectual, and high-rent neighborhood. Wyatt, ever the cynic when it came to his ex, figured she'd curried the favor of some influential faculty member with one of her whacked-out causes, like banning junk food from the university's dining rooms.

After a brief thought of lighting a match and burning the letter unread, he flipped it over and tore open the flap. The note smelled as expensive as the stationery looked.

Dear Wyatt,
I was so saddened to hear of your mother's death.
Before returning to Providence, I'd been in Arizona

for the past year, caring for my own mother, who has been going through some depression. Corinne probably didn't tell you, but Mother and her second husband divorced and she was quite devastated by it.

I wanted to express my sympathy, for Alice was always so good and kind to me, even through our own problems. . . .

Wyatt reread that statement three times. *Our problems? Our? You cheated on me and that was our problem? Spread the blame to minimize your own betrayal? Nice try.*

. . . Corinne has been in touch with me, and she says she has some things for me—just a few mementos that your mother had told your sister that she wanted me to have. . . .

He frowned, trying to recall any time that his mother had offered Paige more than the vaguest of smiles. Alice Landry had never criticized openly, yet she'd never been comfortable around her sophisticated daughter-in-law. His mother felt intimidated and shy, and Paige, to his knowledge, had never done anything to lessen either. Now Paige wanting some trinket or piece of dated junk just didn't pass the sniff test.

And then there was this:

I'll be driving over to Briarwood early next week. Perhaps we could meet and have a drink.
Fondly,
Paige.

Wyatt reread the note four times. The last line about meeting for a drink intrigued him, because Paige knew how much he despised her.

He was curious why she and his sister had kept in touch—true friendship, as Corinne claimed, struck him as a stretch. As much as he and Corinne had their disagreements and arguments, she was his sister and he loved her. Most of the time she was too trusting, and all the time too defensive when she was proven wrong. Paige could sound sincere, ooze empathy, or create whatever sugary emotion she needed on cue. He knew; he'd been suckered by all of them. He simply didn't believe Paige cared about Corinne—more probable was Paige caring about Paige, with his sister simply a vehicle to ride through whatever plan Paige had.

Wyatt sighed. He didn't need this crap, but if Corinne already knew Paige was coming and she didn't appear because Wyatt interfered, it wouldn't be Paige who'd get the blame. He and his sister were already at odds; sandbagging this supposed friendship would not endear him.

Paige had him by the balls, and no doubt she knew it. Nevertheless, he took great pleasure in ripping the vellum in half and tossing it into the trash.

Chapter
Five

*Almost a week after the accident, Jessica remained un-*conscious.

Every day, Tom Egan assured Mattie and Stephen that her condition was slowly improving, although to Mattie, little appeared to have changed. Some of the machines had been disconnected from Jess's body, but they remained nearby, bordering her bed like metal beasts from a *Star Wars* panorama. The most obvious injuries, the bruises and cuts, were healing, and for that Mattie was grateful. Still, worry and fear had become constant companions.

Thank God for Donna. With The Garret covered, Mattie worked out her daily schedule around hospital trips. On each visit, she eagerly anticipated that *this* time she'd find a change to reassure her that Jessica was getting closer to waking up. Yet on every visit, her hope had evaporated into disappointment.

On this sunny late spring afternoon bursting with new life, Mattie's expectancy soared anew. Hannah had actually stuck around this morning and talked about a summer job at the local hardware store where she'd worked the previous year, rather than dashing off, as had become her habit. The phone calls that Stephen had faithfully monitored had lessened, and yesterday, at The Garret, she and Donna had talked for almost an hour before Jessica's name came up. All of this indicated that the immediate shock and fear had dissipated and her daughter's accident was slowly becoming old news. On the one hand she balked at this, and yet on the other hand she desperately wanted Jessica's condition off the "she's doing as well as can be expected" treadmill and on a straight line to full recovery.

"Patience, Mattie," Tom Egan said to her now, as they both stood near the hospital bed. He wore a lightweight sports jacket over a pristine shirt and tie, and his pants were so sharply creased that Mattie wondered if he carried a travel iron in his medical bag. A snotty observation, she knew, but the days of medical stagnation had made her testy. She'd planned this particular visit to coincide with Tom's afternoon rounds; she wanted to be there to see for herself exactly how he examined Jessica.

At the foot of the bed he read her chart, then drew close to her side. He took the stethoscope from his bag and listened to her heartbeat. Next he used what looked like a fat fountain pen with a light on the end to look into her eyes. He took her pulse and felt her skin, gripped her hand and then released it—once, twice, three times.

Mattie watched closely, praying he'd turn and smile or nod or something. Instead, he slipped Jessica's hand beneath the covers and stood for a moment, watching her sleep.

"Any change?" Mattie asked.

"Not the one you want me to tell you."

Her shoulders slumped and she felt dizzy, as if it at any moment her head might spin off into nothingness. She felt as if she were functioning inside a whirling abyss. Tom cupped her elbow and urged her to sit down.

"Mattie, Jessica is better than when she was brought in. It's only been five days."

"It seems like five months. I'm sure she's better than the night of the accident. . . . It's just that it's so slow—the progress, I mean."

"I know this is very hard. You're her mother and you want to make her well." He sighed. "She's been through a traumatic accident that affected her body beyond what we can physically observe. She's healing, but this is going to be a long, slow recovery."

She wished he would tell her something she hadn't concluded herself. "But she doesn't move. Not a finger, not even a blink of her eyes. If I didn't know she was breathing . . ." She let her words trail off, their implication making her shiver anew.

"I assure you she is. Her body is working hard to heal, and we're doing everything we can to help it along."

"Can't you give me some idea of how long?"

"If I give you a time frame and she remains in the coma, how will that help? False hope would be more destructive than uncertainty. Medical science has made a lot of strides, but comas are unpredictable, and right now Jessica's body is on its own timetable. We watch and monitor and learn, but anything as exact as a prediction that could be made about a broken arm simply isn't possible."

"Of course, you're right." And deep down, under all the angst and worry, she believed him.

"You need to be in good shape when she does wake up. If you keep yourself in this high anxiety state, I'm going to put you in a bed and order you to rest."

Mattie's eyes stung, and she twisted her hands together. "I've been a real pain, haven't I?"

"A royal one."

"Oh, God."

He reached down and squeezed her hands. "If you were anything but a pain in dealing with a crisis like this, I'd be disappointed."

She managed a smile.

Then, when she said no more, he asked, "How are Hannah and Stephen?"

"Hannah is better, but still scared and weepy. Stephen has been tireless—everyone's emotional support."

"I'm glad for all your sakes. I know how upset he was about the divorce."

Mattie wasn't sure how to respond. Tom and Stephen weren't close friends; they would be better described as two tennis enthusiasts. They played at the same indoor court and occasionally stopped for a drink at a nearby bar after a match. Stephen had never given these bar stool chats much more than a shrug and a "just a couple of guys discussing bad and good serves" dismissal.

"I didn't know Stephen discussed the divorce with you."

"Not at any length. Frankly, I found it refreshing that he didn't dwell on the details, nor did he in any way descend into angry trash talk about you. He did make it clear that he wished it hadn't happened."

"No one likes to go through a divorce," Mattie murmured, feeling defensive and resenting her reaction. Their divorce had been exceptionally free of charges and counter-charges. But then it hadn't been about one huge issue like cheating or abuse or some sudden exposure of a secret life; it had been about the unexpected changes in Stephen—and yes, in her, too—that piled one upon another until their weight finally crushed their marriage. Mattie anticipated the breakup long before Stephen did, and when it finally happened, she was more resigned and better prepared. Stephen simply expected his remorse and apologies, and her willingness to understand and forgive, to be enough. They weren't.

"You and Stephen have made the best of a difficult decision. Friends that Brenda and I have who've divorced weren't so generous toward their exes. In those cases divorce day was happier than most days of the marriage."

Mattie pondered that; she and Stephen had been happy *many* days, not most. She knew that their contentment had flourished because of their defined roles in the marriage—he worked and made the money, and she stayed home and raised the children. Nothing conflicted. Only when those roles changed, a year ago, had the problems begun.

Tom walked to the door when a male nurse signaled him. They spoke in low voices, then Tom said, "I'll be right along." He picked up his bag and patted Mattie's arm. "I have to go. An elderly patient saw me come down the corridor, and is upset that I haven't been in to see him." He glanced at his watch, then picked up their previous conversation. "You and Stephen should be commended. It's good for Hannah, and ultimately for Jessica, that you've both put whatever differences you've had aside and come together as a family during this crisis." When he reached to pat her again, she stepped away; the gesture made her feel like a clingy child. "Take care of yourself," he murmured, striding out the door.

Mattie sat for a while after he'd gone, thinking about what Tom had said. She had divorced friends, and she knew that above all they loved their kids. She couldn't imagine that even those who had been mired in the messy conflicts of support and custody and property settlements would not put that anger aside if one of their kids were hurt. Tom was singling out her and Stephen for behavior that, given the turn of events, seemed pretty normal to her.

Today's visit had spawned a change—if not in Jessica, then in her. She glanced at her daughter and saw her with the eyes of resignation. The last shroud of denial that any of this could have happened to her daughter slipped quietly away, leaving her chilly and empty. But, remarkably, the vacuum presented new space, for that patience Tom told her she must have. She'd spent days jumping between disbelief and fear for Jessica. Then there had been her desperate optimism that this would be a forty-eight hour crisis followed by a wakeful Jessica, full of explanations about mistaken perceptions. No "actual" lies, not a "stolen" but a "borrowed" car speeding in the night toward disaster, and no "real" pregnancy.

Denial, Mattie realized, clothed itself in many disguises. And as long as she persisted in believing in the lollipop life she'd presented to her daughters, the longer it would take to find out what Jessica had gotten herself into.

And she did want to know. For whatever trouble had brought her daughter to this place, that misfortune had not taken her life. God was indeed good. So from this fresh perspective, she concluded that once she'd assembled the missing pieces, the evidence that now appeared damning would become, at the very least, explainable. How her troubling talk with Kevin fit into this, she had no idea. But she didn't have all the answers yet.

She straightened, optimism crowding out her earlier doubts. At the bed, she bent down and kissed Jessica's cheek. She crinkled her nose at the cloying antiseptic smell, really noticing it for the first time. Tomorrow she would bring some of that jasmine body cream Jessica loved.

Mattie squeezed her hand. "I love you, sweetheart." And because she didn't know what else to say, she kissed Jessica again and left the room.

"Mattie, you have such lovely things. And you're always adding more. It's such a delight to shop here."

"Thank you, Mrs. Crowley," Mattie said as she wrapped the chintz teapot and its lid in layers of yellow tissue. "I try to have unusual and unexpected items. And when Ernie finds something I know a steady customer like you will love, I try to make sure you see it first."

"Well, Ernie certainly did a good job this time." Mrs. Crowley smiled knowingly, as if having a shopping edge with Mattie were as beneficial as being married to a man who could afford her indulgences. "Please tell him to keep looking."

Mattie smiled. "I will."

Ernie, a picker who knew what Mattie liked and was familiar with the merchandise she carried, had found the teapot at a church sale. Known for his buzzard-sharp eye, Ernie had spotted a Pamper Shampoo box shoved beneath one of the tables that sagged with junk. The box advertising an extinct brand of shampoo had been a huge clue that items inside were probably old.

After checking the markings on an assortment of plates and bowls, he found the teapot at the bottom, wrapped in a 1950s newspaper. The fuzzy-haired woman manning the table apologized profusely for the jumble of dingy china— the carton had come in just moments before the sale began. While she chattered on about the impertinence of donations made at the last minute, Ernie smiled engagingly. He offered the woman ten dollars for the box, and as he was leaving, carton in hand, he heard her brag to another worker that she'd gotten rid of that filthy box for much more than it was worth. Little did she know.

When he'd called Mattie and told her he had the chintz teapot—no chips, no crazing, and an intact lid—she was ecstatic. Because they'd done a lot of business, he offered to sell it to her cheap. Of course Ernie's idea of cheap and hers were never the same; so they haggled, made offers, then counteroffers until finally Ernie agreed. Usually the price was less than what Ernie wanted and double what Mattie had hoped to pay, but in the end both got a bargain, considering the current prices for genuine chintz in the collectibles marketplace. Ernie did his usual snarling about how she always got her price, and Mattie reminded him that it was he who taught her how to haggle with a picker. In the end, both made an impressive profit.

The assorted china in Ernie's box sold quickly to other dealers, and at the end of the day, his ten dollar investment brought him an eye-popping 900 percent profit in less than forty-eight hours.

When the teapot arrived, Mattie inspected it for the minutest chip or hairline crack. Ernie, as always, delivered what he promised—mint condition. Mattie had called Myra Crowley, and the moment her customer saw the piece, she paid in excess of three hundred dollars without even a blink.

"You must have quite a collection of chintz by now," Mattie commented as she placed the pot in a sturdy box.

"Oh, I do, but never enough. Here, let me put the lid in my purse." Mattie handed her the tissued item. "I can't wait to have a tea. What fun. Oh, and what else did I want to ask you . . . ?" Thoughtful a moment, she said, "I have it. A cake plate—any size. Do you suppose your Ernie could find one of those? And maybe a server?"

"I'll tell him to look. If any do come in, I'll put them aside and call you." Mattie loved doing her own treasure hunting, but practically speaking, she couldn't run The Garret and be in ten other places. Ernie knew what she liked, and because she trusted him, she often bought from him on his word alone that a piece's condition was mint or nearly so. Not once had she been disappointed. "I must tell you, though, that a chintz cake plate with a server in pristine condition will be expensive."

Mrs. Crowley shrugged off that reality. "You just call me. Promise?"

"I promise."

Myra signed the credit card receipt, and Mattie gave her a copy and the carefully wrapped purchase. She watched with some amusement as the woman stopped and fingered a basket of white linen luncheon napkins, their edges scalloped in dark rose. She turned to Mattie. "I just can't get out of here, can I?"

Mattie laughed.

"Oh, dear, I shouldn't, but they will look so pretty with the teapot . . . for my tea party." She swept up the basket and handed it to Mattie along with a different credit card. "Richard won't notice that I bought this stuff the same day if they're on different cards."

Mattie took care of the transaction, and this time Myra did indeed leave, her backward gaze catching sight of a huge ceramic jardiniere. She looked wistfully, then said, "Maybe next time."

Mattie thanked her again for her patronage. Not until Myra was safely out the door did her smile collapse.

She sat down at the wooden table behind the counter, feeling drained. Keeping up appearances, as her mother would say, was more tiring than she'd anticipated. Usually a conversation like the one with Myra would give Mattie a huge rush. Pleasing her customers so that they came often and spent lavishly not only made the shop a success, but assured her she was building on the base of a satisfied clientele left by her parents when they retired.

But since the accident, her enthusiasm had waned—the scant number of new items on the weekly inventory list attested to that. Mattie was very aware that her regulars came to browse and buy as often as three times a week, and new items were essential. Usually, in a week's time, she had been to a couple of auctions, perused local flea markets, and made the rounds of the weekend yard sales. It was a rare week that she didn't find at least a dozen sure-to-sell items.

But these past days had produced nothing but the teapot, and that was thanks to Ernie. Her customers understood, but even though her own life was on hold, theirs weren't. There were two other shops in Briarwood, and at least thirty others—that she knew of—within a fifteen-mile radius. Her customer base would soon be spending their money elsewhere.

What concerned Mattie was her ho-hum attitude and her amazing lack of interest: the shop, the sales, the hunt for more items, were suddenly irrelevant. Yet at the same time, she couldn't afford to let The Garret flounder and fail.

In addition, the Landry auction loomed. She still hadn't gone through the boxes from Alice Landry's attic, half of which Wyatt had hauled down and placed in the living room to be sorted through. Wyatt had also grumbled about furniture stored in a shed that awaited attention. Completing appraisals of the items in the house had taken weeks—and then Corinne and Wyatt were at odds over what should be sold and what shouldn't, so that presented another delay. And most recently, her conversation with Kevin that left her more confused than satisfied.

She rose, went to the small refrigerator, and took out a can of iced tea. She loved the shop and her work, but it frustrated her that so much of her day was spent here when there were so many unanswered questions about Jessica that she needed to pursue.

The bell jingled, and Mattie looked up, expecting to see Myra back to buy the jardiniere. She was surprised to see that her visitor was Barbara Prescott, Callie's mother. Mattie had called her after the accident, only to learn she was on an unexpected out-of-town trip. Seeing her now filled Mattie with a burst of fresh anticipation.

Trim and carefully coifed, Barbara grinned, then hurried forward, drawing Mattie into a very pleasantly scented hug. Mattie responded in kind, feeling her eyes smart when Barbara whispered, "I came right over, Mattie. I'm so, so sorry. I just got in from the airport, and Callie told me all the dreadful details. You must be absolutely frantic and terrified."

"More numb and worried. I'm glad to see you. How was the trip?"

Barbara peeled off a linen jacket and laid it aside with a needlepoint handbag that she had worked on all winter. "The trip was fine, but the visit was depressing. My sister's ex got remarried, and it really sent Marilyn over the edge. Drinking, crying, hysterically calling him, and then asking me at least a zillion times how he could do that to her. When I said he was a goddamned bastard who probably never gave a thought that his gold-plated wedding to a dimwitted party girl might offend her, she just cried some more. What's wrong with some men, anyway? Are they really that idiotic?" She sighed. "It was a long, stressful week. I wanted her to come back with me, but she refused. I think she's ashamed that her perfect marriage to the perfect man that she bragged about turned into a sleazy nightmare."

"You're a good friend as well as a good sister."

"I hope so."

Their friendship had begun a few years ago, after they met at an auction where they had bid against one another on a Rookwood vase. Barbara had won the bidding war.

"But enough about Marilyn," Barbara said. "I simply can't believe what happened to Jess. How is she? Any change?"

"She's healing, but no sign of consciousness."

"Oh, Mattie . . . and here you are working, when I'd be as worthless as a wool sweater in August. Why don't you get that Donna person in here to handle things?"

"She's here as often as I need her."

"Well, if there's anything I can do. . . ."

"Actually there is. I need some questions answered about the night of the accident."

For a moment Barbara appeared uncertain, then said, "Sure, I'll be glad to help, though I can't imagine what I would know." She stepped back, and Mattie imagined that she would have backed right out the door if she could have done so gracefully. Barbara was a good friend, always willing to help, so Mattie was puzzled by this uncharacteristic unease. However, she had known for a long time that when it came to Callie, Barbara tended to view any conflict that couldn't be solved by a cleaner house or a home-cooked meal as something that, if ignored, would simply fade away.

Mattie said, "I called you after the accident to ask about the sleepover."

"Oh? I was away."

"Yes, but didn't Callie tell you what I wanted?"

"There were a lot of calls, and she and Don took messages. I haven't gone through all of them." Barbara shifted a bit too much, glancing out the door at her cream-colored Mercedes, obviously hoping for some emergency, such as the car alarm going off, so she'd have an excuse to leave.

To slow down any incentive to do so, Mattie hung up Barbara's jacket and slid her handbag away from the sweating iced tea can. "If Callie told you all the accident details, surely she would have mentioned that I called. I spoke with her for about ten minutes and pretty much told her what she told you."

Barbara pursed her mouth, then smiled dismissively. "Oh, you know how kids are. They simply repeat stuff, never bothering to say where it came from."

Mattie decided she was probably splitting hairs, and besides what did it matter? Barbara was here now.

"I need to know some details about the sleepover."

"What about it?"

"Was there one?"

"There was one planned—at least Callie was preparing for one. I was packing to leave, so I didn't pay much attention except to leave money for pizza. She knows she can always have girls for the night, but no boys. I'm adamantly opposed to boy-girl sleepovers," she said firmly, as if her rule would never be broken. And in Barbara's organized world, it probably wouldn't be. "Besides, Don was home. You could have spoken to him. Why is this so important?"

Mattie allowed the statement about Don to pass; she doubted Don had hung around for even five minutes after Barbara's departure. The fact that Don was rumored to have had numerous girlfriends over the years had never found credence with the trusting Barbara. Mattie had vaguely floated the possibility a few times, but Barbara had become so unhinged at the prospect that Mattie had dropped it. Denial, she now realized, could become an addictive salve. "It's important because Jessica told me she was going to Callie's, but instead she was with Arlis Petcher."

Barbara was thoughtful a moment, then aghast. "Are you suggesting that *my* Callie allowed Jessica to use her as a cover to hide who she was with and what she was doing?"

"Yes, and she continues to do so," Mattie said bluntly, too weary and desperate to worry about being diplomatic.

"Now, wait a minute. Callie would not be a part of such a deception."

Barbara, like herself, had always been an embracer of Lollipop Land ideals. But in that moment Mattie realized that maternal naiveté wasn't innocent, but an excuse to hide behind a tangled mass of deliberate unbelief. "They're friends, Barbara, and I understand Callie's loyalty, but I also believe she knows a lot more than she's saying. Since Jessica can't speak for herself, I need to find out what Callie knows. I was hoping she might have told you."

"She hasn't," Barbara snapped, "because there's nothing she knows." She paused, and Mattie remained silent. Then, as though she knew Mattie wouldn't believe her, she embellished. "It's quite simple. She had a sleepover that Jessica was invited to, but didn't come. How you can leap to some teenage conspiracy from one incident is beyond me." Her voice had risen to a squeak, and Mattie knew that if she didn't get her calmed, Barbara would get in a huff, demand her jacket, grab her handbag, and sail out without a backward look. "I really have a thousand things to do at home." She did indeed lift her handbag. "May I have my jacket, please?"

Mattie took her hand and squeezed gently. "Barbara, please. I don't want to argue, and I'm not angry with Callie. I'm sure she and Jessica have a lot of confidences, as most good friends have, and if there weren't these mysterious circumstances around the accident, I would never ask you to try and get information. But suddenly the daughter I always knew is being portrayed as a stranger, and it's very upsetting." Mattie could feel a huge lump forming in her throat, and tried to swallow it. She thought she was cried out, but despite her efforts, her eyes filled. "I'm sorry. I don't want to be weepy and desperate, but I am."

Barbara's guard dropped away. She put her arm around Mattie and squeezed, then handed her a box of tissues. "I didn't mean to snap at you. In your place, I'd be demanding answers, too. And I truly wish I could help, but I just don't recall anything that night that was out of the ordinary." Then her eyes widened, and her hand tightened on Mattie. "Oh, wait. There was something I overheard."

"What? What?"

"But it had nothing to do with the sleepover."

"That's okay."

"And it didn't happen the night of the sleepover. It's probably meaningless, and it's going to sound like I was eavesdropping, but I just happened to be in the hallway, straightening out the upstairs linen closet. I can't believe what a mess it gets in, and Don is the worst. How one man wanting one towel can make such a mess . . ."

"Barbara? Callie and Jessica?"

"Yes, yes. It was an afternoon few days before. Callie and Jessica were in Callie's room, and they were talking kind of loud, like when you're arguing and your voice goes higher. Anyway, I walked closer to the door—okay, call me nosy, but the two of them never disagree about anything, and I was curious."

Mattie grinned at her. "Thank God for curiosity."

"So Jessica kept saying, 'Arlis isn't my best friend, you are, you always will be,' but Callie must not have been convinced, because Jessica kept talking to her. Your daughter does have a lot of friends," Barbara continued. "Then Jessica said something about wanting Callie to trust her the way she did about her boyfriend."

"Whose boyfriend?"

"I couldn't tell. Probably Jessica's, because Callie seems to have a new one every week. Anyway, I heard Callie start to cry. Jessica begged her, saying 'Please, please,' and I guess she convinced Callie, because a few moments later they came out of the room as friendly as ever. Both said hi to me and went downstairs. Apparently it was nothing more than a crisis of friendship that was quickly resolved."

"How did Jessica look? Had she been crying, or was there anything unusual about her? Nervous? Distracted? If she gets nervous, she's fiddles with her clothes."

"I thought she looked tired, but other than that, nothing. What are you worried about? Was Jessica into something dangerous? Oh, God, not drugs."

Mattie debated, then decided to just tell her. "She was pregnant."

Barbara looked shocked. "Oh, Mattie, no wonder you're upset."

"She lost the baby because of the accident. I'm not sure if I'm relieved or sad—a little of both, I guess."

"Well, if it were my Callie, I'd be relieved. You'd think, with birth control hitting you in the face in every drug and convenience store, that these kids would use it. Do you know who the father was?"

Mattie paused. Suspicion wasn't fact, and to single Kevin out when she wasn't sure would be unfair. "That's what I'm trying to find out."

Barbara frowned. "Do you think she confided in Callie?"

"Maybe."

"I'll find out. Maybe the mentioned boyfriend was the father. Don't you worry, Callie will talk or else." Barbara set her face into a kind of determined expression that assured Mattie that Barbara would indeed get an answer.

Suddenly Mattie had a moment of panic. To ask Callie meant revealing the pregnancy, and if Callie hadn't known before. . . . Mattie didn't want it all over town, and telling one teenage girl would open the chatter gates, plus Stephen would be annoyed, and her parents, worried about gossip. And then there was Hannah. Her stomach clutched, and for a long, horrid moment, she felt sick and dizzy. Had Hannah been told? Mattie had started to say something right after the accident, but something had interrupted, and later, after Hannah had gone to bed, Stephen had insisted that she let him handle it. She agreed, although now she wondered what she'd been thinking. She should have told Hannah. Then, as though she'd been prodded by a poker, she realized that she was allowing Stephen more and more responsibility when she should be easing him out rather than letting him become more entrenched.

Well, of course, Hannah knew. Stephen wouldn't want her to hear it from anyone else, and because she had no idea if Jessica had told anyone. . . . Then, as if she'd been stripped of all her maternal hovering, anger flashed. Why hadn't Jessica confided in her? How could she get herself in such an asinine mess?

Mattie eased herself down in a chair. *Get a grip here. You're frustrated, and you want answers that you aren't getting. But anger at Jessica isn't going to bring any new knowledge.*

"Mattie, are you okay?"

"I just remembered a phone call I need to make."

"And I need to go. I'll call you after I speak with Callie."

After Barbara left, Mattie called Stephen.

"Sweetheart, take it easy. I said I would tell her, and I did."

But you didn't tell me *you told her.* Holding down her irritation, she asked, "How did she react?"

"I told you she was surprised and upset. What's the matter with you?"

Surprised and upset? She didn't remember him telling her that. This was ridiculous. She would remember something that important. "Stephen, you did not tell me. I know I'm preoccupied, but not so that I wouldn't pay attention." Or had he, as was his habit, talked about so many things that she, as was her habit, tuned him out? Was it possible he'd casually mentioned telling Hannah and she'd missed it?

" 'Preoccupied' is somewhat of an understatement, Mattie."

She gritted her teeth. *Dumb, dumb, dumb.* She never should have admitted to being distracted. Stephen had leaped upon the word like a dog on a steak bone.

"I do have a suggestion, however," he said.

"Yes, I'm sure you do," she said, wearily.

"Spend more time at home. Since Donna's willing to work full-time, that will free you up to be home with Hannah."

It was one of those comments that, coming from anyone else, she would have immediately agreed with. But with Stephen, there was the hovering, the ordering, the sense that her behavior was the real cause of every family problem. The entire conversation echoed dismally of nitpicky ones in which Mattie was made to feel inadequate by the inference that she should retie yards of apron strings. Thereby she could keep all her daughters' needs paramount, making the three of them perpetually joined like peanut butter and jelly.

An absurd assumption, but of course how Stephen saw their family was what counted, and if she'd only view their lives from his perspective . . . he would be enthusiastically willing to take all the burden, all the chaos, and run everything the way he used to. Then and only then would all of them be leading exemplary lives.

But dammit all, now was not then. "You know what, Stephen? I don't have to listen to all of this. And if you don't like the circumstances at my house, no one is stopping you from leaving."

"Is that what you want? Maybe you'd like me to leave town, too."

"Oh for heaven's sake."

"And when Hannah asks questions, you can answer all of them."

"Stop it. You know . . ."

"And when Jessica awakens and wants to know why her father isn't there, you can explain that you didn't want me around."

"Of all the ridiculous statements! I've never said or insinuated I wanted any of the things you're saying. This sniping at me is neither endearing nor fair."

She didn't hear the long sigh of resignation she expected, but instead an apology.

"Mattie, you're right. I was way out of line. Guess my old habits haven't changed as much as I'd hoped." Then his tone brightened. "Sweetheart, this is all much more important than you and I wrangling over your independence. We are divorced, your life is yours, and I have no say about what you do. The only reason I seem so rigid is anxiety for Jessica's and Hannah's well-being. I know you'd never object to that."

"No, of course not," she murmured, counseling herself about being so touchy. He had been kind and patient and almost like the Stephen she'd fallen in love with. She was the one on edge, and taking that out on him wasn't fair. If she'd somehow spaced out that Stephen had indeed told Hannah about the pregnancy, then she was *definitely* too preoccupied.

"Mattie?"

"Yes, I'm here."

"I'll see you in a little while. I love you, sweetheart."

And then he hung up, leaving her staring at the receiver and listening to the dial tone. What nonsense. Stephen didn't mean he *really* loved her; he was simply caught up in being the good father and the supportive ex-husband, and had blurted out the residue of long-past feelings.

He loved her? No. Affection, perhaps, but not love.

Mattie locked the shop, set the alarm, and walked to her car. As she started the engine, she was still nagged by Stephen's insistence that he'd told her he'd spoken with Hannah.

Perhaps her mind was indeed shutting down. How could she have missed words about Hannah, but clearly heard that love confession? Tuning out his chatter had become a honed skill over the years, so that she could ignore the irrelevant and pick out the important.

But this time, she'd not even heard the important.

The truth was, she hadn't lived with Stephen for over a year. Before the divorce was final six months ago, they'd been separated for almost eight months. Her once honed skills could indeed be rusty.

However, she had certainly gleaned an important nugget from Barbara. Something had been going on with Jessica that was so out of the ordinary that she and Callie had argued.

And Arlis's name being mentioned days before the accident proved to Mattie that Arlis was more than just the girl with the car; at the very least she and Jessica were acquainted and friendly. So much so that Callie not only had noticed and had been hurt, but had believed she'd been replaced.

More pieces to the growing mystery.

And as if that conundum weren't enough, exterior events had popped up and glommed onto her thoughts like mind weights. Stephen staying at the house since that first night, sleeping in the guest room but making it clear, to anyone who took time to notice, that he'd returned home.

A fact she'd artfully dodged when it came to Wyatt. She'd allowed him to assume the obvious—Stephen was around more often because of the accident. Allowing the assumption held its own mendacity, for though she detested the half lie, she shuddered at the brew of conflict that would spill if Wyatt knew about Stephen. Hannah needing her father was the point, and to Stephen's credit, he'd been immensely supportive. Her overriding concern wasn't her ex, but her younger daughter.

Then there were her parents, smiling and nodding their approval of Stephen's return like the doting in-laws they'd always been. They were quick to proclaim that his presence was proof of what they'd always believed—that Mattie had been hasty and the girls ill-served by the divorce.

Hannah, too, had endorsed Stephen's reentry, acting as though the divorce had disappeared along with Jessica's consciousness. Mattie's mother, always with an opinion, couldn't resist noting "Oftentimes good things come out of bad events," and the sooner Mattie recognized that, the less she'd have to stress about. Pinning Louise Rooney down to define "good things" got Mattie a prompt "Don't be obtuse. You know what things. Look at the improvement in Hannah since she sees her father every day."

Mattie guessed the change in Hannah was due more to

the huge amount of attention she was getting as the sister of
the comatose Jessica. At first, Hannah had lurched from
tearful hysteria to moody silence, but most recently she was
bouncing with euphoria at the rush of popularity. Overwhelmed by the burst of new friends, male and female, it
was only human that she would bask in the new attention at
school, where she'd always felt overshadowed by her sister.

Hannah, cute and wholesome rather than vivacious and
beautiful, now found herself in the spotlight. At first she'd
shied away, but as the days passed, she'd gone from disbelief to flattered to glorying in all the notoriety. As a result,
Mattie's once practical daughter had morphed into a bundle
of dramatic sighs and teen magazine smiles.

"Hannah certainly has come out of her shell," Mattie's
mother had observed, leaving it unclear whether she thought
that a good thing or a disaster.

Mattie felt only concern, but what could she say that
didn't sound critical or demeaning? *Shyness becomes you,
and that isn't a bad thing?* Somehow, she doubted that
would sit well with Hannah.

But her mother's observation of Hannah's seemingly positive adjustment raised a sticky issue. How long would
Stephen stay? And if she had to ask him to leave, would that
upset Hannah?

Wyatt, of course, had been her private oasis. Now that,
too, ran the risk of being invaded by her good-intentioned
duplicity. It was weird, but when she focused on the girls
and the upheaval to her family, it seemed, well, acceptable
and reasonable that Stephen was at the house so much. It
was only when she imagined the scenario from Wyatt's view
that Stephen's presence seemed wrong.

"What you need to do is get this straightened out with
Wyatt," she said aloud, as she turned into her driveway. Hannah dashed out of the house.

"Hey, sweetie, where are you going?"

"Later, Mom. Got to meet some friends."

"I thought we'd go in and see Jess together."

"I already went in with Dad. Be home later."

Mattie watched her daughter rush down the street and

around the corner. She walked slowly toward the house, feeling as if her family had been cast adrift. Something was definitely wrong when the only one home was her ex-husband.

Chapter Six

"Some friend she turned out to be!"

"Maybe she was afraid."

"Afraid to tell *me*? Me? I'm her best friend. At least I used to be," Callie Prescott said in a miffed voice. "We told each other everything. How do you think it felt to have my mother ask if I knew? I felt like a jerk."

"What about me? I'm her sister, and I had to hear it from Dad."

"You mean your mom didn't tell you?"

"She was at the store. He wanted me to know before I heard it at school. Others are gonna find out, and then they'll blab it."

"I bet Arlis Petcher knew."

"No way. Jess wouldn't tell her."

"Get real. They were, like, as close as our butts are to these towels. She told Arlis all the stuff she used to tell me. And you know what? I don't even care."

Yes, you do, Hannah Caulfield thought, realizing that Callie, who bragged that she knew everything about everyone, didn't know diddly piddly about her very best friend.

It was a few days after each girl learned that Jessica had been pregnant. Because this was a half-day at school, Callie had called Hannah, suggesting they meet at the reservoir and catch some sun. Proms were coming, and no one wanted to look like a pale freak in her strapless backless. To gain mega ray exposure, Callie wore a skimpy two-piece and Hannah, who couldn't fit into last year's suit, wore a halter top and shorts. Both had slathered on a sticky lotion supplied by Callie that guaranteed to tan an August brown in only a few hours.

Since Jessica's accident, Hannah and Callie had talked, but only polite chitchat if they ran into one another at the hospital. Hannah knew the score when it came to her lowly sophomore status around a senior. Especially a senior in as tight as Callie. She never spent her time with "the lower life," as she called anyone younger than she was. Hannah, riding a wave of popularity because she was Jessica's kid sister, had been rushed by more than one senior looking to find out why Briarwood High's most popular girl ended up in an accident with a loser like Arlis. Given her freshly groomed status, she wasn't surprised by Callie's invitation, only that she'd taken over a week to make it.

After all, everyone else wanted to be with her, so why not snotty Callie? If she'd learned one thing since the accident, it was that with Jess off the stage, the spotlight was greedy for Hannah. And she didn't intend to miss a moment.

Her parents would be horrified by such an unsisterly thought, and Hannah had a few pokes of inconvenient guilt that she quickly rationalized with her cranky conscience that tried to keep her in a box she'd now outgrown. Although she loved her sister, it wasn't fair that she hogged all the flirty guys, got ten times more phone calls, and got invited to all the parties. Now it was Hannah's chance to prove she was pretty and flirty and fun. She knew she wouldn't shine and sparkle forever; when Jess woke up, she'd be the star again and Hannah would be lucky if anyone remembered her name. But for now the glitter and the glow were hers, and she didn't intend to waste a minute.

As the two girls stretched out side by side on a grassy patch near the town's reservoir, it was very clear that Callie had really called to pump for information. Today was all about Jessica, Hannah decided with a ton of disappointment. Too many days, even at home, were all about Jessica.

"Can't we talk about something else?" Hannah asked, suddenly feeling strangled by her absent sister.

"Something else? Like, what else is there in this hick town? I mean, here is Jessica in a coma, and now all this stuff is coming out that no one knew about. Everyone is talking and wondering who your sister really was, and you want to talk about something else?"

Hannah raised herself up, supporting her body on her forearms. Callie, eyes closed, moved her legs apart to tan her inner thighs.

"What do you mean 'who my sister really was'?" Hannah asked.

"Oh for God's sake, are you dumb, or do you just ask dumb questions? What do you think I mean? Her secret life, of course."

What a mouthy snot. Most of the kids who asked her questions were at least polite. Hannah never could figure out why Jess hung with Callie, and when she'd asked her sister, Jessica always defended Callie, saying she talked and acted outrageously because she thought that made her popular. And it did, Hannah surmised sourly, for Callie sure headed the jockette list at school. Hannah remembered all the times her mother had stressed that liking herself was more important than being liked by others. Maybe for adults, but for a kid not being liked was the worst—as bad as face hair and pus-filled pimples.

But the wild idea of Jessica having a secret life intrigued and alarmed her. Why, it was like being two different people, and it sure looked as if she'd been playing that game for a few months. Claiming to be a virgin, then getting pregnant by Kevin, then being in an accident with that snarky Arlis in a stolen car! It was pretty bizarre, and definitely "the dirt" at school. Her mother wanted to believe there were reasons that just weren't known yet, but that was way too tame for Callie. Hannah played along so she wouldn't sound dorky. "Oh, sure. She had lots of secrets."

Callie sat up, breasts spilling from the skimpy top. She'd already started to get pink, and Hannah glanced down at her own thighs. They were disgustingly white and grossly fat. No wonder she couldn't fit into her favorite bathing suit.

"She's told you all of them?"

Popular girls were always thin and buff and tanned. She was suddenly popular, but she sure wasn't skinny, tight, and bronzed. She could be, and she *would* be, Hannah decided. She'd quit eating lunch at school and spend the period sitting in the sun.

"Oh, Hannnnnnnnahhhhhh. . . ."

She turned to Callie, squinting her eyes. "What?"

"Jessica's secrets. Has she told you?"

"I promised not to tell."

"You can tell me. Come on, Hannah, you owe me that after the way your sister treated me. She begged me to trust her, and I did, and then I find out she was a fucking liar. I mean, is that lousy or what? She's my best friend, and she has some secret life and I'm the last to know."

"A couple secrets isn't a secret life," Hannah said, wishing she'd stayed home and tanned in her own backyard. A little Callie was already too much.

Thin and Buff sighed dramatically. "I bet they aren't even good secrets." Then she shifted the topic. "Were your mom and dad pissed about the pregnancy?"

"Secrets, secrets, secrets. Don't you care about anything else?"

Callie gave her a direct look. "No."

Hannah was not used to such direct answers. "Well, Dad seemed more sad and kinda disappointed, but with Jess being the way she is, it's kinda tough to be too hard on her. I think Mom was just shocked."

"Your parents will probably wait till she wakes up to make a stink. So has anyone talked to Kevin?"

"Mom did, and he says it wasn't him."

Callie sat straight up and put on her sunglasses. "Really? Wow, he denied it? That's pretty ballsy."

"Mom believed him. Dad didn't. He said Kevin was covering his ass by pretending to be outraged and innocent. I kinda think Dad is right. I mean, Jess was pretty straightforward about not giving out just 'cause a guy wanted it. But, I mean, Kevin was her boyfriend."

Callie scowled at her as if she'd just arrived on the dimwitted bus. "Not giving out? She was yankin' your chain, sweetie, giving you all that purity shit. She and Kevin fooled around plenty. Anyone who doesn't think that cunt and cock got regular action is a total dumbbell."

Hannah flushed, squirming away from the sleazy image that didn't sound at all like Jessica or Kevin. "You don't know that," Hannah snapped.

"Then how did she get pregnant? By some bee fucking a birdie?"

"You know what?" Hannah got to her feet. "You make me sick. I'm going home."

"Poor little girl can't take the truth," Callie said in a dismissive voice, stretching her slender body into the sun. "Hey, keep living in that white lacy world of Jessica the virgin—why should I care if you're that dumb?"

Hannah opened her mouth to protest, but the objection died on her tongue. Since her sister had gotten pregnant, it was pretty tough to keep playing the virgin tune. And Kevin *was* her boyfriend. She sat back down. "I think Kevin needs to show some guts. She isn't pregnant anymore, so it's not like he's gonna get stuck with a baby."

Callie shrugged. "Why admit guilt when no one is around to prove it?" She slathered on more sticky lotion. Then she looked at her in such a pointed way that Hannah fidgeted with tugging at the cuffs of her shorts. "Let's talk about you."

"Me?"

"You. I saw you flirting with Mr. Fairfax yesterday afternoon."

"I was not flirting," she said hotly.

"Oh no? Flickin' your hair back and leaning against his car so he could see down your blouse. I saw you."

"You're crazy. He couldn't even see the front of my blouse, 'cause I had a ton of books in my arms. He asked me if I wanted a ride home."

"And you went."

"Why shouldn't I? Those books weighed a ton. Anyway," she sniffed, "Kane has given me rides before." *There, Miss jerkhead, I can be just as snotty as you.*

"Excuse me? Kane? You don't call him Kane."

"I do, too."

"Since when?"

Since it pisses you off. She fluffed her hair. "Since he told me to."

"Well, you aren't going to do it anymore. You stay away from him."

"Maybe I don't want to."

Then Callie loomed over her, fury making her eyes darken almost to black. "He's mine, and I don't share. Or maybe you want me to get someone to beat the shit out of you to make it clearer."

Hannah shrank back. *She's serious. She really, truly believes that Mr. Fairfax is her boyfriend.* "Geez, I'm sorry, Callie, I had no idea."

"Of course, you didn't. But now you do."

But Hannah wasn't about to just drop this. She was curious and fascinated. Mr. Fairfax had to be over thirty. The older man—it sounded so deliciously forbidden.

Kane Fairfax was a part-time guidance counselor who always acted more like the kids than a fussy, by-the-book teacher. He'd been married once, a long time ago, but was single now and spent lots of hours at school because all the kids liked going to him. He was cool and laid-back and handsome in a dark, sexy way. He drove a red Corvette.

And the idea of him and Callie was just too juicy. "So, are you going to tell me about how all this happened?"

"I don't know. Jess said you were a blabbermouth."

"I am not! I kept her secrets, didn't I?"

"Okay, but you gotta promise on Jess's life you won't tell."

"I won't. I won't, I promise."

Callie leaned closer to Hannah. "It's so cool, and he adores me. We've been involved for about three months. No one knows—except Jess, of course—so if it gets out, I'll know it was you who blabbed."

Hannah barely breathed out her awe. "I won't. I promise." Then she asked, "Are you sleeping with him?"

Callie rolled her eyes. "No, we hold hands and wish upon the stars. Duh, Hannah."

"But how—I mean, isn't that against the law or something? Stories about teachers and students doing it always end up getting the teacher fired and in jail."

"He's not a teacher. Besides, all those stories are about little kids. I was eighteen in February."

Hannah knew she should be shocked or at least embarrassed, but instead she was fascinated. In her own fantasies, there was always something mysterious and mature about falling in love with a sophisticated older man, but those dreamy thoughts were usually about movie or rock stars, never about anyone she really knew. All the men she knew were dull and gray and boring except her dad and Wyatt.

She liked Mr. Fairfax; he was a cool guy, but she thought he was dating that third grade teacher. True, he was always giving guys rides in his Corvette and flirting with their girlfriends, and she had seen a lot of the girls flirting back. And, truth to tell, she'd had a bubbly, exciting feeling when he'd driven her home—sorta like the first plunge on a roller coaster. Wow, Callie really did have a cool secret, deliciously cool.

"You promise you'll never tell?"

"Oh, I promise." She wiggled closer to Callie. "So where do you meet? Like, I guess he doesn't come and pick you up like a regular date."

"We have a place—it's very private and very romantic."

Hannah envisioned a house that overlooked the ocean down in Newport—a place like her mother's boyfriend had. She could see it all—the sandy beach, a warm summer night, champagne, kisses and touches and sex. . . . Her sigh was audible, and Callie didn't miss it.

Callie reached over and pressed her hand on Hannah's crotch. Hannah jumped back, her face flaming red faster than the sun could have colored her skin. "What are you doing?"

"Seeing if you're as turned on thinking about Kane as I am."

"I'm just sweaty," Hannah sniffed.

Callie laughed. "Uh-huh."

"So what about your parents? I mean, don't they wonder where you are? Even with the divorce, my dad is always quizzing Jess and me about boys and where we're going and when we'll be home. I mean, how do you get around all that?"

"I lie."

"You do? Like *really* lie?"

"Parents are mostly clueless, and they believe what they want to believe."

"Aren't you afraid you'll get caught?"

"Of course. But that's what makes it so much fun."

Hannah didn't know what to say. What Callie was doing sounded wrong, but she sure acted like it was a lot of fun. It wasn't as if he was married or she was some kid. Then again, maybe she was making it all up.

"How do I know you're telling me the truth? You just said you lie to your parents."

"Hey, believe me or don't believe me, I don't care. Meantime, I'm off to have some afternoon delight with Kane. Translated for you children, that means some good sex. Then again, you probably wish you were me, don't you?"

Hannah felt very young and way out of her depth with the older Callie. She tried to picture how her sister had reacted to Callie having sex with a much older man. "Did you ever ask Jess that? If she wished she was you?"

"Everyone wants to be me, kiddo, Everyone." Callie swung her bag over her shoulder and walked across the grass to the street. Hannah watched her until she became a small, bikinied speck.

Callie and Mr. Fairfax having sex. She didn't know if she believed it, but thinking about it gave her a grossed-out feeling in her tummy like the night Darren Munson stuck his disgusting tongue down her throat while he hugged her like he was doing an imitation of a python. Hannah shuddered, recalling her one and only date with the older basketball player. Callie and Mr. Fairfax did all of that and much, much more. That's what Jess and Kevin had done, too, but Jess got pregnant and . . .

It wasn't fair, Hannah thought, stuffing her towel into her bag. Callie was doing gross stuff and got away with it, and Jess was in some stupid accident with Arlis Petcher, of all people, and all this secret stuff got found out. And Kevin, what a gutless loser. Well, she hoped her father didn't let him get away with it. He conned Mom, but no way would he con Dad.

"Mrs. Caulfield, come in and sit down. I'm so glad you came."

Evelyn Fitzgerald, the dean of girls, was a small, sixtyish woman who dressed impeccably and appeared to have come from a bygone era where manners, morals, and responsibility were as significant to the education of young adults as the academic basics of English and math. Though her approach brought plaudits from some, she had her critics who called her insensitive. She maintained that neither influenced her; her job was about making better students, not puffing herself up or appeasing naysayers. From her daughters, Mattie had heard that "Fitz," as the kids called her, always told the truth, even when "a lie worked just as good."

Mattie didn't want good working lies, nor did she want squishy excuses. She'd come for answers, and hoped that the dean, famous for her ability to peg problems, had observed something out of the ordinary in Jessica. "Thanks for seeing me, Ms. Fitzgerald."

The dean closed the door to her office and indicated a chair to Mattie. "How is Jessica? I spoke to Mr. Caulfield right after the accident. From what I've heard here at school, she's still in the coma."

"Yes."

"She's a strong girl. I'm sure she'll come out of this."

Mattie sighed. "If wishing would only make it so."

"If only. How can I be of help?"

"I'm curious about Arlis Petcher."

"So sad for her family."

Mattie leaned forward. "I didn't even know the young girl existed until the accident. That troubles me, because Jessica had never mentioned her. I spoke to the mother of one of Jessica's friends who overheard part of a conversation between her daughter and Jessica. She spoke with her daughter, but didn't find out anything. To be honest, I'm not surprised. But from what I have heard, Arlis was nothing like the other girls that Jessica hung around with. I guess I'm asking if you ever saw them together, and if you did, what you observed."

"What I observed indicated some kind of association. I saw them walking together in the halls more than a few times, and often they sat together in the cafeteria. I must admit their closeness struck me as odd—a bit like Cinderella forming an alliance with the wolf from 'Little Red Riding Hood.' "

"That certainly doesn't reassure me," Mattie said, the image too starkly troubling.

"Jessica is very popular and has her pick of friends, while Arlis was, well, standoffish. One has to labor to get even a minor conversation out of her." Then, before Mattie could comment, she added, "While I deplore cliques, they are unfortunately an entrenched fact of teenage life. The simple truth is that your daughter was very much an insider, while Arlis was not."

"Yet, they had something in common."

Evelyn Fitzgerald nodded. "Perhaps there was some mutual my-trouble, your-trouble bond."

A trouble bond? The more the dean talked, the more Mattie's interest deepened. Finally some answers. "Like what?"

"The Petchers divorced about the same time you and Mr. Caulfield did. That shared emotional upheaval could have created a bond where a simple friendship based on likes and dislikes would not have existed."

Mattie knew the divorce had been difficult for both her girls because they adored their father. There had been some low points when Jess and Hannah had blamed her, but she had resisted defending herself as the beleaguered victim and she had never sunk to trashing Stephen to shore up her own parental standing. Though there had been emotional traps and heated disagreements between them, Mattie and Stephen had been united in their determination that their daughters not become pawns or prizes. She believed they'd done their best, and the suggestion that a troubled Jessica would seek solace from Arlis rather than Stephen or herself gave Mattie serious pause.

"The night of the accident I just assumed they were married because they were there together, and he seemed worried about his wife." *Like Stephen and me*, she realized suddenly. *No doubt the Petchers assumed we were happily married, too*. Mattie had appreciated Stephen's support; no doubt Arlis's mother was glad for her ex-husband's presence.

"Was she loud and unpleasant?"

Mattie looked down. "She was accusatory, but she'd just learned her daughter was killed, and she was devastated."

"Was she blaming you or Jessica?"

"Both."

Ms. Fitzgerald nodded. "Shirley Petcher can be raw and vitriolic. She had a hard life and was never schooled in social graces and the art of polite tears. Having just learned that Arlis was dead—well, a courteous grief would have been ludicrous."

"In other words, she was honest and real," Mattie said, viewing Mrs. Petcher's fury in a new way. "I can assure you, my tears would not have been polite or my grief genteel if Jessica had been killed."

Ms. Fitzgerald smiled. "Then, like your daughters, you and Shirley have some common ground. Her honest reaction may have magnified your own discomfort with Jessica's behavior."

"This is not about me," Mattie said, shifting in her seat, uncomfortably aware of the bull's-eye the dean had hit.

"Nor is it about Shirley Petcher's opinion of Jessica," Ms. Fitzgerald said softly, obviously aware of Mattie's reaction. "You don't want to muddy your determination to find out what changed Jessica with how a distraught woman viewed her—or you."

Mattie got the point. She wanted her daughters—both of them—always to be viewed in a favorable light. They were good girls, and she'd raised them to be kind and unselfish and aware of the impression they made. Though none of that was wrong, Mattie immediately thought of her own mother's constant awareness of appearances, of being socially correct, of presenting herself in such a way as to play down anything unpleasant by blaming the unpleasantness for soiling her life.

"If Jessica had died, I would not have been filled with social graces either."

Ms. Fitzgerald smiled. "Not to put too fine a point on it, Mrs. Caulfield, I disagree. You are who you are, and I doubt even a major tragedy would spiral you into a demented personality."

"That doesn't sound like a compliment."

"Merely an observation of human nature. Generally, what is true of a parent is also true of their offspring. Arlis, like her mother, acted tough and hard because it was safer than being nice and softhearted. Jessica, like you, is polite and not given to explosive outbursts in front of strangers."

"Exactly. Jessica is a lot like me."

"And she certainly resembles you."

"Yes," Mattie said, recalling how Stephen had so proudly pointed that out. Both were blond, of the same height and close in size. And last winter Jessica had said, "Some kids at school say you look like my sister." Then, before Mattie could acknowledge the compliment, Jessica added, "It's so cool that I look older." And Mattie had smiled.

To Ms. Fitzgerald, she said, "That night I listened to Jessica being accused of things my daughter would never do. Stealing a car, drinking, lying . . . and pregnant."

The dean gave her a curious look. "Pregnant. Ah, I didn't know that, and to be frank, it surprises me."

Mattie nodded, then continued, "All the details we learned that night were bizarre. Another strange twist was that she was sneaking off with Arlis when she'd deliberately let me think she was going to a sleepover. And now you're telling me Jessica had some kind of 'trouble bond' with her. I can't reconcile any of those things with the daughter I know."

"Of course you can't, but that doesn't mean they aren't true or don't reveal a problem you haven't yet discovered."

"Oh, God, I can't imagine this getting any worse." Mattie sighed. "It seems the pregnancy was the source of this change in her."

"Perhaps, perhaps not."

Mattie rubbed her temples. "I'm even more confused."

"Until Jessica wakes up and can explain, you must view these details as dots without connectors. You cannot reconcile them without Jessica. If she'd been only slightly injured, all these pieces would be in place, and though not pleasant, they would have context and you would have insight. In the meantime, laboring to find the connectors is natural, but that process will no doubt bring more questions."

The dean rose and walked to her office window, on the sill of which twin vinca vines potted in bright yellow ceramic grew in lush profusion. When she turned around, her face was distressed. "What I'm about to tell you is more mysterious dots, but this is one of those situations that I didn't find disturbing enough to notify you or her father. But now that you say she was pregnant, it could be significant."

Mattie was immediately interested.

"About a month ago, I stopped in the library to get a book and saw Jessica sitting by herself at one of the study tables. She was reading quite intently, and when she saw me, she quickly closed the magazine and tucked it under some papers. She looked upset, and though I make it a policy to not interfere just for the sake of being nosy, something was clearly bothering her. This is a stressful time for seniors, what with finals and proms and college approaching. . . . I knew Jessica was planning on going to college in Boston, so I wondered if she was having second thoughts. Boston isn't that far, but it's a whole different world than here in Briarwood and commuting to URI. Anyway, I assumed something of that nature. When I began to ask a few questions, she nodded in that way teenagers do when they aren't listening but want you to think they are. However, her sad expression troubled me—she looked as if she were alone and trapped. I took it upon myself to sit down. I assured her that I only wanted to help, and that if she needed to talk, I'd be glad to listen."

Mattie felt as if pins and needles were pricking her legs and climbing up her spine, but at the same time she had a deep inner burst of euphoria. "Please tell me what she told you."

"Well, at first she brushed me off, but when I tried again to reassure her, she burst into tears and said Kevin Bonner had broken up with her and now everything in her life was ruined. Drama is hardly a stranger at this age, so when she didn't elaborate any further, I didn't press. I try not to apply platitudes such as 'This will pass,' 'There will be other boys,' or 'Rejection is part of life'; I know that teenagers need to work through a crisis to gain experience rather than be instructed in a lot of worthless generalities. Since I didn't see any other signs of distress following that afternoon, I assumed she'd handled it all right. Now it appears that being pregnant plus the breakup with Kevin explains the 'alone and trapped' expression."

Kevin, damn you, you did lie to me! Mattie felt like a gullible fool. "And you never spoke with her again?"

"No, but I did see her with Arlis about three days before the accident. Apparently the two of them were discussing something upbeat, because Jessica was smiling, and at one point she threw her arms around Arlis—you know the way girls do. Arlis seemed amazed by Jessica's happiness. Now that I think about it, perhaps Arlis was also puzzled by their alliance. Maybe it's a dot or a connector or neither. But I offer the incident to you in case it has some significance."

Mattie stood and offered her hand. "You've told me a lot, Ms. Fitzgerald. The tears over Kevin breaking off with her isn't the same story Kevin told me. Plus he denies he was the father."

The dean's eyes widened. "Really? I have to say I'm surprised he would lie. Kevin has always been truthful. Could there have been another boyfriend?"

"I can't imagine who. No one I've talked to has mentioned one."

When they were at the door, Ms. Fitzgerald added, "Remember what I said about dots and connectors. Kevin's version and Jessica's differing one are two dots. The connector could make them both true or at least better explained."

Mattie thanked her again for her help. As she drove to The Garret, she kept revisiting what Evelyn Fitzgerald had first said about a "my-trouble, your-trouble bond" between the two girls. Whether she liked it not, the trouble bond must have been the divorces. What else could it have been?

How could she have been so blind as to assume that because she and Stephen had managed a graceful divorce—if there was such a thing—Jessica would automatically adjust?

Obviously she had not, and Mattie berated herself for blithely assuming otherwise. And she blamed Kevin. For a kid who swore he'd barely seen Jessica in weeks, his name sure made the rounds of conversation; even Ms. Fitzgerald had assumed he was the father. One thing she knew to be true: dots and connectors not withstanding, Jessica had clearly and tearfully said Kevin had broken up with her.

What would he have to say about that?

Chapter Seven

Wyatt hefted what seemed to him like the fourteen mil-
lionth box down the narrow attic steps and set it with the
others in his mother's living room. The cartons were pushed
so close together that finding a path out of the room would
require a map. "I swear all of Briarwood has stored their
junk in your grandmother's attic," he said to Kevin.

"Nah, they dumped a bunch in the cellar, too."

"Very funny."

Perched on a chair that had come out of the dusty attic,
Kevin chugged down a Coors.

"Easy on the beer."

"My only one."

"Your only one since two boxes ago."

Wyatt, in jeans and a sweat-soaked shirt, looked around
and concluded that his mother was either a hopeless pack rat
or a savvy collector of industrial proportions. It was hard to
concede the latter, given all the years he'd listened to his old
man bellow "Throw it out!" when his mother pondered
whether to display an item or put it away for safekeeping.
He had to smile as he thought of Pop rolling his eyes and
confiding, "My Alice would save shit if she could figure out
how to get rid of the stink."

So much crap, and boxes packed with even more. If not
for his mother's specific instructions before her death, which

were restated in her will, that her things be sold and the money used for Kevin's college education, Wyatt would have handed every last sagging box to his sister and paid the college tuition himself.

But he couldn't do that—either legally or morally. He recalled telling his mother a few weeks before she passed away that she wasn't to worry about college for Kevin. He'd take care of it. She'd given him one of her "You'll do as I say, I'm your mother" looks, followed by the statement that he'd already done too much for his nephew. She was his grandmother, and she'd saved a lot of valuable things just so they could be put to good use. College tuition was the best use.

Valuable things. Christ, he hoped so.

"So when is Mattie coming back?"

"Mrs. Caulfield to you."

"You don't care if I call Paige, Paige."

"Paige is a bitch."

"I think she's cool." He grinned—waiting, Wyatt knew, for him to attack.

"Obviously you and your mother know her better than I do," he said sarcastically, still wincing from Corinne's hysteria when Wyatt told her to uninvite his ex-wife. Thinking his sister would comply only proved his ignorance of her determination to turn every issue with him into a battleground.

"Mom likes ragging on you."

"Now there's a revelation." He took the bottle of beer from Kevin and set it aside. "How about getting some of these boxes emptied so we can make some room?"

"Maybe Paige is coming here 'cause she wants you back."

"Maybe you'd like to shut up and work your hands as fast as you work your mouth."

Kevin grinned and Wyatt scowled, because he knew Kevin expected it. They'd always had a close relationship and a kick-ass guy kind of banter with enough sharp edges to keep it interesting, but at the same time the slice-and-dice talk never mucked up their affection for one another.

Since the accident and the ramifications that spilled onto

him, Kevin had drawn closer, which Wyatt suspected had a lot to do with knowing he could depend on his uncle for no-bullshit advice.

The teenager was worried about Jessica and also deeply offended that she'd allowed some other guy to have sex with her while holding him off. Wyatt had listened more than offered advice, for when it came to sex, Kevin wouldn't talk to his mother and he was too ashamed to talk to his friends. Wyatt got the nod whether he wanted it or not. Some days he didn't.

They unwrapped dishes and knick-knacks, placing them on the dining room table so Mattie could sort and put a value on them.

"And when is *Mrs. Caulfield* gonna show up and do the job you hired her to do?"

Wyatt moved a stack of plates that he remembered watching his mother hand-wash because, she'd told him, they were too valuable to trust to a dishwasher. "You got a boil on your ass about Mattie?"

"You'd be pissed if she accused you of knocking up her daughter."

"You were Jessica's boyfriend; her assumption is plausible."

"It's shit."

Wyatt shrugged. He didn't want to get into this. He knew how steamed Kevin was when he left the meeting with Mattie. He'd half expected a phone call from her, but it never came. In fact, he hadn't spoken with her at all, which worried him. He figured Mattie to be more open-minded than to blame him for trying to give his nephew the benefit of the doubt.

At the dining room window, Kevin's shoulders slumped. "Ahhh, Jesus."

"What?"

"Here she comes. You didn't tell me she was gonna be here today."

"Hey, you were just whining about her not being here. Besides, I didn't know she was coming," Wyatt said, winding his way through the maze of boxes. "Keep your cool, kid. As much as you want to think so, she's not the witch of Briarwood."

"Worse. You got the hots for her, and probably don't believe me."

"Knock it off. I never said I didn't believe you."

"Well, do you?"

Wyatt turned around. Kevin stood stiff-backed and belligerent.

"Yeah," Wyatt said softly. "Yeah, I believe you."

The relief and gratitude in Kevin's eyes reminded Wyatt how important trust was when all the odds made guilt look more credible than innocence.

Kevin kicked some newspapers aside. "Well, she's got no right to accuse me." He grabbed his shirt, balling it in his fist. "I'm outta here."

"Uh, did it occur to you she might have come to see me?"

"No."

"Thanks, pal." Wyatt walked into the entrance hall and held the screen door open for her. "Hi, babe, what a nice surprise."

"Hi, yourself," she murmured, sliding her arms around him, unmindful that he was sweaty and smelly.

"Hey, you're gonna get dirty." But even as he cautioned her, he welcomed the feel of her—and so did his body.

She locked herself onto him even tighter. Figuring that while he had her this close, he might as well take advantage, he lowered his head and kissed her. She clung tighter, if that was possible, and he deepened the kiss.

"Is that missing me I taste in your mouth?" he asked, drawing her against the wall and fiddling with the buttons on her blouse.

"Hmmm. Maybe I'm sex-starved."

"God, I hope so."

She giggled. "Can we run away together? Right now?"

"Absolutely. Truck's full of gas."

She kissed him again. "That's what I like about you. You never ask if it's practical or prudent or right or wrong, you just take what I say and go with it."

"The wisdom of a man in love."

She looked at him, her eyes unblinking. "In love? With me?"

"No, with my truck." He gave her a little shake. "Of course, with you."

He hadn't planned on blurting it out—in fact, he hadn't planned on saying it at all until he was sure it wouldn't freak her out. The last thing he wanted to do was make her feel committed when she already had more obligations than fingers on her hands.

Her cheeks colored and she looked away, as if embarrassed.

"Hey, babe." He bent his knees so that he could look at her, because she wouldn't raise her head. "It wasn't a marriage proposal, and it doesn't mean you have to move in with me, and it doesn't even mean you have to say the same thing back to me."

She nodded. "That's the trouble. I do love you, and I want to be with you and do wonderful things, but there is so much other stuff going on, that I'm afraid you're going to get very impatient and find someone else."

"Not gonna happen. All my 'other women' resources vanished after I found you. Listen, for all this serious talk, we shouldn't be standing in a hall with me dirty and sweaty and making you that way. I like your idea of running away, so let's get to it."

But she didn't move and her shoulders slumped, and he knew that whatever nirvana moment they'd just experienced, it had quickly evaporated. "You have some news about Jessica?"

"These days, everything is about Jessica."

He heard the weariness, and the frustration of "Will this ever end?"

"You know why I want to run away with you?"

"I'm getting hard thinking about it."

"Be serious."

He grinned and kissed her nose. "Okay, I'm serious."

"I want to hide away and wake up and find that Jessica is fine and that there was no accident or terrible questions or heartbreaking surprises. . . ."

"If only I had those secret stones."

That brought a wan smile. "I wish you did, too. At this point I'd try anything."

"Let me lock things up here and we'll go to my place." Wyatt held his eagerness in check despite the fierce wanting that fired up like a meg eighty rocket. They'd have wine, then dinner, then . . .

"I saw Kevin's bike outside. Where is he? I want to talk to him."

He released her, coming back to reality. "I thought you were here to see me."

"I am here to run away with you. I just want to talk to Kevin." She smiled at him, yet even as she did, he sensed the returning distraction of real life as she moved into the interior of the house.

His chill of disappointment iced up into crankiness.

Then, at the wide doors that opened into the living room, she stopped. "My God, were all these in the attic?" He didn't miss the excited awe in her voice, and that further annoyed him. Always the cartons and their contents; they'd become so loomingly large in his daily life that he couldn't complete a sentence without their intrusion. His sister wanted them all, his ex was coming to town to get some trinket, and Mattie looked as if manna had dropped from the attic.

Feeling beyond ornery, he baited her. "They're all filled with worthless crap that's on its way to the dump."

The look of horror he'd seen the last time he'd said that didn't appear. "Don't be silly. You said that about the box that contained the Roseville." At his frown, she added, "Remember that vase you called as ugly as a prize at a cheap carnival?"

"It was uglier."

"It could afford to be. It's worth about two hundred dollars. Not the high end of Roseville pieces, but hardly a dime store vase." She opened the flaps on one of the heaviest boxes.

Two hundred bucks? The old man had once used it for cigar ashes. "Are you sure?"

She looked at him. "If I'm not, then you better hire yourself another appraiser."

He couldn't argue with that.

She opened a newspaper-wrapped object and found a cup and saucer. She turned them over, then walked to a window where the light was brighter. Without comment, she pulled more pieces of the same pattern from the box, then jiggled the box. "This is filled with china, Wyatt. How did you ever wrestle this down those steps?"

"I ate two bowls of Wheaties this morning. Come on, Mattie, you're not going to unwrap all that stuff. If you want to look at dishes, check out the dining room table. Kevin and I already put stuff there."

"I will. But these are Fiesta, and I want to see how many pieces she had."

"Too damn many, if you ask me," he grumbled.

"Stop complaining. Your mother has, I suspect, a trove of items worth a lot of money. Would you rather I charge you a huge appraisal price and you get nothing in return?"

"I suppose not."

"Good. Now, I'll wait for Kevin to come out of hiding."

Wyatt raised his eyebrows. "You're a smart-ass."

"I hope so. I've been a real dumb-ass the past few months. Maybe I'm learning."

She dug more plates and a bowl or two from the box, tossing the crumpled newspaper onto the floor. He watched her, noting a new resolve in her expression. If Kevin thought he was off the hook with his denial the other day, he was in for a serious awakening.

"He's pissed at being called a liar," Wyatt said.

Mattie didn't miss a beat. "Really? I'm pissed that he called my daughter a liar. And since she can't speak for herself or defend herself . . ."

"You're here to do it for her."

"Do you blame me?"

"No. And if I believed the kid was lying, I'd be right behind you, defending her."

"Jessica is not a liar."

"Haven't we been down this road?"

"And we will go down it a thousand times more until I get some answers."

"Fine." Wyatt made his way around boxes and into the dining room. "Kevin!"

In a few moments the boy appeared, glaring at his uncle. "Traitor!"

Wyatt squeezed his shoulder. "Come on. You know you gotta do this. Now or later."

"How about never?"

"Just tell her the truth."

"I did that, goddammit."

"Well, you're just gonna have to tell her again."

"How many times does it take until she gets it?"

Wyatt halted his nephew. "Cut the wiseass stuff. This is her daughter, and Mattie is confused and frightened about all these issues that show Jess to be . . ."

"A jerk."

"All right, a jerk. But if it was you accused and in a coma, you'd want your mom to believe in you and not the stories that make you look like a jerk."

He shuffled his feet. "Yeah, I guess."

Wyatt winked at him. "Let's go."

Half an hour later, Wyatt and Kevin had heard about Mattie's visit to Evelyn Fitzgerald and how Jessica had been in tears over Kevin breaking up with her. Mattie emphasized that Jessica had said that; it wasn't the dean's interpretation.

Kevin sat silently, as though absorbing it. Wyatt straddled an old chair, chin resting on his stacked fists. He knew "Fitz" was reliable and as truthful as the Pope. This didn't look good for his nephew. Mattie stood, paced a bit as if trying to lose the tension wound up inside of her.

Finally, Kevin said, "Okay, I don't know how to make this sound the way you want to hear it, but what Jess told Fitz isn't true." Mattie stared at him, bewildered at his continued denial.

Wyatt intervened. "You knew nothing about the pregnancy?"

"You think I blew her off because I made her pregnant and that's why she was crying?"

"Mattie?"

"It certainly looks that way."

"Well, it's not that way. My old man blew off my mother because she was pregnant with me. I know how tough that was on her, 'cause she told me how she had to make up a dumb lie about my father getting killed so her parents would let her come home. I never want to be an asshole like my old man. If I'd made her pregnant, I would have stood by her. How about you and Mr. Caulfield . . . ?"

"Kevin," Wyatt warned.

"Well, would you have? Jess might have thought you wouldn't. She was always saying how she never wanted to disappoint you. That's probably why she kept the pregnancy secret."

"Then why did she tell the dean you'd broken up with her?"

Kevin clawed his hands through his hair. "Geez, don't you know?"

Mattie looked at Wyatt, who nodded. "Come on, Mattie, you know. . . ."

"If she'd told the dean the real reason, Ms. Fitzgerald would have called Stephen or me."

"She was protecting her secret," Wyatt said. "But she was also trying to keep from disappointing you and her father."

Mattie stared at one and then the other for a long time, then slowly lowered herself into a chair and seemed to dissolve in a puddle of newly born guilt. She covered her face and shuddered. Wyatt knelt in front of her, talking softly. The last thing he wanted was for her to transfer blame about Jessica to herself. First off, he knew that self-blame, no matter how much deserved, was never satisfied. And second, that guilt would cuff her to her ex in a way that Wyatt couldn't break.

After a few moments, Mattie reluctantly allowed him to

pull her to her feet and wrap his arms around her. The heaviness in the air was suffocating.

Behind them, Kevin hadn't moved.

Wyatt drew back, and Mattie straightened. "I owe you an apology, Kevin. I know I've been nasty and unfair to you, but making you responsible for the changes in Jessica seemed so obvious. The real problem is that whoever or whatever caused those changes should have been noticed by her father and me."

"Mattie, she was good at keeping things a secret, and she worked doubly hard to keep you and Stephen from noticing any change. Maybe she was so disappointed in herself that she couldn't bear to see that same sadness in your eyes."

Kevin got to his feet, jamming his hands into the pockets of his dirty jeans as he drew a little closer to Mattie. "Mrs. Caulfield, look, I don't know if this would help, but if you want, I can ask around. There are guys who owe me. . . ." At Wyatt's penetrating look, he said, "What?"

"Owe you? As in how?"

"Just owe me, okay? Don't get your jets clogged. It ain't nothing . . . that's gonna get me shot."

Which didn't reassure Wyatt.

Mattie, however, whizzed right past that revelation as if it were irrelevant. And since Wyatt's main interest was getting Mattie all to himself, he put off his questions to Kevin for a later date.

"Yes, Kevin, I would like you to ask around. You'll be discreet, won't you?"

"Huh?"

"She means don't broadcast the pregnancy.".

"Are you kidding? That's already out there. Another week and even Bugsy the janitor will know."

Mattie looked dumbfounded. "But how? I haven't told anyone except Callie's mother."

"Who told?"

"Well, obviously she talked to Callie. . . ."

"There you are," Wyatt said.

Kevin shrugged. "Hey, it's no big deal. They're all talking more about her being in a coma than being pregnant. Hell, most of the girls have been pregnant or thought they were. None of them have been in a coma, so that's cool."

Mattie sat down. "Most of them have been pregnant or thought they were? My God, maybe Stephen was right when he said the girls should have gone to private schools."

Kevin started to say something and Wyatt shook his head. He took Mattie's arm. "Come on, you and I are running away. Lock things up here, kid. You stayin' at your mom's tonight?"

"I guess, since you're going out."

"You can stay here if you want. Just don't drink all the beer."

"Yeah, sure."

At the back door, Wyatt grabbed the keys to his truck. "Leave your car here. It will be okay."

"Maybe we shouldn't. I should get home."

"For what?"

"I do have another daughter, you know."

"She's a sophomore. She can't stay by herself for a few hours? I promise to have you in by midnight, Cinderella."

"Let me at least call."

"Use the cell phone in the truck."

"And what if she isn't there?"

"Use the redial." He steered her out the front door and toward his truck. "Are we making love before and after dinner, and what are the chances of a snack in the truck?"

She burst out laughing. "We wouldn't be a bit horny, would we?"

"Do that again."

"What?"

"Laugh. I haven't heard it in a long time."

She threw herself in his arms, and they both were laughing as they climbed into the truck cab and Wyatt drove away.

Chapter Eight

Just as he'd promised.

Mattie smiled at the time on the clock in her car: 11:45. Cinderella would be home by midnight. She'd had a grand time running away; just the few hours out of Briarwood had been a welcome reprieve from two weeks of tension and worry and questions waiting for answers.

She was still warm and languid from their lovemaking, and wished she could have stayed the night. Realistically, however, she would have come home even if Jessica's accident hadn't happened. She strongly believed that while she had teenagers living at home, she needed to be there.

But the way Wyatt was able to make her forget or dismiss every concern and obligation was truly staggering. Some wine, all those lingering kisses, and the heady excitement that had enveloped her nearly persuaded her to bury herself in him.

And the fact that he had to remind her he needed to get her home had shown her how hollow all her "obligation" talk was after two or three good orgasms.

"You must have been very sex-starved," she whispered into the car's darkness, holding the lovely memories as treasures from the night.

She turned right, then five houses later turned into her drive to find not only Stephen's car, but also her parents'

New Yorker and Hannah leaning against the fender of a black convertible she didn't recognize, talking to a boy she didn't know.

She felt all her nerves tighten as her reactions ran the gamut of annoyance: Why were they all here? Were they waiting like the moral police for the tardy woman? Then the anger of How dare they! Followed by a flush of terror—had something happened to Jessica?

That last thought had her parking and shutting off the engine and practically leaping out of the car.

Hannah straightened from a lazy lean against the convertible's back fender. "Hi, Mom. This is Conner. How was dinner?"

"Hello, Conner. Uh, dinner was fine. What's going on? Is Jessica all right?"

"Geez, Mom, how come you never ask if I'm all right?" The petulance was thick and immediate, and hit Mattie with the impact of an electrical shock. She blinked at Hannah, who suddenly looked too much like her sister. In fact, wasn't she wearing a shirt of Jessica's? Suddenly Mattie saw all of Hannah's delight over her new popularity as more than just a fleeting indulgence.

Mattie cleared her throat. "Are you all right?" It was a lame question, too little too late, and of course it didn't fly.

Then the pout. "It's always Jessica."

Mattie glanced at Conner, who was taking this all in, and another look at Hannah revealed an even deeper pout. "Honey, I know you don't need to be reminded that Jessica is the one in the coma." It wasn't the most motherly of comments; and in these few seconds, new concern about Hannah became focused. But the remark was for Conner's benefit. Plus, a house full of people wasn't exactly the grace note that should have completed her evening.

She'd have to talk to Hannah about this "it's my turn to be queen" attitude.

"Jessica's okay. Me and Dad saw her around seven."

"Thank you."

"They're worried that something happened to you."

Mattie frowned. "Didn't you tell them I called?"

"Yeah, but that was in the afternoon. You know Dad."

Oh, yes, she knew Stephen—the proverbial clock-watcher.

"You're not mad at him 'cause he was worried, are you?" Hannah asked with some apprehension. Implicit in her question was You're gonna yell and make him leave.

"I'm not mad because anyone was worried." Hannah didn't need to hear her outrage, but she certainly intended Stephen to. She crossed the lawn to the porch steps. But before she moved any farther, Hannah's hand was on her arm. "Mom, maybe you better go in the back way and, well, you know. . . ."

"The back way? Why?"

Hannah drew even closer, and then, lowering her voice so that Mattie could barely hear her, she said, "Kinda fix things. You know, your hair and your clothes. I think they're gonna know."

Mattie felt herself physically shrink back. Humiliation, mortification, embarrassment—they all draped over her like a neon-lit scarlet letter. A cadre of defensive comments jumped into her mind like bad ideas that only made her look worse.

Wait a minute. This was her house and her life, and there was no way she was going in the back door, like she was trying to sneak in after curfew. "Hannah, it's late, and you have school tomorrow."

"It's Saturday."

"Never mind. It's time you were in bed. Conner, it was nice meeting you."

"Sure." He was already headed for the driver's side—a long, lean kid whose clothes were five sizes too big. It was then she noticed the beer bottle in his hand. "Hey, Hannah, tomorrow—okay?"

"Yeah, whatever," she said dismissing him. Then, before Mattie could go inside, Hannah said, "I'm sorry. I shouldn't have said anything."

"No, you shouldn't have."

"But Dad will, or Gran. I mean, it's not exactly a secret

that you and Mr. Landry are, well . . . like Dad knows it, and . . ."

"Hannah, has your father been discussing Wyatt and me with you?"

Hannah shrugged.

Dammit, Stephen, how dare you! "What has he said?"

"Mom, don't be mad, please. He just asked if I liked him, and I said he was okay, but that he wasn't like Dad."

"Neither Wyatt nor I have ever thought about him replacing your father." Mattie was furious with Stephen for putting such an idea in Hannah's head. And if Stephen was so worried about his daughter, why hadn't he done something about sending Conner on his way?

"How old is Conner?" Mattie asked as the black convertible barreled down the street, tires screeching so loudly at the corner that Mattie braced herself for the crash. It didn't happen, and the car whined on into the night.

"He's a senior."

"And a reckless driver. How old is he?"

"Oh, Mom, you sound like Gramps."

"One daughter in an accident is enough for three lifetimes. Now, how old is Conner?"

"Seventeen."

"Not only a bad driver but an underage drinker." And before Hannah could mount her defense, Mattie asked, "Were you drinking beer, too?"

"I had a couple sips."

"A couple sips? How about just a yes?"

"Okay. Yes." Then, in her most belligerent tone, she whined, "What's the big deal? Everyone drinks beer. At least we aren't having sex, like Kevin and Jessica did."

How to explain it all in one simple declarative sentence? Impossible—and why would Hannah believe her anyway? Both she and Stephen had made their feelings known— Kevin was guilty. As for Jessica's pregnancy, she couldn't even begin to speculate with Kevin out of the picture. Right now she was too tired to think. She patted Hannah's cheek. "I'm glad you're not having sex."

"He wants me to. A lot of guys want me."

"I'm not surprised. You're a beautiful young woman."

Hannah seemed taken aback that Mattie didn't pounce with parental warnings. "You're not gonna freak out or anything?"

"No, but I'd love to discuss this with you in the morning, when I'm not so sleepy and you're a little more sober."

Hannah giggled, then threw her arms around Mattie. "I love you. You are so cool."

Mattie held her, hugging her, cherishing her response, kissing her cheek. She wiped a smudge of dirt from her cheek. "I love you, too. Now off to bed with you."

Hannah hurried into the house ahead of Mattie, who waited until her daughter had informed all of them Mom was home. The chatter grew louder as they all made their way to the front hall, like hounds that found their prey.

"Well, it's about time," her dad said, the relief evident.

"After Jessica, we're all on a bit of an edge. We were afraid you'd been hurt." Her mother looked harried and suddenly older, and Mattie immediately regretted worrying them. And words they'd spoken during the divorce suddenly came back to her—"You'll always be our daughter; we'll always be anxious and protective, because parents don't quit being parents when the children grow up."

Mattie especially regretted giving them further unease when she knew how disquieting the past couple of weeks had been for them.

"It *is* very late, Mattie." Stephen, his tie loosened and his usually pristine starched shirt listless and wrinkled, looked stern and official, reminding her of an exhausted truant officer.

"My apologies to all of you." She placed her handbag on a chair. "It certainly wasn't my intent or Wyatt's to cause such chaos." She left it there, allowing them to draw any conclusion they wanted.

Instead of all chattering at once, there was wide-eyed silence from her parents and an embarrassed scowl from Stephen.

Finally, her father said, "Well, you're home and safe now. Louise, we should go. Everyone is tired."

Her mother, always wanting to add a just a wee bit more, said, "We knew you went to dinner with Mr. Landry, but when the evening got later and later, and you didn't come home. . . . Well, Stephen called us, thinking you might have stopped at our house for that price guide you mentioned wanting to borrow."

The price guide. Oh, God, she'd forgotten all about it. She had told her mother she'd stop by for it sometime today.

"Sweetheart. . . ." Stephen came forward. "Don't be angry at them. I'm afraid I alarmed them. I really was worried about you."

Mattie nodded, apologized to her parents, and after hugs and kisses and whispers of seeing her tomorrow, they said good night. But not until she heard their car hum down the street did she turn to Stephen. Her regret did not extend to him.

"You owe me an apology, Stephen, and a damn good explanation!"

His mask of concern disappeared. "Me? I'm home where I should be. Your daughter is in a coma, and you're out fucking some ex-cop for eight hours."

Mattie's cheeks flamed, and in a triggcr reaction, she slapped him. "You bastard! One has nothing to do with the other, and you know it."

And while the smacking sound raced around the room, she wantcd to snatch back her words. She'd blown it—boy, had she blown it. But for heaven's sake, why did she have to make excuses to her ex-husband?

He glared at her, barely flinching. "So you admit it."

Oh, the hell with it. She was tired of jabs and pussyfooting and getting instruction on how she should conduct herself. "And why shouldn't I admit it? I'm not married, and the last time I looked at my driver's license, I was old enough to be out after dark."

And then, to her astonishment, he shoved his hands in his pockets and lowered his head like a beaten animal. "Christ,

Mattie, I'm sorry for sounding like an overbearing ass. Of course you're furious with me, and you should be."

"I don't appreciate your possessiveness," she said, not expecting him to concede the truth so quickly. Her fight energy drained like water through a sieve.

"I know you can date and have sex with other men."

"How generous of you, but my sex life is not a discussion point between us." Then she added, "What did you insinuate to my parents?"

"They drew their own conclusions."

"Ones you egged on."

"I did not. And you can ask them tomorrow."

Which of course she wouldn't, because she didn't want to face the same questions. Nor did she intend to discuss her sex life with them. And he probably knew that.

She locked the front door before heading upstairs.

"Mattie?"

"I'm tired. I'm going to bed."

"Wait, I have to say this."

She glanced at him. His face was drawn and his body slumped as though he were naughty. She felt a pang of softness.

"I love you, Mattie."

"Oh, God, Stephen, don't. Please don't."

"I have to, because it's true. The divorce hasn't changed that, it's only made it more difficult for me to tell you. Since Jess's accident, we've gotten along so well, I guess I wanted to believe that we were becoming a family again, the way we used to be. Hannah seems happy that I'm spending so much time here, and your parents have told me how glad they are that I'm not one of those nasty ex-husbands."

Mattie blinked at this turn of events. He'd taken the past two weeks and fashioned them into cheering accolades of support for himself.

Then, as though he'd read her mind, he said, "This isn't about me, it's about us. Wouldn't it be wonderful if, out of this tragedy, we could put our family back together?"

The concept boggled her mind; he was talking as if he had some family agreement that now depended on her to make it unanimous. "Stephen, I'm fond of you, but putting things back together is far-fetched."

"It's Landry, isn't it?"

"Wyatt has nothing to do with you and me."

"He's in your life and I'm out."

"You make it sound like he caused our divorce."

"He's benefited from it."

"Nobody has benefited. And this is a ridiculous discussion. Good night, Stephen." She climbed a few steps, but he didn't take the hint.

"You don't think he's going to stick around after the auction, do you? Come on, honey, you know better than that."

She did know better—she knew Wyatt loved her. He'd said so. Sure, he probably wouldn't live in Briarwood, but Newport was only half an hour away, and just tonight they'd discussed the possibility of opening a branch of The Garret in Newport.

While she mulled over the choice between discussing what she'd just told him she wouldn't discuss and repeating her "good night," he continued, "Landry's rich and single and has his pick of women."

That made her smart. "He did not 'pick' me."

But he went on as if he never heard her.

"I heard one of his old girlfriends lives a couple of blocks from him in Newport. Handy, huh? And then there's his ex-wife."

"Paige doesn't even live around here."

"He didn't tell you she's coming to visit him next week?"

Wyatt had nothing but contempt for his ex-wife; she couldn't imagine him sitting still for some visit. Kevin had said that his uncle and his mother had argued about Paige, but Mattie had been more concerned with Jessica's relationship to Kevin, and paid scant attention. As for Wyatt not telling her about Paige—why would he? "Where did you hear all of this?"

"I asked around. It's amazing the information one can glean in a small town if one knows who to ask."

"More like small town gossip," she muttered. "And for that matter, why were you even asking around about Wyatt?"

He looked genuinely puzzled by her question. "I would think that would be obvious."

Mattie sighed. It probably was, but she too exhausted to think it through.

"I've asked, honey, because you haven't. We have two daughters, one of whom has been accused of some uncharacteristic behavior. Landry's presence in your life has upset me, so it's certainly possible that it upset Jessica."

"You think she resented Wyatt?"

"I do."

"Well, I don't, and since Jessica can't tell us, it would appear it's a moot point for now." But deep within, Mattie was concerned; this was a concept Mattie had not considered. Jessica had never given any indication; both girls seemed fond of Wyatt. But realistically, Mattie admitted that given Jessica's unhappiness over the divorce in the weeks immediately following, it was plausible that Wyatt's presence in her mother's life disturbed her. Perhaps she was trying to act adult and sophisticated by not complaining or pouting. A kind of "if you're happy, Mom, I'm happy for you" attitude. And because Mattie had wanted the girls to like Wyatt, she would not have questioned.

Now, however, she was disturbed. Stephen's scenario sounded frighteningly simplistic, but it certainly gave reasonable credence to Jessica's odd behavior. The family was broken; the oldest daughter had a broken heart because the father she adored had been sent away and replaced by her mother's boyfriend. And finally Jessica acted out her rebellion, which was discovered because of the accident. God, Mattie thought, it sounded like some dreadful soap opera plot.

But it was also very plausible. She might have been clueless when it came to her daughter needing help, but she'd never believed she'd been deliberately ignorant. Now, for the first time, she realized that if her relationship with Wyatt had truly upset Jessica, then Mattie, and not outside factors, bore the blame.

Mattie shuddered.

"Sweetheart, I don't want to see you hurt, and for sure I

don't want our daughters caught up in some embarrassing situation."

She knew all about embarrassing situations—she'd had more than enough tonight. But the more he talked, the more her mind became mired in confusion and troubling thoughts. She certainly couldn't live her life restricted to those who met some approval standard of her family. On the other hand, she was hardly unbiased when it came to Wyatt. As annoying as it was for Stephen to raise questions, she had to consider them. Truthfully, she really knew little about Wyatt.

Oh, she knew the Landry family and she knew he wasn't a deadbeat. But Wyatt the single man who, no doubt in the past, had slept with a lot of women. . . . But that was then and this was today. . . . Now he was in love with her, and she grew more in love with him day by day. . . . But he hadn't mentioned Paige coming . . . and that had to be because he didn't care. So what if an old girlfriend lived in the vicinity . . . that didn't automatically mean he was. . . . But none of it mattered if the real truth was that Jessica resented him.

Enough.

She was exhausted and not thinking straight. And to blink and duck because Stephen raised some questions was equally foolish. Hannah. She'd talk to Hannah and find out how Jessica really felt about Wyatt. And once Jessica awakened, she'd talk to her, too. If they had negative feelings or resentment toward Wyatt, she would deal with those, but simply to accept Stephen's word wasn't fair to Wyatt or to their relationship.

She walked up the stairs; when she reached the top landing and looked down, he stood at the newel post and she was reminded of all the years he'd done exactly that. Calling up some last-minute detail that she'd usually forgotten before he made sure the house was secured for the night.

And sure enough. "Don't forget to set your alarm. Donna called and wanted me to remind you she can't come in until noon tomorrow."

"Yes, I remember." But she hadn't.

"And Mattie . . ."

"What?" she asked wearily.

"All of this will work out. I promise."

In her bedroom, she stood at the windows, looking out on the starry night. Just a few hours ago those same stars were glorious and romantic and twinkling with approval. She wished Wyatt was here to hold her, to listen, to reassure her. She'd left him feeling buoyant, but now, once again, she felt leaden and swamped. She had to get some answers about how the girls felt about Wyatt.

Then at least she'd know what she was dealing with. She was their mother, and they came first.

Yet a tiny voice inside whispered, *I don't want to let him go.*

On Saturday morning, Mattie waited until Stephen had gone off to play tennis, then knocked on Hannah's bedroom door. She usually opened the shop at ten on Saturdays, but speaking with Hannah without Stephen around was necessary.

"Come on in."

Mattie glanced around at the messy room, glad to see one thing about Hannah hadn't changed. Her daughter was ensconced in the middle of her bed, surrounded by teen magazines, a makeup mirror, and an assortment of gloss, creams, colors, and polishes.

"Sweetie, I want to talk to you."

"I'm sorry about the beer. I didn't have very much, honest."

Mattie sat down beside her. "Not the beer. I wanted to talk with you about Wyatt."

"You gonna marry him?" Hannah asked, her eyes wide—with worry?

"No, but I want to know how you and Jessica feel about him. I've kinda assumed you liked him because he likes both of you and I've never seen any tension when he was around. I remember when you first met him that night he came to take me out to dinner."

"The night Daddy came with the present."

"Yes."

"We liked him okay. It just felt weird seeing Daddy leave and be so sad."

"I'm sorry that happened. I didn't want to make him sad, but coming here unannounced, as though we had a date, was very unsettling."

"I guess."

"How did Jessica feel about Wyatt? Did she resent him?"

Hannah shrugged and peered more intently at her reflection.

Mattie drew closer, sitting on the edge of the bed. "Surely Jessica and you talked about Wyatt."

"Not really."

"Why not?"

"There was nothing to say. You liked him and he was okay. Jessica had her own troubles."

"Such as?"

"You know. Arlis and Kevin and being pregnant."

Mattie rose and walked to the windows that looked out over the backyard. "I'm confused, Hannah. You and your sister always talked and had confidences, yet you sound as if you barely spoke with her in the weeks before the accident."

Again the shrug. Then suddenly, Hannah was off the bed and squeezing Mattie's arm. "I don't want you to get weird or worried. We talked a lot, but you're making it sound as if we talked about *everything*. Even sisters don't always pay attention to each other all the time."

"I suppose."

"You're not mad at me and Daddy, are you?"

Mattie sighed. "No, I guess I'm just disturbed that I seem to know so little of what has been going on in my own family."

"It will work out okay. Daddy's back, and everything will be okay."

"Well, I just don't understand why you're doing all this probing about a nonissue," Louise Rooney said as she placed intricately folded napkins in silver rings across each of the luncheon plates.

Mattie, on her way to the hospital, had stopped by at her mother's request to do the flower arrangement. Today was her mother's turn to host lunch and an afternoon of bridge. Mattie had hoped to avoid the subject of Jessica beyond daily updates on her condition, but clearly that wasn't going to happen. She was still smarting with the realization that her own behavior might have brought all of this on. She'd spoken to no one about it, including Wyatt.

Since Kevin's denial of being the father, both of her parents had adopted the approach that whatever the circumstances that led to the accident, they were now incidental and therefore pointless to pursue. Mattie suspected they feared what might be learned.

She feared it, too, but her greater worry was that the accident had only temporarily interrupted the problems, not eliminated them. And if, as Stephen suggested, Jessica resented Wyatt, Mattie had a decision to make. Her conversation with Hannah had offered her no assurance that Stephen was wrong. Now she faced making a decision that she wanted desperately to avoid.

Denial, Mattie, plain old garden variety denial, because you love Wyatt and you can't bear breaking off with him.

"The pregnancy may be a nonissue now, but her strange behavior and its cause certainly are not," Mattie said, chasing that denial into the back of her mind. "Which bowl do you want to use for the flowers?"

"The one with the violets on it," her mother said, then, like a boomerang, jumped back to Jessica. "Don't you see how asking all these questions makes Jessica look bad?"

"She already looks bad," Mattie said, her own bluntness startling her as well as her mother.

"How can you say that when she's fighting for her life?"

She couldn't argue with that; Jessica's precarious condition trumped all previous behavior. "Why don't you go get gorgeous while I finish up here?" She turned her back, putting the water-soaked Oasis that would hold the fresh flowers into the oval bowl. With green tape holding the Oasis secure, she began placing the flowers.

But her mother didn't go upstairs; she sat down, and Mattie, without turning and looking, knew she was in for some kind of lecture.

"I just don't understand you, Mattie. Why are you acting like this is some silly detective novel plot? It would be so much better to just let all the talk and the rumors die out. When Jessica wakes up, we can all say we love her and we forgive her for whatever difficulty she got herself into, and go on from there. The poor child shouldn't have to wake up and face some inquisition."

"Is that what you think I want? That's what I want to avoid. If we know what Jessica was doing and why, then when she does awaken, we can settle it all quickly. The personal issues can be put aside, but the legal ones cannot. The police are looking for witnesses, and if there are some, we have no idea what they might say. And for sure the police will want to talk to her about the stolen car."

"Oh, phooey on that! Your father and Stephen already took care of that."

Mattie almost dropped the bowl of flowers. "They took care of what?"

"There will be no charges. Surely you didn't think your father and Stephen would stand by and see her charged with stealing a car? Frankly, I don't understand why you weren't in favor of it."

Mattie sat down. "In favor of what? I don't know what you're talking about."

"Stephen said you'd be against them doing anything, so they just went ahead."

"Stephen does not speak for me, and shouldn't be telling you and Dad how I feel about anything."

"Well, we don't seem to see as much of you as we do of Stephen," her mother answered in her best "aggrieved mother" voice. "And I think you're being unfair. He's only trying to help. Jessica is his daughter, too."

Mattie wanted to shake her mother; instead she took the easier tack and acknowledged Stephen's love for his daughters. "What did Dad and Stephen go ahead and do?"

But before her mother answered, a coiling premonition began to unwind within Mattie.

"They went and talked to the Petchers."

"Oh, God."

Her mother's eyes widened to the size of sandwich plates. "Is there a law against them doing that? I hardly think this is worth getting in a ruffle about. All they did was talk to those poor people and offer them some help."

"Help? Like money?" The word "bribery" coiled into her mind like a deadly snake.

"Not money. Although they could use some. They live in one of those dreadful developments where no one has a yard or a garage. Your father and Stephen simply did the decent thing and offered to replace their car."

To Mattie, this still seemed like a payoff, but it was even more insidious. "And in doing so, they acknowledged that Jessica was driving or at fault for the accident or she stole the car. What happened to waiting until she woke up so we could get her side of the story?"

"Oh, dear, I hadn't thought of that." Then she shook her head. "The Petchers aren't too bright, they probably didn't either."

"Just because they're poor doesn't mean they're stupid. What did they say?"

"They said they didn't want anything from the family that killed their baby."

Mattie sighed. At that moment she wanted to kick her ex-husband.

"But Stephen is convinced they'll come around."

"Stephen is an idiot," Mattie muttered, not caring if her mother heard it or not. She picked up the arrangement, walked to the dining room, and placed it on the table. Then she returned to the kitchen. "Mom, I want you to tell Dad that he's not to go and see the Petchers again. I'll talk to Stephen."

"Oh, dear, now he's going to be cross with me."

"He won't be. I promise," she said gently. "I'm sure his intentions were only to help Jessica. All of us want that."

"Yes, we do, don't we?" Then she glanced at her watch. "Oh, dear, they'll be here in half an hour, and I need to dress and do makeup. The arrangement is lovely, Mattie." Her mother kissed her cheek. "Kiss Jessica for me, and tell her that we'll be in after dinner tonight."

"I'll tell her." She watched as her mother hurried up the stairs.

Mattie gathered her handbag, her stomach churning with new knots and new anger and new complications.

Why couldn't she be like every other divorced woman in the country and have an ex-husband everyone despised?

Chapter Nine

*Mattie turned in to the hospital parking lot and was de-*lighted to find a spot beneath an overhanging beech tree. The day was hot, and she didn't relish getting back into the car's heat-baked interior.

She used the visor mirror to check her hair and to put on some lipstick, then gathered her handbag and another bag with items she'd brought for Jessica.

She opened the door, distracted by juggling her parcels and the ever-present hope that she'd see a change today in her daughter. She jumped when a hand eased under her elbow.

"Hello, stranger," Wyatt said as he drew her out of the car. His expression told her nothing, but the very fact that he was there signaled a determination to see her.

She pressed her hand to her pounding heart. "Where did you come from?"

He shoved her door closed. "You drove right past me."

Which meant he'd been waiting for her. He knew she visited Jessica at this time every day, and as he settled against the fender of the black Mazda parked next to her car, Mattie tried desperately to think of some breezy excuse why she'd been dodging his calls.

She glanced around, her gaze landing on his black truck. "I guess I was preoccupied."

"It would seem so," he said, as though that were an understatement.

"Actually, I was thinking about the auction." She was hoping to divert him from a discussion she didn't want to have. "I was at your mom's house yesterday and went through a whole lot of boxes."

"The day that you know I'm down in Newport."

"It seems to have worked out that way," she said, widening her eyes as if the reason for his absence had simply slipped her mind. It hadn't.

"Don't tell me you forgot, because I know you didn't."

"Actually, I got a lot done there by myself," she said breezily, sidestepping his comment and asking herself why she didn't simply walk away.

"The very focused Mattie, huh? Not preoccupied or distracted."

Well, there was no way she was going to touch that—she remembered too well the last time she'd been "distracted" when she'd been working; it had been a rainy afternoon a few weeks before the accident. He'd teased and touched and seduced her into some very innovative lovemaking in his old bedroom, beneath a poster of Pete Rose sliding into second base.

They called him Charlie Hustle.

Like you hustled me up here and into bed, she'd whispered.

Whatever works, he'd murmured with a grin and a wink.

Now he folded his arms, and anyone watching from a distance would only observe two people chatting amicably. He kept his voice low, almost seductively quiet, as though any rise in volume would spook her.

She managed a smile. "In fact, I also have an auction date for us. June fifteenth." Then she added, "That's only a month away."

"I'm sure glad you clarified that. Just in case I couldn't count."

Damn! He was biding his time, waiting her out no matter how many conversation side trips she took. "I contacted George Epperly a few months back. He's really booked, but he promised to try and squeeze us in. The fifteenth was the only date he had, so I grabbed it."

Silence roared between them.

He barely moved.

She had to force herself not to fidget.

Finally, when the tense quiet was raising what felt like a lifetime of perspiration along the back of her neck, he said, "George Epperly. Hmmm, his nephew and I played Little League together. He was lousy at bat, but that season's best first baseman. Hadn't seen him in years, and then we ran into each other at Home Depot. He said his uncle was going to call you with a date."

She blinked. Oh, God, was that why Wyatt had been trying to get in touch? About George doing the auction, and not about their relationship? "You could have mentioned that."

"When? I haven't seen you, and you've ignored my phone calls."

Round and round. God, she felt like a plump mouse trying to navigate a skinny maze. "I've worked with him before. He's cranky and grumpy, but he puts on a real show with the bidders. Plus he's fast, usually selling about a hundred items an hour."

"Terrific. The sooner this is over, the better I'm liking it."

"I'm sure we all feel that way about a lot of things," Mattie said, feeling all thought-tangled and mind-twisted. "We're going to have a tent for the auction. I've set it up so we'll have inspection the day before, and for a short time on the day of the auction. Ads in the local newspaper, plus *The Providence Journal*, should bring a lot of buyers. In addition, I'm running some notices in the trades."

When she said nothing more, he waited the length of time it took an elderly man to park his Cadillac. "Life in auctionland seems to be running smoothly. Now what else is going on?"

"Nothing. I've been busy at the store, plus things at home, Jessica. . . ." Suddenly she was exhausted, and only wanted to get away from him. She had the distinct sensation they'd still be standing here an hour from now if she didn't call a halt. She tried to move past him, but the front of her car was too close to the fence that protected the beech tree for her to squeeze by. Wyatt was positioned to stop her in the other direction. A truly silly need to feign outrage, as if he were holding her prisoner, leaped into her mind. Why did he have to be so persistent? Why did he have to demand answers she didn't want to give? Why couldn't he just give up and go away? But one reason she loved him was his dogged persistence, and she supposed she'd be disappointed if he let her cow him. Nevertheless . . . "Wyatt, I really must be going. Jessica's friends from school usually come in the afternoon, and I want to see her before they all troop in."

She settled her bag strap on her shoulder, gripped her other bag, and started around him. Wyatt slipped his hand around her upper arm and stopped her. "Then let's slice off the horseshit. Something has happened, and I have the eerie sense I'm not going to like it."

Just blurt it out and be done with it. "I think it would be a good idea if we didn't see as much of each other."

"As much? Hell, I haven't seen or heard from you in days. Something triggered this blackout, and I want to know what."

"I just need to work some things out in my mind."

"What things?"

"Will you stop badgering me? You remind me of Stephen. Whether you like it or not, I do have a life apart from you." Oh, God, she sounded bitchy, and she didn't want to. But dammit, she didn't need aggravation.

He, naturally, remained unfazed, even going so far as to gently tuck a strand of her hair behind her ear. He was so casual, so blasé—and by the directness of his gaze, she gauged that instead of her bitchiness being off-putting, he relished it. Well, fine. Better a blowout shouting match than clunky sparring to avoid him.

But then he moved aside; and, relieved, she took a few steps. About five more steps and she'd be out of his range.

She should have known better. Just as she turned to cross behind the row of parked vehicles, he said, "Now I wonder where I got the idea that you had a life with me. Because we're sleeping together? Nah. Sex is no big deal. Ah, maybe because we've said we love each other? Nah. These days, declarations of love are as common as Mom's boxes of junk. Could it be because we're both divorced and know a good thing when it comes along? Yep, that could be it, except for one detail. Just one of us is really divorced; the other one only pretends to be."

While he talked, she returned, annoyed now and feeling childish enough to stamp her foot and tell him to shut the hell up.

"You can be a sarcastic prick, you know that?"

"Bingo."

"I do not want to discuss Stephen."

"I'd like to forget he exists, but he does, so why shouldn't we discuss him? I'm sure he isn't laboring in shyness about me. Besides, you just compared me to him, so I have to assume he's hassling you in that charming 'I know best' ooze he's so good at."

Mattie turned away. Her mouth felt parched and her head began to ache. She didn't need this emotional tug-of-war; she really didn't. Then he did the worst possible thing. He took her purse and the bag, put them down on the asphalt, and pulled her into his arms. He leaned back against the car so that she rested against him. A soft, cooling wind blew across them, and for a pleasant moment she let down her guard and resistance and slid her arms around him.

She felt his sigh of relief clear to her bones.

"Babe, what's he doing?"

She told him about Stephen and her father offering to replace the Petchers' car.

"You're worried they'll accuse them of bribery? Don't. The husband has a rap sheet that would paper a room. If they can get a free car out of this, they'll take it."

"You checked on them?"

"I called a guy I know. He filled me in."

"Why didn't you tell me?"

"No reason to, until now."

"I wonder if Jessica knew Arlis's father had been in trouble."

"Probably not. So what else about Stephen?"

"He's very opinionated, and in the process makes me feel inadequate or guilty—or both."

"At the risk of having an opinion, let me offer this about your ex. The most important thing to Stephen is Stephen. If he's not happy, he'll find a way to blame you and fuck up what happiness you've found."

She gazed off into the distance, watching some boys on skateboards gliding across the lot. Behind them, coming out of the hospital, was a woman carrying a small blue bundle. A man was close by, a diaper bag over his shoulder and flower arrangements in both hands. She and Stephen had taken that first walk as a new family when Jessica was born, and again with Hannah. She remembered her joy at having had healthy, beautiful babies, the privilege of staying home to mother them and watch each of them develop with the awe of a proud parent who was sure no two children had ever been so bright or so talented. She'd been enormously content in her mother role; her love and respect for Stephen and their marriage had been boundless.

"He's not a bad man, Wyatt. He just lost his way when his job went sour. His pride couldn't take not being the family provider. He derived a lot of pleasure out of giving us the things he never had." She chuckled. "I remember when Jessica was a baby, he wanted her dressed in the best clothes and all the baby equipment had to be top of the line. And new. I suggested that we could get barely used, top of the line items at a local consignment store, but he wouldn't hear of it. How did I know they hadn't been tampered with? Where did they come from? No, his kids would have the best, spare no expense. He was like that about everything, even long after he lost his job. Much of the debt came from his insistence that he'd have the money eventually." She fell silent, overwhelmed by how all of this could still deeply sadden her. Wyatt held her close, saying nothing, as if sensing the importance of presenting the Stephen she'd married and had loved for nineteen years.

She sighed with relief and melancholy. "We were so happy for so long that he doesn't understand why we can't be happy again. He's had a hard time accepting the divorce, and this accident has simply clarified for him how much his family means to him."

"Okay, Mattie, I'll concede his good points. He was obviously a man proud of his family and proud of his ability to provide."

"I think that's the first positive thing you've ever said about him."

"I'll watch myself in the future." He grinned, then continued. "Even losing his job and the debt could have been dealt with if he hadn't been such an ass. From what you told me, he was the uncooperative one. He was the one who resented you going to work and using money you'd saved to pay bills when he got laid off. He was the one with an ego the size of Alaska, and he was the one who flat-out refused to go to counseling. Now, I'm speaking as an admittedly *very* partial observer, but this is so obvious to me. You're carrying all the fret and worry, while he's whining and playing the devoted father and reeling you in with his 'let's forget the divorce' nonsense, as if you're the one responsible for dirtying up his new and improved happiness plan."

Mattie absorbed this, realizing that Wyatt's observation framed a truer picture of Stephen. Yes, he had been a wonderful provider of the tangibles such as food, shelter, and the material necessities and luxuries. From her came the emotional support, the understanding, even the discipline. The girls knew the unspoken roles. Dad gives and Mom teaches. Dad is soft and Mom is tough. Dad is the approver, Mom is the improver.

Of course, they'd been happy; Mattie had her role as the responder and Stephen had his as the initiator. This chosen arrangement, untouched by conflict or a necessity to change, had served them well for so many years.

But then it did change, and she stepped into his role. Stephen still resented that, and was trying desperately to recast himself as the perfect provider.

Then something new occurred to her. Of course! Stephen the provider—that was the real reason why he wanted to replace the Petchers' car. It showed him as the man in charge, the father who took care of his daughters. Since the accident, he'd tried to be the man in charge that he used to be, and Mattie had all but let him, grateful he'd handled so many of the tedious details. And because he was once again functioning within the family, he believed he had the right to judge her actions, then criticize and advise.

"He suggested that my relationship with you may have caused the change in Jessica."

"And you said . . . ?" For long seconds his question hung painfully between them.

"Actually, I asked Hannah how she and Jessica felt about you."

"And she said . . . ?"

"That they liked you, but I don't think it's about you being in my life as much as Stephen being out of it." She looked up at him. "All I want is for my daughter to wake up. If that means being willing to look at myself as the source of her problems, then so be it."

He released her, and before he picked up her purse and bag and handed them to her, she saw a resignation in his eyes that she wanted to banish. "You better go if you want to beat her friends."

"You're angry with me."

"No. I'm just sorry you're so determined to blame yourself."

"But what if it's my fault?"

"I can't answer that, Mattie. And no one else can, except Jessica. Including your ex-husband."

He turned, and she watched as he crossed the lot, climbed into his truck, and drove away.

This is what you wanted, isn't it? Not to see him as often? But she feared now that not-as-often had just become never.

"Hey, Hannah, wait up!" Kevin shouted down the empty corridor. School had let out for the day, but he'd stuck around until sophomore tryouts for next year's junior-senior band had let out.

She stopped by the double doors and turned around in surprise. "Hi."

"You make the cut?"

"I won't know until next week."

He halted a foot or so from her and gave her his best "very interested" smile. "You'll make it. You're good."

"Why, thank you," she said, looking flattered.

"At least you don't have to haul your instrument around."

"Yeah, a piano would be tough to get on the bus."

He grinned, and she grinned back. Then an awkward silence settled in.

"I need to go. Dad's picking me up, and he's probably out there waiting."

"Sure. Uh, I just wanted to ask you something."

"If it's about Jess, nothing is different."

"Gotta be tough . . . you know, waitin' and not knowin' what's gonna come down."

"Yeah." She sighed, fiddled with balancing her armload of books, then backed away from him. "I better go."

"No, wait! I wanted to ask you something, something important."

She gave him a puzzled look. "What?"

Kevin had never been a soft-lead-up-to-the-point kind of guy. It took too long and made him feel phony. Of course, what he was doing was phony, but since his rep was creamed into shit anyway, he figured he had nothing to lose. Some guy had knocked up Jess, and Kevin guessed Hannah probably had a name—or maybe a few names. For sure she knew something. Those contacts he'd bragged to his uncle about had been as reliable as going to a cokehead for a loan. Then there was his pride; he was still pissed by her virgin act with him. "I was wonderin' if you wanna go to the senior prom with me."

She frowned, curiosity squeezing her eyebrows together. Actually, he'd been a little amazed when the idea floated into his mind last night, after his third can of beer. Back in March, Jessica was his date, and even though he'd never officially unasked her and she hadn't told him she wouldn't be going, the fact was they probably would have dated on prom night. Dates were made months before, and it would be better to go with an ex than to miss the biggest night of their senior year.

Kevin could have gotten a date; a couple of girls, including Callie, had hinted they'd like to go with him, but the sweet numbing effects of all those Coors, plus wanting some inside info about who Jessica was doing sex with, brought Hannah's name cruising into his mind like an Indy driver eating up the finish line.

"You're asking me?" she finally said, as if waiting for him to take back the invite or say it was a joke. "Why?"

He hadn't expected that. " 'Cause you're a cool kid."

"That's a dumb reason. You just broke up with my sister a few weeks ago. She's in the hospital, and it's kind of weird that you'd ask me out."

"Wow, you're suspicious," he said, trying for an insulted expression.

"Shouldn't I be?"

"Nah. It's a dance, not a lifetime of dates. I liked your sister and I like you. What's the big deal?"

"But I'm only a sophomore," she said, looking relieved he hadn't backed off.

"Uh, yeah, I think I've heard that rumor. You know what the guys say about sophomores?"

She shook her head.

"Sweet, sassy, and sexy."

She flushed, then grinned, then giggled. He braced himself for more questions or an accusation that he wanted to pump her about Jessica. He was sure, despite his swagger and coolness, that his real reason was as transparent as a cheap rubber.

"I'd love to go."

"Cool." He hoped he looked as laid-back as he sounded.

She nearly dropped the armload of books, and Kevin quickly helped her restack them. "You really look at those? I mean, every time I see you, you're lugging a gazillion books."

"I tend to be a freak about studying." At his puzzled look, she quickly added, "I'm not, like, weird or anything—I mean, I wouldn't make you feel like you were bringing a bore to the prom."

"I think it's kinda neat." Then he added, "Jess was always studying."

"I guess so."

"What I meant was that you're her sister, so it's probably pretty normal that you'd both like to do the same things." The more he talked, the deeper he dug himself in. Then he glanced up and saw her father's car. He said quickly, "There's your old man."

"My father," she corrected, and he winced. She didn't look happy, and he was scared to death he'd screwed himself.

Then she asked, "Are you going to call me? You know, so I know when to be ready?"

"Sure."

"You have my phone number, don't you?"

He almost said yes. "Could you give it to me?"

She handed him her books, then from a notebook she tore a piece of paper big enough to list the Top 40. With a red marker, she scribbled the number.

"Thanks." He dutifully pocketed it.

She hurried through the double doors.

"Wait," Kevin shouted. "What kind of flowers do you want?"

She didn't miss a beat. "Yellow roses."

"Got it."

She ran across the cement yard and got into her father's car.

Kevin sauntered outside, tugged a cigarette out of his pocket, then held his hand over the match and bent his head for the light. He leaned against the building and assumed a bored face as the Olds Cutlass pulled away. He couldn't believe his luck. He asked, and without buzzing him with questions, she said yes. Just like she'd been waiting for him to rock into her life.

What a stud you are, Bonner. What a freakin' stud.

* * *

"Hi, Rosebud, have a good day?"

"The best."

Hannah's father grinned. "That's what I like to hear."

She put her books on the floor, the excitement of being asked to the senior prom so unbelievable that she wanted to pinch herself to make sure she was awake. She'd planned to go with Conner even though he hated dances; she'd intended to charm him into taking her. Then, just when she almost had him convinced, he got a warning that he was flunking English and might not graduate. His parents had grounded him. No parties, no dances, no fun.

He was stupid anyway, she decided, curling up with this brand new invitation. *Flashing that beer bottle in front of Mom. What a moron!*

Besides, she'd much rather be going with Kevin. He was so cute. And the way he'd waited for her, like his day would've been lousy if he'd missed her. . . . He could have had his pick of tons of senior girls, and he picked her. Her thoughts spun with plans from getting her nails done, her hair swept up with some flowers, some really cool jewelry so she looked like that model she'd seen on TV. And thank God she'd been working on her tan—it would look great with that white shimmery dress she saw at the mall . . . and shoes . . . and jewelry . . . and yellow roses. She absolutely loved yellow roses, and she was going to keep the ones Kevin gave her forever.

Somewhere deep within her euphoria, a tiny voice warned her that Kevin's invitation was probably more about missing Jessica than rushing her. Still, Hannah intended to impress him. She'd come out of her shell, and a lot of kids said she even looked like her big sister, so Kevin asking her was probably because it would be like taking Jess. Well, so what? She liked Kevin, and having a date with him was, like, major awesome. Maybe he was thinking about Jessica, but she could make him forget. She got the date, and she wasn't going to refuse because he once went out with her sister.

Euphoria back in full flower, she folded her arms and slid down in the seat, not at all sure how she could possibly think about anything but Kevin and the prom.

Her dad turned the corner and pulled into the ice cream palace. Suddenly she sat upright. "Wait, Dad, I can't."

"Can't what?"

"I'm too fat, and if I'm gonna fit into the dress I saw at the mall, I can't eat anything."

"What dress? Come on, Rosebud. You're not fat, and I promised you this morning we'd stop for sundaes."

This morning! Her whole life had gotten exciting since this morning! At her father's confused look, she pleaded, "Don't be mad. It's not that I don't want to, I can't."

He gave her that patient look he'd always given her and Jessica whenever they announced they were too fat. "Okay, I'm sure I'm supposed to know this, but what's so important about this particular dress?"

She was gonna tell her mother first, but maybe this was better. She could talk her dad into anything, and then he'd be on her side when she told her mother. And this was just too cool to keep to herself. "Oh, Daddy, the best thing in the whole world just happened to me."

His eyes crinkled in amusement. "All the more reason to have sundaes, so we can celebrate."

She made herself stop wiggling and sit like a sophisticated *woman* instead of a giggly girl. "I've been invited to the senior prom."

"Ahh, now that explains it all." He smiled that wonderful indulgent smile that said he understood how excited she was. "Who is this lucky guy, and how many others did he have to fight off to get you?"

"Oh, Daddy. . . ." She giggled. "You always say such neat stuff."

"You're a neat daughter. So who's the guy?"

"Kevin Bonner."

His grin slid away and Hannah immediately reached out and grabbed his arm, as though to catch that moment of approval before it vanished completely. "I know what you're gonna say, but it's okay, honest. I mean, this is, like, the coolest thing to have ever happened to me."

"Hannah, I understand your excitement, but . . ."

She was on her knees on the seat, leaning toward him and

pressing her hand across his mouth to stop the "but." "No, you have to listen. He's one of the most popular—I mean, who would ever have thought that Kevin Bonner would ask *me*? If anyone even suggested it, I would have laughed. Of all the senior guys, for sure he would have had a date, right? But he didn't, and he even waited until I finished the band tryouts. It's not like he *had* to ask me. I really, really want to go with him, and you absolutely can't be mad and you can't say no. You can't." She was running out of breath and big deal reasons, and worst of all, she could hear the panic in her voice. "I mean, it's not like I'm stealing Jess's boyfriend . . . like, they haven't dated in weeks." Then she added what she hoped would be the clincher. "I think it's kinda special that he would ask me, and I bet Jess would think so, too."

He gently lifted her hand and kissed it lightly, squeezed her fingers, and folded her hand in his before he released it. Hannah was sure her heart was about to burst from pumping so hard. He had to say it was okay. He had to.

"I think your sister would be disgusted and very upset that you would go with a guy like him."

Hannah felt as if she were drowning. "A guy like him? Disgusted? She'd have no right, not after what she's been doing and the losers she's been hangin' with."

"Don't trash your sister," he said sharply.

"You can't trash trash," she snapped and saw her father's eyes narrow with anger. *Shit, shit, shit.*

"Hannah Marie Caulfield, don't ever talk about your sister that way. It's unfair and cruel. Do you understand me?"

"Yes, sir. I'm sorry."

"That's better."

A few beats of silence thumped between them.

Then Hannah sat back down in the seat and in a whiny voice, asked, "How come she got to do anything she wanted, and I can't even go to the most important dance of the year?"

"I didn't say you couldn't go to the prom. I said I don't want you going with him."

"You can't do this to me! You can't! I already told him I'd go with him. He's going to bring me yellow roses, Daddy. Yellow roses, my very, very favorites."

"Sweetheart, I know you're disappointed, but the Bonner boy is off-limits. And you know why."

"But he said it wasn't him, and Mom believes him."

"Well, I don't."

She locked her arms together and sank deep into the seat. With a pouty mouth pursed enough to wrinkle prunes, she glared out the windshield. "I'm going with Kevin, and I don't care what anyone says."

"Hannah," he warned, "I don't want to hear that rebellion." He opened the car door. "Hot fudge or butterscotch?"

She said nothing.

He sighed heavily, turned, and walked to the take-out window. A few minutes later he returned with two sundaes.

"I said I didn't want one."

"Fudge is hot just the way you like it."

And her tummy did growl a bit, and her glands felt as if they were leaning toward the sundae he held outstretched in his hand. "If I eat it, it doesn't mean I'm not going to the prom with Kevin."

"If you don't eat it, you're not going either."

"I am!"

"Here. Eat." Reluctantly she took it. She'd skip supper tonight to make up for the calories. She dug in, savoring the chocolate on chocolate and wishing she had parents who weren't so strict. Taking a big bite and savoring the warm chocolate, she wasn't feeling so savory about her sister. *This is all your fault, Jessica. If you'd left Kevin alone, Dad wouldn't hate him. Thanks a lot.*

Chapter Ten

Mattie rubbed the jasmine cream into Jessica's pale arms. By this time, her daughter would be well into working on her summer tan. "You know, Jessica, school will be finished soon, and then the summer. I know you had all kinds of plans. Going to the beach, working down at Flamingos, and remember we talked about redoing your room?" She talked on amid Jessica's silence. One of the nurses had told her a few days ago that talking aloud was helpful with coma patients. And just because Jessica didn't show an outward response, that didn't mean she couldn't hear you.

Closing the lid on the jar of cream, Mattie began telling Jessica what had been going on at home, the progress of the upcoming auction and about the estate jewelry she'd just bought to resell. "There's a bracelet I think you would love. I brought it with me." She reached into her handbag and took out a heavy gold piece that was encrusted with rubies. "You always look wonderful in red." She slipped the bracelet on and clasped it, then stepped back to admire it. "It's perfect."

"I would certainly say so."

Mattie glanced up and smiled at the nurse. Casey had taken a special interest in Jessica since that first night. She was about Mattie's age, had been divorced twice, and never had any children; she had a flock of nieces and nephews that she doted on. She checked the chart at the end of the bed.

Mattie said, "My daughter loves rubies. I don't know why, when most girls want diamonds."

"I'm an emerald girl myself, although liking them and having them are about as far apart as Rhode Island and California." Casey replaced the chart. "I'm glad you're talking to her. The sound of familiar voices, the cadence of words coupled with your emotion when you speak—these are good things." She chuckled. "I love it when her friends come. They giggle and chatter about clothes and who's dating who and what's happening at school—it's wonderful to listen to their naturalness, instead of them acting as if this a mourning room."

"Yes, her friends are a lively bunch. I've found that talking to Jessica has had the unexpected benefit of helping me. I have a lot of questions, but I'm trying to keep them to myself. Jessica getting better is what's important. The answers will come later."

Casey gave her a sympathetic look. "I know it's hard. Your husband said basically the same thing the last time he was in."

"He's my ex-husband."

"Oh, of course. I'm sorry. I really did know. It's just so wonderful that you have pulled together during this." She took Jessica's pulse, then entered it on the chart. "I've had patients with divorced parents, and believe me, at times their visits were more like battlegrounds than a time to show concern for their child's recovery."

"Stephen has been wonderful," Mattie murmured, thinking about her talk with Wyatt, and how he would scowl or roll his eyes at her kind words about Stephen. But Wyatt had not witnessed how devoted Stephen had been; Mattie appreciated it even if Wyatt didn't. "Stephen and I have had our problems, but one problem we've never had is fighting over the girls or about the girls. He has been, and still is, a tremendous father."

"How sad that the two of you weren't able to work things out—" Casey closed her mouth and shook her head. "Forgive me. It's not my business."

"It's okay, Casey. My parents are saying the same thing, and most of the time I'm the one to blame."

"But they didn't live with him, right?"

"Right."

"And therein lies the rub, doesn't it? I've had two husbands—neither one worth a bowl of warm spit—but I never could convince my family they were bastards."

Mattie smiled. "Always on their best behavior, huh?"

"Oh, God, yes."

Mattie and Casey exchanged looks of understanding. After Casey left, Mattie thought about what they'd discussed, and decided she'd like to get to know Casey better. She'd not been one to seek out other divorcées for mutual bitch and tears sessions, but lately she'd had too many tangled thoughts about Stephen. Airing them with someone who wouldn't praise or trash him could give her some new perspective. It occurred to her how many threads and cords spring out of the unforeseen. The accident had indeed changed their lives as well as Jessica's. All the unanswered questions continued to tug and nag at Mattie, but there'd been unexpected and welcoming moments, too. Like meeting and getting to know Casey.

She began talking to Jessica again, carefully avoiding any subject that might remind Jessica of her uncharacteristic behavior. If her daughter could hear her, she wanted to encourage her to fight her way back to consciousness rather than frighten her into remaining comatose.

As the afternoon wore on and her daughter's friends began to whisper and chatter outside the room, Mattie gathered up her things. Reluctantly, she slipped the ruby bracelet off Jessica's wrist. She was going to put it in a pretty box and present it to her when she awakened. As she bent down to kiss her, she laced their fingers together. And then she felt it.

Or did she?

It was probably her own hand moving, but when she stared at their hands, she saw Jessica's usually unresponsive fingers bend and tighten against hers. It was the pressure of a weakened child, but pressure just the same.

"Jessica, oh, sweetheart, you moved, you heard me. You really heard me." And if ever there was a signal to Mattie that they'd crossed a significant recovery point, this was it.

She tried squeezing again and again, and there was some response, but not as strong as the first two times. Her daughter was trying so hard to push through the fog that Mattie found herself weeping for joy. She'd cried so much since the accident, but this time they were tears of happiness.

She pushed the nurse's call button. When Casey appeared, Mattie sprang up like a jack-in-the-box. "Oh, Casey, she moved. She squeezed my hand. I felt it and I saw it."

Casey immediately bent to Jessica. "Jess, honey, you hear me, don't you? Remember when I told you that you had to promise me you'd wake up for your graduation? Well, today I want you to keep that promise. I want you to move." No response. "Jessica, squeeze my hand so I know you heard me. Come on, honey, squeeze."

But there was nothing. Mattie, standing to the side, had dug her fingernails into her palms in anticipation. *Please, Jess, please. Show Casey I didn't imagine this.*

Then, as if Mattie's will connected with Jessica's, her daughter moved her fingers against Casey's.

And Casey's smile grew big enough to wrap around the lilac bushes that bloomed outside the window.

"I think I'm really going to cry, Casey."

Casey straightened, and patted Jessica's now limp hand. "You did good, kiddo. You did very good."

Mattie could barely contain herself. "So does this mean she's going to wake up in a few days?"

"Let's not get too far ahead of ourselves. This is very good news. I'll note it on her chart. Dr. Egan will have to evaluate."

Mattie threw her arms around Casey. "She moved, Casey. She really and truly moved."

Casey hugged back. "She surely did." There were tears in Casey's eyes, too.

* * *

By the following day, word of Jessica's hand squeezes had spread as quickly as news of free beer and pizza at a Saturday night party. Everyone from the retired mayor holding court between the tenth and eleventh holes at the Narragansett Country Club to the newlyweds from Buffalo who stopped at the Dairy Mart to ask directions to Newport were talking about the miracle.

And the talk was consumed like coffee and over-easy eggs at Minnie's Diner. It took precedence over mundane gossip and the latest hair rinse at Isabella's Hair and Nails, and even found its way into a few of the neighborhood bars, where regulars like Freddie and Sal abandoned their usual sports or political chatter for the latest on Jessica.

"It sure is a miracle," Freddie said. "Thought for sure that little girl was gonna be locked up like a livin' corpse."

"Caulfields got to be thrilled by this."

"Heard tell the two of them were huggin'."

"Well, what'd you expect? Miracles trump a divorce every time."

"Don't think that ex-cop would want to hear that."

"Yeah, Stephen better watch himself. 'Member when Landry beat the bejesus out of that guy? Right here, not five feet from where we're sittin'."

"Guy deserved it. Messin' with Landry's wife was as dumb as dirt."

"So you think Landry is gonna go after Mattie's ex?"

"Christ, it all sounds like one of them soap operas the missus watches. Will Stephen survive if he does? Will Mattie leave Wyatt and return to her ex? Will Jessica wake up and tell all her secrets? Will Briarwood ever be the same? Who needs TV when we got our own melodrama right here in town?"

They guffawed, ordered another beer apiece, and tossed back a few pretzels. Freddie and Sal, both in their sixties, spent most afternoons hawking their opinions to one another. They chewed on cigars and swilled down bottles of Bud as they perched on stools at the Blue Seagull Bar, known locally as the BS Bar. The owner had substantially improved his bottom line when he tore out the wooden front and replaced it with a mammoth picture window shaded by a red and black awning. Customers could keep one eye on the Sox or the Patriots or the Celts, depending on the season, while keeping a hand wrapped around a cold one and another eye on the comings and goings on Briarwood's main street, if they had a mind to. And today the topic was all Jessica, all the time.

Across the street was the hospital, and about four blocks down was the police station. The town hall, fire and rescue station, and one of the first indoor malls in Rhode Island spoked out on the map like a crooked triangle to anchor midpriced housing, family-run businesses, and the Narragansett Country Club. Sidewalks were old and rich with "break your mother's back" cracks, and pedestrians, whether by habit or by design, avoided stepping on as many as they could.

Watching the passersby on this Tuesday afternoon, Freddie and Sal saw Landry's nephew and a girl come out of the front entrance of the hospital and head toward the parking lot.

"Not a bad kid, that Kevin," said Sal.

"Girls like him, that's for sure. My sister's youngest went out with him for a while, until he dumped her for Jessica. Hey, ain't that her kid sister with him? Yep, it sure is."

"Kinda nice that they're in visitin' together."

"Sure looks like more than nice to me. Looks like the kid is double-dippin'."

As Freddie and Sal watched, Hannah Caulfield suddenly tried to hug Kevin, who, thrown off balance, grabbed her shoulders so they both wouldn't end up on the ground. Kevin steadied them. They stood, gazed at one another, then Hannah leaned forward and kissed him. Kevin never moved.

The kiss—not a mushy-gushy liplock, but what the boys in the BS would call a kitty-cat kiss. A purr and a smack that surprised Kevin.

Freddie and Sal watched as Kevin took that kitty-cat kiss, then kissed her again—this time, it was a big-dog kiss.

"Kid don't waste no time."

"Hey, when the babe is takin' the lead, no guy is gonna back away."

"Times don't change much."

"Nope."

They nudged one another as saltier memories revived thoughts of their Navy days when they'd R&Red their way through busty babes with hungry thighs that opened eagerly, as if every dick were a banquet.

Freddie and Sal paid for their beers, moved off their stools, and walked outside. The sun was summertime warm, and the two men stood, hands in their pockets, about to go their separate ways. Freddie, home to cut the grass, and Sal, off to his grandson's ball game.

Hannah and Kevin parted company, Hannah disappearing around the corner and Kevin heading for a bicycle that was locked to a chain-link fence.

Just as Freddie and Sal began to turn away, their thoughts jumping to chores and family obligations, a movement in the parking lot caught their attention.

"Whoa, whoa. Will ya take a look over there."

"Uh-oh."

"We maybe oughta stick around."

"Zippety stickety. We better mosey on over and see what's going down."

Kevin unlocked the bike, the taste of Hannah's mouth still rolling through him. He shouldn't have kissed her that way, but he figured that if she was gonna throw out all those "hot for his body" signals, then she better know what she was getting.

Having sex with her wasn't gonna happen—a little harmless flirting, yeah. A kiss or two, uh-huh, but nothin' heavy.

Actually, he'd begun to regret asking her to the prom; she was too eager, and though she had all the big girl curves and moves, she was a kid. Fifteen and so stud-struck, Kevin was embarrassed. He'd gone into the hospital alone, and he hadn't been with Jess for more than five minutes when she appeared. He wondered if she'd followed him, then decided he was thinking like a crazy dude.

As they walked out together, he made sure he didn't get too close. Then she loses it and throws her arms around him like he was some savior, and tells him he's the coolest guy in the world.

Yeah? he asked, liking that she was so impressed.

I still can't believe that I'm going to the prom with you.

Yeah, well, gettin' lucky happens. . . .

That was a thank-you kiss.

That's what it was? Whew, I thought it was a real kiss.

You think I don't know how to do real kisses?

Not unless you been kissed by me.

It had been a dumb-ass, ego-header thing to say, because she dared him to prove it. Course he could've backed off, but hey, what was one kiss? Besides, he figured he might scare her off if he did his bad boy thing. So he'd smoked her mouth.

Had she been scared or shocked or snippy? Like she should have been? Nah, she'd given him some shit-eating grin followed by "I like being kissed by you." Then she skipped away as if she'd just been crowned prom queen.

Kevin shuddered now. *What a dumbshit you are!* Kissing her at all was stupid. But kissing her like that, when not once, either before he asked her to the prom or since, had he ever thought about anything more than a maybe a chaste good night kiss? Seeing her was about Jessica, that's all. Just Jessica.

Well, he was ass-high in this hot spot now, but he wasn't gonna fry. No way. She'd just have to take the bad news. No sex, and he wasn't gonna be her boyfriend. And she better wise up, or some scumbag goon was gonna take her like flies buzzin' fresh meat on the rack.

He turned his bike, ready to head home, when he saw old man Caulfield coming toward him. Now what? He looked all steamed and overcooked. Whatever was boiling him, Kevin knew he wasn't gonna like it.

"Kevin, you've got some explaining to do."

"Sir?" Kevin kept his face blank, giving him his best stupid look. Oh, shit, he probably saw him kissing Hannah.

"You seem to have remade yourself into full-fledged innocent to my wife and Hannah. But we know better, don't we?"

Remade himself? Full-fledged innocent? What the hell was he talking about? Kevin pondered a moment to at least give the impression he had a clue. Finally he frowned. "I don't know what you mean, sir."

"I'm talking about my Jessica. My beautiful daughter who's in a coma, thanks to you."

"Now wait a minute. I had nothing to do with the accident. I hadn't even spoken to her in three weeks."

"Let's cut the bullshit."

Kevin shrugged. He guessed from the flames in Caulfield's eyes, he was supposed to cower in fear. "Cut it any way you want. It's your party."

"You're a cocky little bastard."

"Hey, look, Mr. Caulfield, I don't know what you want from me."

"Try the truth."

"About what?"

"Getting my daughter pregnant and then denying it."

"Ahh, Jesus, not that again," he murmured under his breath, then tried to get on his bike. Caulfield grabbed the handlebar and yanked it, sending the bike smashing to the ground. Kevin swore and tried to get by him, but Caulfield hauled him back, fisting up a handful of Kevin's T-shirt.

"Yeah, that again," he snarled.

The guy was no lightweight, and his hothead attitude only ginned up his fury. Kevin knew if he didn't get him calmed down, he was in for some serious busting up.

Grabbing for some reason, he said, "Look, I don't blame you for being pissed. I am, too. But it wasn't me, I swear it. I told your wife that."

"She might have swallowed that stupid story, but I don't. You're lying to protect your own ass. You fucked up, kid, and you're not gonna get away with it."

The scared-not-quite-shitless sweat rolled down Kevin's spine and circled in his gut like rats rounding up for the kill. Begging sounded like a good idea, but he didn't think Caulfield would go for that; besides, Kevin did have some pride. Guy probably had a glass belly—one punch and his lights went out. But he didn't want to fight him, he just wanted him out of his face. He'd tried reason, and all he got was Caulfield thinking he owned the space.

With his best cocky swagger, Kevin balled his hands into effective fists and shoved both into Caulfield's gut. He let go of Kevin's shirt with a pained surprise.

"I don't wanna hurt you, so get away from me. Try findin' the punk who did this to her instead of hasslin' me." He moved to the side.

But not far enough. Caulfield roared back, cuffing Kevin in the jaw. "Hey, kid, I don't want your sass and I sure as hell don't want your opinion. I want the truth from you. Got it? And I want it now. You knocked up my daughter. Now admit it!"

Kevin felt the huge fist that had turned his jaw to paste pressing into his windpipe. He backed up as far as he could, but Caulfield pushed and pushed until Kevin was wearing the imprint of the chain link on his back. "L-let me go . . . I-I can't b-breathe."

But Caulfield only twisted his fist tighter. And whether fury, desperation, or terror fueled Kevin, getting choked by the bastard wasn't gonna happen. He brought his knee up and jammed it into Caulfield's balls.

The yelp was painful to hear. Caulfield loosened his grip and Kevin took some deep, deep breaths. He retrieved his bike, only to have it once again flung aside. Caulfield was coming at him like a bull after a red cape.

The two struggled, hitting the ground and rolling, fists flashing and connecting, neither about to yield or give up.

Passersby stopped, some kids who knew Kevin cheered him on. Freddie and Sal and a dozen others rooted for Stephen, figuring anytime a guy in his forties took on a street-tough teenager, he needed a cheering section. Punches went back and forth with Stephen holding his own. When Kevin got a bloody nose, Stephen grinned in triumph, but then Stephen got a fist in his eye and the victory died. They wrestled on, punching, name-calling, swearing, and landing more blows.

The crowd grew bigger. A woman began to wail that someone should stop it. Cheers and moans rose, laughter and a scream. But no one tried to break it up.

Then a police cruiser rolled into view. Two officers came running; one grabbed Kevin by the scruff of the neck and the other hauled Stephen up by his arm. Both were dirty and bloody. When the cops suggested they call the fight a draw, they went back at one another, and once again the cops broke it up.

"I want this punk locked up," Stephen ordered, spitting out dirt and saliva.

"Me! You started all of this." Kevin used his shirt to wipe his bloody nose.

"Hey, settle down, both of you."

"I'll settle down when he admits the truth," Caulfield snapped.

"Truth, hell, you got the truth. You just wanna bust me up 'cause you don't like it."

The two cops looked at one another, and nodded. "Okay, we're gonna take you both to the station where you can cool off."

"You're arresting me?" Stephen bellowed, as if the cops were playing a joke. "He's the one you should be hauling in."

"Oh, he's going, too," the mustached cop said. "Call it a mutual detainment."

"What the hell does that mean?"

The clean-shaven cop looked at Kevin. "You know what it means?"

"That the rest of my afternoon is fucked up."

"A wise boy, wouldn't you say, John?"

"Wise, Hank. Very wise."

Chapter
Eleven

At The Garret, Mattie and Donna were rearranging a corner after a customer had bought a pair of small wing chairs, freeing up some much-needed space.

"I'd about given up on selling those," Mattie said. "When I saw them at Brimfield last fall, I was sure I could turn them around before Christmas."

"They were just waiting for the right customer."

"I guess." She studied the space, which got the morning sun. "I know, let's move that garden bench in here."

"And that oval wicker table?"

"Yes, plus the lemonade set, a few linens, some pillows— we can do a summery tableau." The two women moved in the pieces, adding a galvanized sprinkling can filled with lilacs. When it was all placed and arranged, Mattie stepped back and folded her arms. "You know, Donna, we should be in business."

Both women laughed.

Donna moved on to cleaning some silver and Mattie fiddled with angling the bench. The phone rang, and she walked into the office area.

"Sweetheart, it's me."

"Stephen? I thought you were at the country club."

"Yeah, well, I didn't quite get there."

"Are you okay? You sound funny."

"I'm a little banged up."

"You're hurt? What happened?"

"A fight with that punk Bonner. I'm at the police station."

"The police? You were arrested?"

"In the hospital parking lot."

Mattie sat down hard. "Oh, God."

"Is that worry I hear in your voice?"

"Of course, I'm—" But then a small, cautious click way back in her mind gave her a start. *What Stephen does benefits Stephen.* Wyatt's biased opinion, yes, and absolutely incongruous here. Stephen wouldn't deliberately get himself hurt, but then again, if he did . . . *Stop*, she chastised herself. *You haven't even got the whole story.* "Well, of course I'm concerned."

"Thank God. I was afraid you'd screech because it was the Bonner kid."

"Screech? Me? Don't be ridiculous."

"I'm sorry, I'm just upset. I hate having to bother you, but I don't have my car and my left eye is pretty swollen. I probably shouldn't be driving."

"Oh Stephen. . . ."

"Could you come down and get me?"

"I'll be there in about ten minutes."

And three miles away . . .

"Corinne, this has gotta stop." Wyatt Landry looked around at the way the boxes had been emptied. When he and Mattie did them, all the items went onto tables to be appraised. Corinne, by contrast, had set aside a measly six for the auction. "You're giving me grief on every item."

"I don't want to sell all my mother's things. Is that so hard for you to understand?"

"Corky," he said, using a nickname from their childhood, "if this were up to me, I'd give it all to you, but I can't. We've been through this more than a dozen times. Mom wanted the money her stuff brings to go toward college for Kevin."

"Then why didn't *she* sell it all and just give Kevin the cash? Instead she held onto everything, as if they were all heirlooms and she couldn't part with so much as a salt shaker."

"Because it was easier for her not to deal with the emotional complexity of the decision, and if she'd gotten past that, there would have been the sorting and the selling."

"I would have helped her sort and sell. It's almost as if she didn't want me to have anything."

"Maybe she didn't know that you were interested," Wyatt said carefully as he studied the markings on the bottom of large platter. Mattie turned every piece of china over to examine marks, and she recognized almost all of them. To him, they were as mystifying as his sister's daily nag and pout about instructions in the will.

"She didn't know because she never asked," Corinne muttered.

"Okay, but you running out the door every time she brought out her stuff sent a big negative zero."

"You didn't hang around either."

"But, sweetie, I'm not salivating like a hungry monkey over every item in every box."

"Fuck you."

Unfazed, he shrugged. She sighed heavily and sat down on a dining room chair.

Wyatt looked at her, pained and irritated by the continual go-around and her near fiendish obsession with stuff she hadn't given a rat's ass about when their mother was living. Corinne always wanted new things, whether it was clothes, furniture, or dust-collecting bric-a-brac. Wyatt recalled clearly his sister's attempts to get Alice Landry to get rid of her growing accumulation. Their mother had never argued, but the glare of possessiveness she'd level at Corinne for the mere suggestion needed no words. Back in those days, it was Wyatt who tried to head Corinne off. If Mom was happy with her junk, then let her alone. Now, his sister had done this incredible reversal and hovered over each piece as if selling anything was a crime against family values.

He wished she was as particular about her personal life. She was thirty-five, single, and pretty enough to send usually well-spoken men into fractured syntax. No grubby clothes or messy hair. She always wore makeup, always dressed as if an important moment or person would appear unexpectedly, and she always smelled wholesome and sexy at the same time. Even here, in the midst of crumpled newspaper, dusty boxes, and humid air, Corinne in navy shorts and a white sailor blouse looked more like she was on her way to a tennis match down in Newport than mucking around through sixty years of accumulation.

Despite some extra pounds, he knew she had no trouble getting dates, although the guy was always a bit stunned to learn she had a seventeen-year-old son. "He said I looked seventeen myself," she would declare while admiring herself in the mirror. She relished their astonishment and followed it with her story of being a teenage bride, a teenage mother, and a teenage widow all in the short space of a year. The fabrication had been delivered so often that Wyatt knew she'd come to believe it herself.

Her dates were all suitably impressed, sympathetic to a fault, but few were interested in serious—as in marriage. This rejection never seemed to get her down—"always lots of men" was her attitude—and privately, Wyatt doubted she wanted a permanent relationship. Corinne loved the rush of dating, the flirting, and the power she believed she had when it came to sex. Make them wait, make them beg, and then make them grateful.

And as long as she was on that train, marriage was not, and would not be, the next stop. Though his sister regarded the disappearance of one guy and the entrance of the next as some kind of female instinct that she'd honed into expert judgment, Wyatt saw it more as a cover for her fear that if she let down her guard and fell in love, the guy would dump her as Ricky had.

He rarely raised the issue, and only rarely did he point out her shallow using of, in his opinion, some really nice guys. In fact, his sister never dated jerks or losers. "Who has time for jail-and-bail types" was her attitude. Nope, her dates all had good jobs, reliable incomes, and, in some cases, serious money.

As with the issue of their mother's things, Corinne

viewed these men through her own creative conscience. *I want him, and therefore I should have him, and when I don't want him anymore, then he should have the brains to go away.*

Now, giving him the benefit of her best pout, she said, "I did so much for Mom and Dad. You'd think I would have gotten something back."

"Come on, Corinne, Kevin getting an all-expenses-paid education is a helluva lot of something."

"Why don't you throw that at me one more time?" she snapped. Wyatt, passing the point of patience, felt like walking out.

Instead, he fired back. "Why don't you try thinking about someone besides yourself?"

"You have a lot of nerve asking me that. I, dear brother, was the one here. I was the one who took them to appointments, I came and cooked for them and did their laundry. I would say that was a lot of years of thinking about someone other than myself." She folded her arms and glared at him. "So what did you do?"

Wyatt bristled. This was where he usually acknowledged that she had indeed done more physical work for their parents; that yes, he should have been here more than he had been; and that, absolutely, she'd been a faithful and devoted daughter. He believed that as strongly as he regretted his own preoccupation with Paige's affair, her lover, and his doomed marriage that had scalded his perspective and left him less than useful for too many years. But he'd had one use, and today he sharply reminded her. "I paid the bills."

"Big deal. You've got more money than God, so I don't see how that was any great sacrifice."

"Corinne, let's leave it, okay?"

She gave him her best triumphant smile; she'd won the round, and she knew it. She picked up her can of Diet Coke. "Paige called me this morning."

He could feel her watching him for some kind of reaction. "Ahh, that must mean you're about to tell me when she's due to arrive."

"This afternoon," she smoothly. "I thought we could all have dinner tonight."

"All? Like including me? Forget it."

"Oh, Wyatt, don't be such a baby. It's just a dinner. She wants to see you, and you know how persistent Paige can be when she wants something. I thought by arranging it this way, it would make seeing her easier."

"I don't want to see her at all, and to me her persistence isn't worth a bottle of rancid water."

"Well, what was I supposed to do? Tell her you hated her guts?"

"Yes, on the very slim chance she's forgotten why." He could feel his ire rising.

"I think you protest too much."

He gaped at her, truly at a loss for words. Christ, was she deluded into thinking he had some hidden reserve of care for his ex-wife? "Corinne . . ."

But she steamed ahead. "I made reservations at the Briarwood Inn. Kevin can join us. And don't you dare not show up. After all the giving-in and compromising that I've done on Mom's things, this is the least you can do for me."

The entire concept of a happy, or even a polite-faced, endurance of Paige was so beyond his comprehension, he had not a scintilla of an idea how to counter Corinne's fictional scenario. "Why in God's name are you doing this?"

"Because I think you still love one another."

"Jesus."

"And," she continued as if his own thoughts were a deep secret to him and an open book to her, "if you weren't so goddamn stubborn and pissy about her, you just might find out I'm right."

His mind boggled. If there was one constant in his whole screwed-up life, it was his absolute disregard and dislike of Paige. But since Corinne was hell-bent on some reconciliation mission, and believed that if he was a no-show, that meant he cared. . . . He shook away the tangle of logic. *Don't think about it, just go, endure, and leave.* Besides, in a macabre way, he was curious about Paige. How many other marriages had she wrecked besides her own and Bobby Dodd's?

"Okay, I give up. What time?"

"Six. Oh, Wyatt, you are a dream," she said, grinning as though she'd moved a mountain. Actually, she probably had. "Tell you what, I'll bring the cameo I planned to give to her. She borrowed it a few times from Mom, and I thought it would be nice to have it go to someone we know rather than a stranger." She paused. "Unless you insist on selling it with everything else."

"Do whatever, Corky. You won. I'm too beat-up to argue with you."

She hugged him fiercely. "I love you."

He returned the hug. "Yeah, yeah, yeah."

And for just a few moments he was reminded of the closeness they'd had as kids. He usually did give her what she wanted—which, now that he thought about it, was exactly why they were at loggerheads about their mother's things: he wasn't letting her have her own way.

She glanced at her watch. "I wonder what happened to Kevin. Wasn't he coming here after visiting Jessica?"

"He'll be here."

"I have to run an errand, plus I told him I'd order his flowers for the prom. I'm so glad he's going. Too bad Jessica has to miss it. I think I'll get some roses for her, too."

"An excellent idea."

She pressed her hand to her chest. "You mean I actually had a good suggestion?"

"I'm memorizing the moment."

She punched him in the shoulder and then waltzed to the door. "Don't forget tonight."

"Corinne?"

"What?"

"Make sure this is only dinner. You got me for an hour. Then I'm leaving."

"We'll see. Maybe you won't want to leave."

Then she was out the door and Wyatt was shaking his head at the absurdity of sitting down to dinner with Paige. One consolation was that they wouldn't be alone. And to make sure the reunion was as short as possible, he decided to make plans to see Mattie.

Just as he started for the phone, it rang.

"Hi, Kevin, what'd you do, take a side trip to see Hannah?"

"I hate saying it, but you were right about asking her. Shit, what a mess."

Since Wyatt had learned Kevin was taking Jessica's sister to the prom, he'd given his nephew grief about Hannah getting the wrong idea. Kevin had countered with his trademark: *I can handle her.* "Hey, lately being right has gotten me grief." Then he heard some yelling in the background. "Where are you?"

Kevin talked and Wyatt listened incredulously.

As his nephew related the events in the hospital parking lot, Wyatt felt the cold curl of anger. "What is he, nuts? Yeah, okay, I'll be down. Your nose broken or just bloody? Good. See you in a few minutes."

Wyatt pulled on his shirt, his disgust with Stephen Caulfield rising to a new level.

Christ, the man was insane.

The Briarwood police station had seen very little of Wyatt Landry since his blowup with the now retired chief five years earlier. Given a choice between a review board turning his underwear inside out to investigate his brawl with his partner in a downtown bar and leaving the force, Wyatt chose the latter.

The chief had been Lou Sidney, but the man at the root of Wyatt's career change and his divorce was still there, and no longer a detective. Bobby Dodd had been appointed chief two years ago.

The possibility he'd encounter Dodd existed, but Wyatt had his cold, blank stare perfected when it came to his former partner.

Wyatt got out of his truck just in time to see Mattie cross behind two patrol cars and head for the double doors into the brick building.

"Mattie!"

She turned, then stopped and waited while he jogged to her.

"Isn't this just lovely?" she commented with disgust, falling into step with him.

"Yeah. Terrific."

He held the door for her, and they stopped at the front desk. The desk sergeant, whom Wyatt knew from his days with the department, was in his mid-fifties and waiting out his retirement far from the rigors of stakeout or street repair detail that, though lucrative, killed you with boredom.

"Wyatt! Hey, guy, good to see you."

The two men shook hands.

"Yeah, it's been a while." Five years probably qualified as a while. Wyatt asked about Kevin and Caulfield.

"Oh, yeah, the two wanna-be street fighters." He grinned his "we cops see this deal about fifteen times a week" smile. "They're here, and about as cranky as two wet tomcats. No sign they're on an 'all's well, now we're pals' highway, like in the movies."

Mattie scowled, as if she'd expected that at least there'd been a guarded agreement that they'd both been wrong. Wyatt couldn't imagine Caulfield apologizing; more like conniving a way to blame Mattie for the entire thing. A little out there, Wyatt admitted, but the day wasn't done yet.

"Down the hall, third door on the left," the sergeant said.

Wyatt glanced to his right, at the chief's office; the door was closed.

"Dodd's out. Should be back in a few minutes. Want me to tell him you're here?"

"No."

The sergeant looked mildly embarrassed, as if he suddenly remembered the old fracas. "Hey, sure, whatever you say."

Mattie had walked on ahead, and gone into a small room where Stephen and Kevin were seated on opposite sides of a beat-up wood table of questionable heritage, scarred with years of slices, scratches, and gouges. An officer sat so that he could watch both of them. His arms were folded, face menacing, weapon holstered but obvious. To Wyatt, he looked immensely official, and he recalled with some fondness when he'd had that exact same attitude while guarding a drug dealer with more escape moves than Houdini.

Kevin sat slung back in his chair, body sprawled, head down, blood from his nose spotting his Red Sox shirt. One arm was scraped, and there was a new rip in his jeans. He didn't look as much hurt as furious.

Caulfield huddled over the table, looking like he'd climbed out of a Dumpster after a night of brawling. Getting beat up in your forties tended to make you look permanently constipated, and Wyatt felt almost sorry for him. Face bruised, two shiners still in their infancy, clothes dirty, shirt torn, and one hand full of scuffed knuckles.

"Stephen! My God, you look terrible!" Mattie went toward him and looked closely at his eyes and the other bruises. Caulfield lapped up the hovering sympathy.

Kevin and Wyatt exchanged glances.

"Yeah, I don't feel so hot either," Caulfield muttered.

Mattie looked at the officer. "Is it okay if we leave?"

He got to his feet. "Both of them need to be officially released."

"Who does that?"

"Well, ma'am, today it's the chief. He'll be back in about twenty minutes."

Wyatt raised his eyebrows. "Isn't that a bit over the top? These two aren't on the FBI's Most Wanted list."

"Got my orders, sir."

Wyatt nodded; Mattie look baffled. "So we just wait?"

"Yes, ma'am."

Mattie sat down next to Stephen as if he were a juvenile in need of maternal support. They spoke in whispers, Caulfield managing his best "I've been a bad boy" look. Kevin looked as disgusted as Wyatt felt.

He started for the door, and before Mattie could ask, he said, "I'll be back."

At the front desk, he said, "Mind if I wait in Dodd's office?"

The sergeant scowled at this change in attitude. "I don't know. Better take a seat over there. He'll be in shortly."

And so Wyatt sat and waited and wondered if there was some kind of conspiracy tackling his life. First dinner with Paige, and now Dodd. All in one freaking day.

Fifteen minutes later, Bobby Dodd came in the side door. Tall, grayer, still sporting the rugged-craggy-too-much-sun look that bespoke his farming heritage. Bobby's dad had owned the dairy farm next to the acres of potato fields belonging to Wyatt's father. The boys had grown up together, not best friends but fishing buddies until high school. Then they'd had a rivalry over a girl, and for one summer they never fished together and rarely spoke. Wyatt won the girl, but the relationship lasted barely three months. By the time school opened in the fall, Wyatt and Bobby were friends again and the girl had moved away.

He and Bobby turned their backs on farming, much to their fathers' disappointment. They both wanted to be police officers, and long after the rivalry over the girl had passed, the two men found themselves beat cops on the Briarwood police force. Their friendship was renewed, and after each had married, their wives joined the same health club. Soon the four of them took cruises together, walked the beaches in Newport, and then, on an impulse that laid the tragic foundation for disaster, they arranged their vacation so they could join other friends for one long weekend party on Cape Cod. Dodd and Paige had teased and flirted with far more seriousness than either Wyatt or Dodd's wife suspected. Only later had Wyatt concluded that the seemingly harmless intimacy set in motion quadruple consequences—an affair, an end to a friendship, and the death of two marriages.

Now Wyatt rose to his feet, his practiced blank face firmly in place and unforgiving.

Dodd said something to the sergeant, who watched both men as if a brawl might erupt and he didn't want to miss it.

Then Dodd turned, walking toward his office, and, as if they were two pals who'd just shot the shit the day before, he motioned to Wyatt.

Inside his office, Dodd closed the door, and when it was

obvious Wyatt wasn't going to pull it back open and storm out, Dodd offered his hand.

Wyatt might have been hypocritical enough to have responded in public. In private, no way.

Dodd said, "I'm disappointed. I thought we'd hated each other long enough."

"What the hell is this, anyway?"

"When I heard your nephew had called you, I figured I'd extend an olive branch."

"You fucked my wife for a year, and now you want to be pals?"

Dodd winced, and for a passing moment Wyatt regretted his crudeness.

"Actually," Dodd said, "I thought if we just tried being acquaintances, it would be a start."

"Not interested. Just release Kevin so I can get outta here."

But instead of following through on that, Dodd changed the subjects. "I heard around town that you're dating Mattie Caulfield."

"You planning on taking her to bed, too?"

"That was a cheap shot and not worthy of you."

"Spare me your opinion of my worth. Me dating Mattie is relevant to you because . . . ?"

He shrugged. "No relevance. Just that her ex-husband is not going to sit by and watch you walk away with her."

"What a surprise."

Dodd leaned against the edge of the desk. "I understand Stephen has been living at the house since the accident."

Wyatt wished like hell he could have hidden it, but he knew his surprise swept across his face. He knew Caulfield spent time at Mattie's . . . but living there? He was too stunned to be angry. Why hadn't she told him? Yeah, sure, and he would have nodded his understanding and never once thought that if Stephen was back in the house, how soon would he be—or was he already—back in her bed? Wyatt wasn't sure if he was more pissed at Caulfield or at Dodd for telling him.

Dodd didn't move. "I figured you didn't know. Mattie's

dad mentioned it—with much approval, I might add—when we talked about the accident investigation. We located some witnesses, and with the good news that Jessica has shown some response, we hope to question her soon."

"Why are you telling me this?"

"Thought I'd give you a heads-up."

"Your concern brings tears to my eyes."

"Christ, you don't quit, do you?"

"Just give me a reason that sounds marginally credible."

Dodd looked straight at him and spoke softly and carefully, as though he were walking a steel girder a hundred feet in the air and Wyatt were removing the rivets beneath him. "Because once upon a time I had a helluva good friend and I threw him away, along with what good sense and morals I once possessed, for a goddamn affair that never was more than that. I wrecked your marriage and I wrecked mine."

And now you want forgiving redemption from me? But he didn't say it. His friendship with Dodd might have tanked, but this cautious confession surprised him. Rather than make any response, Wyatt turned away and walked to the door. "Just release Kevin, and I'll be on my way."

Dodd sighed, then went to his desk, signed the form, handed it to Wyatt, and said, "Give this to the sergeant."

Wyatt left the office. His heart was pounding and his mouth tasted like pee. It was exactly the same feeling he'd had before he'd practically killed Dodd in that bar fight. But this time fighting wasn't his reaction. Now he felt a mixture of curiosity, a begrudging respect that Dodd had the guts to say what he said, and, most of all, a rickety sense that the confession had changed something. Changed how, he didn't know. But changed.

Why did Dodd bring it all up now? Wyatt had been in town off and on since before his mother's death. Of course he'd thought about Bobby; he was chief of police. His name was in the newspaper all the time, and sometimes even his picture. But Wyatt's thoughts had all tied into Bobby's affair with Paige; in that context, his musings had not been friendly or forgiving or reasonable despite the passing of time. If anything, he'd become more entrenched in his hatred of both of them.

And his hatred was still in good health, thank you very much. He wanted nothing from either of them. Nothing. Ever.

He handed the paper to the sergeant, who sent another officer to pass the word.

While Wyatt waited for Kevin, he mulled over Dodd's words. So Paige dumped him, too. Or did he dump her? Why did he care anyway? Besides, he had enough to freak about with Caulfield back in Mattie's life.

Kevin came down the hall, and behind him were Mattie and Stephen, their heads together, their voices low and muted.

"Thanks," Kevin muttered. "I'd like to kill the son of a bitch."

"Yeah, I know the feeling. Come on."

Outside, Kevin climbed into the truck, wincing when he bent his bruised knee. Wyatt waited long enough to see Mattie help Stephen into her car. As she rounded to the driver's side, she glanced up and saw him. Wyatt walked forward, and to his relief, she joined him so that they stood about halfway between the two vehicles.

"I want to see you tonight," she said, not quite pleading.

"I was going to say the same thing."

"I've missed you," she said softly. "Sometimes, I feel so trapped and alone and unsure."

"Oh Mattie . . ."

"Don't be too comforting or I'll bawl."

Wyatt laid his palm on her cheek, and she rubbed her face across his hand, sending about two million erotic sensors racing deep into his body. "My ex-wife is in town and Corinne has dinner planned for all of us."

"When can you get away?"

"I can meet you by 7:30."

"At your mom's? I don't think I should leave town, plus I'm going see Jessica at six."

"Mom's is good. I'll bring the wine."

And then, to his astonishment, she reached up and kissed

him. Wyatt kissed back, holding her and loving that she didn't try to pull away. "Thank you for not getting pissed about me coming down to get Stephen."

"Since we're being honest, I'm more worried about what you're getting yourself into."

"So am I." She kissed him again. "I'll see you tonight."

As Wyatt walked to the truck, he turned and glanced back at the windows along the side of the police station. The sun bounced off the glass on all of them, but not so brightly on one.

The one where Bobby Dodd stood watching him.

Chapter Twelve

*Mattie called her father and asked him if he'd mind get-*ting Stephen's car at the hospital parking lot. He and her mother stopped by for the keys, and although Mattie had already given a sketchy account over the phone, her parents were startled when they saw Stephen so bruised.

"My God," Carl said, drawing closer to have a look at his puffy, blackening eyes. "I hope you knocked his block off."

"I held my own."

"Good. The little punk ought to be locked up."

Mattie, who'd listened to both of the "he started it" versions at the police station, said, "Dad, there's enough blame for both of them."

Her mother, looking sickened by the entire episode, couldn't take her eyes off Stephen. Finally, she scowled at Mattie. "Why are you defending that boy?"

"I'm not, I'm blaming them both."

"Well, you shouldn't be. Stephen could have been killed."

"That's not likely."

Her mother set her straw purse on a side table, the tiny thump signaling her ire. Louise Rooney never got angry; she lectured, and Mattie heard it coming. Trying to deflect was as effective as locking a broken window.

Nevertheless. . . . "Please, it's been a tough day."

"Well, of course it has, especially for poor Stephen. What are you doing about it?"

"Me?" Even for her mother this accusation was bizarre.

"Yes, you. It's your continual contact with the Landrys that's causing all of the problems."

"Now wait a minute," Mattie began, deciding her brothers had been brilliant to have moved a zillion miles away.

Her mother barely took a breath. "The entire Landry family has brought nothing but conflict and despair to our family. I don't believe I need to list all the tiresome details. That teenage troublemaker probably gets his nasty thuggery from his uncle. He practically beat our chief of police to death."

Mattie felt a whole basket of outrage spill over her. "Mother, for God's sake, stop it. In the first place, you don't know what you're talking about. Bobby Dodd was not the chief of police at the time, and as far as Wyatt hurting him— he had a damn good reason."

"Good reasons are nothing but oily excuses," her mother snapped, charging on. "And you should know better. Under that logic, then Stephen would have *good* reason to beat up that Wyatt person." And just as Mattie's outrage at the comparison boiled even higher, her mother raised the heat one more notch. "What's truly troubling is that my daughter is defending the use of violence."

"Mother, shut up. Please, just shut up."

Louise Rooney reeled back as if Mattie and hit her. Her father stared in amazement.

Stephen became the peacemaker. "No one is defending violence, Louise, least of all Mattie. My God, she gets squeamish over roadkill. And though I'm no fan of Wyatt Landry, Mattie is right; he did have good reason." Then, beaming the charming smile that emphasized his dimples, Stephen said, "Mattie and I are divorced, and she has as much right to date as do I."

"But you haven't dated," her mother said.

"Only because Mattie spoiled me so that there aren't any women that attract me."

Talk about splitting hairs, Mattie mused, as her mother embraced his words as if they'd been delivered by Moses.

Of course he'd dated, and what man would date a woman who didn't attract him? Mattie had seen him with other women, and though at first it gave her a painful jolt, she'd also been happy that he wasn't alone, that he'd pulled out of the melancholy he'd wrapped himself in after the divorce. In fact, she'd felt more freedom to see Wyatt.

". . . her back."

Mattie scowled. "What did you say?"

"I said, I was going to have to work harder to win you back."

Her eyes widened at this revelation. Her mother smiled approvingly, and her father looked surprised but pleased.

"The Caulfield family is going to be fine," Stephen assured them, oozing confidence. "What we all need to do is put these bumps in the road behind us and concentrate on helping Jessica."

"Always the voice of calm and reason," Carl said warmly.

Louise Rooney walked over and kissed Stephen's cheek. "I'm just so upset by all of this. And to see a fine man like you get beaten—well, it's very disconcerting."

"It's okay, Louise," Stephen soothed. "Next time I get in a brawl, I want you in my corner."

That pleased her mother to such an extent that Mattie half expected her to blush or giggle. Then both her parents looked at her.

Waiting. . . .

And sighing. . . .

And waiting and sighing louder. . . .

Stephen, his gaze supportive but also indicating he'd done all he could. It was up to her.

"I'm sorry I told you to shut up," Mattie said, not in the least repentant for her outburst but aware that the unspoken nuances were not nearly as important to her mother as what was said.

"Well, I should think so," her mother said, coming over and drawing Mattie into her arms. "This has all been a stressful time for our family, and sometimes things are said that, well, just shouldn't be said."

Like what you said about Wyatt, she thought, keeping the

comment to herself. Her father took Stephen's keys, her mother made him promise to call Tom Egan, and then assured Mattie that they'd be back quickly with the car.

"That's not necessary, Mother. Tomorrow is fine."

"You don't want us?"

Truthfully? No. "I'm going to see Jessica."

"You're not taking Stephen!" Her mother looked horrified.

"No."

"At least that shows some sense. Jessica shouldn't see him that way."

"Jess is in a coma. She can't see him."

"What if she woke up while you were there? She'd be terror-stricken."

If Jessica did indeed wake up, Mattie was pretty sure that a bruised father wouldn't terrify her. She wasn't five years old. "Yes, Mother," Mattie said, too weary to argue.

"And you know how gossip flies in a hospital. Everyone will want to know what happened to him."

"They probably already do," she muttered.

"Thanks to that boy, who has most likely bragged to all his friends."

"I appreciate you getting Stephen's car." And, she decided in that moment, *I don't intend to be here when you bring it back.*

"Make sure Stephen calls Tom. Better yet, you do it."

"Yes," she answered. She'd vigorously argued for seeing Tom all the way home from the police station, but Stephen said no. Wanting to end the conversation, she said to her parents, "I should go and see if Stephen needs anything."

Both smiled in approval, and Mattie finally closed the door. She leaned against the wood, feeling as if she were sinking under the weight of falling bricks, her name on each one of them.

What had happened to her smoothly running life? The divorce had been mostly amicable, her business was flourishing, and she'd fallen in love with Wyatt. Then came Jessica's accident.

Now, everywhere she looked, conflict raged: worry about Jessica, her parents' views, new worries about Hannah and Jessica's adjustment to the divorce, on-and-off disharmony with Wyatt. Only with her business and with Stephen had there been few problems. Even the issue of her working hadn't been mentioned by Stephen in weeks. Which, now that she thought about it . . . why hadn't he? Had he changed that much? She sighed, discouraged. Just what she needed, another oddity to ponder.

So what did it all mean?

Was Stephen at the center of this complicated wheel?

Was Stephen the constant?

He'd certainly proved himself to be the perfect ex-husband.

And now, with this most recent pronouncement, he was the perfect ex who was trying to win her back.

As far as her parents were concerned, he was certainly the perfect son-in-law. Hannah adored him and Jessica had always believed her father was the best.

So what's wrong with you?

She rubbed her temples and could feel herself sinking under the tensions that she'd carefully tucked into a distant place in her subconscious. And amid the turmoil, she found herself contemplating the idea of taking Stephen back just to make peace. In fact, in some ways, she'd already taken him back. He was living here, insisting on buying groceries, spending time with Hannah, and occasionally going with her to see Jessica. And, of course, he was basking in all the praise of how fortunate Mattie was to have such a considerate ex-husband.

And truthfully, how different was it now than when they were married? Not much. Except for one thing. There'd been no lovemaking, and to his credit, he'd never made a sexual move on her. Yet Mattie knew that if she gave him the least indication of interest, he would.

She felt as if she were swirling through a whirlpool of emotional circumstances, all tangled and snarled. She wanted out of the complications, she wanted her daughters back the way they used to be. Hannah being Hannah instead of a carbon copy of Jessica, and Jessica awake and smiling. And she wanted Wyatt.

She wanted the secure safety of being with him and shutting out the noise and rifts and unpleasantness, of having him tell her how much he loves her and wants her forever, of no conflict beyond their ongoing banter about whether his mother's things are worthless junk or valuable treasures.

Yes, she most assuredly wanted Wyatt.

She went to the phone, and when he answered, she almost burst into tears.

"Mattie, are you okay?"

"No. I'm cranky and miserable and lonely and overwhelmed, and I wish you were here so you could tell me I'm not crazy and make me believe that someday all this stuff will be over."

"Ahh, sweetheart." His sigh and whispery words of support made her long for him as though he were her resting place; he'd made the world special just because he loved her. "Look, come on over. Kevin's at home with Corinne, who's cuddling and yelling at the same time. I'm all alone. We can get in some holding before you go to see Jessica."

Mattie glanced at the clock. It was nearly five o'clock.

"But you have to go out to dinner."

"The hell with that. Being with you is more important."

Mattie felt a rush of joy, and clutched it as though it would fly away. "I'll be there in a few minutes."

She hung up feeling flushed and so rejuvenated that she almost giggled. She went into the downstairs bathroom, where she brushed her teeth and refreshed her hair. Then she peeked in on Stephen. He was ensconced on the couch, pillows tucked behind his head, the new copy of *Time* in his hand, and the early news on TV.

"I'm going out. I'll be back. Want me to bring you something for supper?"

"I'm not hungry. Going to see Jessica?"

"Yes." It wasn't really a lie; she was going to see Jessica after she saw Wyatt.

"Go on, then. Hannah will be in, and if I need anything, she can get it."

Mattie was through the kitchen and walking toward her car, anticipation of seeing Wyatt running like thick, warm syrup through her, when Hannah came hurtling around the corner, flying past her and slamming into the house.

Oh, God, what now? And while getting in her car and driving away dragged at her, she couldn't.

She returned to the house in time to see Hannah burst into the living room, coming to a halt in front of a bewildered Stephen.

"Rosebud, what is it?" he asked, flicking off the TV and sitting up.

"How could you do this to me?" she cried, horror twisting her features. "Beating him up like he was an animal, like you were an animal, just because he likes me. Everybody's talking about it." Her voice rose to a shrieking shrill. "Poor Hannah," she mimicked, "has a daddy who treats her like a sugar baby."

" 'Sugar baby'? What does that mean?"

"That my father thinks I'm too virgin for Kevin."

"Too virgin?" Stephen nearly jackknifed off the couch. "Goddammit, you better be a virgin. If he's touched you, I'll kill the son of a bitch."

For a few seconds Hannah appeared stunned by her father's harshness. Mattie, too, thought Stephen was being overly severe, but she took advantage of the lull and intervened. "Honey, the issue between Dad and Kevin wasn't about you."

Hannah swung around, glaring at her mother as if she, too, were the enemy. "It was, too, about me. He hates Kevin, and he wants me to hate him like he does. I don't and I won't, and if he ever hurts Kevin again, I'll hate him forever."

Alarmed at this vitriolic side of Hannah, Mattie said, "That will be enough, young lady."

"You're on his side!"

"Hannah," Stephen said, "your mother is right. This was about what the Bonner kid did to Jess and his lie about it. I thought if I confronted him and demanded a confession, he'd be scared enough to break down and tell the truth. He didn't, but that doesn't change my belief that he's lying." He held up his hand to silence her when she began to protest. "But I was wrong to have fought with him. That was childish, and it was embarrassing for your mother to have to come and get me."

"I don't believe you."

"Hannah!"

"And what would it take for you to believe me and forgive me?"

Mattie was amazed at this reversal from blustering to steady calmness, and his willingness to let it appear Hannah would get her way when, in fact, Mattie couldn't imagine Stephen backing down about Kevin. Especially after this afternoon.

"What do you mean?" Hannah asked warily.

"I messed up and I've upset you, and more than anything I can think of, I don't want you to hate me. I want you to forgive me so we can be like we used to be. I don't want to lose your love or have you mistrust me, so I want to know, what can I do to make things right?"

Mattie found her own throat closing up at the heartfelt emotion behind Stephen's words. But it was Hannah who embraced his words like a promise. She rushed to her father, throwing her arms around him. Mattie saw Stephen wince at the assault on his sore shoulder. But he drew her close, kissing her on the top of the head the way he'd done when she was a little girl.

"Oh, Daddy, I didn't mean it. I love you. I'll always love you, no matter what."

"And you forgive me?"

Though Hannah might have been soothed by her father's confession, she hadn't forgotten what he said. Wielding her recently acquired coquettishness, she said, "You asked what you could do."

Over Hannah's head, he gave Mattie a "guess I'm stuck" look. "Okay, Rosebud, name your price. Should I take out a small business loan and have more closets built?"

She giggled. "It's not money and clothes."

"A private phone in your room?"

"You already told me I could have that."

"Ah, I've got it. A Jeep when you get your license?"

That one she pondered, but finally said, "Not that either."

"A date with Ricky Martin?"

Now she looked at him at him as if he were magical. "You could do that?"

"I could try. I know a guy who's good friends with his agent."

Hannah was so impressed that she slowly sat down on the edge of the coffee table, and in a tone filled with awe, managed a long, drawn-out "Wow."

Stephen peeked around at Mattie. "Maybe I should mention this to Jessica and it would wake her up."

Mattie smiled. "I don't think so. She doesn't like Ricky Martin."

"Oh."

Hannah said, "That's okay, Daddy. Jessica is weird anyway."

The comment about her sister was typical teenage blather, but given Hannah's vagueness of late about anything Jessica, Mattie asked her, "What do you mean 'weird'? In what way?"

"Huh?"

"Hannah, don't look at me as though I have the IQ of a potted plant. Why is Jessica weird?"

"She just is. I mean, she had a great boyfriend, lots of super friends, and she was popular. She threw it all away to hang with Arlis Petcher. I mean, how normal is that?"

"Obviously there are things we don't know."

"You always take her side."

"And I take yours, too. Have I given you any grief for this new 'look' of yours that is more your sister than you?"

Hannah appeared chastened. "Jessica knew how to be popular, and now lots of her friends like me, and I'm popular, too. Is that so terrible?"

"Not if they like you for you. But do they? It's hard to tell if you're Hannah *honoring* her sister, or Hannah *trying to be* her sister."

Stephen rattled his magazine. "It appears to me to be a little experimenting. When I was a kid, I wanted to be a soldier, so I wore fatigues, slung a toy rifle over my shoulder, collected all sorts of military stuff! That lasted about six months, until I decided I wanted to be an astronaut. I imagine you're doing a little of the same thing, aren't you, Hannah?"

But instead of simply agreeing, Hannah looked at her mother. "I could have decided to copy Arlis—she smoked and drank beer, and, well, other stuff."

Mattie said, "And that would have concerned me, too."

Stephen sighed in obvious exasperation. "I thought we were talking about a date with Ricky Martin."

"That would be way cool," Hannah said, making no effort to hide the fact she was tuning out her mother. "But even a date with Ricky . . ." She hesitated, as if making sure she truly wanted to let go of such an awesome possibility. Then, "That's not what I want. I want you to say I can go to the prom with Kevin."

Once the words were out, she held her breath, as if the room might collapse around her.

Mattie waited, too. She and Stephen had gone a few rounds on this ever since Hannah had come home in hysterical tears after Stephen told her she couldn't go with Kevin. She'd told her mother that going to the prom with Kevin was the most important thing that had ever happened to her, and if her father stopped her, she was leaving home.

Mattie usually took fervent threats in stride, knowing they were emotional levers shoved between two parents to get one's own way. Mattie and her brothers had used the very same strategy with their parents. And any other time, she would have told Hannah that if she wanted to move out, she better start packing. In the past this countering had always worked with both girls.

But this wasn't any other time. Stressed emotions, hotheadedness, and wild threats in a family already fractured by divorce and with one daughter in a coma had Mattie very wary of calling anyone's bluff—even Hannah's teenage bluster. Now, however, in the light of other changes in Hannah, she decided to say something.

"Hannah, why did Kevin ask you to the prom in the first place?" Hannah looked horrified, and Mattie immediately wished she'd phrased the question with a little more finesse. "All I meant was that when I spoke with him, he gave the impression he still cared about Jessica. Isn't it a little strange that he would invite her kid sister? Perhaps he might be hoping to gain some information from you."

Hannah clamped her hands on her hips, her lower lip pouting. "I don't believe this! You're accusing him of using me? Like I'm some dolt and would let him?"

"Hannah, I'm not saying that. I'm just asking you to think about other motives than the ones you want to be true."

"There aren't any," she snapped. "I asked him."

Uh-huh, like he would admit he was using you. But she didn't say it aloud. What was the point? Mattie took a deep breath, and decided to drop the issue. She had never really objected to Hannah going with Kevin, and since Stephen had drawn his line of absolutes, Mattie had stayed out of the controversy. Now with this new flare-up, she found herself exhausted by the bickering. And with Stephen watching her as if waiting for her to agree to his concession, she nodded.

Hannah was still frozen in place, like a defendant awaiting the verdict.

"All right, you can go with Kevin."

Hannah's dizzy happiness over this victory had her hugging Stephen again. "Oh, Daddy, you're the best."

"But no scx."

"Yes, sir."

"And no letting him talk you into something you know is wrong, beer and drugs included."

"Yes, sir."

"And you have to promise one more thing."

She looked wary. "Daddy, I'll be good, I promise."

"One more thing, Hannah?"

Her shoulders drooped. "What?"

"Promise me you'll get that dress you wanted at the mall."

As his words sank in, Hannah's face lit up. "Oh, D-daddy," she cried, sitting beside him on the couch and crying. Stephen patted her head, looking so proud that he was back in his daughter's good graces.

Mattie watched for a moment, then crept out of the room. At least one thing today turned out to have a happy ending.

Half an hour later, Mattie was curled up in Wyatt's arms, telling him of the events at her house.

"Aren't parents supposed to stick up for their own kids?" Wyatt asked. "I thought that was some unwritten rule."

"They have never liked the fact that we divorced."

"But why blame you?"

"I don't know if it's blame or confusion. Stephen doesn't fit the mold of the angry ex-son-in-law. In fact, in some ways he's been a better ex-husband than he was a husband."

"Or more adept at manipulation."

"Your dislike is showing."

"I don't want to talk about Stephen," he said kissing her and nuzzling her neck. "I want to take your clothes off and find out if you're as aroused as your eyes tell me you are."

"I could just tell—"

He silenced her with another kiss. "Not half as much fun," he murmured, then opened the first button of her blouse and kissed the dimpled place in her throat where her pulse beat. She sighed, and he slipped the next button free. She arched up, and he brushed his mouth across the beginning of her cleavage, drawing deep on the sweet scent of rose soap that always swirled around her.

The blue lace of her bra intrigued him, and he ran his thumb across the airy fabric, then traced the cup edges to the bottom band and opened a third button.

She moved restlessly against him, speaking as if she lacked oxygen. "Wyatt . . ."

"Hmmm."

"Could you not take so long?"

He chuckled. "That anxious, are we?"

She reached to open his jeans, but he stopped her, loving her pout of disappointment. "I want to."

"So do I." They were on the couch in the living room,

more conducive to a make-out than full-out sex, but here they were and Wyatt didn't want to burst the moment by taking her upstairs. He stretched out, easing her with him, too aware that his body was in high gear and racing. She, too, was hot, and her heat was devouring him.

"There's time," he whispered, sliding off her blouse and bra and tossing them so that they landed over the edge of a packing box. Her hands again were busy at the snap and zipper of his jeans, and this time he didn't stop her.

She grinned at her victory, clasping her hand around him and stroking. Wyatt thought the top of his head would implode. If he didn't slow her down, he was going to come, and for sure he wasn't going to let that happen. He wasn't fourteen and in perpetual heat. Then again, with Mattie . . .

He lifted her, and her eyes widened as he positioned her on top of him. Before she could grin her victory at disarming his control, he hiked up her skirt and got rid of her panties. He noticed, as they flew to join her blouse and bra, that they were the same lacy blue.

His hand slid over her, finding moisture pooling and warmth grasping when his fingers slid inside.

"Most definitely aroused. More than your eyes told me."

She stiffened, and he felt her tiny climax. Mattie had done this since the first time they'd made love; he figured she was blessed with the ability of double pleasure, but she'd always seemed as amazed as he was. Then, when she revealed that it happened nearly every time they made love, she'd double-thrilled him when she'd said it had never happened with Stephen. It was as though, she'd told him, he'd discovered and touched some erotic pulse in her body that she'd had no idea existed.

Now, she pushed closer to him, and Wyatt accommodated her by guiding himself easily inside of her. She closed tightly around him, and he swelled into the tight, hot fit.

She kissed him, then lifted her head and licked her lips. She was beautiful—all tossled and slick and eager.

"You sure do the best sex," she said, touching her tongue to his.

"You ain't so bad yourself."

"I don't ever want to lose you."

"Never gonna happen."

"I'm sorry I've been so bitchy."

"You had a right. And you know what?"

"What?"

"You talk too much." He gripped her, and their motions came without effort, without concentration, just a natural rhythm of two lovers in perfect sync.

She watched him, lifting herself, wanting to see as he had taught her. Wyatt kept his gaze on her eyes, looking for the pop and then the lazy glaze of satisfaction. They'd found a mutual intimacy and enjoyment in the locked gazes that made their climaxes even more profound.

When her eyes slid closed on a long, mewling sigh, Wyatt's pleasure followed immediately.

Minutes later, lying in a tangle, Mattie's eyes closed. "What time is it?"

"Time to tell me you love me."

"I love you."

"That's my girl."

"I need to go."

"Not yet."

Then she pulled back. "Are you really going to have dinner with your ex-wife?"

"Not if I can stay here with you."

She drew close and kissed him. "I wish I could stay all night."

"I wish you could stay for the rest of your life."

"Oh, Wyatt," she cried, hugging him close, as if in some way that would bond them when reality couldn't. He held her, taking pleasure in the warmth and the moment and the woman.

Later, as she dressed and Wyatt lay sprawled on the couch watching her, he glanced at his watch. He needed to move. He didn't want to piss off his sister, and he had told her he'd be there.

Mattie went into the bathroom, and while she was gone, he tugged on his jeans and walked over to the last box that he'd brought down from the attic. He'd just finished hauling it down when Mattie had called. While he waited for her, he'd unpacked the items, never expecting to find what he had.

Now he reached inside the box and lifted out the old sock.

"What do you have?" Mattie asked. "Please tell me it's an original Tiffany."

"It's pretty incredible."

"Oh, be still, my heart. Finally he admits to finding something valuable." He heard the laughter in her words and slid his arm around her when she drew close. "What is it?" she whispered.

"I thought the old man threw these away. I wonder why he didn't."

"What? What's in that old sock?"

"I wonder if Corinne remembers them."

"Wyatt, what?"

"The secret stones."

Chapter Thirteen

"Well, it's about time."

"I got delayed," Wyatt said to his sister.

Kevin grinned, his body surely sore, his nose, definitely swollen. Then there was Paige. "Hello, Wyatt," she said, pitching her voice low, as if they shared a secret.

Wyatt was at a loss as to what to say. The standard greetings, from *It's nice to see you* (which it wasn't) to *You're as beautiful as always* (which she was), were as phony as the forced cordiality of this dinner. Nevertheless, he'd told his sister he would be nice, and he knew he'd catch all kinds of blistering hell tomorrow if he wasn't.

"Paige, you're looking lovely and prosperous," he managed in his best neutral tone. It worked. Paige beamed, and Corinne let out a long, relieved breath. Kevin looked puzzled.

Then, before Wyatt sat down, Paige set her martini aside and rose. She was as thin as one of those supermodels and dressed in a white silky something that dipped low into her cleavage. A circle of what he knew had to be diamonds lay around her neck, their sisters were in her ears, and their cousins were around her wrist. Paige in zircons was as likely as this dinner being memorable to him. The display was ostentatious and most likely deliberate, to flaunt her bagging some poor bastard who was delusional enough to believe he'd bought her fidelity. Her hair was darker than he remembered, and caught up in some fancy do that he figured emptied her alligator purse of a C-note or two.

She came to him, her fingers touching his forearm as she reached up and brushed her mouth across his cheek. Wafts of a pricey French perfume filled the space, and he thought of the rose soap that Mattie used, realizing he had never much liked perfume, even when Paige wore it when they were married.

"It's been a long time," she whispered, as if she'd been on an extended trip.

Not long enough almost tripped off his tongue. But he'd promised himself he would be placid and tolerant and keep his words clean.

"It has been that," he muttered.

"You did get my note?"

"Yes. I was sorry to hear about your mother's depression." And he meant it. "Helene has always been a classy lady. Give her my best next time you talk to her."

"What a kind thing to say."

"It wasn't said to be kind, Paige. I always liked your mother, and she *was* a classy lady." *Unlike her daughter.*

Wyatt held her chair while Paige sat back down and then settled in himself. It was going to be a long night.

He glanced at his nephew, who looked about as prickly as a dog who'd gotten too friendly with a porcupine. "How are you doin'?"

"Sore and pissed."

"Kevin," his mother warned, "we're not going to discuss your deplorable behavior with Mr. Caulfield." Then, as if Wyatt might have wondered, she added, "I already explained it all to Paige."

By "all," Wyatt assumed the fight details.

"It's amazing how relationships can become so entangled with other relationships," Paige said, then looked directly at Wyatt. "Isn't it?"

He shrugged. "Is it? Sorry, that's my area of avoidance. One entangled relationship cured me."

She pulled her gaze away, scraping off her smile, and turned to talk to Corinne.

Wyatt leaned close to Kevin. "I'm surprised you're here."

"She forced me."

"Yeah? And here I thought it was Paige and her charms."

"She is seriously hot-looking."

Seeing his ex through the eyes of a seventeen-year-old should have had him agreeing, but even that narrow view left Wyatt empty. Not only the lack of any kind of lust, but the cold absence of any feeling at all—even his five years of hatred.

"Wanna know the real stuff?"

"As in?"

"What Mom was nervous about?"

"My breathing is on hold."

"She was 'fraid you wouldn't show."

"She was almost right."

Then Kevin leaned closer. "I think she was, like, panicked that Paige wouldn't be cool with just her."

Wyatt glanced at his sister, who was sipping a piña colada and looking too much like a very young Corinne trying desperately to impress. Wyatt was amazed that she'd worked so hard to gain a friendship with a woman as shallow as Paige. It wasn't as if his sister had no female friends. She had plenty, so what was going on? The way she'd presented this particular evening to Wyatt came across as more about Paige wanting to get together. Wyatt now guessed it was the other way around.

Christ, did she really believe her own "you two still love each other" bullshit? Or had Paige floated some idea that she wanted him back, and was she using Corinne's always romantic heart as the wedge?

Corinne signaled a waiter for refills. She ordered another piña colada. Paige nodded a yes to a second martini, and Kevin, a Coke.

"I'll have a bottle of Coors."

They also ordered dinner, and while the waiter took orders, Wyatt glanced across the room to a table for two by the windows that looked over the gardens. It was occupied by a couple who looked fresh out of college. Wyatt recalled the first time he and Mattie had sat there.

That was the night Stephen had shown up at her door, surprising Mattie with a birthday gift, hoping to entice her on a date. Wyatt had met the girls for the first time just moments before, and he remembered thinking that Mattie and Jessica had looked more like sisters than mother and daughter. Jessica had been charming and lively, and Mattie—she'd been so beautiful with her big eyes and captivating chatter about going on their first real date.

But then Caulfield had sulked himself into a dejected state when Mattie refused the gift. Their dinner, rather than being a romantic first date, had Mattie tied in knots. Wyatt spent a good part of the evening reassuring her that she shouldn't feel guilty or anxious about saying no to her ex. Privately, he was amazed that she wasn't royally pissed at his gall. When did a divorce translate into a "let's try again" date complete with gift? Wyatt, of course, assumed a barrel of questionable motives while Mattie defended Stephen as always remembering birthdays, anniversaries, and even less notable events, such as the day Jessica got her driver's license and the date when Hannah, at age nine, had announced she intended to be the first woman president.

Talk about micro thought data, Wyatt had mused, despite being reluctantly impressed by the man's stunning memory. However, he still didn't like Stephen.

After the others, the waiter took Wyatt's order of steak, baked potato, and a Caesar salad. He then hurried away, promising their drink order would be right out.

Corinne said, "You could have had something fancy."

"Steak isn't fancy enough?"

"I meant to drink."

"I like beer."

She shook her head as though tolerating a kid with no sense of adventure. "That's my brother—nothing elegant, nothing different." She laughed nervously. "Just the same old drink."

"But so very Wyatt," Paige said, as if his choice needed a defense. "He's always preferred beer, and no matter how hard I tried to wean him, I never could."

Wyatt stared at her. Wean him? Into what? Her world of sloshing down martinis like they were Coke? No, thanks. He'd never been a true hard liquor guy, and Paige's only comment on that fact had been once when she'd had a few too many of her beloved martinis and told him he had adolescent sex fantasies because he drank adolescent beer. It was the kind of idiotic comment that Paige could deliver— even when she was whacked—as if she were quoting Shakespeare.

Without raising his voice, he said, "Knock it off, Paige."

That brought a few moments of nervous silence. The drinks arrived, and after everyone took sips and swallows, Kevin leaned forward. "Is that Porsche really yours?"

Paige nodded. "You like sports cars?"

Wyatt rolled his eyes, and even his sister blinked. Asking a teenage boy if he liked fast cars was as silly as asking some poor working stiff if he wanted more money.

Kevin, to his credit, didn't fall off his chair in a hysterical belly laugh. "Well, sure. Doesn't everyone?"

"My boyfriend hates them. He likes big cars—lots of chrome and lots of room."

"Geez, that sounds like what old men drive," Kevin said. "Wyatt has a cool truck, and even that total creep Caulfield drives a convertible."

"How nice," Paige said, bristling.

"Kevin," his mother corrected, "you're being rude."

"What's rude about saying how it is?"

"Don't talk back to me, young man."

"Jesus," he muttered, embarrassed and looking as if he wanted to slide under the table.

Their dinners came, a welcome reprieve. For the next twenty minutes, they all ate while Corinne insisted that Paige tell all about her recent trip to France. And she did. By the time the plates were cleared and coffee brought, Wyatt had heard an eternity of details about Paris fashions, two street artists who'd insisted on painting her in the nude, and some French ambassador who'd begged her to marry him. The bullshit temperature had broken the record.

Kevin was awed and Corinne was fascinated. Wyatt was just tired. Next came the presentation of the cameo that had belonged to his mother. To Paige's credit, she was gracious to a fault, and even reminisced about how kind Alice had always been to her.

When the bill came, Wyatt picked it up and left a bundle of bills. Corinne led the way out; then, spotting a guy who waved to her, she excused herself and walked over to speak to him. Kevin went to drool over the Porsche.

Wyatt started toward his truck, concluding that while he could have thought of thirty other better ways to spend the past ninety minutes, the dinner hadn't been totally unbearable. In fact, since it was over, he could afford to be generous and end it on a polite note.

"Paige?"

She stopped and turned, and before he had a chance to say anything, she did. "I was wondering when you'd make a move."

At first Wyatt didn't get it; and then, incredulously, he did. And suddenly he was embarrassed for her. God! He should have just headed for the truck and kept his mouth shut.

She drew close, her voice seductive. "You're very sexy and handsome. I'm so glad you didn't get fat and bald."

"Paige, you've got the wrong idea."

"Surely you didn't think I wanted to have dinner in that stuffy inn unless you came? I knew you would. My God, you didn't think I came to town to see anyone but you?"

Furious with himself for walking into such an obvious trap, he leveled his best shot. "Dodd's still in town. Try him."

For a few seconds she appeared confused, then said, "I'll have to call and say hello," dismissing Bobby as if he were as irrelevant as a grain of sand on the beach. "Where can you and I meet?"

"You're really serious."

"Of course, I am!" she snapped. "I want you, and I saw

the look in your eyes. You want me, too. You've always wanted me. Corinne told me about Mattie—that is her name, isn't it? Or was it Pattie? No matter. I can make you forget her. I could always make you forget everything, but us."

To his astonishment, Wyatt felt sorry for her. She saw him as a conquest she'd once had, and now wanted to prove she could get him again. Acquiring, discarding, and then returning to reacquire, as though to assure herself she always got just what she wanted when she wanted it.

"Paige, don't do this."

But instead of the embarrassment she should have demonstrated, she discreetly pressed her hand against his fly.

Wyatt jerked as if touched by hot poker. "For Chrissake, what the hell are you doing?"

She laughed. "Relax, no one saw. You always were a prude about anyone knowing how much we liked sex. Remember how horny we used to be? All the places where we made love? Like that time in the stacks at the library?" She giggled, and Wyatt felt like he'd been plunged into the middle of a horror show. "You almost toppled that shelf when I went down on you." Then she whispered an obscenity that sounded like a climax line in a porno movie.

Wyatt wasn't appalled or disgusted or insulted; he was merely sad and tired and bored. How often he'd played out a scenario where, in some encounter with Paige, he'd blister her with venomous words, make her beg for his forgiveness just so he'd have the pleasure of telling her to fuck off. Revenge was indeed best served cold, and his had been on ice for five years.

Now here he was. His sister was out of earshot, so he could verbally blister his ex. Kevin was examining the Porsche like a buyer with cash in his pocket. No more need to be cordial or pleasant; he could say what he wanted, call her every vile name that had tripped through his mind in the past half-decade; he could belittle, degrade, and mortify her.

Yet no words came. His finely honed hatred had vanished, leaving him looking at her as though she were a stranger; she stirred nothing in him. Zip. Zero. Nada.

And so he did what an hour ago he couldn't have imagined, even with a gun pointed to his head. He took her by the shoulders and kissed her, but with no passion, no tongue, and a polite kind of energy reserved for old girlfriends at a high school reunion when even remembering their name was a hazy exercise.

"Good-bye, Paige. Enjoy your diamonds and your Porsche and your life."

"But I thought we could—"

"I know what you thought and what Corinne thought."

"You bastard!"

He squeezed her shoulders and then stepped away from her. "Good night."

"I hate you," she hissed. "Maybe I *will* call Bobby. He was always better than you. Every time. Every goddamn time."

But Wyatt walked on.

It was all over. Gut-deep over. And he felt like a brand-new man.

Reflection, the mirror of the heart, had been a fruitful friend to Mattie. She'd fully embraced it during the separation from Stephen, depending on that honesty—which was sometimes brutal—to reveal the true direction of her life and that of her daughters. In these past weeks, serious reflection had been trampled upon by conflicts and unwelcome surprises, as well as occasional spurts of happiness to keep her sane.

So on this Saturday morning, Mattie made herself a fresh mug of coffee, had a few words with Hannah about summer job hunting before her daughter hurried out the door to meet friends, and switched on the answering machine. She went to her bedroom, where she closed the door and locked it.

She opened the windows to draw in the harmony of the chattering birds and warm honeysuckle breezes, then settled into the pretty Queen Anne chair to let her thoughts find ground. She had some decisions to make; recent events had presented troubling directions.

Like last night, when both of her brothers had called

within an hour, a sure sign that her mother had prompted them. Louise Rooney couldn't understand why they hadn't immediately flown home, and though Mattie understood her mother's theory that "families need each other in a crisis," she reassured them that they could do nothing. Why not wait to come home when Jessica regained consciousness, so she could enjoy them and the family could celebrate? They'd agreed. Those conversations had taken place within days of the accident.

Since then, she'd been in touch weekly with both, giving Jessica updates, and had just spoken with them after Stephen's fight with Kevin. So the calls last night seemed superfluous. Mattie told them both so, but they wanted to know about her; Mom had casually mentioned—uh-huh, Mattie believed "casual" about as much as she believed in summer snowstorms—that there could be a reconciliation between her and Stephen. Yet the idea must have rooted somewhere in her mind, because she wasn't surprised or annoyed by the suggestion, only puzzled by how it had nudged tighter and so naturally into her consciousness.

Geoff, ever the cynic, told her she was crazy, and Mark, brimming with his usual logic, suggested she just live with Stephen and forget that old marriage trap.

Mattie, wobbling and uncommitted, found herself somewhere in the slippery middle—not quite crazy, but not willing to live with Stephen either.

Which, she realized in this reflective moment, was exactly what she *was* doing. She was once again Stephen's wife, but with no sex. That was reserved for Wyatt, whom she loved but didn't live with. Placing the relationships side by side had her seriously concerned as to how she gotten herself into such a dilemma. Why in heaven's name had she allowed Stephen to take over the house, play the husband, treat her as if she needed him?

She scowled, and for the first time understood exactly why Wyatt was appalled; it had nothing to do with liking or disliking Stephen, it had to do with watching her sink further and further back into a relationship that had failed. The truth was that Mattie had allowed Stephen in because it was easier than keeping him out. She certainly didn't want to create more problems when Jess's condition was mountain-size. And Stephen had been . . . well, helpful and kind, and she'd seen changes in him since the accident. He wasn't drinking heavily, there'd been no whining about his old company letting him go. In fact, he had put in resumés at two new tech companies and the hiring managers had been impressed, or so Stephen had said. Best of all, his belittling of her career hadn't been the first words out of his mouth these past weeks.

And then there was the fight with Kevin; pure and total stupidity on Stephen's part. Like his suggestion to her father that the two of them visit the Petchers and offer to replace their wrecked car. Mattie had headed that off, and Stephen had agreed it could have landed them into a legal nightmare if the Petchers charged bribery or an attempt to silence them about bringing charges against Jessica. Good intentions notwithstanding, Stephen knew better.

But not until Mattie had stepped in and asked him if he was out of his mind had he realized how wrong a move like that could be. That seeming cluelessness puzzled Mattie, especially because she hadn't had to argue to convince him; he'd agreed almost immediately.

Just like with the fight. All the way home, he'd grumbled, calling Kevin everything from a fucking bastard to a goddamn liar. Mattie let him rage, knowing his pride and ego were as bloody as the cut on his lip. But then, to Hannah, he came across as the naughty boy who had made a huge mistake and now regretted his actions—and, most of all, regretted embarrassing Mattie.

Admittedly she'd been impressed; honest confession of his mistakes and his faults to his daughters had always been one of Stephen's hallmarks. She knew that his openness with them accounted for their respect for him and the closeness they felt toward him.

Two stupid moves by Stephen that he'd immediately turned into positives for himself. Linking them probably

would not have occurred to her but for a phone call earlier
that morning to his sister, who was in upstate New York for a
weekend of antiquing.

Elise Caulfield Dankin was a year older than Mattie; she
was a financially comfortable widow, and enjoyed spending
her money and time at flea markets, auction houses, and antique malls. Home for her was a big, rambling Victorian in
the northern part of the state, where she stayed long enough
to sort the things she wanted to keep from the things she no
longer wanted. The unwanted were then sold to dealers, a lucrative recycling business that made money all around.

Mattie had sold a number of Elise's treasures, and Elise
had purchased from Mattie. In fact, it had been through
Elise's purchase of a battered dresser that Mattie had transformed with some paint and fancy hardware, that Mattie had
met Stephen. She'd been in college, working summers at
The Garret. Stephen had been three years out of college and
working for a start-up computer company. He'd come to the
shop to get the dresser, and within a week, he and Mattie
were dating.

After the divorce, Elise had come to the shop and Mattie
had braced herself, expecting conflict. Yet, to her surprise,
Elise had been sympathetic. And it was that conversation
that Mattie now recalled both vividly and chillingly.

Elise had been soft-spoken, but presented the authorita-
tive knowledge only a sibling would have.

"I'm not taking sides, Mattie, although it will sound like
I'm using the clichéd excuse of blaming family background,
but when our father abandoned us, Stephen became the man
of the house. And in that role he tried to create some ideal-
ized fantasy of the perfect family. This was to make up for
our father's failure and our mother's bitterness. Of course he
couldn't."

"I don't think there is such a thing," Mattie had said.

"But when he couldn't do it with us, he was determined
that he would do it with his wife and children. He also had
an obsession to succeed. Not the worst obsession to have,
but you know what happened when the success got shaky."

"Yes, he got very upset, and he resented me working."

"Which then led to him getting depressed and angry and frustrated. What he needs is for his old company to call and say It was a mistake, we want you back, let's start over."

"Yes, and Stephen would go in a minute."

"Because he's a huge believer in forgiveness ending all arguments, dissolving disagreements, and wiping out all mistakes.

"But sometimes forgiveness isn't enough, or one can have forgiveness but not change the damage that's been done." Elise paused, thoughtful. "For example, the drunk who gets in a brawl and loses his eyesight. He may have learned valuable lessons, quit drinking, become the model citizen, but he's still blind. Choices and their inevitable consequences can be far-reaching and permanent. One can forgive, but not always forget. One can forgive but not restore a friendship or a marriage or a job back to the way it was before."

Mattie had viewed this take on Stephen as interesting, probably accurate, but somewhat extreme. Wanting forgiveness was hardly a bizarre human need, and so Mattie had tucked the conversation aside until this morning, when Elise called to inquire about Jessica. Stephen had answered, laughing at his sister's surprise when he told her he'd been staying at the house.

Mattie paid no attention at first, until he began telling his sister about the fight with Kevin. When Stephen said Mattie had forgiven him and that's what counted, Mattie remembered the "forgiveness" talk.

True, Mattie had accepted his apology, but what he was telling Elise was clearly a fabrication. And his jocular and glib rendering of the fight with Kevin had transformed a nasty brawl into a minor skirmish.

"Oh, come on, Mattie, it's over," he said, after he'd hung up and she questioned him. He dismissed her concern about his bogus account. "Must you dissect every word I say? I bet that Bonner punk is taking plenty of credit with his loser pals." He poured himself a fresh mug of coffee. "What time are we going to see Jess?"

"Around noon."

"I'm going out to the porch to read the newspaper."

And watching him move around the kitchen, sorting through her mail on the counter, commandeering the newspaper she'd planned to read, then going out to sit on her porch so that he could wave to the neighbors and discuss the frustration of growing roses with Briarwood's expert, eighty-year-old Florence Witherspoon. . . .

Suddenly Mattie, comfortably tucked into her bedroom, felt an uncomfortable sense of claustrophobia; Stephen was everywhere, entrenching himself, inserting himself back into her life with an ease that she'd allowed not because she'd fallen back in love with him, but because of Hannah and Jessica and even her parents. The lovely family bond reconnects to weather a crisis. Such an emotionally charged sentiment, she realized, had become more threatening than fulfilling.

Whether the decision that came immediately to mind was hasty mattered less than her need to make it and act on it. She left her bedroom and went down the stairs and out to the porch, where Stephen, newspaper abandoned, was gazing down the street.

She didn't lead into it and she didn't mince words. "Stephen, I want you to move back to your own apartment."

"Why? What have I done?" he asked, looking hurt, as though she'd suggested he leave the country. "I thought we were getting along well."

"We're divorced, and you being here isn't right."

"Why?"

She wanted to scream. "Because I don't like my growing dependence on you."

"Dependence as in being together for Hannah and for Jessica? You don't mean that you want me out of their lives?"

"This isn't about the girls. This is about me."

"And me moving back to the apartment will be easier on you?"

"Yes." And she braced herself for a shower of logic and reasoning on why his staying was better for her.

He stood, as though contemplating six possible responses. Finally, he said, "All right. It's done." With that he smiled, dimples flashing. Mattie knew she must have looked amazed at his easy compliance. No argument, no hassle, no pressure.

"Thank you," she muttered, wondering why he'd been so amenable and then chastising herself for being suspicious. This was what she wanted. *He isn't arguing, so count your blessings and don't mess it up with a lot of explanations.*

"Is it okay if I finish the newspaper before I leave?"

No argument, almost an agreeable pleasure. If it wasn't so ludicrous, she would have almost assumed that she'd given him exactly what he wanted.

Back in the house, Mattie returned to her bedroom and glanced out the window. Stephen was now deep in conversation with an across-the-street neighbor.

Mattie went to her closet and reached up on the shelf where she'd hidden them. And even while she was pulling down the sock of secret stones, she was embarrassed by their mythical significance to her. Was this over the edge or what? Probably, but she believed in miracles, and since God often worked in mysterious ways, then if some talisman like secret stones strengthened her belief, who was hurt? It certainly couldn't make this stagnant limbo where Jess was living any worse.

And though she hated to admit it, her daughter's movements of last week had lost their power to excite her. Yes, Tom Egan had warned her this would be a long path to full recovery, but of course he'd say that. It made his job easier and avoided the risk of giving a prognosis that might not turn out positive. Practical and patient—that was Tom.

But Mattie wasn't practical, and she was tired of the waiting, weary of being patient; she wanted Jessica to wake up, and it was this very simple desire playing cat-and-mouse in her mind that brought Mattie to this new possibility. It also seriously challenged her reasonable views of how life worked.

But for Jessica life wasn't working, and Mattie teetered so close to the edge of hopelessness that she was willing to try anything.

Even a sock of secret stones.

Chapter Fourteen

Would he ever get to the end of it?

Wyatt figured the barn would be nothing more than pickings for the dump. Instead he found furniture done in by years of dampness, rusted metal items ranging from an old coal stove to a twisted sharp something that looked as if it came from a stash of fifteenth-century torture tools.

He stood in the dark, cobwebby barn where his father had once stored farming equipment—everything from cultivators to enough burlap to bag the state. The cultivators and most of the planting equipment has been sold when the old man had been forced into retirement by bad health—just in time, Wyatt thought grimly, to free up space for his mother to store more junk.

Kevin poked around a warped walnut tabletop, his sneakers crunching some broken glass. Behind the table top he found a rusted Narragansett Brewery sign from the fifties. He also disturbed a few mice, who scurried into another corner.

"Hey, this is cool. Can I have it?"

But Wyatt was looking up at the rotting rafters where some chairs had been hung. "Kevin, come over here and help me get those down."

Kevin tucked the sign by the door. "How'd she get them up there?"

"Who knows? Maybe they were born there."

"I don't think Mom is gonna want these," he said as he took the first one from Wyatt and put it on the floor.

"I'll probably have to pay the guy at the dump to take them." Though neither the legs nor chair spindles were broken, the woven seats were shredded, coated in mouse droppings and some ancient bird shit.

Once all eight of the chairs were on the floor, Kevin brushed his hands down his jeans. "Now what?"

"Let's put them in the back of the truck. I've got an appointment at the office on Monday. I'll drop them at the dump on the way."

"Some big-time investor, huh?"

"He won a bundle in a lottery and he wants to buy stocks."

"If he's one of your guys, he's gotta be rich already. What's he doin' buyin' lottery tickets?"

"Actually, he didn't buy it. He got it in a birthday card and was going to toss it. His daughter took it, checked the numbers, and found out it was worth a cool twelve million."

"Wow!"

"That's what I said." Wyatt dusted the cobwebs off his clothes and dragged his forearm across his sweaty forehead. "Right now, I could use a cold beer."

"Me, too."

He eyed Kevin, who eyed him right back.

"You're gonna get me in trouble with your mother."

He shrugged. "So what's new?"

Wyatt chuckled. "Can't argue with that."

He picked up two chairs and led the way out. Kevin picked up the sign.

"Now that," Wyatt commented, putting the chairs in the truck bed, "is probably worth some bucks."

Kevin looked horrified. "You're not going to show it to Mattie?"

Wyatt went back for two more chairs, and Kevin followed.

"Come on, I want the sign. It's a piece of junk. All dinged and rusted."

Wyatt nudged the chairs at Kevin and picked up two more. "All set for the prom?"

"Huh?"

"Prom? A dance with pretty girls in fancy dresses and usually held in June?"

"Yeah, yeah," he said, his lack of interest blatant. "What about the sign?"

Wyatt chuckled. "Good thing Hannah isn't here to hear that."

"Can I have the fuckin' sign or not?"

"It's yours."

"Geez, why do you do that?"

"To yank your chain." Wyatt closed the tailgate. "Let's go get that beer."

Well, of course, expectation that a sock of secret stones could affect Jessica was goofy. Way out there ridiculous. Grasping at desperation. Absolutely contrary to Mattie's usual good sense.

All of those and more, and yet the discovery of the secret stones had given Mattie a euphoric hope that even she couldn't explain. It wasn't Wyatt's sweet story of gathering the stones and crediting them with getting his kid sister out of trouble, when in fact it was him working behind the scenes. It wasn't Corinne's fierce childhood belief in their power to keep her from harm. Nor was it that their father, of the no-nonsense practical generation, seized them and threw them away. That was an incident that brought a smile and a bit of reverie on the beliefs and faith of children.

What had snagged at Mattie and now made her a believer was the fact that Wyatt *knew* his father had gotten rid of the stones; he'd seen him dump them out and throw the sock away.

And yet there they were. Seven white stones tied in a black sock, reappearing in a most unlikely place—in the middle of a carton of delicate china. Who would pack rocks with china? Certainly not Alice Landry.

And if his father got rid of them, as Wyatt had witnessed, then how had they managed to reappear?

And. And. And. All those facts put together made for more than an incident; they were a mystery, and Mattie couldn't help but wonder if there was some force at work here.

Since Wednesday, when she and Wyatt found the stones, Mattie had pondered her reaction and where she should go with it. Obviously she hadn't grabbed the sock like the Holy Grail and rushed to the hospital, expecting that if Jessica touched the stones, she'd magically awaken and her ordeal would end.

But pondering, which was Mattie's practical way of thinking through either a conflict or a difficult decision, rather than cementing doubts about the secret stones, had done just the opposite.

She didn't want to consider what Wyatt must have thought when she'd called him last night and asked him if she could borrow the stones to show Jessica.

"Babe, I'm afraid I don't have the power to work behind the scenes on this one."

"I know that." And she'd laughed the way one does when trying to cover straw-grasping with practicality. "In fact, I'm going to bring Toadie, too."

"Toadie?"

"Jessica's old teddy bear."

"Always room for one of those."

"I'm not losing my mind."

He laughed. "I know."

But still, after she'd hung up, she guessed that going on to tell Wyatt that her daughter once had a teddy bear Jessica swore could talk and keep her safe probably had him wondering what that had to do with secret stones.

Childhood and all the wonders of belief and faith without questions. Corinne understood that. Jessica had, too.

When her daughter had been four, Mattie had overheard conversations about fairies and witches and animals that could talk like people. She knew the two voices were Jessica, but her daughter always swore that whenever she was scared, Toadie would tell her not to be afraid and that he would never let anyone hurt her.

Mattie recalled that when Jessica had been bitten by a dog, it wasn't the doctor or the shot that made her feel better, it was Toadie. Once she'd gotten lost in the mall and Mattie had all the security people searching. It hadn't been one of the rent-a-cops who had found her; according to Jessica, it had been Toadie who showed her where it was safe.

Stephen and Mattie had indulged her, believing that a healthy and active imagination was integral to childhood. They understood that she would outgrow Toadie and whatever powers she'd thrust upon him would evaporate.

Jessica still had Toadie—raggedy, one ear torn and droopy, his color faded, in a place of honor on her bed—at least Mattie thought she did. Until she went into Jess's bedroom to get him and he wasn't there.

Planting her hands on her hips, she frowned. "That's funny," she murmured. "I would have sworn the bear was here."

And while she wondered where Jessica had put Toadie, in came Hannah, modeling the dress she'd bought for the prom.

Mattie was a bit taken aback by her very grown-up daughter. Hannah twirled in a swirl of slippery white satin trimmed in pale yellow lace. It embraced her pretty figure rather than clung, and because of the style Hannah wore no bra. Spaghetti straps that looked less substantial than real spaghetti held up the bodice. The dress draped and flowed with expensive simplicity.

"Ta-dahhhhhh," Hannah sang, turning in front of the full-length mirror so she could catch her own pleasure and her mother's smile. "Am I gorgeous or what?"

"Stunning."

"Thank you, thank you. And the prize for beauty, poise, grace, and cool goes to Hannah Caulfield."

"You forgot humble."

"Humble? Yuck. Humble stays home. Only we stars are attending."

Then she dropped the posing and hugged her mother.

"I'm so happy. And you and Daddy are just the best parents. Callie told me you'd never let me buy this dress."

"You're not home free yet. Dad hasn't seen you in it."

"Oh, I'll charm him into loving it."

"I'm sure." Then, changing the subject, Mattie said, "We're going to see Jessica. Why don't you come with us?"

"Can't. I'm going to the beach." Examining herself in the mirror, she scowled. "I need a really scrumptious necklace. Can I wear your ruby one?"

"No. But I have some pearls that would look lovely."

"Pearls? Ugh." Hannah grimaced as though Mattie had suggested a dog collar. "I want something that nobody else wears."

"Your sister never minded wearing pearls."

"That's because everyone copied her. She was the one everyone wanted to be."

"Including you."

"I don't want to be her, I just want to be as popular as she was. And I am." Then she wrinkled up her face and made her eyes beg. "Please, Mom. I won't lose it or let anyone touch it. It would look so fab with my dress."

Mattie hesitated—a big mistake.

Hannah zeroed in. "Mom, say yes. I bet Daddy would say it's okay, and he gave you the necklace. Please, please."

Mattie hadn't worn the necklace since the divorce, and in fact probably wouldn't wear it again. She'd planned to give it to Jessica, but she'd already gotten her that bracelet. "How would you like to have the necklace?"

Hannah stared, stupefied. "You're gonna give it to me? For keeps? Forever?"

Mattie laughed. "Yes, for keeps."

And with that, Hannah was hugging her and dancing away and then dancing back. "I can't believe it, and I love you. Oh, I just can't believe it!"

"It's in my jewelry drawer, in a white flat box."

Hannah raced out and was back in about ten seconds. Mattie took the necklace, laid it around Hannah's neck, and connected the clasp in back. Hannah held her breath until Mattie stepped away.

.

"Oh, it's so beautiful."

"Yes, it is, and it looks lovely on you."

"Thanks, Mom," she said so seriously that Mattie felt her eyes tear. And for a few moments they were both silent, Mattie feeling as if some lock had been broken. This was good. Yes, it was another break from Stephen for her, but more important, it was a bond with Hannah. She'd always intended her daughters to have her jewelry. Why not now, and why not pieces that had come from their father?

Now, Hannah stepped closer to the mirror and rubbed her palms across her breasts.

Mattie blinked. "What are you doing?"

"Making my nipples hard," she said blandly. Then she stepped away and smiled. "There. Perfect."

And her nipples were indeed hard and visible. Mattie was left speechless. At Hannah's age, Mattie would have been embarrassed, not proud.

"Hard nipples are a little too provocative," Mattie said.

"But that's what I want. Sexy and glamorous and provocative. Jess dressed like that when she was going to a dance or a party, so I can, too."

Mattie sighed. Short of telling her she couldn't wear the dress, Mattie was at a loss. "Speaking of your sister, I think it would be nice of you to visit her."

"I did. On Wednesday."

"Which was days ago."

"Geez, Mom, it's not like she can talk or even care if I'm there."

"That's not the point." Mattie searched through the mounds of stuffed animals. "Do you know where Toadie is?"

"That old bear? No."

Mattie headed for the closet, opened the door, and shuddered.

"Gotta go, Mom."

"Hang that dress up and don't get sunburned."

"Yes and no," Hannah called back, while Mattie ventured into the closet. The airless space was tangled with clothes, bags, shoes, boxes, and more boxes. It reminded her how disorganized Jessica was about her closet; the girl had an affinity for boxes, but a seeming aversion to putting anything in them. She started on the shelves and worked her way down to the floor, which was where Stephen found her.

"What are you doing?"

"Looking for Toadie."

"The bear? She doesn't still have that."

"Yes, she does." And Mattie held it up.

"Now what? She's not four, Mattie. Surely you're not planning on taking it to the hospital."

"I was."

"Oh, for God's sake."

"I have some secret stones, too." She hadn't planned to tell Stephen, but she didn't care. He was leaving, her house and her life were hers again, and if she wanted to believe in secret stones, it was her business.

"What?"

"I figured that between the stones and Toadie, we might just work some magic and get Jessica to open her eyes." But he wasn't looking at her or the bear. "Stephen? What are you looking at?"

"That box that was under the bear."

Mattie looked down. It was a small box and undoubtedly empty. A piece of tape that had been on it had stuck to the bear's fur. She lifted the lid, and there in the soft cotton lay a thin gold bracelet. "Where did this come from?"

Stephen was turning away.

"Stephen?"

But he plunged his hands in his pockets and wouldn't look at her. She got to her feet and walked to where he stood. "What is it?"

"Christ, I can't believe it."

"What?"

"The newspaper. I just read a story about that part-time guidance counselor, Kane Fairfax, being arrested for allegedly having sex with one of the high school girls. Gene and I were just discussing it."

"There must be some mistake," Mattie said, shocked. She'd met Kane numerous times, as well as the teacher he was currently dating.

"According to the news account, he swears he never forced her, says it was always consensual."

"But that doesn't matter if she's under age. But why are you telling me this?"

"The newspaper said he often gave them jewelry."

Mattie glanced down at the bracelet. "You think Jessica and he—that Kane gave her the bracelet? That they had sex?" She sat down on the bed, the enormity of that possibility overwhelming her.

"Hell, I don't know, but a bracelet hidden in the closet, a pregnancy with no visible father, and her behavior the past month sure makes it look like a possibility."

"I just can't believe that Jess would get involved with a man twice her age. It's just not something she would do."

"As I recall, we've faced a lot of things that Jessica wouldn't do."

She looked down at the bracelet and the bear. "My God."

Chapter Fifteen

By Sunday evening, Mattie felt as if she'd spent the weekend on a runaway roller coaster: dizzy, elated, and scared all at the same time. There'd been the shocking news on Saturday of Kane Fairfax being arrested and Stephen's conclusion, after seeing the bracelet hidden under Toadie, that Jessica might have been one of his victims. Mattie had called Wyatt, who promised to find out what he could.

In the meantime, she'd vacillated between wanting to learn it was Kane—then she'd have a target for her frustration and at least one plausible reason for the strange change in Jessica—and not wanting to learn that her smart, savvy daughter had been so foolish and, well, just plain stupid. If it was true, her involvement with Kane added an unsavory dimension to the mystery of who her daughter had become.

Stephen was livid; his anger made Mattie glad Kane had already been arrested, for Stephen surely would have killed him. And that reaction was based only on the possibility that the man had been with Jessica. God knows how he would react if Jessica had really had a relationship with Kane.

After venting to her, Stephen called Wyatt on Sunday night, asking questions that Wyatt did his best to answer while reminding Stephen he wasn't a lawyer.

Wyatt summarized what he'd learned from a contact at the police station. Kane had been brought in for questioning and formally arrested Friday night. The complaint had been made by a high school girl, accompanied by her distressed parents. They'd found her drunk in her room and wailing that Kane had broken her heart. They got a rambling tale of afternoon sex and gifts and promises of forever-after love. But apparently it had all soured when, the week before, she claimed, Kane told her he didn't want her coming around anymore. The girl was still not officially identified, but most in town knew it was Emily Olson, the daughter of a local businessman and his wife. Emily was known to have had drinking bouts in the past, but by all accounts she'd gotten her life together until this latest episode.

Apparently Emily saw Kane with another girl from school, became distraught, started drinking, then finally told her parents and then the police.

"While this sounds like a slam dunk," Wyatt said, "it really isn't. The new girlfriend has emphatically denied it."

"Who is it?"

"Couldn't get a name."

"Shit."

Wyatt continued, "Fairfax is outraged and maintains all he'd ever done for this 'young woman,' as he called her, was give her a ride home from school a few times. It could be a 'he said, she said,' or it could be the romantic delusions of a kid with a big-time crush who came on to Fairfax and he told her to get lost. She could have decided to hurt him the way she perceived he hurt her. Fairfax swears that the jewelry gifts the newspaper mentioned didn't come from him."

"So what do you think?" Stephen asked.

"I don't know. He could be a sleaze or she could be setting him up. Bottom line is that Fairfax has a hotshot lawyer, and we all know what miracles they can work."

"You mean even if he's guilty, he could walk?" Stephen asked in outraged astonishment.

"He could."

"Jesus." Then he said, "Hang on a minute, I want Mattie to hear this." He handed her the cordless while he went into the den for the other phone.

"Hi," Mattie said to Wyatt.

"Hi, yourself. He sounds pretty pissed."

"I am, too, but I don't think I've ever seen him so angry."

"Wyatt, you still there?" Stephen asked.

"I'm here. I was going to say this. Even if Kane had a lousy lawyer, he could beat this. If it were proven by strong evidence that he did have sex with the Olson girl, her case is weakened by her willing participation. This isn't the fifties, and most young women are sophisticated. Many have had a lot of sexual partners by age seventeen. The term 'minor' doesn't have the punch it once had, and a savvy, sexually active, almost-adult minor raises few eyebrows."

Stephen muttered, "Why the hell even bother with an arrest or have a law if they can't enforce it?"

"A question, Stephen, every cop asks when some asshole walks who should be locked up."

"No wonder you got out."

"Yeah, well, that's another story."

Mattie quickly asked, "So what happens now?"

Wyatt said, "I'm not a lawyer, but it's probably pretty safe to say this. If Fairfax does escape legal punishment— and I say if—he's probably cooked in the public opinion arena."

"Maybe," Stephen muttered. "Look at the way some of the pond scum in the limelight turn their disgusting behavior into a popularity magnet."

"I know, but we're talking Briarwood. Small town, involved parents, good kids for the most part. Take yourself. You're furious, Mattie's furious, and you both want answers and action—I'd say you're pretty typical. If Fairfax's behavior were commonplace, it would have been on page six instead of page one. Trust me on this, Stephen, the phones at the police station are in meltdown."

"I want to kill the goddamn bastard."

"Yeah, well, I have a feeling the line is already forming."

They hung up, Wyatt promising to call if he heard anything.

"He's a good man," Stephen commented. "A good man." And after that accolade to Wyatt that left Mattie catching her breath, Stephen went back into the den, packed his clothes, and took them out to the car.

"Do you want to go see Jessica with me?" Mattie asked, glancing at her wristwatch. It was nearly four, and Mattie wasn't happy that she hadn't seen Jessica since Friday. They'd planned to go Saturday, but this thing about Kane had overwhelmed the day.

"Do you mind if I don't? I'm so pissed and so keyed-up I don't think I'd be very good company."

"Please don't get drunk," she said, an automatic reaction to Stephen's old method of coping with things he couldn't deal with. She berated herself for sounding clutchy and far too maternal, but she recalled too vividly his heavy drinking before and during the divorce. Happily, she hadn't seen Stephen really drunk since the night she was on her way out with Wyatt and he unexpectedly appeared at the door. Still, his potential for recklessness could be revived by today's news.

"You read my mind."

"You know it won't change anything."

He shrugged. "Hey, some nights a bottle of bourbon can be a good friend. You could get blown with me. I remember once, right after we got married, we got smashed together and had some, um, uh, shall we say creative, sex." When she scowled, he waved away her look of confusion before she verbalized it. "I know, you don't even remember. That, my sweet, is the beauty of it."

"I think you're confusing me with one of those girls who chased you before we were married."

"Hey, whatever. It's not important."

"Promise me, Stephen, okay?"

He slid his duffel into the backseat, followed by his briefcase and his tennis racket. When he straightened, he said, "Tell you what, I'll promise not to embarrass you."

"That doesn't reassure me."

He grinned, dimples deepening. "It's encouraging that you even want to be reassured about me."

Mattie pushed away a clamor of thoughts about asking

him to stay; if she did, it would make it that much more difficult to later ask him to leave.

Yes, these were new and frightening circumstances, but at the same time she'd made a decision and he'd agreed. To reverse herself now would make that resolve look more like a hotheaded demand than a principled action. Besides, she wasn't his baby-sitter; she'd already played that role in an effort to save their marriage. It hadn't worked then, and it surely wouldn't work now.

Stephen closed the back door and then turned to slide into the front seat.

Mattie touched his arm. "Don't overdo it. And call me tomorrow, okay?" Implicit was her expectation that he wouldn't be so hungover, he couldn't.

He squeezed her hand, then slipped his palm around her neck. His thumb stroked along the base of her earlobe and then, lowering his head, he murmured, "You always have worried about me, haven't you?" Then, as though his question inspired some new depth of feeling between them, he drew her closer and kissed her.

The intimacy flustered Mattie, because they were standing in the drive so any neighbor who chose to look could, and also because the kiss was sweet and warm and familiar and so like the Stephen she'd fallen in love with nineteen years ago.

And for a few sentimental seconds she allowed it, almost welcomed it. Then the import of what she was doing swept away the cobwebby mush.

This wasn't nineteen years ago. This was now, and she was in love with Wyatt. Good God, he would wonder about her sanity if he drove up and saw her at this moment. "Stephen, don't—"

"Shhh. Don't spoil this. I love you. I've always loved you, and I always will. I want you back, I want us to be a family again. I want to make it all up to you and Hannah and Jessica. Please, sweetheart, don't deny me the right to a second chance."

Mattie had seen the edges of his desire to reconcile for

some time; she'd blithely pushed it aside because the idea had no place in her life. Even if it had, the environment of Jessica's coma was not the best one for such a major decision.

Then, as if he understood her resistance, he added, "I don't want you to make a decision today, but I want you to think about it. Will you at least give me that much? Give our family, especially Jessica, that much?"

Again he drew her into his arms, and she went because she didn't know what else to do and letting him hold her didn't seem so wrong when their daughter was the reason.

And while a neighbor watered her flowers and another mowed two passes in his front yard and a dog yapped at passing cars, they stood with their arms around one another, not moving, not kissing or caressing, just a gentle communion that held all they had in common and none of what they didn't.

He kissed her forehead, then eased back, looking deep into her eyes. "Call me if you hear anything, okay?"

"Yes," she whispered, then watched him drive away.

She actually felt dizzy, emotions tumbling, plans with Wyatt suddenly feeling askew and off-balance. And most hazy of all was the idea that maybe she should consider a reconciliation.

Just for a while.

Just until Jessica was awake and home again.

Twenty minutes later, Hannah came home from the beach long enough to shower, change clothes, and announce she was going to Callie's and absolutely couldn't be late.

Nevertheless, Mattie halted her at the kitchen door. School would be out for the summer next week, and though Mattie had dropped hints, and recently some pointed suggestions, her daughter had done nothing, to her knowledge, about finding a summer job or checking into summer volunteer programs. Either would have been acceptable; what was not was doing neither. So instead of delaying, which no doubt was what Hannah hoped, so that she could happily claim all the jobs were taken, Mattie asked her when she planned to start looking.

Hannah backed up as if she'd been insulted. "A job? You mean, like, *working all day*?" Then, in the tone that announced her mother had no clue how a kid was supposed to spend her summer, she said, "Mother, I have a zillion plans. I have no time for a *job*." She said it as if the word itself caused hives. "I will not be made to sweat and labor. It's disgusting."

Mattie sighed. "Oh, my, that's too bad, because either a paid job or a volunteer one is what you're going to have to do."

"Why are you being so mean? You sent Daddy away, and now you're forcing me to work?"

"Your father and I agreed that his moving back to the apartment was best."

"Not best for me."

"You can still see him anytime you want, Hannah. The apartment is only a few blocks away."

"It's not the same," she muttered.

"I understand that," Mattie acknowledged, not knowing what else to say. She knew Hannah wanted her father home permanently, and Mattie was leery of saying too much in favor of Stephen, so as not to give her daughter the impression that a reconciliation was imminent.

When Hannah didn't respond, Mattie again addressed the summer job.

"I don't wanna work," she whined.

"You worked last year." Mattie also recalled Hannah talking about a job just a few weeks ago. Then it had been about spending money, and sweaty and disgusting weren't mentioned.

"But I was a baby then." At her mother's raised eyebrows, she added, "You know what I mean. And anyway, how am I going to see Kevin if I'm working?"

"See him when you're not."

"Like, that'll be never," she muttered.

"What about Benjie's? I was in there last week, and Mr. Wikson said he hoped you'd be interested in coming back. He told me you were one of his best employees. And I do believe the hardware store is air-conditioned. You know, to prevent sweat and heat stroke from overcoming the employees."

Hannah shuffled her feet, and Mattie could hear her mind spin as she hunted for a plausible reason to argue.

Mattie finished putting away clean dishes from the dishwasher as she delivered what she hoped would entice Hannah. "Oh, and I saw Kevin buying some nails while I was in there. Seems to me a guy would be impressed with a girl who knew her way around a hardware store."

Hannah thought about that for a few moments, then looked at her mother, her teeth tugging on her lower lip. "I'll have to think about it."

"Or you could mow lawns," Mattie added helpfully. "I saw some ads in the paper."

"Girls don't mow lawns."

"Really? I thought girls could do anything the boys could do."

"Not that."

"Ahh. Then Benjie's is your choice."

"No."

Mattie closed the dishwasher with a little slam. "Then I suggest you start looking on your own tomorrow after school, because you are not going through the entire summer sleeping until noon and hanging out all night."

"None of my friends have to do this. Callie's parents want her to have fun."

Meaning, of course, that Mattie was in favor of summer drudgery. "We've covered the details. End of conversation."

"Shit."

"Hannah Marie," she warned.

"You say it."

"Not to my mother," she said, glad Hannah hadn't been here when she told Louise to shut up.

"It wasn't to you, it was 'cause this is gonna make my whole summer crummy."

Mattie considered a remark about how easy and unconflicted her daughter's life was if a summer job was the crummiest thing that she ever encountered. "A cross you'll have to bear."

Which of course sailed right over her head.

"Okay, okay, I'll go talk to Mr. Wikson," Hannah said reluctantly.

"Good. And you know he's pretty lenient with days off."

"Yeah, he's okay."

Mattie patted her cheek and kissed her. "Now, you can go on over to Callie's. I'm going to see Jessica."

"Mom, when's she gonna wake up?"

"Soon. I just feel it. She's going to wake up soon."

After Hannah had gone, Mattie went upstairs and gathered up Toadie and the sock of secret stones. With her bag slung over her shoulder, she grabbed a bottle of water to drink on the way and was almost out the door when the phone rang.

"Mom, I can't talk now, I'm on my way to see Jessica."

"This will only take a moment." Her mother's moments never lasted less than twenty minutes.

Mattie sighed. "All right."

Her mother asked if she'd heard about Kane Fairfax, then, before Mattie could answer, she launched into her own opinion, speculating that with a man like that working in the schools, it was no wonder the kids were messed up. And how could he get away with such stuff and where were the parents and what did Stephen think and on and on.

Mattie wished like hell she hadn't answered the phone. She slid her bag off her shoulder and placed it, along with the stones and Toadie, on the counter. She took a doughnut from a box in the refrigerator, settled herself in a chair, and uncapped the water.

"You're not saying anything."

"I think you've covered it all," Mattie said with a dollop

of sarcasm. "I'm sure the legal system will take care of Mr. Fairfax."

"Yes, well, I should hope so. Do you know who the girl was? Is she friends with Jessica or Hannah?"

"I don't know. Mom, I really have to go. Was there something else?"

"Else? Oh, yes, dinner. Your father and I want you and Stephen and Hannah to come tomorrow night."

Tomorrow night she wanted to do a final inventory for the auction, and she hoped to see Wyatt. "Mom, it sounds great, but I have a backlog of things that I need to do."

"Please tell me when you don't have 'things' to do."

It was just the kind of remark that had Mattie clenching her teeth. Perhaps she was suffering from a battle fatigue weekend or was just weary of her mother's industrial-strength opinions. "I won't when the auction is over, when Jessica is home, and when my life once again becomes my life."

"It's just a few hours for a family dinner," her mother said, and Mattie could hear the hurt in her voice. "Your father wants turkey, and no one cooks a turkey for two people. I thought it would be nice if Stephen and Hannah and you joined us. Do you know how long it's been since you've been here for dinner?"

Mattie sighed, regretting her shortness. None of this was her mother's fault, and though she often had a too direct bluntness when it came to expressing her opinions, at least Mattie was rarely left wondering what she thought.

"Okay, Mom, we'll be there for dinner tomorrow night."

"Oh, I'm so glad. If only Jessica—but I know she'll be here in spirit."

"Yes, she will." Then she almost said she'd call Stephen, but stopped herself. She'd never get off the phone if her mother learned that Stephen had moved back to his apartment.

They set the time and Mattie finally hung up.

Once again she picked up the secret stones, Toadie, and her bag. Then she remembered Stephen was going to get drunk, which meant he'd be less than interested in a night with her parents. She should call and tell him what was planned; again she set her things down. But then, irritated by her own "fixing" of Stephen's image, she grabbed up her stuff and marched out the door.

If he didn't show up tomorrow night or if he was hung-over, let him explain it.

In Jessica's room at the hospital, Mattie sat on the edge of her bed. She drew her daughter's hand into hers and tucked the bear between them. She told her the story of the secret stones and then poured a few in her daughter's palm, closing her fingers around them.

Keeping her voice soft and even, she began to talk, em-phasizing how much she and Stephen loved Jessica, and that no matter what had happened or what she'd done, their love and faith in her were secure and solid. She spoke of her own teenage angst, of once being so angry with her parents for some rule they were enforcing that, to prove she could do as she pleased, she let herself be picked up by a guy she didn't know. She hadn't cared about safety or good sense or those "deranged strangers" parents warned about but rarely were seen.

When the guy stopped and smiled and was in no hurry to drive away alone, Mattie saw just three things. He was cute and sexy, and older, and he had a tattoo on a very muscled forearm.

"Well," she continued, rubbing the stones against Jes-sica's palm. "After I got into the car and he started to drive, I was scared, but I was also feeling pretty sure of myself. I was sixteen, but I told him I was eighteen. He said his name was Denny and he was from Providence and he was twenty-two. We talked, and then he stopped outside of town and began kissing me." Mattie paused, realizing her confession of reck-less behavior probably appeared quaint by today's stan-dards, but the underlying principle of the foolish notion of "I can take care of myself" still held true.

"I let him kiss me, Jess. And I let him touch me, and he wasn't rough or forceful. It was very arousing, and I remem-ber thinking that this was like in the movies—a sexy stranger seduces a willing young woman, they fall in love, and they live happily ever after. I believed that all of it was serious and that we'd been chosen for each other in some mystical, magic manner." Mattie cleared her throat, realizing that she was about to tell Jessica something she'd never told anyone.

"Denny made love to me. I gave this stranger my virginity. And you know what? I don't think he even noticed. Later he dropped me off at the same place he picked me up. I wanted something more—a promise we'd see each other, even if it was in secret. Actually, I liked the whole idea of a secret—more exciting and more romantic, and yes, more dangerous. And then you know what? He gave me a chain necklace he was wearing, kissed me, and told me he loved me." Mattie almost smiled at this recollection because she'd been so sure he meant it, so sure that she and Denny were destined for a long and happy future.

"For weeks I believed. For weeks I wore the necklace. For weeks I existed on the memory of every touch, of every kiss, of how it felt to be with a man. But you know what? I never saw him again.

"Inside my soul I was devastated and unhappy, and I felt betrayed. I began to make excuses for Denny. He'd been in an accident and couldn't come back and find me. Another girl had found out he loved me, and he didn't come back because he was afraid she'd hurt me. And he'd tried to find me and couldn't, but he'd keep looking, and one of these days we'd be together."

Mattie felt some tension in Jessica's fingers as she related the story. That spurred her on; she knew her daughter was hearing and probably understanding, and once Jessica was awake and talking, Mattie knew she'd get a bombardment of questions about Denny, but that was okay. Sometimes showing vulnerability made the kids more aware that parents, too, made bad decisions, took perilous risks, and faced consequences that couldn't be changed. Mattie would welcome the questions, and she dearly hoped that Jessica would answer some for her.

Making sure the stones were in Jessica's palm, Mattie said, "Sweetheart, I have to ask you a very important question, and I want you to try extra hard to answer me." Again she pressed the stones. "I want you to squeeze the stones if the answer is yes. Can you do that right now, so I know you're hearing me?"

Mattie held her breath, her gaze riveted on her daughter's fingers for any sign of movement. When she saw a slight movement, her heart pounded so loud she heard it as much as felt it.

"Oh, Jessica, sweetheart, that's wonderful." Mattie's tension was building to such a crescendo she had to make herself stay seated. "All right, Jess, I don't want to wear you out. I know this must be difficult. I have only one question. Remember, squeeze the stones if the answer is yes."

Mattie took a breath, framing her question in her mind so that she didn't confuse her daughter or phrase it so it wasn't clear. *Okay, okay, calm down. Don't chatter, don't junk it up with too many words.*

"Jess, did you ever have sex with Kane Fairfax?"

With her heart now stopped totally, and her breathing suspended, Mattie waited and waited and waited. There was no motion, no squeeze, not even the minutest pressure. She stared hard enough at the stones and her daughter's fingers to meld them together, but still there was no motion.

Mattie asked the question twice more, repeating that Jess should squeeze only if the answer was yes.

Her daughter's fingers remained still.

Mattie leaned down and hugged her. "I knew you wouldn't have done that. Oh, Jessica, thank God. Dad was ready to kill Kane."

Then Jessica squeezed the stones. For a moment, Mattie was confused, then realized that Jessica was simply agreeing with her. "You understand, don't you?"

Another squeeze.

"Do you want to keep the stones and Toadie?"

Yet another squeeze.

Mattie let go of her hand, removed the stones, and returned them to the sock. She placed the lumpy bundle against Toadie's belly and tucked them both where Jess could feel them.

She kissed her cheek, squeezed her hand once again, and said, "I love you."

And this time Jessica *really* squeezed back—hard.

Chapter Sixteen

On Monday morning, Wyatt stopped at The Garret on
his way down to Newport.

Mattie glanced up, startled to see him in a coat and tie—
from where she was standing, the back of his truck looked as
if it was either coming from or going to the dump. The town
still had a walk-through dump, which was as much a gathering place for friends and discarded treasures as an outdoor
flea market.

"I'm going," he said, noting her questioning expression.

"In those clothes?"

"For twenty bucks one of the guys at the dump will haul
the stuff out for me. You should know me well enough that
me picking through someone else's trash is as likely as you
locking the door and having sex with me right here on this
ugly couch."

"Oh, damn," she said, playing along. "You read my
mind."

"About sex or the ugly couch?"

"Sex, definitely. I was hoping you'd help me make this
very expensive Victorian feel loved."

He raised an eyebrow as he walked closer to the stiff, ornate love seat. "On this contraption, a guy wouldn't be able
get his knee out of the way so he could get his cock in."

"I'm sure that was a painful problem for men in pursuit

of Victorian ladies," she said, always amazed she could have these outrageous conversations with Wyatt. She'd never thought of herself as a prude, but she and Stephen had rarely engaged in sexy chatter.

Wyatt examined the couch as if he were measuring it for lovemaking comfort. "Unless she sat on his lap or got on her knees—"

She clamped her hand over his mouth and grinned. "I get your drift."

He kissed her palm and winked at her. "So why don't you close up and come with me?"

"With our clothes on or off?" she asked blandly.

"You're quick." And then he groaned at having just set himself up.

She couldn't resist. "Only when you're ready."

He laughed. "Okay, Miss Smart-ass, here's the deal. I have a meeting but should be done by noon. We could go to Flo's for clams, then the beach, then there's that nice king-sized bed at my place. We could open the doors and smell the ocean and practice some new positions."

"Sounds very tempting."

"Then give in and say yes."

She sighed. "I can't. Today is the worst possible day. I have a lot of work here, plus I'm expecting a call from the tent people. They set up on Friday, and I'm trying to get a bigger tent so the bidders aren't packed in if it turns hot. And then dinner tonight at my parents." She paused. "Although I do have some news you'll like. Stephen moved back to his apartment yesterday."

He grinned. "You're right. I like that."

She told him what had happened and how wonderful Stephen had been.

"I'm glad he didn't give you a hassle."

"Actually, he's been pretty amazing . . . considering."

"Considering . . . ?

"He could have been a real jerk. My parents, the girls, the neighbors—they all think he hung the moon. In other words, if it had come down to what he wanted versus what I wanted, he would have won."

"And Stephen usually gets what he wants."

"He didn't this time."

"If you say so."

"You're not going to rub the moss off that old manipulation theory of yours."

He shrugged. "I'm just not ready to declare him pure and holy."

"What does he have to do, Wyatt, give you his blessing?"

"He doesn't have to, he already has yours. He's got you bragging about his extraordinary behavior, when all he's done is what any decent guy would do."

"Because he's a decent guy."

"And so it is written," he muttered, then he held his hands up. "I concede. You called this good news, and so do I. The details aren't that important."

As she started to say something more, he took her by the shoulders and kissed her, murmuring, "I love you, That's what's important."

He was right. That's all that was important.

They discussed the auction, set for the following Saturday. It promised to be a hectic few days, what with the prom Friday night.

Then she asked, "Nothing on Kane, huh?"

"They're keeping it pretty buttoned up."

"Well, Jessica wasn't one of his victims."

"You've found out for sure?"

"I found out from Jessica, thanks to your secret stones."

He glanced at his watch, then folded his arms and leaned against the counter. "Walt won't like waiting, but this I gotta hear."

And so she explained the whole scene with Jess, and how Mattie had known the stones had significance because they appeared when they did; because they were found in a place no one would ever put stones—a box of china, and because Jessica had responded when she'd held them in a way that convinced Mattie they worked.

"Babe . . ."

"Don't you dare tell me I'm crazy, or tilting at windmills or believing in something that's out of the land of fairy dust.

I saw what I saw, and Jessica responded. It's true and it worked and dammit. . . ." Then, to Mattie's horror, she felt tears well up in her eyes. Even as she listened to her own account, it sounded exactly as if she was desperately embracing the unbelievable.

"I wouldn't dream of questioning the power of secret stones," he said, tugging her into his arms as though she were a child who'd been told there were no miracles, but he had something even better. Faith in the impossible.

"If you'd been there and seen her reaction, then you'd . . ."

"Babe, you don't need to convince me. I believe you."

She clung to him, loving him and wishing she could indeed go to Newport with him. "What about getting together right after the auction?"

"I'm gonna have to wait that long to make love to you?"

"No, silly. I mean to spend a day in Newport. Maybe even a weekend."

He looked elated. "Man, those secret stones did work some magic. You choose the weekend and I'll be ready."

They laughed together, and she walked with him to the truck. He kissed her once more. When she glanced into the truck bed, her eyes widened in disbelief.

"Oh, my God! They can't be! It has to be a mistake." As she chattered, she was unlatching the back and climbing into the truck bed, heedless of the dirt and junk. She scrambled onto a mound of broken boxes to look more closely. "I don't believe my eyes, and I'm looking right at them."

Wyatt blinked. "Looking at what? What the hell are you doing? You're going to get filthy."

"These chairs . . . where did you get them?"

"In the shed, hanging from the rafters. Hey, they're crap, busted seats and—"

"They're stunning."

Wyatt stared at her as though unsure whether he should drag her out of the truck or hose her down to bring her to her senses.

"Well, don't just stand there. Help me get them out."

"Get them out? For what? Please don't tell me you want

to put them in your store. Those things make that ugly sofa look like a cover shot for one of those decorating magazines you sell."

But even as he talked, she was very gently lifting the first chair from among the trash that, judging by her relieved expression, must have acted as a cushion.

"Put this one inside the door," she said, handing him the first one. "And for heaven's sake don't hit it against anything—a broken leg would be a disaster."

"A disaster," Wyatt muttered as he gingerly took the dirty chair, trying to keep it away from his clean clothes. "How could they be any more of a disaster than they already are?"

"Trust me, okay?"

She was perched on top of all the trash, her hands carefully pulling away the junk he and Kevin had loaded late Saturday afternoon. Ripped bicycle tires were tossed aside, rusted tools carefully placed far from where she was working to free the chairs. Wyatt repositioned the remains of a chain-link fence and shoved aside a once upholstered chair now rotted and filled with mice droppings. Then she found the box of empty beer cans. As she pondered them, he shook his head.

Finally, after examining each can, she lifted the box free and said, "Here, take these and put them aside. Old beer cans are often collectible. These aren't mint, but they are Narragansett Ale, and they'd probably have regional interest. I'll need to check—yes, George would know."

"You mean you don't have a handy booklet on the value of rusty beer cans?"

"I know it sounds crazy."

"Kevin found a Narragansett Ale sign that he went nuts over."

"I hope you told him to keep it."

He nodded.

"Good. And you need to let Corinne take the things she wants. The auction will bring in more than enough to educate Kevin at Harvard."

"And how did you conclude that?"

"I know. I just know." And with that mysterious answer, she smiled and went back to freeing the chairs.

Wyatt took each chair and carefully carried it into The Garret. When they were all clustered together against the background of the pretty pieces Mattie was selling, they looked like they been dragged through three Dumpsters.

"Would you like me to carry in that old stuffed chair, recent home to most of the mice in Briarwood? A few pillows and a can of air spray, and no one would even notice."

"I have to call George."

"She's not even listening," he mumbled to himself. "Who's George? A furniture repair man?"

She looked aghast as she punched out George's number, "George is our auctioneer, remember? You played Little League with his nephew."

"Oh, yeah."

"As to repair? These chairs? No way. They're perfect just the way they are." She walked around them, staring and touching as if they were jewels on display. Then, into the phone she said, "George, you have to come over to The Garret. No, right now. Yes, it's about the auction, but it's too incredible to tell you on the phone. I want to see your face. Hurry."

She disconnected, then started to punch another number. "Mom will be stunned."

Wyatt plucked the phone from her hand and set it down. "Oh, no, you don't. You're going to tell me what is so earth-shattering about eight dirty chairs with rags for seats."

"You better sit down."

"I think I can take the news on my feet."

"These are nineteenth-century Windsor chairs and they—"

"So they're *old* dirty chairs with rags for seats."

"Will you shut up and listen to me?"

"Yes, ma'am."

She took a deep breath. "These chairs . . . oh, my, it just makes my heart pound looking at them. These are going to bring in somewhere around a hundred thousand dollars at the auction."

The figure rolled off her tongue with such surety that Wyatt thought maybe he should have sat down. Now he studied the pieces as if there was some obscure detail like gold nails hidden in the grime. "Mattie, babe, I know you're sincere, and I know you want the auction to make a lot of money, but a hundred grand? I don't think so."

"Do you believe I know my business? Was I right about the Rookwood?"

"Yeah, but that at least looked useful—these aren't even good firewood."

"How they look, as in pretty and polished, isn't the point. The value is in their age, their scarcity, their historic significance, and their superb condition. They're probably about a hundred and fifty years old. Oh, I wish I knew who owned them. If we could document some history . . . but that's probably too much to hope for." She touched the arm of one in awe, as if Abraham Lincoln might have once rested a hand there. She continued, "There's nothing broken, no one tried to refinish them—thank God."

"Not a good thing?"

She shuddered. "It reduces the value by as much as seventy percent. These are perfect—finish is original, and the wood is dry and solid. No one left them in water. You did say they were on the rafters, right?"

"Uh, yeah." He scowled. "What about the seats?"

"A professional who knows Windsors could restore them so the seats look like the originals."

"So there's a difference between refinish and restore."

"Absolutely."

"And you're sure these things are worth money?"

"Such unbelief," she chided as though he were an antiques agnostic. "Let me prove it to you." She walked to the door; outside, an old Plymouth Fury the size of an aircraft carrier had lumbered up and halted beside Wyatt's truck. A shabby, scruffy guy got out, slammed the car door, and stalked toward the shop, looking as if he'd chewed railroad spikes for breakfast.

Mattie beamed. "What took you so long?"

"Long! Hell, there ain't no freeway between there and

here. I drove through three stop signs and almost hit some bald buzzard in a wheelchair." He stomped into The Garret, cigar stub twitching, shirttail just barely inside khaki pants that bagged at the knees and were held up by a frayed belt of no recognizable color. His hair had more snarls than a cheap ball of twine, but his eyes were alert and sharp. Wyatt remembered that Mattie told him Epperly didn't give a great first impression, but he was the best in the business.

Epperly plucked the cigar from the corner of his mouth, glaring down at Mattie, who stood so that the chairs, which Wyatt had placed around the corner, weren't visible. "If this isn't a showstopper, my shit list just got a brand new name."

"Oh, George, you're such a wonderful old grouch." She laughed and hugged him and he hugged back, but he didn't prolong it.

"Don't dance them pretty eyes at me, missy," he snapped, jamming his cigar back in and shifting the stub to the other side of his mouth. "Always did have eyes too pretty for your own good."

Wyatt grinned. He liked George—and oh, did he know how those pretty dancing eyes could influence a moment.

"Where you get off orderin' me over here like I got nothin' better to do?"

"You'll be happy, I promise."

"I was happy before you called. Just so you know, I left an Internet auction that's gonna end in twenty minutes. I was high bidder on some Heisey I've been huntin' down since that porked-up, back-stabbin', hunker-in-the-sewer skunk Borden—"

"Borden's one of his best friends," she side-mouthed to Wyatt.

"—oinked my Cora into trading that glass for a lot of linen that ain't worth a crotch of sour sweat—" George came to an abrupt stop when Mattie stepped aside and flipped on a light. His cigar drooped, his eyes sparkled like a kid with his first two-wheeler, his voice softened to a cadence of reverence. "Sweet Christ almighty . . ."

"Aren't they gorgeous?"

"Where did you get them?"

"Oh, well . . . ," Mattie said breezily, twining her fingers together as if valuable Windsor chairs—a hundred grand valuable still boggled Wyatt—found their way into her shop at least once or twice a day. "They were on their way to the dump, and I rescued them."

"The dump?" He looked as horrified as Mattie had when she spotted them in the truck. "Like in-the-garbage dump? Jesus, Jesus. . . ." George's face turned puke green and then the pale color of old cheese. Recovering, he chomped down on his cigar, walked around each of the chairs as though they were enclosed in angelic light, and then bent down with an agility that told Wyatt he spent a lot of time looking under furniture. "They're perfect."

"I know."

"They're gonna bring a bundle."

"I know."

"You gotta get on the horn and get the word out."

"I was just waiting for your opinion."

Then he grinned. "Course you were. I ain't been an expert on Windsors for my health, you know."

"George, you're an expert on everything."

"Goddamn right. And call Parker in Buffalo. He was cryin' and moanin' at Brimfield about never seein' anythin' that made his heart go bumpety-bump."

"These will do it."

"Probably give him a friggin' heart attack."

After another tour around the chairs, he looked at Mattie. "The dump . . . Christ, I'll be tellin' my grandkids about this one. So tell me what moronic dumbbell would take these to the dump?"

Wyatt stepped forward and George scowled, seemingly noticing him for the first time. He gave Wyatt the kind of once-over reserved for an intruder. "Who the hell are you?"

"I'm the moronic dumbbell."

"Louise, that was a delicious dinner, as always." Stephen leaned back and laid his folded napkin on the table.

Her mother beamed. "Thank you. I'm just so happy you all could come."

"Saying no to you is never easy," Stephen said with just enough sincerity to make it believable rather than a son-in-law pander. Former son-in-law, Mattie reminded herself, realizing that the word "former" had been left out of most of her descriptions of Stephen lately.

The evening was breezy, warm, and framed with an incandescent sunset of such intense reds and gold and oranges that no human artist could have created it. They were on the Rooneys' back porch, seated in wicker chairs cushioned with plump pillows in a pink and green hydrangea pattern. On the house's clapboard siding hung a collection of colorful birdhouses that her father had decorated to empty out the palette of paint cans in the garage. Antique urns planted with geraniums, vinca, and pansies softened the corners. Citronella candles flickered on the tables and a trio of rabbits chased each other across the meticulously cut back lawn.

As the conversation drifted to the Red Sox, Mattie sat back relaxed, half-listening, recalling sweet summers on this porch before the divorce. The four of them came for cookouts, or mega events like the Fourth of July and Labor Day picnics, family birthdays or any other occasion when her mother could find an excuse to get everyone together—from luring Mattie's brothers home so she could spoil them, to a pair of great-aunts from Providence, assorted and quirky two or three times removed cousins, and always close friends such as Cora and George Epperly, whom the Rooneys had known since The Garret had opened.

But since the divorce, these gatherings had, for Mattie, been forced, and she'd carried an inner tension that usually peaked with a mountain-sized headache. Those times when she'd reluctantly agreed to family get-togethers, she'd begun counting the moments until she could escape almost as soon as she'd arrived. Though she'd attended and smiled and laughed, it had all been an illusion. Tonight, she didn't have the impatient itchiness of wanting to leave; she had no desire to clarify for the zillionth time to her parents that though

Stephen remained a stellar father, she'd embarked on a new life without him.

Yes, tonight was different because she was different. She'd changed, and this realization sprang from the progress she'd seen in Jessica and Stephen's unfailing cooperation and support since the accident, which had climaxed when she'd asked him to move back to his apartment and he'd given her no argument or hassle.

And today, the Windsors.

The find had been made even more breathtaking by the excitement she'd heard in the voices of dealers and potential buyers when she'd called them.

All of these weren't just unrelated events—they'd made this night different, they'd mirrored the awareness of the change within her. Or had this inner change made the night so rewarding? Either way, this turnabout didn't surprise her or smack her like some emotional lurch, but affirmed its place within her as if a light had driven away all the darkness. This illumination gave her pause and drew her into some serious consideration of a reconciliation with Stephen.

All right, maybe she didn't love Stephen with the wonder and eager passion that she felt for Wyatt, but she had at one time. And she wasn't so blissfully romantic that she didn't know that all the erotic energy, delicious anticipation, and just plain fun of being with Wyatt would fade in time. She loved him, yes, but she loved her daughters and her parents—and perhaps, if she opened up to the idea, she could come to love Stephen again. She dismissed the idea of sacrificing her own wants—that didn't automatically mean dissatisfaction and unhappiness; real sacrifice meant exchanging life for death. And it certainly wasn't death for her to put the girls' needs before her own. Perhaps Jessica would have never gotten into trouble if Mattie hadn't been so close-minded about taking a second look at her divorce decision.

If she did this, it would not be a relinquishment, but merely getting a grip on priorities, she concluded. And as moonlight follows sunset, she could no longer automatically dismiss the possibility of a life again with Stephen.

"You're awfully quiet, Mattie," her father said. "All this talk of the Red Sox season bore you?"

Mattie glanced up. "Actually, I was just doing some thinking."

"About lots more family summers on this porch, I bet."

She smiled. "Yes, about family summers." She then rose to her feet as her mother began to clear the table.

Louise served coffee while Mattie loaded the dishwasher. Hannah carried out a tray of desserts: chocolate mousse served in a set of pink Depression glass Mattie had found for her mother at the big antique mall in New Jersey.

The conversation from dinner resumed over coffee; once again there was amazement over Mattie's incredible find of the Windsors. They pondered the latest on Kane Fairfax—his continued denial and the fact that no one else had come forward to support Emily Olson's story. Stephen had told her privately that he'd heard at a local diner that that there were some holes in the accuser's version that weakened her charges. Mattie felt a small sense of relief—she'd hoped from the moment she'd first heard that there'd been some horrid mistake, that Kane hadn't done what he'd been arrested for.

Of course, there'd been no mention of a potential connection of Kane to Jessica, and Mattie was relieved that Stephen hadn't said anything. Her parents would only be upset and worried, and because Mattie was convinced there was no truth to the possibility. . . . Of course, she still couldn't explain the hidden bracelet, but there was plenty of time for that after Jessica awakened.

"If only she were here," Carl Rooney said, when the conversation drifted back to Jessica, "this would be just like old times. I remember, when she was a little girl, she would curl up in that old swing we had—it was right over there. Remember, Lou?"

Louise's features softened. "She loved to ask all those questions we never knew quite how to answer. Like why couldn't she have been a boy."

"That was the tomboy period where she refused to wear anything that resembled girl's clothes," Stephen added.

"And she got all her hair cut off."

Mattie shuddered. "It was dismal."

"But what a change when she hit her teens."

Hannah, frantically dieting for prom night, had quietly switched her father's empty mousse dish with her full one. Tucking one leg beneath the other, she said, "Yeah, she goes from a gross-out fake boy to the perfect Miss Prom Queen even when there aren't any proms."

"And you, Rosebud, the princess of shyness, have finally quit hiding and let us all see how popular and beautiful you are," Stephen said.

Hannah grinned. "You really think so, Daddy?"

Mattie rolled her eyes as Stephen nodded in the expected affirmative.

Hannah's recent need for reassurance about the obvious had begun to disturb Mattie. Yes, she'd come out of her shell since the accident because the spotlight had turned on her, but she hadn't come slowly—more of a burst as if she'd been trapped and suddenly flung free. No slow transformation like the caterpillar to the butterfly for her daughters. One day a tomboy, the next a prom queen. One day shy and reserved, the next outgoing and dating Jess's old boyfriend.

And while the change in Jess had been inevitable—tomboys grow up—the change in Hannah had come not because she'd outgrown her reserve and shyness but because her older sister was out of the picture. Mattie was very aware that the less outgoing Hannah had always felt overshadowed by Jessica. However, if Mattie had been thinking about how their family had been affected by Jessica's accident, she would have thought that Hannah would become more shy and more reserved, if only because the mass of attention she got from almost the beginning was so overwhelming.

"Well, I'd say you've had quite a run of attention," her grandfather said. "And I can tell you've used it wisely."

"I have?" Hannah sat up as if wisdom were a new accoutrement she hadn't realized was hers.

"The prom, all the new friends you've made, even managing to wrap your dad around your finger the way Jess has always done."

"He's the best dad, and when I grow up, I want to be just like him—smart and kind and honest. I wish our family could always be as happy as we are tonight. Jess would want that, too." Then Hannah looked at her mother. "She hated that you divorced Dad." At her mother's astonished look, she shrugged. "I didn't want to tell you before, but now I do. She and I talked about it a lot, and I bet that when she wakes up and sees you and Dad for the first time, she's gonna think you got back together. She's gonna really be pis—uh, upset—when she finds out you guys didn't."

Mattie's eyes widened at this out-of-nowhere confession, then wondered if it was a bit of payback because she'd insisted Hannah get a summer job. A kind of "make me do what you want, and I'm gonna push you to do what I want."

Her daughter tucked herself deeper in the chair, clutching a pillow to her chest, and gave her mother a miffed look. Stephen, obviously uncomfortable, pushed the half-finished mousse aside and wiped his mouth. Louise and Carl studied their cooling cups of coffee.

Mattie rose. "It would seem I'm the bad guy in this picture."

"Honey, no," Stephen said, tossing a warning look at Hannah. "She's just being honest about what she thinks Jessica feels."

"What she thinks Jessica feels?" Mattie's temper tipped, and she grabbed at it because she didn't want a scene.

"She hated you for divorcing Dad."

Mattie's breath caught. "Hannah, this is neither the time nor the place."

"Well, when is? You're always with Wyatt Landry."

"I am not!" And the moment Mattie said it, she wanted to pull it back. God, she sounded Hannah's age—and worse, she sounded defensive.

"Hannah, you owe your mother an apology," Stephen said sternly. When it didn't come immediately, he snapped, "Right now, young lady."

"I'm sorry." But before anyone could draw a breath of relief, she came right back. "Why do I have to say I'm sorry for telling the truth?"

"Christ," Stephen muttered. Mattie knew that the end of the evening would not mirror its perfect beginning.

Carl and Louise got to their feet. "We'll just finish up in the kitchen. This sounds like a family discussion, and though all of you know how much we, too, would like to see the four of you reconciled, I don't think our opinion is relevant right now." They walked, away, leaving Mattie with a sympathetic Stephen and a sulky Hannah.

"Was all of that necessary?" Mattie asked Hannah when her parents were out of earshot.

"It's what I believe."

"Your belief or disbelief doesn't make something true."

"This is all true!"

Give it up, Mattie concluded, but when Hannah squeezed the pillow tighter and fell back into the chair as though a calm strategy would work better, Mattie braced herself. Now what?

"Don't you think it would be cool if Jessica woke up and found us a family again? I mean, wouldn't that be the best? She'd be so happy."

On their own, Hannah's comments sounded warm and wishful, but Mattie didn't like the subtle underlying inference. "We did not stop being a family because of the divorce." Mattie strived for matter-of-fact, but she was feeling besieged.

Hannah glanced at her father, then speared her mother with another glare. "Yes, we did. A family lives together. And we were doing that until you decided you didn't like that. You couldn't even let Daddy stay at the house. You had to throw him out."

"What?" She looked at Stephen. "What did you tell her?" And when he didn't reply immediately, she answered her own question. "I did not throw your father out. And he knows that, don't you, Stephen?"

"You asked me to leave, Mattie, and when Hannah wanted to know why I wasn't staying, I told her you wanted your space. What did you expect me to do? Lie?"

At that moment she wanted to smack them both. "No, of course not."

"Then it's true."

Mattie sighed. "Whatever you want to believe." She was too weary to even try to explain. Besides, what was the use?

Hannah said, "Well, I think it stinks."

"I'm sure you do."

"Maybe you're not, like, you know, seeing the whole thing?"

Mattie raised her eyebrows. "Obviously not. You, of course, are."

"Well, sorta. I mean, if you really wanted to know, it could help."

Hannah the reconciler, Mattie thought with no small amount of irony. And with that thought came the next. Somehow in this emotional melee, Mattie had managed not only to alienate her daughter, but also to set herself up for advice on her life.

"Let's say it was like this. Maybe God made the accident happen so we could be a family again. I saw on TV where two people who were best friends had a big fight and they hadn't talked to each other in over two years. Then one of them was in an accident and the other one was scared he would die before they could be friends again."

"Your sister is not going to die!" Mattie snapped.

"How do you know? Lots of people die without waking up from a coma."

"Don't tell me, another TV show."

She sniffed. "Mrs. Draper told me that."

Mrs. Draper was Hannah's guidance counselor. "And why would she even venture such a possibility when we have no evidence that's going to happen to Jess?"

"Because I asked her, and I told her I didn't want a wussy lie to make me feel better."

Stephen got to his feet. "I think this has all gone far enough."

Hannah tossed the pillow aside, jumped to her feet and grabbed her father's hand. "I want to come and stay with you."

"Hannah!"

"Honey, you belong with Mom, and you know I don't have enough closets for that department store of clothes you have." He grinned and patted her cheek.

But his attempt at lightness didn't work. "I don't like it when you're not home," Hannah pleaded, ignoring her mother. "I thought you'd be there to take pictures on Friday when I'm all dressed and when Kevin comes. If she won't let you be there, I don't want to live there anymore."

"Come on, Rosebud, you don't mean that."

"I do. I really do!" And when she started to cry, Stephen soothed her while Mattie stood motionless, feeling as relevant as shredded plastic, a mother in name only.

Chapter Seventeen

"How did it all come to this?" Mattie asked, much later that night, in her kitchen. She'd poured wine for herself and bourbon on the rocks for Stephen.

"I don't know, but I don't like it."

"It's not that I think she shouldn't live with you."

"I know. But this is her home and this is where she belongs. Besides, I have only one bedroom, and she wouldn't like sleeping on the couch."

On this issue she was glad for his support. "But I can't force her to stay here. She's not a toddler."

"I'll talk to her."

"You tried that before she went to bed."

"Let her cool down a bit." He sipped his drink and then sat down opposite Mattie. He reached across the table and squeezed her hand. "I knew she wasn't happy about me returning to the apartment, but blaming you wasn't fair."

"Stephen, I don't care if it was fair, I care if it's true. Oh, not about the apartment, but what she said about Jessica. And if it is . . ." She swallowed, trying to dislodge the emotional boulder from her throat. "If all that about Jessica hating me for divorcing you—if it's true, it doesn't exactly make me appear very bright when it comes to knowing my own daughters."

"Teenage dramatics to get a rise out of you," he said, dismissing her concern. "Drink some wine. It'll relax you."

"Well, her performance worked," Mattie said, sipping the merlot.

"Not all of it did. As I said before, I'm not going to allow her to move in with me."

Though she was grateful Stephen agreed, Mattie wasn't assured that Hannah would meekly back off from her threat. And if she didn't? Mattie hadn't a clue what she could do. Ordering her or dragging her back sure wasn't appealing— nor, she guessed, would it work. At five, yes, but not at fifteen.

"I don't suppose you have an answer if she refuses to stay here. We have to do something. I simply can't chance Hannah taking things into her own hands."

"You think she'd rebel, as in running away?"

"I don't know, but we already have one daughter whose rebellion has her in a coma with God knows what kind of outcome, plus a bunch of unanswered questions. And you know what? I'm sick of it. I'm sick of waiting and hoping and watching like some hovering, hand-wringing mother who stands by like a saint. I don't feel even remotely saintly, and I'm exhausted from trying to figure it all out, because accepting that Jessica became some whacked-out creature while I was too busy or too clueless to notice is ridiculous."

"Mattie, you're being too hard on yourself."

"Am I?"

"It will work out."

Mattie sighed, staring down at her half-finished wine. She wasn't interested in banal, meaningless comments. It would be so easy to agree and salvage some of her pride. Or she could disagree and spend the next hour rehashing all that had happened in the past few weeks, as if reruns brought clarity or insight. She was tired of talking and analyzing and never getting past zero. She'd done some reconsidering at her parents' house; it was time to put some action behind her thoughts.

"Stephen, I think it would be best if you came back here."

She waited, not sure what to expect, but a leap of joy wasn't forthcoming. "You do know what I mean. Back here to live."

Stephen slipped his hands into the front pockets of his jeans and walked to the back door. He stared out into the night, and Mattie, who'd expected some reaction—*any reaction*—was now even more confused. "You don't want to?"

"I want more than just being a houseguest."

"Sex?"

He turned, looking at her with such openness that her defenses, which would usually have roared forth, meekly remained sheltered. "I want us to be a family again."

Now Mattie felt shallow and embarrassed. "I'm sorry. That sex comment was crass."

He chuckled. "But an honest one. And if you can be honest with me, we're making more headway than I thought."

Mattie wasn't quite sure what that meant. She thought she'd always been honest and straightforward, even after the divorce. He had been the one who had done things that confused more than enlightened. The fight with Kevin that was so juvenile for Stephen, then his playing the victim with her and his sister, but the hero with her parents.

Then there'd been the other side—his almost total compliance with whatever she asked of him—such as his easy willingness to return to his apartment. *The many sides of Stephen Caulfield*, she thought with some measure of amusement. And here she'd believed for years that he was pretty uncomplicated. *What a dope.*

It occurred to her that if she didn't even know who her husband was—ex or otherwise—how could she have known her own daughter?

"Mattie, I detect a another judgment on yourself."

She pushed away the troubling thought. "Let's talk about what you said about being a family again."

He grinned. "I could talk about that all day. But basically, to me, being a real family again means our remarriage."

Remarriage? That possibility fell on her like a surprise thundershower, yet she should have expected it. Nevertheless, she suddenly felt swamped by the implications of her own decision. Stephen moving back, which then would become reconciliation, and obviously sex, and then a remarriage.

She pushed her chair away from the table, as if that could distance her from answering. "You're going too fast for me."

"I just want to make sure it's clear what I want if I come back."

Suddenly she was jumpy and nervous, not wanting to say anything that he would misinterpret. Her answer here would immediately resonate with huge importance. Reconciliation was one thing . . . the rest, a mountainous mass impossible to scale with a simplistic response. "You want an answer from me tonight on whether I'll marry you?"

"Not necessarily tonight, but shortly. I don't want any misunderstandings about the final outcome."

"Shortly? Like a few days, a week, a month? I can't give you that assurance."

"Why not?"

"Because I don't know, and if I say that yes, shortly, I'll remarry you, I might as well say yes tonight."

He looked at her, his gaze focused and intense. "Because of Landry?"

At the mention of his name, Mattie shuddered. She'd not wanted to think about Wyatt because it was too painful. Letting him go would be akin to scraping out her heart. And what about Wyatt's reaction? She didn't think it would be far-fetched to guess that he'd be devastated. And as that potential rumbled through her, she realized just how much hurt would come to both of them if she reconciled with Stephen.

On the other hand, she had no intention of discussing her love for Wyatt or his love for her with Stephen.

"It's not because of Wyatt, it's because of me. Dammit, Stephen, my mind and my responsibilities and my worry over Jess, and now Hannah, haven't left me with a lot of objectivity to make life-changing decisions."

He thought about that for a moment, then nodded. "Will you at least keep an open mind about us?"

Isn't this exactly what she'd decided at her parents' house? Hadn't she resolved her own questions about whether a reconciliation might be feasible as a start? All right, perhaps she hadn't leaped as far ahead as marriage, but no one reconciles to eventually split up. Besides, given Hannah's behavior and attitude, she'd just as soon have Stephen here. He would help, and Hannah would be a lot more obedient if his presence was physical and constant. And then there was the haunting element that Hannah had injected. Jess waking up and learning her parents had reconciled. Certainly her expected euphoria would be better medicine than the reminder of the divorce.

"All right, I'll keep an open mind."

His grin was wide, his dimples, deep. He crossed the kitchen and took her into his arms. Mattie stiffened.

"Too soon for even a hug?"

"Yes." Did she sound like a skittish prude, or what?

He settled for kissing her forehead. "Everything is going to be all right. Mattie, you've made me very happy."

After he left the kitchen, she sat down at the table, her half-empty wineglass looking as sad and lonely as she felt. Just where did the happiness meter register in her own life? Happy. Very happy. Somewhat happy. Not happy at all.

Grow up, she scolded herself. *You haven't made this decision to be personally happy*—personal happiness involved Wyatt. *No, this decision is for your family, for your daughters, for everyone.* . . .

Mattie put her hands over her face and cried.

As the auction drew closer and the excitement over Mattie's discovery of the Windsor chairs grew, Wyatt had stayed in Newport for two days to clean up some work in the office. Lottery winner Walt and his wife had told Wyatt how much risk they wanted in their portfolio. Wyatt had pointed them to some growth stocks as well as some new dot.coms that were moving up and turning quick profits. Walt was the kind of client Wyatt respected: aggressive with some percentage of risk capital, but also an investor in safe securities, such as the dozen or so conservative blue-chip companies that Wyatt added.

Once the auction was over, he'd have to return to the office for real. These few weeks of vacation had started a paper growth on his desk. He'd sorted and filed and tossed, made some phone calls, and dumped a bunch of energy stocks for a client who walked away with a quarter of a million profit. By the time he left at two o'clock on Wednesday afternoon, he felt productive, organized, and downright euphoric.

He wanted to see Mattie. See, hell—he just plain wanted her.

But first things first. And talking to Corinne came first. Or at least it did until he spent most of the day trying to track her down.

Finally he reached her at home. "Where have you been?" he asked, his tone exasperated.

"Excuse me?"

Wyatt sighed. "Okay, none of my business, but I was worried."

"I'm all grown up, remember?" When he didn't say anything, she added, "I'm sorry, didn't mean to snap at you."

"I asked for it."

Then he heard the catch in her voice. "Corinne?"

"Oh Wyatt . . ." She broke into a halting kind of crying. "I b-broke up with the g-guy I'd been s-seeing. He's nothing but a lying prick—it just took me a little time to find out."

"I'm sorry."

"I don't think I'm ever going to find anyone."

"But you don't want just anyone, you want the right one. A married guy promising to divorce his wife . . ."

"I know, but I really believed him."

"So what changed your mind?"

"The two of them went on a second honeymoon."

"Uh, yeah, that will do it."

"He tried to tell me they didn't have sex. It was insulting, Wyatt. So I told him he could extend his fucking honeymoon all the way to forever, because I wasn't going to be his sex toy anymore."

Wyatt smiled. "Corky, I'm proud of you."

"Yeah, I guess I'm kinda proud, too. It wasn't hard to tell him, but it was damn hard trying to decide to do it. So . . . why were you trying to get me?"

"I have something to tell you. Can you meet me at the house right now?"

"You found more boxes?"

"God, no. Come on over."

When she walked into their mother's house twenty minutes later, the suspicion Corinne had honed to a science was evident on her face. "This stuff doesn't look all inventoried for the auction."

"Actually, it mostly is. The lot numbering is finished, but a few of the more valuable items are being done tomorrow. Mattie insisted we get some specialist appraisals done so George would have a range to open the bidding."

"The more valuable, huh? Like the sign? You're going to make Kevin give back the sign, aren't you?"

Sign? What sign? And then he remembered. "Of course, I'm not. It's his."

She sighed in relief.

"Actually, this is about you and the things you didn't want to sell."

"Oh?"

He grinned. "Ahh, more suspicion of my motives."

"Because you're not always honest with me."

"Perhaps because you tend to try and finesse whatever position you're in to a better one."

"And you don't approve. Well, tough shit, big brother. I don't have the advantage of forty gazillion bucks to keep me happy and worry-free."

"Give it a rest, Corinne." Then he walked around the tables that had been set up and were brimming with china, glassware, silver, vintage bric-a-brac, books, old magazines, and enough odds and ends to open three antique shops. "I want you to take whatever you want."

Three loaded tables stood between him and his sister. She was dressed in a sunflower-print dress and white sandals that made her look more like a teenager than a woman in her thirties.

"Did I hear you right? You want me to take what I want?"

"Anything."

"What's the catch?"

"None. Mattie has assured me the chairs are going to sell for enough to give Kevin a buffet of colleges to choose from, so we won't need the money that these other items will bring."

Still she didn't look convinced. "And what if the chairs bring nothing?"

"They will."

"But you don't know for sure. An auction can be chancy."

"Yep, sure can." He picked up some silver pieces that Corinne had eyed from the moment they'd been unpacked. "Why don't you start with these?"

She came forward as if he were holding a snake that fascinated her and made her uneasy at the same time.

"And I won't have to give them back?"

"Nope."

"Ever?"

He tugged a curl that slid out of its comb. "Forever and forever."

Then she glanced around at all the items, her gaze moving slowly, as if to absorb the enormity of what he'd just told her. She pointed to a collection of glass. "Even that?"

Mattie had told him it was Heisey, which meant nothing to him, but he recalled George being pissed at losing out on some at an Internet auction.

Wyatt nodded to her. "Including the Heisey."

And then she was flinging herself into her brother's arms with the enthusiasm of a lottery winner; the exact reaction of Walt's wife when Wyatt had suggested that Walt give his wife a chunk of the winnings simply to spend. Investing the majority was prudent, but a lottery win should bring some fun and frivolity, too.

"Oh, I can't wait to pick and choose."

"Leave a few things for the bidders," he said sagely.

She walked from one table to the next, touching items, picking some up and leaving others. She glanced up. "You know, this is like being let into a locked-up candy store. There's so much I want, I can't choose."

"Well, take your time. I'll be back later to help you repack and move the stuff to your house. I'm going to try and hook up with Mattie. I tried a bunch of times when I was in Newport, but no dice."

His sister, in the midst of examining a pair of ornate lamps, glanced at him, her expression a bit odd.

"Have you seen her?" Wyatt asked.

"Uh, no."

Now Wyatt was scowling and walked closer to her. "What's the matter?"

"You and Mattie. I thought it was over."

"Corinne, I told you that Paige and I aren't going to get back together. She knows that, and believe me, I know it."

"No, I didn't mean because of Paige. I meant because of Stephen."

Wyatt shook his head, trying to clear it of this convoluted conversation. "Let's back up. I'm divorced. Mattie is divorced. Mattie and I are involved. Apart from Stephen being the father of her two daughters, I don't see where he is a concern of Mattie's and mine."

Corinne sat down on a small side chair. "Jesus, you don't know."

"Don't know what?"

"Oh, Wyatt, I'm so sorry. I just assumed you knew that Mattie and Stephen have reconciled."

There had to be a mistake or a misunderstanding or just a lousy piece of gossip gone amok. Christ, she'd told him on Monday that Stephen had moved back to his apartment. Now they were reconciled? No way. This was only a little more than forty-eight hours later. No, he wasn't buying it until he spoke with Mattie.

Corinne told him it was all over town, although Wyatt had his doubts about that. To his sister, "all over town" meant the beauty parlor circuit.

He drove his truck to The Garret, but only Donna was there. Mrs. Caulfield was going to the hospital, she told him, and then home to do some alterations on Hannah's prom dress. Mr. Caulfield thought it was a bit too sexy, and wasn't it wonderful to see a father who cared so much, and wasn't it wonderful that she and Mr. Caulfield were working things out?

"Breathtaking," Wyatt muttered. So much for his theory on beauty parlor gossip.

"It's like a real romance," Donna said dreamily.

"Or calling shit sugar."

"Pardon me?"

Wyatt managed a smile. "Nothing. I'll catch up with her another time."

Back in his truck, he drove toward her house. *And when, Mrs. Caulfield, were you planning to call me and tell me what the hell was going on?* He tried her cell phone, but she didn't pick up. He tried the house and got Stephen; he hung up without saying anything.

At her house, Stephen's car was in the drive but no sign of Mattie's. He could stop and wait and have a showdown right in her backyard, which gave him a jolt of energy that fizzled just as quickly. Or he could simply kill Caulfield. Except his gun was locked up down in Newport. A knife was too messy. He could just beat the shit out of him; he knew how to do that. He knew that move like he knew his own name.

Yep, that would be a good move, Landry. A real solution for his ego, but a lousy one for the future. He wasn't a hot-headed kid or a wronged husband, like when he almost wasted Bobby because of Paige. This time he was just the boyfriend, just the guy who'd fallen in love with her. Not even a blip compared to the saintly ex-husband and perfect father and marvelous son-in-law and faultless neighbor. . . .

Wyatt had almost swallowed that touching story of Caulfield moving out. The guy was a goddamned master at finessing others to his way of thinking while making himself look like the reasonable and caring family man.

He jammed the truck into gear and then, just as quickly, shoved it back into park.

He scrubbed his hands down his face. What had happened? That's what he wanted to know. What had changed Mattie in forty-eight hours? He sat in the truck, combing over every detail of his last conversation with her. Nothing even remotely pointed to her making this kind of decision; the last time they'd been together, she'd even spoken of a weekend together after the auction.

He sighed, and more gently this time, put the truck into gear. He had to talk to her, but not here. He was going to be calm and rational and listen to what she had to say.

He loved Mattie and she loved him. On that basis he would approach her.

Chapter Eighteen

Prom night arrived with all the anticipation and terror of an opening night on Broadway. Mattie had been to one of those back in the eighties, and she remembered the electricity and the tension and the hope that a megahit would be born.

According to Hannah, this dance was the megamoment of her entire life, and though Mattie and Stephen tried to not chide her for over-the-top exaggeration, she did push their patience. Her hysteria over her "yucky" hair, the "gross" line on her shoulder where the sun hadn't tanned her, the perfect dress (just that morning) that had, by afternoon, morphed into making her look like "a fat cow," and finally, if Kevin wasn't "wildly" inspired and impressed, she'd be "mortified." All this female frenzy sent Stephen off to hide in the den with a "Call me when you want me to take pictures" and Mattie grateful prom night wasn't a monthly occurrence.

"What am I gonna do about this stupid line?" Hannah cried to Mattie, as if the barely visible mark were a mammoth blotch of bleached skin. They were in Mattie's room in front of a long, oval-shaped mirror. Hannah was near tears.

"Let's try some tanning stain," Mattie said softly, trying for calm and reason. "Slip the straps down while I see if I can find the cream."

"But it will look yellow or a yucky brown, and then everyone will think I used that instead of the real sun."

Mattie cupped Hannah's chin and tipped it up so she had to look at her. "Honey, I want you to take a deep breath and calm down. Do you think I'd just slather the tanning cream on like I was frosting a cake?"

She took some deep breaths. "I guess not."

"I promise I'll make it blend."

"I know. It's just that I want tonight to be perfect."

"It will be."

Another deep breath and sigh. She scowled again at the spot, as if it had stubbornly refused to tan just to ruin her night. "I should have taken my top off; then it would be perfect."

"You already look perfect, and by the time everyone sees you in your lovely dress, you'll forget all about the spot on your shoulder." Mattie tipped her head to catch Hannah's facial reaction and commented, "I would hope you wouldn't take your top off on a public beach."

"It's no big deal. Lots of kids do it."

"Not my daughters." She paused, eyeing Hannah. "Does she?"

She shifted from one foot to the other, a sure sign she'd done something Mattie wouldn't like. "I undid the back and unhooked the straps, but I guess one of them didn't get tucked away. Callie took hers all the way off and a couple of guys sneaked up, grabbed it, and ran off. I was laying on my top so they couldn't get to it."

"A wise move on your part," Mattie said, deciding that some things never change. Similar antics had gone on when she was in high school. "So who is Callie going with tonight?"

Hannah shrugged. "I don't know."

"She's practically become your new best friend and you don't know who her date is? That's hard to believe."

"She and her boyfriend are kinda not seeing one another. Mom, are you gonna get that stuff or not?"

"I'm going." Mattie went to find the tanning stain while Hannah wiggled out of the bodice. Stephen's concern about the dress being too sexy had been docilely accepted by Hannah. Mattie had expected fireworks, especially since Hannah had waited until the last minute to model it for her father, thereby allowing no time for a seamstress to do alterations—or if bad came to worse, the purchase of another dress.

"You can fix it, can't you, Mom?" was the plea. Mattie had spent the better part of the past three days putting a second lining in the bodice, which actually improved the drape of the fabric. But better yet, on-display nipples were no longer prominent.

Mattie returned to the bedroom and stopped in the doorway, admiring her grown-up daughter. She was truly awed by the fresh beauty and a quickening innocence that, as a mother, she wanted to protect and proudly show off to the world. Her youngest, once skinny with a dirty face and snarled hair, now stood on the cusp of womanhood. Her hair styled and caught up with silver combs and tiny yellow rosebuds, the white slip dress with thin straps against her tan, and the silvery pumps combined to make a stunning presentation..

"Oh, Hannah, you're lovely and so grown-up," Mattie said, wondering where the years had gone. Rompers and skinned elbows and scraped knees seemed like yesterday.

Basking in her mother's praise, Hannah then did exactly what Mattie expected—she wanted approval from her father. "You think Daddy will like it?"

"He's probably going to insist on being your chaperone, and for sure he's going to worry until you're home safe."

She giggled. "Dads always get goofy about daughters and boys, don't they?"

"No doubt because they were once boys and remember what they were doing to someone's daughter."

"I like it that he's that way. . . . You know, wanting to protect and sorta get in my space to make sure I stay okay. Like when he fought with Kevin—it made me like, well, proud."

Mattie raised her eyebrows. Proud wasn't exactly what she would have called Hannah when she was "mortified" by Stephen's behavior. But then Stephen squared it all away with his apology and allowing her to go to the prom with Kevin. Mattie decided she could probably take a few lessons from Stephen about keeping the confrontations at a minimum. Then again, she usually had a solid base of reason for the rules she laid down for the girls, and she wasn't compulsive or erratic—she never made it up as she went along, and sometimes she had a sense that Stephen did just that. The fight with Kevin was certainly impulsive and stupid, and yet Stephen managed to turn it to his advantage with a self-deprecating charm for her parents, and ingratiating humor with Hannah.

Quite a performance, Stephen, she decided in retrospect. Splash and dash and emotional wizardry made for a good show, but to what end?

But if she questioned Stephen, she knew she'd get one of those dismissing comments: *Really, Mattie, must you scrutinize every move I make?*

Hannah, sounding like the ultimate authority on paternal behavior, said, "You know, some fathers don't care what their daughters do."

"I don't think there's too many of those around."

"Well, mine is the best. The absolute best."

Mattie smiled, then made her sit down. She gently applied the tanning cream to the white line, assuring Hannah that once it dried, no would know.

After a final check of hair and the dress and another dab of lipstick, she was ready.

In the den, Stephen was reading the evening paper when Mattie came in and turned, sweeping out her hand. "I present Miss Hannah Marie Caulfield. Drum roll, please."

Stephen sat up, did a hand-slapping drum roll on the coffee table, and, on cue, Hannah swept in with all the drama and panache of a leading lady wowing her public.

Mattie expected Hannah's usual tadahhhhhh, but tonight she was all grown-up and sophisticated, and Stephen was the more-than-impressed father.

"Wow!" He rose and walked around her, his gaze proud. "Who is this gorgeous woman?"

Hannah beamed and laughed. "Oh, Daddy."

"I don't know if it's safe to let you go alone. What do you think, Mattie?"

"Oh, I absolutely agree. This definitely calls for, uh, let

me think. . . ." Mattie tapped her cheek with appropriate thoughtfulness.

"I've got it. A chaperone."

"Perfect."

"Yep," Stephen said, taking both of Hannah's hands and kissing them in a grand gesture. "I think I better go along and chaperone."

He said it with such a straight face that Mattie followed with a nod. Hannah threw a panicked look at both of them.

"Daddy? You're not, like, *really* serious, are you?" She laughed nervously.

"I sure as heck am. What do you think, Mattie? Should I go in the limo or follow in my car?"

"Definitely the limo," she said.

"You *are* serious! Oh, my God!" Hannah nearly dissolved into apoplexy. What she thought funny in her mother's bedroom now was ghastly and traumatic. "You wouldn't, you couldn't do that. I would absolutely die!"

He let her dangle for a few seconds, then grinned and reached for the camera. "Well, we can't have any dead prom queens, can we?" He walked over and took her hands. "You're beautiful—the perfect prom queen," he said simply.

"Jessica is the prom queen," she said, still not quite over her father as a potential chaperone.

"Can't I have two daughters who are prom queens?"

She smiled then and hugged him fiercely. Angling for that last compliment, she asked her father, "You think Kevin will think I look beautiful?"

"If he doesn't, he's a blind idiot. Come on, let's get those pictures taken."

Mattie watched as Stephen took pictures, then took more when Kevin arrived. The yellow roses, three of them wrapped with baby's breath and white trails of ribbon, added just the right finishing detail. Stephen took one last photo as the two of them stood by the back door of the black limo.

She recalled Hannah's excitement that the car was black and not white, and when Mattie had commented that black limos reminded her of funerals, Hannah supplied the obvious reason. White prom dresses show up better in pictures when the limo is black. "I mean, Mom, white against white is dull, dull, dull."

The dress, the dress, the dress, Mattie had thought, but she had to agree when she saw Hannah and Kevin show-cased beside the black limo. It was a stunning contrast.

As Kevin waited for Hannah to slide onto the plush leather seat, Mattie drew closer to him. "That was very thoughtful to send yellow roses to Jessica."

"Yeah, Mom said she liked that, too." He looked acutely embarrassed, so Mattie squeezed his arm, letting that be her thanks.

Good-byes and blown kisses, "Have fun" and "Love you," and the perennial standard of every parent, "Behave," floated around the limo like a spritz of perfume, and then the car slipped away. Watching, Mattie was struck by how a month ago this would have been Jessica waving and blowing kisses. And it would have been Hannah shy and waving good-bye. Though the accident had affected Jessica directly, it seemed to have influenced Hannah mightily.

And if the talk of the past few days was executed, the accident had also reshaped her divorce into a reconciliation.

In the kitchen, Mattie poured herself some iced tea while Stephen foraged through the refrigerator, looking for sandwich fixings.

"What time is she coming home?" he asked, juggling roast beef, tomatoes, lettuce, mayo, and a jar of green olives to the counter.

"Late. Parties afterward—one at Megan Forest's house and another one over on Drury."

Stephen assembled his sandwich. "It's going to be a long night."

"Yes, and by the time tomorrow is over, I'll be ready for about three days' sleep. I can't believe I set the auction for the day after the prom."

"Maybe we could go away for the weekend," he said casually, and Mattie immediately thought of her promise to Wyatt about a weekend. "I don't think so."

Stephen looked at her. "It wasn't a subtle way to suggest

sex, Mattie. It was a suggestion to relax for a couple of days."

"I'm sorry."

"So am I." He put his sandwich on a plate, added a handful of potato chips, took a bottle of beer from the refrigerator, and returned to the den. A few seconds later she heard the television.

What did he mean by being sorry? Sorry he'd asked her, or sorry she was so suspicious? She wiped the counter, debating whether she should reconsider. Then she scowled. Here she was feeling bad because she hadn't leaped at the idea of a weekend with her ex. And why, for God's sake, was she feeling bad? She'd made it clear when she agreed to the reconciliation that she wouldn't be rushed into anything serious or intimate. If she blithely accepted a getaway weekend, he'd take that to mean she wanted more than conversation and meals together.

Then once the weekend was over and she was stressed with second thoughts and disgust at her spineless cave-in, Stephen would be apologetic and say it was all his fault for seducing her, and that though they probably should have waited, didn't this all prove they had a second chance for happiness together?

Ahh, yes, all the "Stephen" signs were there, lit up for perfect viewing, and Mattie had no intention of being fooled.

And Wyatt. Where did she put Wyatt in all of this? She wanted things left as is, but going out with Wyatt and invariably tumbling into bed with him while rethinking her divorce was pushing the "having it both ways" theory so far that Mattie was astonished she could spend even five seconds thinking about it.

But she had. Right or wrong, proper or indecent, she wanted Wyatt, and she loved him desperately. And yet she was just as desperate to have her family be okay, and if the latter meant being with Stephen. . . . She sighed, a kind of sadness filling her. She could adapt, but enthusiasm was something else again.

She missed Wyatt, and she felt uneasy that she hadn't spoken with him since last Monday. She'd tried to call him in Newport on Tuesday, but got his voice mail. And she wasn't going to leave a message about the events of Monday night. She had asked him to call her, but either she'd been out or her machine had been off. Phone tag, and she hadn't given it much thought beyond annoyance that they hadn't made contact until she went to the shop on Thursday and Donna told her he'd stopped by late Wednesday afternoon.

"What did he say? Was he going to come back, or did he leave a time I could reach him?"

"He didn't say much. Just that he wanted to talk to you. I told him you and Stephen were back together, and he looked a little funny. Then he left."

"Oh God. . . ." Mattie could only imagine what "funny" must have looked like.

"Mattie, did I say something wrong?"

"I should have made sure I spoke with him, or at the very least left the message for him, last Tuesday."

"Huh?"

"Nothing. Just that I've probably hurt him badly, and I didn't want to do that." Mattie had felt the hot sting of tears clear down in her throat, tears for Wyatt and tears for what would be lost.

Now, standing in her kitchen, she debated whether to drive over to see him—she knew she should, but at the same time she knew it would not be pleasant.

He'd be furious and confused and rag her out about letting Stephen manipulate her. But he'd also be hurt and cranky and sad. . . . She'd see him tomorrow, but she should try to call him. Maybe they could meet somewhere. He deserved at least that. She just hoped she could make him understand that the difficult choice she'd made was the right one.

But after trying the Newport house, his mother's, and even his cell, she got no answers. She tried all the numbers again ten minutes later, but still no answer.

Mattie turned out the lights in the kitchen, peeked in the den, and saw Stephen immersed in a baseball game. She glanced at her watch. It would be hours before Hannah returned. She wanted to go over her checklist for tomorrow, but right now, she would go upstairs and put away all the preprom equipment. And she wanted to try and call Wyatt again.

Close to an hour later, Mattie finished getting her bedroom straightened and took a quick pass through Hannah's room. Looking around the messy room and then walking into Jessica's room, which remained basically as it had been since before the accident, accentuated with chilling clarity Jessica's absence. The sterile orderliness emphasized the vacuum in their lives. One daughter was missing.

Mattie turned out the lights and left, haunted again by all the questions that still had no answers. In reality, she knew little more than she'd learned that first night. She'd concluded that Jessica must have been a master at fooling her friends into believing nothing was different about her. For sure, her daughter had fooled her.

As she lifted a basket of dirty clothes and started down the stairs, deciding she'd try Wyatt one more time, she heard a vehicle slow down in front of the house. She looked out the upstairs hall window just as headlights swung into the drive.

Oh, God," she whispered, abandoning the basket, racing down the stairs, and throwing a glance in the direction of the den. Stephen was still immersed in the game. She hurried into the kitchen just as the knock came on the back door.

She opened it, and there stood Wyatt—cool and unfrazzled.

Mattie had always been impressed by his laid-back manner, a trait she knew he'd worked hard to cultivate after he nearly killed Bobby Dodd. Tonight, not unexpectedly, he displayed no signs of physical stress; no rumpled clothes and boozy breath spawned by fury and hurt and angst; there wasn't even an explosion of expletives and temper.

Before she could gather her wits to say his name, he said, "Well, well, well, this is a productive evening. Mrs. Caulfield, I believe? Fancy finding you. I was sure either you were missing or your memory had maxed out. I brought a map of Briarwood in case you have trouble finding the auction tomorrow."

"Very funny." Wyatt might be cool and laid-back, but that razor sarcasm was in good form. This was not going to be a quiet discussion, and the last thing she wanted was a three-way with Stephen. "I've been trying to call you." She glanced behind her. "We can't talk here."

"Talk? Now there's an innovative concept. Did it just occur to you, or have you been practicing your betrayal explanations?"

"Wyatt, please. I'll explain. Can we please go outside?" Then, when he made no move to accommodate her, she flattened her hand on his chest to ease him away from the doorway. Rather than the resistance she expected, she encountered the jackhammer vibration of his heart. He wasn't just furious, he was scared and frustrated and hurt. And that made her heart crack and break.

She stepped outside and pulled the door closed behind her. "I know you're angry," she said.

"I passed anger days ago. I went to Newport thinking we had a future, and came back to learn you threw me over for your ex. The missing piece in that picture is big enough to swallow my truck."

"I tried to call you, but when all I got was voice mail, I didn't want to leave the news that way."

"So I find out from my sister and Donna? Gee, I wonder why that didn't make the bombshell less explosive."

"Believe me, I didn't want that. You think I planned it that way?"

"No, I don't think you planned anything. And I don't even give two shits if there was a plan. I want to know what he did to convince you. Lay on the guilt while he played the poor beleaguered victim? Or was it more basic, like wine and candles and a creative fuck?"

Mattie glared at him, her defensiveness loosening and roaring forth. "Stop it, Wyatt. You think this has been easy for me? Here I was feeling bad that I haven't had a chance to explain, and all you can think about is whether I had sex with him."

"Yeah, funny how that works."

"Well, I didn't, okay? And if you really believe any of this was about sex with Stephen, you're not the man I thought you were. There was no 'creative fuck' with him, there wasn't even a kiss. I haven't, and I won't. If I had my way, I'd reconcile with him and limit all that creativity to you. . . ." Her voice broke, and she looked down at her fingers gripping his wrist. She was mightily aware of the heavy beat of his pulse. That, accompanied by the tactile warmth and familiarity she'd come to love and expect, became a sweep of regret for all that she was about to lose.

"Fine," he said, as though he'd heard her words and either missed their significance or just plain ignored it. He tried to pull away, but she tightened her fingers.

"Please, Wyatt, you have to listen to me."

"For what? I already don't like the direction."

"Please?"

"I must be nuts. . . ."

"I know you're not feeling very receptive to anything I have to say, or even what I feel about you, but I love you. That hasn't changed, and it won't. But I'm dealing with more than just you and me. The accident has undone my family by opening up areas I thought were okay. Now I know they aren't, and worse, they weren't long before the accident. I can't ignore the problems because they might interfere with what I want with you. And if you weren't so angry and hurt, you'd agree with me. I know you would. If there's a possibility, even a remote one, that the reconciliation will solve some of those family issues, then I have to try."

That seemed to undo him; he sagged back against one of the porch columns and folded his arms as if chilled. She drew close and slid her arms up and under his so that he had to unfold them. "Please don't hate me. I couldn't stand it."

"Christ," he muttered, then enfolded her as though she were cracked and broken. "I don't hate you. If I did, I wouldn't be here. Okay, family trouble and you trying to fix

it—that I can buy. What I want to know is what are you trying to fix?"

"Hannah and Jessica both had a lot of trouble with the divorce—"

"According to who?"

"I know what you're thinking, and it wasn't Stephen.
Hannah told me."

"How do you know he isn't behind this? That he hasn't
coached Hannah or whined on her shoulder and done to her
just what he's done to you? Created guilt where none
should be."

Mattie sighed. "I don't know. But your explanation is
hardly objective, and though Stephen can be trying at times,
even for him that kind of behind-the-scenes ploy is over the
top. No, since the accident, it's become more and more clear
that if Stephen and I can put our differences aside and try
again, perhaps there's still time to repair . . ." Her thoughts
trailed off along with her voice; it all sounded forced, felt
forced, but she wasn't doing this for the glory of marital
bliss. "I know what you're thinking."

"Yes, I imagine you do."

"But it doesn't matter. Don't you see? I'm doing this for
the girls, not for Stephen and some kind of hollow happiness. And certainly not for myself."

"Ahh, Mattie, you're leaping onto the funeral pyre with
both eyes wide open."

"Why does it have to be sacrifice? Why can't it just be the
right thing to do?"

"Because it's all wrong for us. Okay, I'm a selfish bastard
for not wanting to lose you. But watching you get rolled by
your ex-husband, who's played on your heart and your maternal instincts and skillfully wormed his way back into your
life—I don't know how to fight that."

"I don't want you to fight it, because it will make it all the
more difficult for me. You think I'm not going to miss you
and that I don't wish there was another way? I do. But for
now there isn't. Hannah has been somewhat of a problem,
and Stephen is the only one she listens to. She told me Jessica hated that we divorced and blames me."

"So in turn you blame yourself for her behavior change and the resulting accident."

"Yes."

Wyatt let out a long, deep sigh, and she knew he understood that what had once been a flourishing relationship between them had now reached a finale. Mattie should have felt relief, a sense of release, even a recognition within herself that her decision had been correct; instead, emptiness poured through her as if her heart and soul were porous clay.

"I have to give him credit," Wyatt finally said. "Stephen is a master. And adoring daughters sure do help. Competing with family values and a guy who wants his wife back isn't a contest I'm going to win."

"I'm sorry."

"Yeah, guess there isn't much more to say, is there?"

She reached up and kissed him. He returned the intimacy.

"I don't suppose I can lure you away for a couple of hours."

She hesitated. "I shouldn't. It would only prolong the difficulty of saying good-bye."

"Probably, but take pity on me. I'm settling for a few hours instead of the lifetime I want."

Still she was reluctant, for though she'd made her decision about Stephen, it had a vacuous quality that, if Wyatt chose to exploit . . .

Then, as if he'd absorbed her unease, he said, "I'm not Stephen. I hate your decision, but I'm not going to bleed your heart over it." Then he took her by the shoulders, his voice softening, comforting her in that wonderful way he had. "Look, it's over, and I'm not gonna hang around and harass you or make you feel torn or try to pressure you into coming back to me, although God knows I don't like what's gone down. But at the same time, you've made your choice, and you're the one who has to live with it. I don't see how a couple of hours is going to change that, but I sure as hell would like to end this someplace other than in Stephen Caulfield's backyard."

She couldn't resist his plea and she didn't want to. "Wait for me. I'll be back in a few minutes."

"You're going to tell Stephen?"

"Actually, I am. I'm not ashamed of my relationship with you, and since I'm not going to have it anymore, I certainly have the right to end it my way."

His grin gave her a flush of satisfaction.

Five minutes later she was in his truck and they were driving away. Half an hour after they'd gone, the phone rang at Mattie's, waking a dozing Stephen.

"What? Jesus! Yes, I'll be right there."

Chapter Nineteen

"How could you not have called me?" Mattie was out of breath and clammy warm, her emotions in turmoil.

"Called you where? I don't have Landry's cell phone number. I don't even know where he lives, for Chrissake."

"Both numbers are in my address book."

"And where is that? It wasn't by the phone I answered. Pardon me for not doing a house search for your boyfriend's phone number."

"Don't start, Stephen. I told you where I was going."

"I'm not starting anything. I just hope you finished whatever it was that needed finishing."

"It's finished," she snapped.

"Thank God."

Stephen had met her at the front entrance of the hospital, where Mattie had arrived in a frantic rush after finding the note from Stephen that Jessica had awakened. A scrawled message, "Jessica's awake," taped to the back door was not how she'd envisioned getting the news.

"So when did it happen? How is she? What did she say?" The questions rolled out of her as they rode up in what had to be the slowest elevator in the state.

"They called about an hour after you left. I came right in, and there she was, looking as if she'd just awakened from a good night's sleep."

Mattie's euphoria was twisting and clamoring and jumping, as if she had suddenly been given a new life. "And you talked to her and she answered?"

"Yes. She's pale and she's confused about all that happened, but she knew me and she wanted to know where you were."

Immediately the euphoria tanked. Not only had she missed Jessica's awakening, but her absence was hardly justifiable to the seventeen-year-old who probably resented Wyatt. "What did you tell her?"

"That you'd gone out, and that as soon as you read my note, you'd be here. I think she was a little hurt you weren't home."

"I wish I had been."

"A funny quirk of fate, wouldn't you say? Of all the nights when you should have been."

"You're being a prick, Stephen."

He flicked off the comment as if it were a piece of lint. "Me? No way. A real prick would have told her you were with Landry. I'm not that kind of nasty. And while I didn't make a stink about tonight, Mattie, you can't be sneaking out to see him, not if we have any hope of making this work."

"I've never sneaked out, and you damn well know it. I told you Wyatt and I were finished, and I'd appreciate it if you'd quit the barbs and the jabs."

He shrugged. "I was just making an obvious point."

Mattie clamped her mouth shut. He wanted the last word? Well, fine. But it infuriated her that he acted like she was a bonehead who needed direction and a lecture. Then again, what did it matter? The reality was that Stephen had been home and she'd been out with her now ex-boyfriend. No matter how much Mattie wanted to shade those facts, she couldn't.

They stopped at the door of Jessica's room. Casey came out with a broad smile on her face and some dampness in her eyes. "It's truly a miracle, Mattie. Dr. Egan was here just a few minutes ago. He was very impressed by her response, and told me to tell you he'd talk to you tomorrow. Must have had something to do with prayers and Toadie and that sock of secret stones she was clutching when she awakened."

"Secret stones?" A puzzled Stephen looked at Casey while Mattie slipped by them and entered the room.

"Mattie didn't tell you? Oh, she must have." Casey's voice hummed behind her, then the nurse launched into the story before Stephen could escape. *Good*, Mattie thought. She wanted to see her daughter alone for a few moments.

Jessica was sitting up, her hair had been brushed, and she was wearing a favorite T-shirt Mattie had brought in weeks ago.

Her eyes filled with tears when Jessica smiled. Her daughter's eyes lit up, and she said the most precious of words. "Mom, I've been waiting for you."

Immediately, Mattie was beside her, pulling her into her arms. "Oh, sweetheart, it's so wonderful to see you awake and okay. We were so worried about you."

"I'm sorry."

"No, no, don't apologize. It doesn't matter now. All that matters is that you're out of the coma." Mattie sat back, her eyes examining every inch of Jessica, her hands gently touching her daughter's face and throat and arms. She glanced around when Stephen walked in. He pulled up a chair and sat down. "Hi, honey. Are we wearing you out with all the visiting?"

"No, it's okay."

"Doesn't she look wonderful?" Mattie asked.

"Both of you look wonderful." Stephen smiled, and she could see the love and pride in his eyes. "Hannah is going to be thrilled when she hears."

"Where is Hannah? I thought she was coming with you, Mom."

Before Mattie could say anything, Stephen did. "She'll be here tomorrow. She went to the prom."

"The prom?" Jessica blinked as though the word were foreign, and Mattie had a moment of terror that the coma had snatched part of her memory. "But that isn't for a few weeks."

Relieved, Mattie relaxed.

"Those few weeks have passed, honey," Stephen said, leaning forward. "We'll have plenty of time to talk about all that's happened."

But Jessica didn't ask about the past. "I've been asleep for weeks? The coma the nurse was talking about?"

"Yes, but now you're awake and back with us. Oh, Jess, this is all so wonderful."

Instead of a nod and a smile, she scowled, as if trying to get her memory working. "But how could she go to the prom? She's a sophomore."

"Kevin Bonner asked her," Stephen said, and Mattie immediately wanted to kick him. But then nothing would be accomplished in keeping that from her. She'd hear it from Hannah for sure, and though Mattie didn't think her younger daughter's motives were purely nasty, she also knew that Hannah had become very popular since the accident. Now that Jessica had awakened, Hannah might feel she was about to be pushed from the spotlight. She wanted to believe Hannah would be so overwhelmed with joy that her sister was going to be okay that nothing else would matter, yet realistically she understood that Hannah had grown comfortable with, and now expected, all the attention. She'd want to chatter and brag about her new status, especially the prom and going with Kevin.

"He's a good guy," Jessica said softly.

"And he cares a great deal about you."

"Once he did. No more."

"Why?" Mattie asked.

Stephen intervened. "Don't you think it's better if we wait on the deep questions?"

He was right. And Mattie did have a lot of questions. "I just want Jess to know that Kevin still cares a great deal." She looked back at her daughter. "He's been worried. He's been in to see you just about every day."

"He has?" This seemed to amaze her, but then, in a matter-of-fact tone, she added, "I wonder why."

"He sent you flowers, honey." Mattie pointed to the vase

of yellow roses, and Jessica glanced at them, but without enthusiasm. "What happened to me?"

"You were in an accident about four weeks ago."

"An accident?"

"A car accident, near Route 95," Stephen said.

Jessica closed her eyes, and Mattie and Stephen exchanged glances.

"You don't remember?" Mattie asked.

"I don't think so."

"You were with Arlis Petcher."

"Arlis . . . ? Oh, yes, I remember her. . . . She drinks too much sometimes."

"Honey," Stephen said, "Arlis was with you. She died in the accident."

Jessica stared at him for the longest time and then began to shake her head, tears leaking from the sides of her eyes. Mattie rested her hand on Jessica's cheek.

Stephen rose. "This is too much too soon, Mattie. We're bombarding her."

But Mattie held her hand tight. "Sweetheart, we don't believe it was your fault."

But instead of the nod or some more weeping, Jessica stared at her hard, desperation filling her voice. "How do you know it wasn't my fault? You weren't there. You didn't see. You don't know."

Mattie sat back, bewildered by the accusatory burst. Stephen stood, and slipped his hand beneath her elbow to bring Mattie to her feet.

"I think we've done enough visiting for tonight. It's nearly eleven o'clock."

Mattie again touched Jessica's cheek, knowing Stephen was right but still wanting to stay. Nevertheless, she said, "We'll be in tomorrow."

Stephen chuckled. "Not quite. I'll be in. Your mother has an auction to run."

"Please bring Hannah."

"I don't think I could keep her away." He leaned down and kissed her cheek.

Then Mattie said, "The auction will be done by noon, and then I'll come in for the afternoon. I imagine that by tomorrow it will be all over town that you're awake and the room will be filled with your friends. Mom and Dad will want to see you, too."

"Mattie, ease up, you're exhausting her. Maybe she doesn't want a lot of visitors just yet."

When Jessica didn't say anything, Mattie cupped her daughter's chin and gently turned her head sc she could see her expression. It was bland—neither enthusiastic or wary. And that worried Mattie. "Are you okay? You want me to call the nurse?"

"Where's Toadie and the stones?"

"Right here," Mattie said, tucking the bear close and tugging the sock of stones from where it had nearly disappeared beneath the sheet.

Jessica seemed to relax, as if a friend and a talisman had been returned. She closed her eyes, and Mattie and Stephen quietly left the room.

Mattie stopped and asked Casey to check on Jessica, and then they took the elevator down and walked out of the hospital.

Since their vehicles weren't parked close together, they stopped at the point where they had to go in different directions.

"What did you think?" she asked Stephen.

"I'm grateful she's awake, and now that she is, all the unanswered questions don't seem very important."

"For now, maybe not. But those unanswered questions are what got her into the accident in the first place."

"We're assuming that. It's possible she and Arlis were just cruising around, not on some mysterious adventure."

Mattie frowned at him. "Well, this is certainly a change in thinking for you."

"I don't see why. The answers are pretty clear. I've been saying all along that she resented the divorce. Christ, Hannah made that pretty clear the other night. On that basis, it's not too big a leap to presume she didn't like you dating

Landry. Those two things, combined with being hurt by Kevin's rejection . . . it all adds up to some clear answers. Maybe Arlis had some difficulties—God knows her parents are no prizes—and she and Jessica were doing some mutual advice-seeking."

"You're amazing, you know that? For the guy who got in a fistfight with Kevin and practically wanted Kane Fairfax castrated, now you're the benevolent Stephen Caulfield. When did this huge change take place?"

"I believe it's called forgiveness," he said, appearing just a bit offended. "And don't give me such a suspicious look. The guy who asks for forgiveness should also be willing to grant it."

"Very commendable. I certainly agree with you. I'm just puzzled as to why and when all of this occurred to you."

"When I walked into that hospital and saw my daughter awake and okay. Maybe it's not a hundred-watt miracle to you, but it sure was to me."

Mattie almost hugged him. "What a wonderful thing to say. I apologize for being suspicious."

He put his arm around her. "Apology gladly accepted. Let me walk you to your car."

And so they made their way through the dark parking lot to where Mattie had parked her car.

Stephen continued to talk about Jessica and his attitude change. "I got the definite impression she was uncomfortable talking about the accident and Arlis. What about you?"

"She did seem agitated."

"Let me offer this as a solution. Jessica is going to be fine, and we could risk her continued improvement if we badger her about something she probably wants to put behind her. That kind of approach seems a lot like grinding salt in a healing wound to me. I think we should just let it go, and get on with putting this family back together."

"I'd agree with you except for one thing."

"What?"

"Who got her pregnant?"

"Maybe she doesn't know."

"Stephen! How can you even suggest such a thing?"

"Because it's possible. Let's see, we've suspected the Bonner kid, and then Kane Fairfax. . . ."

"It's not Kane." She started to tell him about the secret stones, but she wasn't in the mood for one of his "that's ridiculous" comments, so instead she said, "Wyatt told me the police were releasing Kane."

"What?" He looked both astonished and outraged.

"Emily dropped her charge on the advice of her lawyer, because the other girl he supposedly was involved with said she wasn't, and wouldn't change her story. Plus Kane's girlfriend signed a statement saying he was with her on two of the nights in question. His attorneys also found some eyewitnesses who backed up the girlfriend's story."

"Leave it to the lawyers. So now what?"

"Nothing, I guess. Kane is free, and the girl . . . It's really sad, because she took a lot of grief for coming forward, and now it appears she was either fantasizing or lying. I think she's going to have a difficult time. Wyatt said she'll get a lot of hassle from her friends, and that any credibility she had is shot. She's not going to be very popular in town for bringing charges that couldn't be proved, plus bringing them against a guy everyone liked and trusted."

"I'd say he was one lucky bastard."

"I feel sorry for her."

"For her? You were the one defending Fairfax when this first broke."

"I know, and I still find it hard to believe Kane would be that stupid, but Stephen, this poor young woman . . . I mean, why would she make up something like that if there weren't some truth in it?"

"I'm sure her parents are wondering the same thing." He squeezed her arm. "Come on, let's go home. We have some wonderful news to tell Hannah."

"Yes, we do. We certainly do."

Chapter Twenty

Auction day arrived. Mattie, in a state of euphoria, had to break herself away from all the calls at home about Jessica, only to be swamped with hugs and tears when she arrived at the Landry house. Cora Epperly, who rarely went to George's auctions because it made her nervous watching him, made an exception just to see Mattie. Her parents had come, following a visit in to see Jessica. Even Stephen and a sleepy but smiling Hannah were there.

Hannah's smile, however, wasn't due to her joy about her sister waking up.

Mattie and Stephen had told her about Jessica when Kevin brought her home around five. Mattie had so hoped that the news would be greeted with honest happiness. Her daughter tried, but Mattie saw something that truly disturbed her. Disappointment.

So while Stephen made phone calls to spread the news, Mattie took her youngest up to her bedroom and closed the door. She wanted to shake her and demand to know how she could be so selfish. Instead, she warned her, "I want you to listen to me, Hannah Marie, and listen closely. When you go to see your sister, I don't want you doing or saying anything to upset her. Do you understand me?"

"Jessica!" She spat the name. At Mattie's look of horror, she shrank back. "Okay, I'm glad she's awake. I'm glad she's okay. So now can we, like, quit blabbing about her every fucking minute?"

"Hannah!"

"I don't care, I'm sick of it. She's all anyone ever wants to talk about. At the dance about a zillion kids asked about Jessica. And Kevin was the worst." She sniffled, and her eyes filled. "I mean, all I heard from him, Mom, was Jessica, Jessica, Jessica—until I wanted to hit him."

Mattie's annoyance evaporated. So her instinct about Kevin's motives had been right. Inviting Hannah was really about Jessica. "Oh, Hannah, I'm sorry," she said, drawing her daughter into her arms. That gesture brought the tears, and Mattie held her tight, thinking that it had been too long since Hannah had been so open with her.

"He d-didn't ask me to the prom 'cause . . . 'cause . . . 'cause he liked me. H-he asked me to find out s-stuff about Jess."

"That was wrong," Mattie whispered.

"I hate him."

"Yes, I imagine you do. I'm disappointed in him. I thought he had more class."

Mattie handed Hannah some tissues, and she wiped her eyes. "I know you think I hate Jess, too, but I don't. I just hate what's she done to our family."

"Sweetheart, she hasn't done anything but get herself hurt. The accident wasn't deliberate. And if anything, it has made some good changes. Dad and I are going to try again, and I know that's what both of you wanted."

Hannah pulled back and, with her eyes still glistening, she asked, "For real? I mean, you're going to get married to him, not just let him live here like he's been doing?"

Mattie was at a loss as to how answer the marriage question. Hannah's feelings and questions weren't couched in nuances or subtlety that allowed Mattie to avoid answers that later she might regret. "We're working on a future together."

"What does that mean?"

"It means we're going to try again."

"Like getting married?"

The question wrapped around her and knotted. When

Stephen broached this, she'd said it was too soon; Hannah, she doubted, would be as accepting of such a general statement. Besides, Hannah would view "weasel words" as an adult excuse to avoid an answer—to her, a reconciliation meant an inevitable remarriage. End of story.

And in reality, Mattie had already put the pieces in place for that eventuality when she broke off with Wyatt. Her ducking and dodging from a verbal commitment was a "just in case" maneuver, which now seemed flimsy and self-protective; a clumsily wrapped, noncommittal cloak. Mattie had always honored her word; when she said something, she followed through. And that was the problem here. She wasn't absolutely sure.

Yet right now, seeing how much Hannah needed it, Mattie wanted to give her daughter reassurance, some confidence to ease her deep fear that her family wasn't going to hold together. Offering her that pledge seemed more important than any reservations Mattie had about her future with Stephen.

"Yes, like getting married," she said quietly.

"Oh, Mom!" And, as Mattie knew she would, an elated Hannah hugged her even more tightly, whispering, "I love you. I love you and Dad and Jessica, too."

And Mattie was glad she'd given this hope to Hannah. Now it was settled, and she felt the inner rightness of having chosen this moment with Hannah. Remarriage was the finale everyone wanted. Her own enthusiasm would come; it was just that right now, the breakup with Wyatt was still too raw and sad.

Now, watching Hannah and Stephen at the auction, any qualms dissipated.

She turned around when someone tapped her on the shoulder.

"Mattie, babe, I just heard the great news," Wyatt said, turning her around and hugging her. It probably lasted a little longer than necessary, but no one noticed except the two of them.

"Isn't it wonderful?"

"Fabulous."

"By the way, you were a help. She was clutching the secret stones when she awakened."

"What can I say?" He shrugged with an amused puff of pride. "When I picked out those stones on the beach, I made sure I only took the ones with secret powers."

She laughed, and it felt relaxed and good.

"Those white stones should get the credit—the hell with those guys who went to med school."

"I agree," she said chuckling. "But seriously, they've become a real talisman to her, along with Toadie."

"Who would have thought? I'm glad I found them, and I'm glad they still work."

"I'm glad your father didn't throw them away."

"Me, too."

And suddenly they were out of conversation; they stood awkwardly, like two old friends with too many differences, or two broken lovers with too little to say.

Wyatt broke the silence. "So now the question is if I borrow them back from Jess and sleep with them a few nights, am I gonna wake up and find you?"

Mattie winced, wishing she'd moved away sooner. "Oh, Wyatt, don't. . . ."

"Guess their miracle-working capacity doesn't extend to us, does it?"

She stepped away from him. "I have to go."

"Mattie . . ." She moved farther away, and he stopped her. "Hold on a minute."

"We've been through this, and I can't do it again." She saw Stephen in the distance, watching them. Not overtly—he was chatting with Hannah and a couple who lived across the street—but Mattie knew his body language. His attention was definitely focused on her and Wyatt. No doubt she'd hear about this later, and from his viewpoint, she couldn't blame him for being irritated.

Wyatt followed her gaze. "The hell with him."

"Oh, Wyatt, you're making this very difficult."

"Talking is difficult? Christ, you're acting as if I had my hand up your skirt."

She sighed. "I'm talking about appearances, and you

know it. It's about having some consideration for Stephen and my daughter and anyone else who cares to glance over here."

Wyatt stepped back. "All right. Let me just tell you this. I'm going back to Newport after all the details are finished here. Promise to call me if you . . ." He shook his head as if reminding himself of his new no-longer-her-lover-and-friend status. "You know where I am if you—oh, hell, never mind. Thanks a lot for everything here—the auction, all your hard work when you had other things more important." He paused, clearly uneasy and struggling for words of departure that were both generic and meaningful. Finally, he simply said, "Take care of yourself, babe."

Mattie, for reasons that made absolutely no sense, was more touched by this rambling, not very cohesive moment than by their more precise talk the previous night. He'd been more stoic, almost determined not to pressure her, and had gone out of his way to not trash Stephen or to criticize her decision. Here he seemed more fragile, if such a term could be applied to Wyatt. Fragile and vulnerable and melancholy.

A suffocating regret closed in on her, and she was grateful for the approach of Corinne.

"Mattie, what fabulous news about Jessica."

"Fabulous indeed."

"Kevin was bouncing when I told him. Hannah, too, I bet."

"Yes, yes, she was." Someone called her name, and Mattie took that opportunity to excuse herself and move away.

A huge tent had been set up, and the 300 chairs were filling fast. Sticky notes with names scrawled by those who reserved the seats were on almost all of the empty ones. Lois, who worked for George Epperly, was assigning numbers and taking names and addresses of potential bidders. The runners, who held the items up for bids while George described them, were moving about, making sure all items were numbered and tagged. One runner hadn't shown up, and when Epperly fumed about incompetent help, Wyatt decided to volunteer.

When he approached, he was greeted with a bushy-browed scowl. "Ah, yes, the moronic dumbbell," Epperly observed.

"I'm trying to improve my image."

The auctioneer chomped down on his cigar. "Call me before you make any more dump runs."

"Absolutely."

Epperly nodded. "Okay, work with Marvin over there. He's gettin' too old to be heftin' furniture, but I can't get rid of him. Christ, on one hand I've got muscle that don't want to work, and on the other hand geezers who don't want to do anything but."

He gave Wyatt a few more instructions. Just before he started to walk away, Wyatt asked, "When do the chairs go up?"

The furniture had been set on a platform behind where George would call the auction. A man in red suspenders sat beside the pieces with all the authority of someone guarding the contents of the Sistine Chapel.

"At ten o'clock on the nose. I got four phone bidders, and that's when they'll be called. Ever been to an auction before?"

"Yeah, long time ago."

"I call 'em fast, so stay on your toes. I got to be out of here by noon at the latest."

"Noon! All this stuff by noon?"

"Even if your sister hadn't pulled what she wanted, I'd still be done by noon." George glanced at his watch, then hitched up his pants, that same no-identifiable-color belt not quite doing its job.

"I'm amazed."

"Damn right you are. And you'll be more amazed later." And he clomped off.

Mattie was running here and there, checking on some lots that would go first, accepting more hugs from well-wishers excited at the news about Jessica. He also watched Caulfield cruise around with Hannah; he looked cocky and satisfied.

Hey, why not? He won the lady; if that fact had been presented to Wyatt a few weeks ago, he would have laughed at the ludicrousness of it. Mattie reconciling with Stephen?

About as much of a chance as him remarrying Paige. He shuddered at that thought. But the ending with Mattie, for that he was sad and depressed.

An hour into the auction, Epperly was true to his word that he called 'em fast. Wyatt, helping Marvin lift a mahoghany desk onto a platform so those in the back rows could see it, was impressed by Epperly's ability to get bids and get them high, as well as by his interaction with the bidders. Wyatt soon learned this was part of Epperly's shtick, a showmanship that bonded him to his audience through the combination of a salesman's flair and a hustler's charm.

One lady—Ethel Pastoria—whom Epperly had earlier charmed into bidding on a child's rocking chair for her granddaughter, took to his attention like a bird finding its nest.

She'd bought not only the rocker but a sterling dresser set as well. "Shine it up, Ethel, and you'll have some pretty pieces." She took it with a high bid of seventy dollars. Then came a maple hutch, a kitchen piece that Wyatt and Kevin had pulled muscles hauling out of the back shed. It was dirty, it smelled, and the idea of putting anything edible in it caused him to shudder, but Ethel was all the way up to three hundred when she dropped out. Other bidders pushed the price even higher, and the piece finally sold for eight hundred bucks to a woman who looked more like she shopped Ethan Allen than tent auctions.

Marvin, the runner Wyatt was helping, leaned over and said, "Ain't it amazin'?"

"That she bought it?"

"Nah, that your mama saved it. That kind of old stuff is worth lots of moola."

"Who could have known?" Wyatt muttered, thinking about all the stuff he saw his old man secretly dispose of when his mother wasn't looking. No doubt a small fortune had been unloaded and buried at the town dump.

Marvin nudged Wyatt. "Watch what this one goes for."

"This one" was a pie safe; the wooden cupboard was

square, with a flat top that was scratched and dented, and
had no decorative details. Traditionally, the piece had two
shelves behind doors that framed punched tin, open slats, or
screening. This one had a door missing. The piece was used
a century ago to cool pies and keep out flies and dirt. The
construction was primitive; it was built for utility and probably assembled from scrap wood, including pieces of broken
furniture.

"What am I bid? Let's start it at five hundred."

"Hey, George, it's missing a door."

"Vintage AC."

"Who's gonna start this? Ethel, how 'bout you?"

"I don't bake pies."

Epperly leaned forward. "Now, Ethel, you got a country
kitchen with lots of them roosters and apple baskets, and I
bet you even got a bunch of purty linen from back in the forties."

"Well, I have some."

"And I bet you ain't got a place to put it."

"I have a drawer."

"Nah, you don't want a drawer. Ain't no one gonna see it
in a drawer."

"Hey, Epperly," someone called from the back, "fifty
bucks?"

"You must think you're at some armpit auction." Epperly
appeared insulted but took the bid. "Okay, I got fifty. Who'll
give me a hundred?"

Wyatt whispered to Marvin, "What's an armpit auction?"

"Where bedroom sets go for a fin. Smoke, beer, and
cheap eats. You can pick up some good deals, but you can
get your ass cleaned, too."

Wyatt chuckled. "No Ethels, huh?"

"They'd get eaten alive. George is good to the old
ladies—a lot of callers couldn't be bothered."

Epperly presented the wonder of the pie safe, trying to
garner bids. "I got a hundred. One fifty. Ethel, get in on this.
Two, and now three to the lady in the red blouse. I have
three. There's three fifty. Ethel, I'm losin' faith in you, dar-

lin'—I can see this beauty in your kitchen holding all that purty linen."

Ethel shook her head, firmly holding out as the price climbed higher and higher, until finally, "Sold! To the lady in the red blouse for seven hundred and fifty."

"What'd I tell you?" the runner mouthed to Wyatt.

"Incredible."

"Okay, we got those bidders on the phones? Okay, settle down out there. We've got some Windsors up here that predate even me. Old Henry, snoozing over there by the tent flap, says these beauties are like some his great-great-grandpappy used for kindling one winter. Old Henry talks regular to his grandpappy, so I'm taking his story for gospel. There are eight of them. Original finish. No strip-happy refinisher spent a Sunday with steel wool and paint remover. The dirt has a heritage, and I have an opening bid of seventy-five thousand. Here we go."

The 300 auctiongoers who were seated, plus those standing, stopped talking. Attention was riveted on Epperly. There was no teasing with Ethel, no mid-bid chatter. This was serious money, and distractions—unless to place a huge bid—weren't allowed.

Wyatt watched in astonishment as the bids climbed in thousand-dollar increments. All four phone bidders stayed in, and three people in the audience. At one twenty-five, someone made a bid of one thirty-five, and for a moment there was silence. Whispering on the phone, followed by a shake of the head; one phone bidder was dropping out.

Epperly leaned forward, his voice low and serious; he could have whispered and been heard, it was so quiet.

"I have a hundred thirty-five here in the tent. Do I hear a hundred and forty?"

Silence stewed and simmered, then one of the phone bids went to one forty.

"We're at one forty. One fifty?" Silence, and Wyatt was sure his hammering pulse could be heard all the way to Providence. Epperly looked around, checked the phones. "Are we all done at one forty? I have one forty once, last chance. One forty once, twice. Sold for one hundred and forty thousand dollars to the phone bidder from—" Epperly glanced down at a paper— "from Virginia."

Wyatt was staggered by the sum and by the fact that someone would spend that kind of money on chairs they hadn't seen. But from what he'd heard about Epperly, the phone bidders were secure because they'd spoken with Epperly and been assured of their authenticity. Mattie, of course, had known they were authentic, and he believed her, but in his gut he couldn't imagine anyone paying even a grand for the chairs. A hundred and forty simply blew his mind.

He glanced up, and saw Mattie grinning.

He grinned back.

Nothing more needed to be said.

Chapter
Twenty-one

With the auction a financial success for the Landrys and a professional one for Mattie, she would have enjoyed a little time for basking in glory. Instead, she found herself flung headlong into a flurry of phone calls and requests for her services to organize and set up estate sales. One in particular involved a couple who had been to the Landry auction and were inspired to tackle clearing out their own home. Accumulation, plus the lure of retirement in Arizona, propelled Fannie and Edgar Bryant to seriously downsize. They had no children, but their "treasures" were like offspring, except they brought only pleasure and no problems. Mattie could certainly relate to the "problem" aspect of kids, but the choice of things over children struck her as not only sad but also not completely truthful. She guessed there was much more beneath their choices than avoiding child-raising problems.

After a walk through their very crowded two-story home and viewing the massive amounts of collectibles and a cupboard sagging with Heisey glass, Mattie eagerly agreed to handle the auction setup. Not surprisingly, after the Bryants had watched George's spectacular work at the Landry auction, they insisted on having him. When Mattie called and he grumbled and cranked about being on vacation, she mentioned the abundance of Heisey. George's silence reverberated, then was almost immediately followed with "Hell, what are you, some kind of wizard? First the Windsors and now Heisey."

"Actually, there's this sock of secret stones with all kinds of magic powers. . . ."

"What?"

She chuckled. "Never mind. I just did a general inventory of the house, and in one of the bedrooms was a cupboard. Mrs. Bryant opened it, and there was the glass."

"You're sure it was Heisey?"

"Was I right about the Windsors? Perhaps they have a few Civil War swords stashed in an old trunk."

"Or Civil War bodies wrapped in Oriental rugs. Don't change the subject. How much Heisey?"

"Hmmm, I'd say fifty pieces. Mint—no chips or cracks or dings."

"Jesus."

"But if you're booked, I'll give Borden a call," she said breezily, referring to the auctioneer who had traded linen for Heisey with George's wife.

"Don't get smart-mouthed with me, missy. Give me the date."

She laughed, and gave him the details.

Other than the Bryants, Mattie had turned down most of the other requests, passing them on to colleagues. Her plate was simply too full, and she'd reached her limit.

Getting Jessica home and their lives as a family back on course became more than just a logical unfolding of events. Mattie had expected a smooth transition, and the following few weeks had been anything but.

The police spoke with Jessica three times as they attempted to put together the timing and the circumstances of the accident. Jessica couldn't remember how fast she'd been driving, but because it was dark and she wasn't that familiar with the curvy I-95, she'd been cautious. She recalled glancing over at Arlis when she opened another can of beer. In those seconds, another car cut her off on a curve, and she'd lost control. The car careened into the guard rail and flipped over once, the heaviest impact on the passenger side. The investigation at the scene showed skid marks that indicated speed, but not excessive speed. What had been shown was the inexperience of the driver; Jessica had overcorrected when she tried to regain control.

On the Petchers' auto theft charge, and the drinking, she'd been emphatic in her denials.

Mattie had prepared herself for every worst-case scenario, from Jessica being arrested to a lawsuit by the Petchers to a protracted investigation. In the end, the witnesses knew both girls. They were neighbors of the Petchers and told the police they'd overheard Arlis, outside her house, saying she was going to take the car because she knew her mother would rant and rave about her going off with Jessica, "that fucking prom queen." To Arlis's mother, her daughter had no reason to be hanging with "the likes of her," and that "rich bitch" would just get her into trouble. The witnesses also saw Arlis drinking and saw Jessica take the keys and insist on driving.

Witnesses were an unexpected bonus for Jessica, but hardly a dividend for the Petchers. Mattie and Stephen braced themselves for a variety of accusations, from bribery and collusion to flat-out denial by the Petchers of their daughter's actions, with all of it leading to endless legal wrangling. But the police declared the investigation closed, and although it was indeed an unfortunate accident, there wasn't evidence to arrest and charge Jessica. The lawyer for the Petchers advised them that, given the eyewitness neighbors and the at-the-scene police report, a lawsuit would be expensive and a long shot. Whether exhausted or simply facing the reality of the odds against them, they reluctantly did as their lawyer advised.

Stephen was surprised by their cave, as he called it, for if the reverse had occurred—Arlis had lived and Jessica had died—he said, "I'd've sued them six ways to Sunday."

"For what? They don't have any money," Mattie said.

"On principle, because losing a kid means losing a future filled with potential—never mind the permanent damage to the family." Then he was quiet for a moment. "What if we did something for them?"

Mattie was touched by his generous spirit. "Like what?"

"I know it could look like since we won, we can afford to be nice, but they lost their daughter. I think we need to offer them something. They could probably use some money."

Mattie nodded, recalling that earlier idea of replacing their car. The timing on that could have been disastrous, but now that Jessica had been cleared, there would be no appearance of trying to buy off the Petchers. But then there was another angle. "It shouldn't be given directly. I think they'd perceive it as some sort of payoff. And in their place, we might feel the same way."

"Okay. What about anonymously?"

"Yes, I like that. We could do it with a cashier's check. The Petchers could simply be told that there were people in town who had been saddened by Arlis's death and wanted to do something for the family."

"And with straight cash, they'll be too busy contemplating how to spend it to worry about where it came from."

"That's a cruel remark. I'd rather believe they'll just be relieved and grateful for some extra money."

Stephen called their lawyer and set it all up, with the amount to be five thousand dollars. When Mattie suggested the amount, Stephen thought it was too much, but when she asked him, "How do you put 'too much' money on the priceless life of a daughter?" he agreed.

As for Jess, physically, she had made wonderful progress, and to those who saw and visited with her, she seemed almost her old self. Mattie, however, sensed otherwise. But then again, she was the only one who still wanted some answers to some old but still pertinent questions. Not about the accident, but about the weeks before.

On this, however, she and Stephen disagreed vehemently.

"Mattie, just forget about all the goddamn questions," Stephen wearily insisted, as if she'd done nothing since Jessica came home but pepper her. In reality, she'd asked very few, wanting to wait until Jess got her bearings and the police investigation was finished.

"I can't wait any longer."

"Or won't."

"Fine, phrase it however you want to, but bad things happened to her, whether by her own doing or someone else's. If those things hadn't happened, she wouldn't have been in that accident. Her silence worries me; I think she's hiding something. I didn't press because of the investigation, but that's finished. These are questions about who she was and what made her make the choices she did. I still haven't learned why Jess suddenly became friends with Arlis but never mentioned her to us. Why lie to us about going to the sleepover at Callie's, and then go out of town with a girl who was drunk?"

"Did it occur to you that all of this might have been to help Arlis? That Arlis swore *her* to secrecy? That *Arlis* had a problem? Maybe Jessica was being kind and considerate— you know, like helping the girl out of a jam or, even more like our daughter, honoring a confidence?"

"Of course that all occurred to me. In fact, it was the first thing I thought of. But Arlis wasn't the one who seemed to have undergone a personality change, and Arlis wasn't the one who was pregnant."

"And Jessica isn't pregnant anymore, thank God."

"But that doesn't change—"

Stephen threw his hands in the air. "For Chrissake, Mattie, can't you just leave it? I'd sure like to forget it, just like Jessica would. You harping on this proves you haven't been listening to your own daughter. Don't you hear what she's been saying? 'I don't want to talk about it' has been her answer since you started your daily quiz."

"It is not a daily quiz!"

He paid no attention. "To her credit, she wants to get on with her life, and the rest of us would like to see her do just that. But you're keeping everyone chained to old issues that are no longer relevant."

Stephen's bombardment wasn't enough; Mattie heard the identical comments from her parents, and Hannah, too, leaving her feeling like the proverbial nag. Her parents siding with Stephen wasn't a surprise, but Hannah's attitude was.

She'd expected that her youngest would pout over her sister stealing the spotlight once again, but Hannah seemed genuinely happy Jessica was home.

But then, as though to single-handedly prevent any more family division, Hannah took it upon herself to announce to anyone who would listen that her parents were getting married. Mattie's parents and, of course, Stephen pounced on that and immediately started making plans.

When Mattie raised an initial objection, suggesting they wait a while, the choruses of "For what?" were deafening. She finally conceded the inevitable; wedding plans soon took precedence, and her nagging questions were shunted to the back of her mind.

But Mattie did take Jessica aside after Hannah brought home the study sheets she needed to take her final exams. She'd missed them, and though she hadn't graduated with her class, her teachers had assured her that once she passed her finals, a diploma would be awarded.

Following Jessica to her room, Mattie closed the door while her daughter fussed with arranging papers and folders.

"You haven't said much about the wedding. Are you happy about it?"

"I guess so."

"That doesn't sound like a ringing endorsement."

"A lot has happened to me, Mom. I guess getting excited about a wedding is a little hard."

Mattie took her daughter by the shoulders. "Look at me." When she did, Mattie said, "I know you don't want to talk about what happened to you. That troubles me, but this coming wedding is too important for you to not have an opinion."

"What about you? Are *you* sure, Mom?"

"I'm sure I want what's best for you and Hannah."

"I'm starting college in the fall, so I won't even be around. You don't have to get married for me." Then she stood and crossed the room. "Daddy and Hannah are excited. I can't get excited about anything right now."

"Jessica—"

"Mom, please. Stop nagging and pushing me! I really

have to get some studying done." She turned away, effectively ending any chance Mattie had of getting a straight answer.

Hardly the best emotional atmosphere to plan a wedding. Mattie wanted to wait, but Hannah and Stephen and her parents pressed and pushed and nagged and whined until Jessica's unspoken objection became a muted note in a blaring brass band.

And so a date was set; the ceremony and reception planned for two weeks later. Still too fast, in Mattie's opinion, but waiting seemed pointless, too. Friends and neighbors all gushed about how special a wedding was that would reunite a divorced couple and reconstruct a family.

It was all a little too gooey for Mattie. Though she was committed to reconciling in her head, her heart wasn't quite there yet. When she tried to tell her mother this, Louise Rooney rattled off some goofy metaphor about Mattie being on a plane coming in for a landing, and instead of enjoying the ride, she was quibbling about the choice of runway.

Of course the analogy didn't work, because Mattie did have a choice. She could say no. But then what? Whether the marriage was in two weeks or two months, she was already resigned to the fact that it would happen.

Hardly an enthusiastic bride-to-be, she thought, pulling back memories of Wyatt and what she'd given up. But then, when she thought of the girls and the family chaos that would ensue if she backed out now. . . . Choices and consequences. Well, she'd made the choice; now she just prayed the consequences would be beneficial to her daughters.

However, Mattie did insist on keeping the event small, with the ceremony and an outdoor luncheon reception held at her parents' home. Her mother went all-out, delighted and enthusiastic about handling all the elegant accoutrements, from vases of flowers to real linen on the tables. Mattie hired a caterer so the cooking and cleanup wouldn't be a burden. During all of this, happiness seemed to be buzzing and building among all the participants except her and, Mattie often noticed, Jessica. The mysterious and distant Jessica.

Three days before the ceremony, Stephen and Hannah

had gone to do some last-minute shopping. Mattie took advantage of the empty house to seek out Jessica in her room.

She found her by the window, the sock of secret stones on the sill and Toadie in one arm.

"Jess, why won't you talk to me?"

Her daughter looked up, then away, then "Oh, Mother, please. Not again."

"I don't understand your silence or your stubbornness." When she shivered and tightened her grip on Toadie, Mattie said, "Just like what you're doing now. You freeze up and shut me out. We always talked things out before."

"Yeah, well, I don't have anything to talk about."

Mattie wanted to shake her out of this tough girl attitude that she suspected was more fake than real. Their earlier talk about the wedding hadn't been so harsh. Then again, Jessica hadn't objected to discussing the marriage—she had *always* balked at discussing those weeks before the accident.

Now, Mattie wanted to tell her she knew she was lying and the telltale flush on her neck proved it. She'd never been able to shade the truth without flushing. But to point out a lie in this already badly frayed atmosphere would get Mattie nothing but snarling and silence.

She crossed the room and knelt beside Jessica's chair. Her daughter fiddled with the hem of her shorts, turning it up and then down. Her fingers were unsteady, and when Mattie took hold of her hand it was cold. Jessica didn't pull away, and Mattie had a strong sense that if she pushed just a bit more, she'd learn at least some of the truth.

"Sweetheart, I won't punish you or even scold you, but this wall you've put around yourself frightens me." Jessica showed little reaction, but since she hadn't stormed to her feet and flounced away, Mattie continued, selecting her words carefully. "I know you're troubled, and while I hope you would trust me enough to talk with me, maybe someone else would be easier. I think that once you've opened this closed door inside of you, you'll really be able to get on with your life."

Mattie winced at her choice of words—it all sounded like prepackaged psychobabble. And while she would have settled for a nod or even a neutral silence, what she got was a narrowed, cold look that served as a fiercely self-protective shield.

"On with my life? Why do parents always think it's so easy? Tears and hugs and a few pats, and all is forgotten and forgiven. So is this where I'm supposed to break down and blubber and confess all my sins? Then you'll have all the stuff that's jammed into every corner of my fucked-up life. Then will you be happy? Your nosiness satisfied?"

Mattie shrank back. The sarcasm of Jess's words was staggering, but Mattie also sensed a crack. This wasn't cold detachment; this was an emotional crater. Again she spoke so as not to incite. Quietly and steadily, she said, "I've never said anything about sins."

"But that what's you're thinking, that's what everyone is thinking."

" 'Everyone' doesn't matter. You matter. And what about you? Is that what you're thinking? Because if whatever happened in those weeks before the accident was just some garden-variety rebellion, you'd have blown it all off and told us what happened. But this, whatever brought it all on, is not garden-variety rebellion, is it?" Jess neither confirmed nor denied, and Mattie continued, "When you stay so apart, keep so much to yourself, and then deny that anything is wrong, those who love you worry that something is very, very wrong."

Jess leveled a hard look at her mother. "You just don't give up, do you?" When Mattie simply looked at her, Jessica screamed as if a bomb had ripped open her gut. "All right! Here it is. Arlis was taking me to an abortion clinic in Providence! Okay? Is that what you wanted to hear? Are you happy now?"

Mattie wasn't surprised, and in fact had wondered if this was a possibility when she'd first heard Jessica was pregnant. "Who was the father, Jess?"

"Noooooo!"

But Mattie pressed. "Kane? Jessica, was it Kane? Are you protecting him?"

"I already told you it wasn't," she cried.

"But you were in the coma, and maybe—"

"It wasn't Kane," she snapped. "I never had sex with him, so how could it be?"

"Then who?"

She burst into tears, then swept the sock of stones off the sill, their weight hitting the floor with a thump. Then she flung Toadie so that he tipped over a bedside lamp and both fell to the floor. Mattie didn't move. Jessica turned her back, sobbing, shoulders heaving. As much as Mattie wanted to take her into her arms, she didn't. She feared Jess would push her away, but she feared even more that she would comfort too much. Jessica needed to get rid of whatever was strangling her, and once she'd done that, Mattie's comforting arms and maternal understanding would be welcome.

Still Jessica wouldn't face her. "If I tell you, will you promise not to ask me any more questions?"

What an odd request, Mattie thought, for surely, if the questions were answered, there'd be no need for anything further. Certainly not promises. But she kept that thought to herself. She was too close to getting answers to chance Jess closing down again. "No more questions."

"Then here it is. I don't know who knocked me up. There were a lot of guys."

This did stun her, and she stared in disbelief. Hadn't Wyatt said something like this? Hadn't Stephen alluded to the possibility? Mattie had been adamant in her belief that Jessica wasn't, and had never been, promiscuous.

"Shocked, aren't you? Good! Then this should end all your questions."

"Yes, I guess it does," Mattie said softly, reaching to touch Jessica.

"Don't! Don't mother me."

Mattie wanted to cry. Instead of feeling some sense that talking would help Jessica, she feared her insistence had just made things worse.

She turned and slowly walked out of the room, pulling the door closed behind her. No more. Stephen was right. The probing was doing more harm than good.

* * *

The morning of the wedding arrived, bringing sunshine and excitement. Mattie, in her bedroom, had laid out the pale green linen dress. There was also a hat with a wide brim, trimmed in flowers and ribbons. Mattie would have chosen something less dramatic, but her mother had ordered it from a milliner who had just opened a business in town. The young woman had been thrilled over the publicity she would get, and Mattie had to admit that the design and details were exquisite. Hannah loved the hat, the ceremony preparations, and all the excitement that surrounds a wedding. Mattie had asked her if she wanted to be her maid of honor with her sister, and Hannah had been thrilled.

Jessica, however, refused and Mattie hadn't insisted.

The tension between mother and daughter lingered even though Mattie asked no more questions. Her concern, however, hadn't lessened, but she was beginning to wonder if her imagination had built up the mystery to such an extent that no answers would be good enough.

A promiscuous daughter, finding herself pregnant, did indeed support what Mattie had initially heard from Kevin, and from Jessica's counselor at school about Jess in tears over Kevin breaking up with her. Sex with other guys wouldn't sit well with a boyfriend. Still, it all seemed so unlike Jessica.

No more, she told herself. *You have your answers, and though you don't like them, they are believable. And you don't like them because her answers reinforce your own denials: You've been out of touch with your daughter and haven't even known it.*

Now, she slipped into the dress and her shoes, and rechecked her hair before settling the hat in place. She knew she looked more than attractive and that Stephen would call her beautiful and that someone else would say she was radiant. No one would notice that, deep down, she was far closer to being a reluctant bride than an excited one.

Stephen had planned a short honeymoon, and Mattie knew that would include sex. She couldn't think about that now, and not thinking about lovemaking but just doing it appealed even more. A lot like when she was a kid, and she and two of her friends would jump off a neighbor's garage roof into the honeysuckle bushes. If she thought about the jump and the landing, she got scared, but if she just raced up the ladder, scrambled to the roof's peak, then raced down the side and leaped wide into the fragrant vines, she was fine. But if she hesitated, if she thought about it, if she couldn't just do it, she panicked.

How silly that such a childhood memory would be triggered by the idea of sex with Stephen. *So what was the point here? Just do it, and when it's over, you might even enjoy it.*

The tragedy was that her tenseness about it had nothing to do with Stephen and everything to do with her. In their first marriage, she'd found him to be a good lover; considerate, gentle, and always aware of her satisfaction. Mattie had no reason to believe this marriage would be any different. She took a deep breath, allowing a lingering thought of Wyatt to flutter through her mind. She glanced at the silver box with the engraved "M" that he'd bought for her right after they'd met. It needed cleaning, she noted, the silver darkening with tarnish, Perhaps it was time to put it away, just as she'd put him away. A love that came and soared and ripened and now had vanished.

She walked out of bedroom when she heard the limo Stephen had ordered to take the four of them to her parents' house, to her wedding.

The house and the gardens and all her mother's fussing were impressive. Guests had arrived, including Stephen's sister, Elise, and Mattie's brothers. They had both come to see Jessica and had remained for the wedding.

"You sure about what you're doing?" Geoff had asked when he heard of the remarriage.

"Who can be sure about anything these days?"

"Seems to me, marriage ought to be sure at least at the get-go."

She'd kissed him and said lightly, "I'm a big girl. I want you to wish us the best and be happy for us."

Geoff didn't appear convinced, but the discussion closed. Today, she noted, he seemed to be past any of his reservations as she saw him mingling with the other guests.

A large blue and white striped tent was festooned with ribbons and flowers. Hannah bounced around, her happiness contagious. Stephen, looking handsome and proud and content, spoke to friends and kept his hand firmly clasped with Mattie's. Jessica was helping her grandmother with last-minute food items, although apparently it was more to stay occupied than out of any enthusiasm.

Finally the justice of the peace arrived and a bridge partner of her mother's began to play a rented piano. Mattie and Hannah took their places; Stephen and Tom Egan, whom Stephen had asked to be his best man, took their positions beside the justice.

The wedding march began, and Mattie and Hannah walked slowly down the aisle. To Mattie it all felt surreal, like some kind of crooked fantasy.

Then they were all in place, and the music trailed off and the guests quieted.

The justice began. "Dear friends and family, we are all gathered here on this joyous occasion to witness the joining of Stephen and Mattie in marriage—"

Someone screamed.

Everyone turned.

"My God, what happened?" someone whispered.

"Is somebody hurt?"

"Jesus, he didn't even get to the 'who objects' part."

"How utterly embarrassing."

Then Hannah hissed, "How could she do this?"

"Shit," Stephen muttered.

Most rose to their feet, straining to get a better view of the commotion. Mattie watched in astonishment as Jessica fled the tent.

Chapter Twenty-two

For a few moments the guests remained in their places, still and stiff, as though a January cold snap had banished the summer heat. Then a buzz of whispers, followed by low chatter and all eyes swinging toward Mattie and Stephen.

The justice closed his wedding ceremony book. "Oh, my, I've never had this happen in the thirty years I've been doing marriages."

"I'll talk to her," Stephen said. "All the excitement must have just overwhelmed her."

Mattie started after him.

"No, you stay here. She doesn't need a crowd of people descending on her."

"People? I'm her mother."

"Who will ask her *more* questions."

She glared at him, then handed her flowers to Hannah, who stared in the direction that Jessica had fled. Mattie pushed past Stephen.

He grabbed her upper arm, stopping her. "Please, honey, let me handle this."

With everyone watching as if this were a new soap opera installment, Mattie conceded. He strode quickly past the guests and disappeared into the house.

Mattie's mother came rushing forward. "What is the matter with her?"

"I don't know."

"How can *you* not know? You're her mother. And what are you doing standing here? You need to see what's going on. You know I love Stephen, but a hysterical daughter is better dealt with by her mother."

Her mother's bluntness punched away her inaction. Mattie took off the hat, handing it to Hannah. "You're right, Mom. You're absolutely right."

"She's a bitch," Hannah whispered to her mother. "She's ruined everything."

Mattie ignored her. One problem daughter at a time.

She hurried into the house, through the kitchen where the caterers were working. They barely glanced at her as she moved past trays of food and a three-tiered wedding cake, then into the living room, where gifts were piled on a white-linen-draped table. Mattie had specified no gifts, and the sight of them annoyed her—all the hoopla over a remarriage, as if there was some renewal of love and devotion. She briefly wondered how many raised eyebrows she'd get if she returned them.

Muffled voices came from upstairs.

She climbed the stairs, went past her parents' bedroom and a guest room. She walked a little farther, and the voices got louder. They came from where the girls always slept when they spent the night. Mattie knew the room well—all frilly and pink and lacy; both girls loved it, although both would have balked at the same decor at home. But at their grandmother's house they loved playing the Queen and the Princess.

The door was closed, but she distinctly heard Stephen's low, modulated voice and she heard Jessica weeping.

"Do we have this all clear and straightened out?" Stephen asked, a hint of exasperation in his tone.

Mattie stopped just short of barging in. Outside the closed door, she listened.

"I can't d-do t-this." Jessica's voice was halting, breaking. And then a sob.

"Sweetheart, of course you can. Come on, now. Dry those tears. You're not a baby. You can't hide in here."

"It's not that, Daddy, you know it's not—"

"Enough. I don't want to have to have this conversation again. I thought I made that clear at the hospital. You and I have a deal, and I'm going to be extremely upset if you break it."

"I know I promised, but—"

"No buts. A promise is a promise. Now I want you to dry your eyes and get yourself together and come back outside. This is your mother's and my wedding, and you're too grown-up to spoil it."

"I can't."

"Jessica . . ."

Was that a warning tone in his voice?

"I can't," she cried. "I can't just sit there and pretend. I can't do it anymore." And Mattie heard her start to cry again.

My God, she didn't want this marriage! And Stephen wasn't listening. Well, of course he wouldn't, he'd try to get her to cooperate. He'd been on this reconciliation campaign, boosted by Hannah's approval and apparently by what he believed was Jessica's also, since just after the accident.

She pushed the door open and Stephen swung around, his expression changing from surprise to fury so fast that if Mattie had blinked, she would have missed the transition.

"I thought I told you to let me handle this," he snapped.

"This is handling? She's in tears."

"She'll be fine. Just give us a few more minutes."

"You've had your few minutes." She walked around him, and he gripped her arm to stop her. "Don't start with your questions. Do you understand me? That's what got her so upset in the first place."

"In the first place, she screamed and ran out of the tent. Let go of my arm."

He didn't.

"What's wrong with you? Let me go."

Jessica was huddled on the edge of the bed, her head down, sniffling.

Mattie jerked her arm free and took Jessica by the shoulders. The instant she touched her, Jessica wrapped her arms around her, trembling and gripping her mother, then sobbing as if Mattie had rescued her from some deranged demon.

"Oh, Mom, please, please don't hate me, please, please don't. . . ."

"Hate you? My darling child, I could never hate you." She soothed and held her, aware of how close and connected this embrace was, compared to others in the past few weeks. That cold, tight attitude that had been her daughter since she awakened from the coma had fled as surely as she'd screamed and fled the tent.

Mattie had found Jessica's wishy-washy response about the wedding a little unsettling, but she would have never guessed this vehemence. Jessica had never wanted this remarriage. "Shhh, it's okay. The wedding can be postponed. It's okay."

"Postponed!" Stephen, hands low on his hips, glared in disbelief. "That's ridiculous. It can't be stopped, it's in progress. Everything's arranged and ready. You're not going to postpone it because of some selfish hysteria."

Mattie turned around. "Well, what would you suggest? We go down and get married while she stays up here and cries? Be reasonable."

"Reasonable is not letting a kid dictate our life."

"I'm remarrying you because of the girls. If Jessica is miserable, then we better do some rethinking."

He threw his hands up and rolled his eyes.

Jessica still gripped her, as if her mother might disappear. "Mom, you don't know, you don't understand."

"Jessica, don't do this. Don't," Stephen pleaded.

"I c-can't, Daddy. I c-can't do it anymore."

Mattie loosened her grip enough to look at Jessica. She was white and terrified, and as tense as a coiled spring. Then she glanced back at Stephen; he, too, was pale and scared and agitated.

"You can't do what, honey? What's going on?" Mattie's voice was barely above a whisper.

Jessica curled deeper against her mother. Stephen plunged his hands into his pockets, turning toward the door. "I'm not listening to any more."

"It was his," Jessica whispered.

"Oh, shit," he muttered.

"His?"

"It was his, because there wasn't anyone else."

Ten seconds of confusion turned inside out and twisted around Mattie like a suffocating stench. "The baby? The baby was your father's?"

And Jessica looked directly at her. "Yes."

The single word pounded over Mattie with all the force and horror of waking up in a thousand nightmares. This couldn't be true, this was too far beyond any outrage Mattie had ever imagined.

She held the weeping Jessica, and a few feet away Stephen stared at the floor—never speaking, never denying. *My God, if he wasn't denying it, if he was just standing there, just staring at the floor . . . not denying, not horrified . . . then in that very nonreaction he was admitting . . .*

From somewhere deep within her arose such a visceral response that she knew if she'd had a gun, she would have shot Stephen without hesitation.

She eased Jessica's arms from around her.

"Don't leave me," she pleaded.

"I won't. I promise."

She rose to her feet, a slow-motion act that countered the raging pressure inside of her. Stephen was still staring at the floor; Mattie rushed at him, pushing him, pounding on him, screaming, "You goddamn bastard!"

"Mattie, listen to me. . . ." He reached for her wrists, trying to deflect her flying hands.

"How could you have done such an evil thing? How could you?" She couldn't even say it, so foreign and so repugnant was the concept of incest. "She's your daughter! Your flesh and blood. How could you do this to her?"

"Don't look at me like I'm some serial child molester. It happened once—"

"Once is horrifying!"

"Let me finish." And suddenly he was calm and reasoned, and that appalled Mattie even more. "Jessica and I dealt with this. She knew then, and she knows now, how sorry I was. She watched me cry and beg her forgiveness. She promised me that we would forget it and put it in the past."

"Put it in the past? Put it in the past, as if it were some misunderstanding? Are you insane? That's the most breathtakingly ignorant comment I've ever heard."

"Mom, he's right."

"What?" She looked at Jessica as though the child had grown two heads. "You're defending him? He did this, and you're justifying it?"

"I'm not. But it's not like this happened every day."

"Oh, God."

"It only happened once, and it was sorta my fault because well, I felt bad for Daddy because you were going out with Wyatt and Daddy was so sad. . . . I kept thinking about him while I was at Callie's, and then I'd been drinking champagne and I was sorta wasted, and I stopped at Daddy's to see how he was and . . . I-I-I stayed because if I came home, you'd be pissed . . . and I know he didn't mean it. . . ."

Her words tumbled out in one continuous mass, and Mattie's head was reeling as if she'd been tossed in some dizzying whirl of black space.

"This was your fault, Mattie," Stephen said, picking up on Jessica's support of him. "I wanted you and it was your birthday and I bought you a present and wanted to take you out for dinner and dancing, but you were with Landry. . . ."

The night he'd shown up unexpectedly and she'd rejected him and his invitation. He'd been angry with her, yes, and no doubt hurt, but to—

"I wouldn't go out with you, so you raped Jessica?"

"It was not rape."

"It was rape, Stephen. She's seventeen years old. And she's your daughter." Even knowing the truth, she couldn't grasp it. "My God, she's your daughter."

"I was drunk, and so was she."

The excuse was so outrageous, Mattie was speechless. Could he possibly believe that because they were both drunk and he later apologized, that would be the end of it? Yes, she realized with the clarity of instinct. That was Stephen's pattern. Do harm, apologize, beg forgiveness, and then put it out of his mind. But this—this was indefensible.

Mattie looked down at Jessica, cupping her chin so that she could see her face. "I want you to tell me what happened."

"I'm leaving," Stephen announced.

"Good. I can't stand the sight of you. And tell the guests to leave, too," Mattie said without taking her eyes off her daughter. "The wedding is canceled."

He slammed the door. Mattie sat down beside Jessica, taking her chilled hands and warming them. This time she didn't have to be prodded. It all spilled out like a flood of water no longer dammed up.

"I'd been at a party at Callie's and I drank too much champagne. Her parents weren't home and we were kinda drinking from the bottles her father had." Mattie scowled, wondering why this would even matter, compared to Stephen having sex with her. "All the kids were doing it, and it wasn't like I was going to drive or anything."

"Who drove you to your father's?"

"Kevin had his mother's car. He was going to take me home, but I was worried about Daddy and I couldn't let you see me that way. You would have freaked. I figured Daddy would scowl and maybe lecture, but then he'd tell me to go to bed while he called you and said I'd decided to stay there."

Stephen had called and left a voice mail message about Jess stopping to see him, and they'd gotten to talking and she was practically falling asleep on her feet. He'd sent her to bed, he'd told Mattie, and he'd send her home in the morning.

And where had she been while her daughter was being raped? Having sex with Wyatt.

"All right. Kevin took you to your father's. Then what?"

"He was drinking. Not drunk, but just kinda laid-back. I was being silly and kinda flirty, like Hannah and I do with Daddy, but he wasn't funny and teasing the way he usually is. He kept calling me 'Mattie,' and I think he really thought

I was you. I knew he wanted to take you out for your birthday. He even gave me the bracelet he bought for you, and told me you didn't want it or him. I felt sorry for him because he was so sad, so I took it." The bracelet she'd found with Toadie, the bracelet that Stephen tried to connect to Kane. Jessica shuddered. "I kissed him good night and went to bed. Then . . ."

Mattie held her breath. She didn't want to hear any of this, but at the same time, listening didn't even come close to the trauma of the actual act.

"I was almost asleep, and the champagne made me groggy, so I wasn't sure what was happening until I felt him on top of me. I tried to stop him, and pushed and shoved at him, but I couldn't." Jessica's eyes pleaded. "I know if I hadn't been drinking, I could have stopped it."

Mattie shook her gently. "I don't want to hear any self-blame. I don't care if you were stone drunk and dancing naked on the bed, he's your father and he has no defense."

"Mom, he didn't mean to hurt me. I think he really thought it was you. And then he cried and begged me to forgive him. I'd never seen him cry, and I didn't want anyone to know. I told him I wouldn't tell, and he swore it would never happen again. And it didn't. It was our secret."

"And the pregnancy?"

"No. I never told him I was pregnant. I couldn't. He was getting his life together without you, he'd been interviewing for some jobs, and every time I saw him, he was just like he always was. Sweet and generous and interested in my life. It was like that night never happened. Telling him I was pregnant—I don't think he would have believed me."

"So you let people think it was Kevin."

"No! I never told anyone I was pregnant but Arlis. And the only reason she knew was because she was going to help me. I quit seeing Kevin. I was so ashamed, and Kevin had been pushing me to make love and I said no." She lowered her head, her skin washed out. "We did do a lot of heavy making out. I really loved him and I wanted him, but I didn't want to do it. I just didn't . . . oh, it doesn't matter now. I know he hates me, and I hate myself for being so nasty to him those weeks, but I couldn't tell him. I couldn't tell anyone."

And then, as if it couldn't be any more devastating, the logical question came to Mattie. "Were you a virgin?"

It took more than ten seconds before Jess nodded yes.

And Mattie had to hold on to her daughter to stop herself from flying down the stairs and clawing out Stephen's heart.

They stayed together, Mattie holding her, rocking her, wanting to make right what could never be right again.

Then she said quietly to Jessica, "If the accident hadn't happened and you'd gotten the abortion, you would have never told anyone about that night."

Jessica nodded her head with a determination that disturbed Mattie. "I couldn't tell that my father—I couldn't. I just couldn't."

Mattie hugged her again and then rose. If not for that terrible accident. . . .

"What are you going to do?" Jessica asked.

"I don't know."

"You're not going to tell, are you?"

"Jessica, this isn't a secret, it's an abomination. We need to call the police and have him charged with child molestation."

"No! He's my father, and I love him. I can't do that to him."

"Jessica—"

"I can't and I won't, and if you get him in trouble, I'll hate you forever."

"Sweetheart, this can't be left just as if it were some minor infraction, like ignoring a parking ticket."

"It's all that stupid Arlis's fault. If she hadn't been whacked out on beer and pukin' on the floor so that I looked over to see if she was okay, we'd've gotten to the clinic and no one would ever have known. There wouldn't have been an accident or a coma, and you wouldn't have decided to remarry Daddy." Then she looked at her mother. "I thought I'd be okay with it, but I couldn't watch it. I knew you were only doing it for Hannah and me. I knew you really loved Wyatt."

Mattie's eyes filled with tears. "Maybe that was part of it, but I think, deep down, you wanted this terrible experience told. That took a lot of courage, and now—"

Jessica backed away from her mother. "I said no. I'm not telling. I'm not."

Mattie quit pushing. Today had been traumatic enough. In a few days, Mattie would talk to her again. Jessica had to change her mind. Stephen could not be allowed to get away with this.

Stephen moved out, and Mattie called a professional service to clean the den where he'd been sleeping. Undoubtedly a little overkill, but the smell of him whenever she entered the room made her nauseated.

The canceled wedding was explained by Stephen as an unavoidable change in plans due to Jessica's recovery, or at least that was one version she'd heard. It infuriated her that Jessica got the blame, and she told him so. "Then you clarify it. Our daughter will be so grateful."

He had her cornered, because he knew as well as she that Jessica was paranoid about keeping silent. Mattie sent all questions to her back to him. She certainly wasn't going to make something up and she couldn't tell the truth, not with Jessica being terrified that her father would be humiliated and ostracized. And though, personally, Mattie didn't give a damn whether Stephen's crime was reported on the evening news, realistically, an airing would be mortifying and traumatic for his daughters. It was a twisted dilemma that fundamentally changed Mattie.

No longer was she sweet and patient and understanding; what blossomed now was a fanatical frustration. Stephen would simply walk through life with no punishment, no retribution, while those who knew him continued to believe he was a wonderful father.

However, Mattie told her parents; one more defense of "poor" Stephen, and she would literally scream.

Not surprisingly, her mother refused to believe it.

"You think I'd make this up?"

"Stephen wouldn't," her mother insisted. "I know he wouldn't."

"Now, Louise, Jessica wouldn't tell a lie like that." Mattie hugged her father fiercely, so grateful that he didn't doubt Jess.

Louise Rooney turned to her husband. "You're on their side."

"This is not sides, there's only one side if a father . . . well, if he did such a thing."

"But he loves them both," Louise said, although clearly her husband's different view had rattled her loyalty. "He's been a wonderful father, and they love him."

"I'm sure he does and I'm sure they do, but that doesn't change what Jessica has said."

Her mother turned to her, and Mattie saw her mouth tremble and the horror of dawning realization in her eyes. "Oh, dear, if it's true—oh, my poor Jessica." Then she covered her face and sobbed. Mattie put her arm around her, understanding her distress.

Then she drew herself up as if jabbed by her blindness. "All this time, I've loved him like he was my own son. I've defended him and comforted him, all the time blaming you for being unreasonable and selfish and stubborn."

"None of that matters now. What matters is Jessica. She refuses to do anything, and I don't know what to do. I'd like some advice."

"Well, honey . . . ," her father began, his words trailing away before he really said anything.

"I think he should be shot," her mother said. Carl Rooney, clearly undone by his wife's bluntness, looked at her as if she were a stranger.

Mattie smiled. "I'm with you, Mom."

Mother and daughter nodded to one another as though making some pact.

"Now, girls—"

"You have a better idea?" her mother asked, deliberately

misunderstanding the cautious tone in her husband's voice. "A lynch mob, maybe?"

"Hold it," Mattie said. "We have to be serious here. His punishment has to begin with the absolute; he can't get away with this. We all agree with that, but Jessica refuses to deal with it. She's convinced she'll be the one responsible if his life is ruined." Mattie felt her throat go raw. "I'm frustrated and angry and outraged. Jessica has withdrawn, and Stephen . . . what does he do? He takes Hannah shopping. Shopping for clothes and ice cream and videos, for God's sake! When I objected, he told me that one mistake didn't negate all the good things he'd done as a father. I mean, he's just moved on. He's working at a new company, stops for a drink with his colleagues, and calls me as if nothing happened. I can't stand it."

"Is Hannah safe?" her mother whispered, fear widening her eyes.

"Mom, they're in a public mall. Don't worry, she's not spending the night at his apartment."

"You haven't told her about this, have you?"

"I have, but she refuses to believe it, and all I'm hearing is her ongoing list of Stephen's sterling qualities."

"So now what?"

"I keep trying to convince Jessica that her continued silence is hurting her. I suggested counseling, and she agreed to that, but it has to be out of town. She's terrified someone will find out."

And so the days passed in a stagnant atmosphere that grated on Mattie to the point where she wanted to literally drag Jessica to the police station, inject her with truth serum, and be done with it. Logic reminded her that she needed to get a grip, but her anger was consuming her.

Two weeks later came a turning point.

Mattie caught up with Jessica at the front door, struck immediately by how sallow she appeared. She'd lost weight; her beautiful blond hair, usually lightened and sparkling from the summer sun, was limp and drab. Her eyes were tired and listless. Mattie wished she could conjure up Stephen and make him look at her, make him see what he'd done that couldn't be undone. Fury at him bubbled anew.

"Sweetheart, where are you off to?" she asked, keeping herself in check. She'd gotten too damn good at that.

"Callie called. I'm going over to see her."

"All right."

"I'm fine, Mom. I know you're worried and upset, but it will all work out."

Mattie willed herself not to react. "Is that what the therapist told you?"

"Sorta. She said you should see someone about your own anger, that although what Daddy did was wrong, he isn't a bad man. And that as long as you have anger and hatred issues with him, well, that's hurting me."

Mattie, who'd never had high blood pressure in her life, in that moment knew hers had climbed into the stratosphere. Of all the therapists in the state, she'd picked one who didn't want to make judgments except when it came to her.

"Say hello to Callie for me," she said, kissing her daughter's cheek, then watching her walk away before closing the door.

Going into the kitchen and pouring herself a glass of wine, despite it being two in the afternoon, she considered that a year from now, she and Jessica would be true casualties and Stephen would be happily living and working and laughing and shopping with Hannah.

Wyatt had been right. Stephen was a master at manipulating and benefiting himself. Where was *his* punishment? She drained the glass of wine. It was long past time she found out.

Chapter
Twenty-three

That evening Mattie began to execute her plan.

At close to eleven o'clock, after Jessica was asleep, Mattie looked in on Hannah, who was curled up watching one of the videos Stephen had bought for her.

"I'm going out. Will you be okay here?"

"I'm fine. These are really cool videos."

"Yes, I'm sure. I'll be back in a couple of hours."

"Where're you going?" Then she pouted. "Oh, forget I asked. I know. Now that you've blown Daddy off, you're going back to your old lover."

Thank you, Stephen. You're doing a stellar job of warping Hannah, too. To Hannah, she said, "You know what, young lady? You've become a brat of mammoth proportions, and I'm getting very tired of your nasty attitude and your smart mouth."

She actually looked chagrined. "I wanted you and Daddy to get married, and she ruined it."

"Jessica ruined nothing. Your father and I couldn't get married. End of story." And when Hannah neither scowled nor asked, Mattie figured Stephen had fabricated some story that benefited him. The propped-up lies continued, and Mattie shuddered at how the truth, in a few months, would be so revised and papered over as to be nonexistent.

"Lock the door when you go to bed."

"Yeah, yeah," Hannah said distractedly, her attention back on the video.

Half an hour later, Mattie turned into the driveway, glad to see lights on in the house. She got out of the car, walked up the curving brick path, stopped at the front door, and took a deep breath before ringing the bell.

A few moments later the door opened, and there he stood.

"Mattie!" And then he frowned. "What's wrong? What's happened?"

And though she swore she wouldn't, though she'd promised herself she'd be calm and measured, seeing him was her undoing and she burst into tears. "Oh God, Wyatt. . . ."

Disturbed and puzzled by the outburst, he tossed aside the analysis of a start-up company he'd been reading and tugged her inside, enveloping her in his arms. He didn't talk or question, he simply held her while she cried and cried and cried.

Finally, she was in the living room, seated on his lap in a huge chair, and her sobs slowed.

"You don't have to talk to me, sweetheart. That you're here is enough for now."

"Oh Wyatt, it's—it's—I don't know where to begin."

"Corinne already told me the wedding was canceled, something about Stephen and you deciding that since Jessica wasn't herself, getting remarried wasn't a good idea."

" 'Jessica wasn't herself. Jessica wasn't herself.' God, if I hear that one more time—of course, she's not herself, and that son of a bitch caused it and then turns around and blames her."

Wyatt scowled at her rant. Then, as though walking through a minefield, he said, "Tough, raw words coming from you. Me, I always thought he was an asshole. So what really happened? He fucked up and showed his true colors?"

He tipped his head to one side, his hand stroking her shoulder. He could feel the tenseness and the anger and something else. . . . Desperation?

Mattie? Talk to me. What did he do?"

"He raped Jessica."

* * *

Wyatt stared with the kind of wordless astonishment he hadn't experienced since that moment he faced the truth that Paige and Bobby were having an affair.

Of all the wrongs he might have accused Stephen of, raping his own daughter was so out there that Wyatt came close to scoffing at Mattie. But he knew her, and this kind of accusation wouldn't even take form in her mind, never mind bluntly coming out of her mouth, if it weren't true.

"I don't know what to do," she said.

"You mean besides slicing off his balls?"

She sighed and almost smiled. "Besides that."

"Go to the police and charge him with rape."

"My first thought. Unfortunately, it's not that simple." She then told him all the sordid details, plus Stephen's determination to put it all behind them and move on. "The most troubling is her silence and continued protection of him. I don't know what to do to make her see that she needs to report this."

"From what you've told me, Jess is more worried about him than about herself."

"It's truly sad, and I can't shake her out of it. My parents know, and they believe Jessica. Hannah was told, too, but she either refuses to believe it or else she simply won't deal with it. Either way, she's taken her father's side. And in addition, she's being such a pain in the butt. . . ." She paused, looking tired and overwhelmed by the avalanche of troubles. "I'm worried about Hannah, too, but this thing that Stephen did is eating me alive."

"Okay, take it easy. You said Jessica is seeing a therapist, so she isn't totally averse to discussing it."

"No, she's not. Although personally I think this therapist cares more about making Jessica forget about it than giving her the emotional tools she needs to do something about it."

"Is she as angry as you are?"

"Gee, does it show?"

"Just a bit," he said, giving a small grin. She relaxed against him, and he felt her tension subside.

"Well, I seem to have enough fury for both of us. As for

Jess, you couldn't find her anger if it was dripping in uranium and you used a Geiger counter."

"It's there, I promise you." Wyatt was silent for a few moments, then said, "My old partner and I worked a couple of incest cases. In one, the victim reacted very much like Jessica. It's like an internal denial—she knows the truth, but doesn't want it to hurt anyone, so she tries to show she's dealing with it, getting past it, and in the process she begins to physically deteriorate."

"I'm seeing that, and it frightens me."

Wyatt nodded. "I'm only speaking from what I observed working those cases, but the pattern was consistent. For Jessica, remaining silent gives Stephen power over her. She's helping him get on with his life while she's mired in guilt mixed with terror that her father will be destroyed if she tells."

"Exactly, but I can't get her to believe that."

"Then you came to the right place. I know somebody who can."

Getting Jessica to agree to meeting with Bobby Dodd took skill and promises and constant reminders that she didn't have to do anything but listen.

To make the meeting less stressful, Wyatt arranged for Jessica and Mattie to meet with Bobby at Wyatt's house in Newport. Out of town, out of sight, out of any gossip loop that might be fed if Mattie and Jessica appeared for no particular reason at the police station.

Bobby arrived first. "Your phone call surprised me."

"Yeah, I suppose it did."

"Is the hatchet getting buried, I hope?"

"The hole is dug."

"Ahh, progress."

Wyatt offered him a can of beer, which Bobby refused. "Don't touch the stuff anymore. Took a bath in it after you and I hit the fan."

"I swam in Scotch. And I always hated the hard stuff."

The two men studied one another in an open silence that each was perfectly comfortable to let stand. Wyatt recalled that old Simon and Garfunkle hit, "The Sounds of Silence." "Hello, darkness" had been a five-year mantra for him when it came to hating Bobby. That murky isolation, he now realized, had begun to slide when the anger at Paige tumbled away after that dinner his sister had arranged. He'd taken a step toward Bobby when he contacted him for information about Kane Fairfax's arrest. But Wyatt hadn't been aware of how little of his rancor toward Bobby remained until he'd agreed to come and meet with Jessica. He'd asked no questions, shown no hesitation or even a suspicion that Wyatt had some deeper motive.

In retrospect, Wyatt conceded Bobby had never been the one spewing the fury. Even when Wyatt had beat the hell out of him, Bobby had taken the pounding as if he deserved it. Which he did. Wyatt hadn't changed his mind about that. But instead of grabbing on to the useless "bruised ego" crutch and carrying it like a poisonous grudge, Bobby concentrated on getting his life and his reputation back. And it had worked, Wyatt acknowledged. Bobby was now the police chief, well respected in town, plus he was a man to be trusted. Even Wyatt knew that, as evidenced by his instinctive suggestion to Mattie that Bobby could help.

Now, Bobby walked to the doors that led to the porch. The view of Easton's Beach fanned out to the Atlantic in the distance. "Nice place you've got here." Then he smiled nostalgically. "Remember when we were kids and we used to hitchhike to Easton's and meet girls? Do guys do that anymore?"

"Nah, the girls all come to them now. My sister says they call Kevin all hours of the night, wear clothes that should get them arrested, and promise to get on the pill before the first date."

"Shit, you and I were born way too soon."

"Or we were dating the wrong girls."

They both chuckled, and that hatchet moved a little closer to the hole.

Bobby turned his attention back to the reason for his being there and asked Wyatt, "You believe this girl?"

"I believe her mother, plus Caulfield admitted it the day Jessica told."

"And that was over two weeks ago."

"Yeah."

"If he's questioned now, he'll probably deny it ever happened."

"Probably."

"Which puts this into a 'he said, she said' not unlike the Fairfax case."

"Except that Mattie heard him admit it."

"That'll help, but a good lawyer will present a vigorous defense."

"I know. And the poor kid is gonna get trashed if his lawyer can find a way to do it."

"And he will. Caulfield might try to object, but when it comes down to whether he does time or not, he'll slide into the lawyer's pocket as slick as a greased dick. She's got to understand that this isn't TV, where the good guys always win."

Wyatt glanced out the window as Mattie drove up, and she and Jessica got out of the car. "Here we go," Wyatt murmured.

And for the next hour, the four of them sat on the porch of Wyatt's house while the beach beyond played host to the Atlantic's rolling surf. A pitcher of lemonade and iced glasses, freshly painted Adirondack chairs that Wyatt had finished just two days before, and baskets of Wave petunias suspended from the porch beams made it appear that the four were enjoying the bounty of a summer day.

At first, Jessica was reticent, but, as Wyatt knew he would, Bobby eased her fears and promised her absolutely that what she said would go no further without her permission. The details Jessica gave were the same that Mattie had told Wyatt, and that he in turn had told Bobby.

Bobby asked, "Jess, what really scares you about charging your father? I know you love him and don't want to embarrass him or humiliate him. Has he threatened you or said anything about this to you since you told your mother in his presence?"

She shook her head. "He doesn't talk to me."

"And that's okay with you?"

"I want it to be the way it was before. I want to be his daughter the way Hannah is."

Mattie's hand covered her mouth, and Wyatt felt his own throat tighten.

Bobby leaned forward. "Jessica? Jessica, look at me."

She slowly lifted her head.

"Sweetheart, it can't be that way because of what he did, not because of what you couldn't prevent."

Jessica twisted the tissue in her hands until it was in shreds. "But if I don't tell, maybe it can. Someday, maybe it can."

Bobby said nothing more, not willing to beat on her like a drum for what she clearly wasn't ready to accept.

Bobby moved on. "Are you afraid to tell for other reasons? Like what people would say about you? If you'd be believed?"

For a long moment, she was still, then looked up at Bobby and slowly nodded.

"I understand that."

"You do?" She seemed amazed.

"No one likes to be accused of lying and making up stories."

"Like what happened to Emily."

"Yes."

"But she wasn't lying and she didn't make any of it up, and going to the police didn't help her. It made everything worse. Now everyone hates her and won't talk to her."

"Sometimes that happens. Are you afraid of that if you go to the police?"

"No one would believe me."

"I believe you. Wyatt does. Your mother does."

She shrugged. "But you don't count. Emily's family believed her, too. Telling the truth doesn't get you anything," she said, as if the truth had lost credibility. "There *were* other girls, and I told Callie she'd be sorry she didn't support

Emily, because Kane would dump her as soon as he found some new chick."

"Callie was involved with Kane?" Mattie asked, wondering if shocking news had become her shadow.

Jessica looked at her mother as if she were slow. "Is."

"You've known, and said nothing?"

"Mattie," Wyatt said softly, "let's not get off track."

"Hannah knows, too. Callie just had to brag. . . ."

"Oh, God," Mattie muttered.

Wyatt and Bobby exchanged glances.

Jessica turned her glass round and round, as if wisdom lay in the condensation. "Callie's stupid. She thinks he loves her. I mean, come on. He could almost be her father, and she really believes that one of these days he'll ask her to marry him."

Bobby said, "Then I'd say that Fairfax has really brainwashed her."

"I told her she should get some guts and call the police."

"You told her that?" Mattie asked, amazed that her daughter's good sense about Callie didn't translate into the same reaction toward her father.

"And what if you were to do that about your father?" Bobby asked, as if absorbing Mattie's thoughts.

Jessica shrank back.

Bobby didn't. "Can I tell you straight out what could happen?"

"You said I didn't have to tell."

"Absolutely, you don't. In fact, when I finish, my guess is that you won't ever want to tell."

Mattie scowled at Bobby, then whispered to Wyatt, "What is he doing? He's scaring her."

"Yep, he sure is." Wyatt sat back, a grin sliding across his mouth. "He's a fucking genius."

Bobby wasted no words, nor did he couch anything he said in pretty emotions or soft explanations. "So here's the deal, Jess. Say you decide to press charges against your father."

"I can't!"

"I know. This is just a hypothetical. You know what that means?"

She nodded, swallowing hard.

"Okay, let's say it happens this way. The police will take your statement and any evidence you have to prove your father did this. He'll be brought in for questioning, and for a while it might even look as if you have a strong case. But your father is not going to pronounce himself guilty and go off to prison. He's going to say he's innocent."

"But he did it."

"I know he did, sweetheart, but he will hire a lawyer who will convince him that even if he's guilty, that doesn't mean he has to go to jail. If it gets to a trial, then his lawyer will point out that you were drunk—"

"So was he," she cried.

"You were flirting—"

"Hannah and I always flirted with Daddy."

"You were dressed in sexy clothes—"

"I'd been to a party!"

"And you were having sex, as evidenced by the condoms found in Kevin's pocket."

"How would he know where Kevin keeps—" She cut herself off. "You tricked me."

"And so will your father's lawyer," Bobby said gently.

"But I didn't have sex with Kevin."

"Never?"

"No!"

"Oh, then it was with other boys?"

"No!"

"Can you prove that?"

"No, I mean yes." She covered her eyes. "I don't know."

"You said your father gave you a bracelet he was going to give to your mother."

"Yes."

"Did he give you expensive gifts often?"

"Sometimes."

"And did you hug him and kiss him to thank him for those gifts?"

"Sometimes."

"And what about the bracelet? You were drunk and flirting, you admitted that. Did you go just a little further when he gave the gift to you? Did you act a little too provocative?"

"Stop it," Mattie cried, "stop badgering her."

"That's enough, Bobby," Wyatt said softly, his eyes on Jessica. She was pale and shaky.

Bobby cupped her chin and she jerked away, pushing herself up and out of the chair. "You're a horrible man, and I don't want to listen to you anymore. I never did any of those things, and if my father says I did, he's a liar. You have no right to make things I did sound dirty when they weren't."

"But his lawyer will, Jess," Bobby said softly. "His lawyer will ask just those kinds of questions, or as many as he can get away with. And the jury—well, it could go either way. It could convict your father if there are enough who believe you and are sufficiently horrified by the testimony. Or, if the jury is more forgiving, they might say that since it only happened once, he's entitled to one mistake and a second chance."

Jessica wouldn't look at him and turned away to walk to the porch railing.

"If you decide to do this, Jessica, it will probably be the hardest decision you will ever make, but once made, the ordeal will be equally difficult. I don't want to paint any rosy outcome here."

"I want to go home," she said flatly.

Bobby said, "Before you go, I want you to tell us who else you told about what your father did."

Mattie stared at Bobby. "She hasn't—"

"Let her answer, Mattie," Bobby said, holding his hand up. "Jessica?"

She lowered her head and began to cry. Mattie started for her, but Wyatt stopped her.

Bobby took a few steps and rested his hands on Jessica's shoulders. She had her back to him.

"I never should have told. She didn't believe me, and now she hates me and what does it matter anyway?"

"Who, Jessica?"

"Hannah. I told Hannah the day after it happened."

Chapter Twenty-four

Hannah knew. All this time, Hannah had known.

On the trip back to Briarwood, Mattie was reflective. She'd expected to be confused and rattled by Jessica's revelation. And she wasn't angry. The fact that both daughters—one the victim and one the keeper of the secret—had carried this knowledge for more than four months brought home to Mattie the power of Stephen's hold on their love, of their refusal to believe anything bad about him and of their ferocious desire to protect him.

"Please don't push at Hannah," Jessica said.

"I guess I've done a lot of that at you, haven't I?"

"Uh-huh." She gave her mother a sidelong glance. "Are you going to talk to her?"

"Yes."

"I made her promise not to tell, but she never believed me anyway."

"I think she did believe you."

Jessica vigorously shook her head. "She's been a bitch to me since I told her, and since the accident, she's, like, tried to steal my life. Making friends with *my* best friend, going to the prom with *my* boyfriend, and trying to show everybody that she was Daddy's best girl."

Mattie nodded, amazed at how the pieces of Hannah's insensitive and boorish behavior that had so annoyed her were now perfectly in place. She was almost relieved.

Almost.

At home, she found Hannah on the phone.

"Where were you?" Hannah asked when she'd hung up.

"I told you Jessica and I were going for a drive."

"You didn't tell me where," she said, as if she'd been left out.

"We were at Wyatt's."

Hannah gave her a disgusted look. "Can't you stay away from him when my sister is with you?"

A few hours ago, Mattie would have snapped back at her. Now she simply added, "We were meeting with the chief of police."

Hannah's eyes widened and shifted, then she sniffed. "Who cares what that's all about? I sure don't."

"Hannah, I know."

"Know what?"

"Jess told you what happened with Daddy."

And for three heartbeats Hannah crumbled, then quickly recovered.

"It's not true. I don't care what she said, what anyone says. It's not true. Daddy wouldn't do that. I know it, and I've proved it. I've been alone with him lots of times, even when he's been drinking. And he never, never, never did anything disgusting like *she* said he did."

"Honey, if you were so sure he was innocent, why were you trying so hard to prove it?"

Hannah burst into tears, and, when Mattie tried to take her into her arms, shoved her away. "Jessica always got all the attention, she was always the one everyone looked at. The most popular, the one all the boys liked, the smartest, and the prettiest. Even the accident made her some kind of dumb hero because of that stupid coma. But then Daddy came home, and I thought we were going to be a family again and all that horrible stuff that Jessica told me was as stupid as the coma. Everyone wanted to be my friend and I was the most popular. Me, not Jessica! It was my chance to be popular, to be better than Jessica, and I took it. Is that so awful?"

Mattie thought it was appalling, but expressing that now would be more harmful than helpful. "And this need you had to prove your sister was lying about your father . . . why did you wait until after the accident?"

Hannah looked down at her sandals, and Mattie did, too. Lavender-painted toenails, matching gold toe rings, and a gold ankle bracelet. The rings and the bracelet were recent purchases when she'd been shopping with Stephen. Things. Always he'd given them things, and then gloried in their gratitude. And Mattie remembered the fuss about Hannah going to the prom with Kevin. Even then Stephen was giving Hannah what she wanted. Saying no, and then letting her talk him out of it so that he would be more loved. Even giving Jessica the bracelet meant for Mattie. A gift followed by raping her, then begging Jessica to forgive and still love him. Mattie shuddered.

"Hannah?"

"Because he came home."

Mattie scowled. "I don't understand."

"When I knew we were going to be a family again, I wanted to prove that would be okay. Then she had to ruin everything—the wedding, our family. And now Daddy has some airhead girlfriend and we won't hardly ever see him."

Pray God that comes true.

"And I did prove it—he was okay," Hannah said emphatically. "And then Jessica ruined it all and you let her."

"Hannah, the fact that your father never touched you has nothing to do with what happened to Jessica."

"I gave him lots of chances."

Suddenly Mattie was disturbed. "Chances to do what?"

"I had to prove it, didn't I?" She lifted her chin, then added, "He even got mad a couple of times and told me I was acting slutty."

"Oh, Hannah!" Mattie drew her into her arms and hugged her, and Hannah's hug back gave her a renewed faith that just maybe there was an end to all of this. "My sweet, sweet daughter."

"He never did anything to me, Mom, honest to God he didn't."

"I believe you."

"But you believe Jessica, too."

"Yes, and so do you."

Hannah began to shake her head, but Mattie cupped her daughter's chin and stopped her. Although she raised her head, she kept her eyelids lowered.

"I know how hard this is, honey. I know your heart doesn't want to believe it happened, but I also know that deep in that same heart, you're terrified because you know Jessica would never make an accusation like that unless it was the truth."

She said nothing, and Mattie could almost feel that shield Hannah had erected between the truth and her instinct to protect her father falling away. Then she started to cry. Deep and hard and devastated. She clung to her mother, and Mattie clung back.

"I d-don't, like, you know, r-really h-h-h-h-ate her . . . ," she whimpered, her voice raspy and breaking.

"I know that, but I also know that she would sure like to have you tell her."

Hannah nodded, and after blowing her nose and giving her mother one more hug, she went to find her sister.

Days passed into weeks, and Mattie, trying to keep busy at work, continued to fret about Jessica. If ever there was a standstill, she knew her daughter stood firmly in the midst of one. Jessica still refused to press charges, and Mattie tried to convince herself that the renewed closeness of the two sisters would eventually lead Jessica to change her mind.

She and Wyatt began seeing one another again, and she loved his support and his letting her vent without trying to shut her up.

"Wyatt, you've been so patient about all this."

"I've loved you for a long time. Patience comes with the territory."

"Some days I think it will never end. Then I see Stephen

going around as if life's a beach. He's dating some redhead who clings to him like he invented charm, and I heard the other day that he got a big promotion at his new job. His daughters are in limbo, and he's chalking up one success after another. He acts as if he's home free."

"And he is."

"Unless Jessica comes forward."

"Yes."

A few nights later, Mattie was propped up in bed with the most recent Jeffery Deaver novel when there was a knock on her bedroom door.

"Come in."

The door eased open, and Jessica stood there in an over-sized T-shirt. Her skin had lost its sallowness and her eyes were brighter. Seeing her standing there brought a rush of memories of all those times when Jessica had come to her room to talk—mother-daughter confidences more precious to her than "quality time."

"I see you brought friends," Mattie said, taking note of Toadie and the sock of secret stones in her hands.

"Can I talk to you?" she asked.

"You know you can always talk to me." Mattie book-marked her page, laid the book aside, and patted the edge of the bed. "Come and sit down."

Jessica climbed up at the end of the bed and folded her legs beneath her. "I've made some decisions."

"Oh?"

"It's time I gave the secret stones back to you to give to Wyatt." And before Mattie could comment, she added, "And I think Toadie needs to go away, too."

"Any reason?"

"Because they're kid stuff and I'm not a kid anymore."

"All right. I can understand that," Mattie said, treading carefully.

"There's no magic in keeping that silly stuff. They don't make the wrong things go away, and they don't make the right things come easy."

"You're right. Life is more complicated and sometimes risky, and doing the right thing isn't always easy, but it's always right."

Jessica looked down, then pushed Toadie away, followed by the sock of stones.

"I'm going to press charges against Daddy."

Mattie's eyes widened. Where had this come from? "Another decision?" she asked cautiously, feeling as if she were walking on glass. She certainly didn't want to do anything to cause Jessica to retreat.

"Yeah, the hardest one."

Mattie's eyes filled, for she knew that what Jessica faced would be humiliating and heartbreaking and soul-shattering. But here was her very brave daughter making this decision. She wasn't crying, she wasn't shaking, and most of all, her eyes were clear and determined.

"What changed your mind?"

"A lot of things. I guess they were sorta piling up in my head. But then today, while I was at the mall, I saw him with that woman. He was laughing, and she was giggling and they were, like, acting goofy like no one would notice. I noticed and I watched them, and finally I walked up to him and said hello. He looked at me as if I'd ruined his day, like I was some pest from his past who might screech out what he did to me. Then he just blew me off." She took a breath, and her voice began to tremble. "I felt like such a jerk."

Mattie's insides were seething. How dare he? Dammit, how dare he?

"I kept thinking how he doesn't come to see me or call me or even ask Hannah about me. And face to face, he can't get away fast enough. It's as if I don't exist because I told."

"And now you're angry," Mattie said, saying the obvious because she could see it in Jessica's eyes.

"He pissed me off. Now he's out there with his martinis and girlfriend, making a new life, and I'm miserable because of what he did to me."

Mattie nodded. There wasn't much to say. Beating up on Stephen—well, she'd done that and done that some more.

Feeding Jessica's anger wasn't necessary; it was there and focused and wonderful.

"What do I have to do next?"

"We'll call Bobby, and I'll go down to the police station with you tomorrow morning."

Jessica crawled up close to her mother and sighed. "I'm scared, but I know I have to do this."

Mattie glanced over at the sock of secret stones, abandoned, no longer needed to perform miracles. And there was Toadie cast aside as a childish comfort. Outside was a perfect summer night. But the best was right here beside her. A daughter who had taken the hardest step of her life.

The days ahead would be difficult, Stephen and his attorney would make that so; but Mattie knew she and Jessica, and Hannah, too, would get through it. Jessica would be more than a survivor or a victim; she would face this and heal and emerge stronger.

Mattie knew that.

She knew that for certain.